AMISH FOSTER GIRLS 4 BOOKS-IN-1

COMPLETE AMISH ROMANCE SERIES

SAMANTHA PRICE

Amish Foster Girls Boxed Set

(includes):

Amish Girl's Christmas

Amish Foster Girl

The New Amish Girl

The New Girl's Amish Romance

AMISH GIRL'S CHRISTMAS

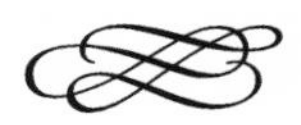

AMISH FOSTER GIRLS BOOK 1

CHAPTER 1

Who knoweth not in all these that
the hand of the LORD hath wrought this?
Job 12:9

ELIZABETH RAN from the house to the barn with two cookies clutched in her hand while snowflakes softly fell around her. Once she got safely into the barn without anyone calling her back, she looked at the house hoping no one would notice her missing at least until she ate her snack. Spotting a bale of hay, she pulled it closer to the door, so she would be able to see if anyone approached.

The white Amish farmhouse looked pretty as the snow settled on the roof. The Grabers' home wasn't large compared with some of their neighbors, but there were four small bedrooms, enough for the Grabers and their three foster children, of whom Elizabeth was one. She'd been with Gretchen and William Graber for ten years. Before that, she'd been placed with the Wallaces briefly and then the O'Briens. She much preferred Gretchen and William Graber as foster parents. If only there weren't so many chores all the time.

She stared at the smoke spiraling from the single chimney and breathed in deeply. The smoke mixed with the smell of the baking bread and the sight of the fresh snow gave Elizabeth a sense of comfort. Most of the memories of her parents were now faded, but she remembered some of their Christmases together.

Recollections of her father teaching her to skate on the ice were the clearest of them all. He'd bundle her up and allow her to sit in the front seat of his truck while he drove to the skating rink. Then it seemed like they stayed on the ice for hours while he patiently taught her the proper movements—how to slide one leg out and then the other. When she'd gotten it right and skated alone, she remembered her squeals of delight as her father cheered her on, grinning from ear-to-ear at her efforts. Sadly, they only had a few seasons together.

Remembering those years tugged at her heart. Many years had passed since her parents had died in the accident. Fortunately, she had no memory of the accident and had been told she'd been thrown clear of the car during the wreck. Her parents weren't that lucky and had both died at the scene. Having no known relatives, Elizabeth was immediately placed into foster care.

She nibbled on a cookie while her eyes settled again on the smoke that came from the wood-burning stove in the kitchen. Elizabeth was continually amazed that one stove was able to generate enough warmth to heat the entire household.

When she'd finished the cookies, she dusted off the crumbs from her hands, pulled the hay back to where it had been, and then headed back to the Graber house where she lived with two other foster children, Megan and Tara, who were around the same age.

Gretchen's head whipped up from sharpening some knives at the kitchen table when Elizabeth walked back inside.

"Don't you have work at the coffee shop this morning, Elizabeth?"

"No. I'm not scheduled for today."

Megan and Tara were sitting beside Gretchen, having a break from their chores.

"Where have you been?" Tara asked.

"I just stepped outside for a moment."

Megan, the quieter of the girls, asked, "Would you like some hot chocolate?"

"Yes, please." Elizabeth took a seat at the table, pleased she'd arrived back in time for another break from daily chores.

Megan was always doing things for others, and fussing over people like a mother hen. Tara was forever talking about boys, mostly when Gretchen was out of earshot.

Gretchen said, "I know it's hard for all of you at this time of year."

Elizabeth nodded. "I still miss my parents."

"At least you have some memories," Megan said as she poured the hot chocolate into a cup.

Elizabeth knew that Megan's father had died suddenly when she was a baby, and her widowed mother had been in poor health and unable to handle single-motherhood. There hadn't been any relatives who were able to help her mother or to give Megan a home.

"I know." Gretchen's eyes moistened in sympathy as she listened to the girls.

"Well, I've got no one to miss." Tara's words were firm and cold.

Tara had only been with them for three years, and had never known her parents. She'd been adopted twice and then twice given up when each family's circumstances had changed. Elizabeth had never asked and neither had she been told what Tara had gone through, but given her harsh exterior she guessed it was something horrid. The Grabers' house was a haven for the three of them. Unable to have children themselves, Gretchen and William opened their home to children who needed to be loved.

Megan looked out the window. "It's snowing, *Mamm!*"

Megan had adapted quickly to the Amish ways, calling her foster parents *Mamm* and *Dat*. Tara and Elizabeth called the Grabers *Onkel* William and *Ant* Gretchen. After all, they weren't Elizabeth's real mother and father, and Tara must've felt the same.

Something in Elizabeth's heart held her back from throwing herself into the Amish ways. Her parents weren't Amish, so she wasn't sure if this was where she belonged. Thinking about whether God had placed her with the Grabers because He wanted her to be Amish made her head spin sometimes. That would mean that He didn't prevent that dreadful accident, and He spared her so she'd be placed here, and thinking if all of that could be so...it then caused her to feel dreadfully guilty.

In a year or two, she'd have to make up her mind what to do. If she chose to live amongst the people in the world outside the community, where would she live? She had no known relatives, no connections to her parents. The only place now that felt like home was with the Grabers. Every Amish woman got married young—it was the Amish way to marry and have many children. The choice was clear—she'd have to find an Amish man to marry, or leave the Amish community and make her way as an outsider—an *Englischer.* She already had a job in a coffee shop, so that was a good start.

"Here you go, Elizabeth."

Elizabeth looked at the hot chocolate that Megan had just placed in front of her. *"Denke,* Megan."

"What are you girls doing today after your chores?" Gretchen asked.

"I'm going into town," Tara announced with a secret smile hinting around her lips.

Elizabeth guessed she was most likely going to meet a boy somewhere.

"What about you, Megan?"

"I think I'll just stay around here and catch up on my sewing."

Gretchen smiled at Megan's response. A real Amish girl would've most likely stayed home and sewed. Gretchen would prefer if the three of them stayed in the Amish community rather than go out into the world.

Elizabeth said to Gretchen, "I'm going ice-skating today. It's been a long time."

"Okay, *gut.* I know how you like your skating. I'm almost finished making the quilt I've been working on, so that's my project for today."

"Gut! We can sew together, *Mamm."*

Gretchen smiled warmly at Megan.

After a period of silence while they drank their hot drinks and ate cookies, Gretchen said, "Tara, you might as well take Elizabeth to wherever she's going to skate, and you can fetch her on your return. That way we only need use one buggy."

"Okay," Tara said. "I don't know exactly how long I'll be."

"Just come and get me whenever you're finished."

STARING OUT AT THE ICE, Elizabeth fought back tears. Two children playing in the snow near the pond provided a good distraction. Elizabeth knew she'd been like one of those carefree children many years ago.

"Okay, here I go," Elizabeth whispered looking down at the skates on her feet.

As soon as her foot hit the ice, joy rippled through her body. Elizabeth could never explain what it felt like to be on the ice. All she understood is that she'd never truly be happy if she didn't skate. It was like flying—as free as a bird.

She soon gathered speed at the edge of the frozen pond, listening to the steel hit the ice with each stride. Chips of ice flew behind her as she increased her speed and readied for what her father had called her 'special move.'

Lifting one leg into the air, Elizabeth stretched out her arms and leaned forward with her leg out behind her as far as it would go within the confines of her long dress. Allowing the momentum to move her, she floated on one skate with the bitter wind hitting her face, freezing her tears onto her cheeks. When she lowered her leg to slow down, applause rang out from behind her.

Startled, Elizabeth came to a halt as soon as she could and then spun around to see where the commotion was coming from. On the other side of the ice stood a young Amish man. Embarrassed, Elizabeth stood still, wiped her tears, and then moved off the ice.

"You're really good," he called out.

Elizabeth gave a nod in a polite response, before looking for her bag containing her boots. The man must've been a visitor to their community because she'd never seen him before. Out of the corner of her eye, she saw movement from his direction. A loud thud followed by a painful whimper echoed through the air. The man lay on the ice, holding his leg.

"Are you okay?" Elizabeth asked as she quickly moved toward him.

Reaching for Elizabeth's outstretched hand, he answered, "Bruised, but not broken. I hope."

Elizabeth helped him to his feet and led him off the ice.

"You sure you're okay?"

"Dumb move, I guess. I didn't think walking on the ice would be that hard."

"Well, why were you walking on it? Where are your skates?"

The man turned crimson and laughed. "I was walking to talk to you. I wasn't thinking straight."

Elizabeth's eyebrows flew up, "Talk to me? Why?" He was handsome and she guessed him to be twenty or a little older.

He sat on a wooden bench and looked up at her. "You looked sad. Are you okay?"

"I'm fine, and I have to go." She saw her bag, walked over to it and proceeded to take off her skates and put on her boots. She'd never been good about talking with strangers.

"Don't go yet."

"I should. I have people waiting for me."

"Well, wait," he said rubbing his leg, "I don't even know your name." He limped over to her.

Elizabeth paused, and he continued, "I'm Joseph." He held out his hand for her to shake.

Elizabeth gave his hand a quick shake while sadness surged through her. Joseph was her father's name and here she was at the ice, their special place. She willed herself not to cry.

"I'm Elizabeth. I should go." Turning to leave, a shiver ran through her body. She hoped it wasn't noticeable and started to walk away hoping that Tara would see she was already gone when she came to fetch her, and would go home too.

"Are you freezing?" Joseph asked.

"It's been so cold for so long, I've gotten used to it. Goodbye," she called over her shoulder as she walked faster.

"You shivered. So, if it's not the cold, then what is it?" Joseph moved to follow Elizabeth. Catching up to her, he continued, "Look, I'm not trying to be rude or anything. I just saw a girl I'd like to get to know and made a fool of myself before I could give her my name. Can we start over?"

Elizabeth stopped in her tracks and turned around. "Start what over? You fell. I helped you. I'm Elizabeth. You're..." Tears welled in her eyes and she swallowed hard.

"Oh! I'm sorry. Did I say something to upset you?" Joseph asked.

Embarrassed, Elizabeth wiped her tears. "*Nee*. Sorry. It's not you. It's...well; it's complicated. I...um...it's... Never mind." She picked up her pace, ashamed of herself for reacting the way that she had. It wasn't his fault that he had the same name as her father. If she were going to function normally, she'd have to learn to control her emotions. Aunt Gretchen was always telling her she let emotions get the better of her.

"You can't walk anywhere in this cold. I'll drive you wherever you're going. My buggy is behind those trees."

He was right; it was too cold to walk and if Gretchen knew she'd walked so far in the snow, she'd get into trouble. Squinting in the direction he was pointing, she made out the shape of a buggy behind the trees. Before she could refuse or accept his offer, she heard a buggy and was pleased to see that it was Tara coming to collect her.

"I have to go. That's my friend who's come to get me." She'd never been so pleased to see Tara.

"I hope we meet again, Elizabeth."

She didn't answer and moved faster to meet the buggy.

CHAPTER 2

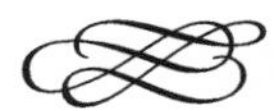

Yea, though I walk through the valley of the shadow of death, I will fear no evil: for thou art with me; thy rod and thy staff they comfort me.
Psalm 23:4

Eighteen years ago in an Englisch home.

"You know, Janice, some women can only have girls."

Janice stared at her mother-in-law, trying to get over her dislike of the woman, but how could she do that when everything that proceeded out of the woman's cruel, thin mouth was designed to put her down?

"I'm sure it'll be a boy." Janice placed her hand on her large baby bump. She was only weeks away from giving birth; she already had two girls, and she knew her husband desperately wanted a boy.

"I hope so for your sake. Lyle has always wanted a boy to carry on the family name and take over the dynasty. I don't think I need to remind you, but when Lyle has a boy, he'll be Lyle Doyle the Fourth."

"I know. You remind me every single day." It had been Lyle's idea to have his mother come to live with them when his father died.

Charlotte Doyle pulled a lace handkerchief out of her dress and dabbed at the corners of her eyes. "My Lyle would've liked to have seen our son have at least one son. Janice, a boy is what you need to give your husband. Who will take over from him?"

"Lyle and I have always said we're stopping at three. It's dangerous with my blood group and he said he doesn't want to put me at risk for a fourth." She'd made that up, the bit about the blood group, hoping it would put an end to Charlotte's rantings.

"You hear all the time of marriages that break down over these things."

Janice's heart pricked with fear. "What things?"

"Women who can't have boys. Their husbands divorce them and try again with another wife. There are many women who'd gladly marry him you know."

"Why would you say something like that to me?" Janice wasn't usually so outspoken, but she had grown weary of the woman's constant jibes.

Charlotte pursed her lips. "As I said, some women can only have girls."

"I believe that biologically speaking, it's something in the man's sperm that determines the sex of the child."

Charlotte gasped and now was using her lace handkerchief to fan herself. "How could you say those vulgar words out loud, Janice?"

"What, 'sex?' I'm not talking about the act; I'm talking about sex in the sense of boy or girl. And if you're talking about sperm, it's the sperm that determines the sex."

"There you go again." Charlotte averted her eyes as though she were terribly disappointed. "It's not necessary to say those words in polite company. I'll leave you to think about your actions while I have a lie down."

"Okay."

When Charlotte was halfway out of the room, she turned around. "I just don't want to see Lyle disappointed, if you have another girl. That'll be the third time he'll have been disappointed." Charlotte turned back and continued through the doorway.

Once she was gone, Janice was able to relax. Although Charlotte was annoying and probably deliberately trying to upset her, what if she was right about her husband leaving her for another woman?

Three of Janice's friends had been divorced after their husbands left them for younger women. At every social event she and Lyle had been to, women threw themselves at him even with her standing right next to him. What would these women be like if she hadn't been there? It was a constant worry, particularly with Lyle going on so many business trips so far from home.

To make matters worse, Lyle had often talked about having a son who would be able to take over his business concerns. How she hoped their baby would be a boy.

It was early Christmas morning when Janice's water broke. Her husband hadn't been able to get home the day before because the airports were closed with the snow. He was held up in New York. This was one birth she'd have to go through alone.

She called her sister, Jane, to look after her two girls, and as soon as she arrived, Janice took a taxi to the birthing center where her good friend and homebirth midwife, Margaret, would deliver her third child.

When she arrived, she got herself settled into one of the rooms and called her husband.

"I'm still trying to get there. I've hired a car."

"How did you get a car? Aren't the roads closed too?"

"Don't worry about me. Concentrate on you and the baby."

"Lyle, don't be reckless. Don't drive too quickly."

He chuckled. "I'll be safe. Here's hoping for a boy."

"What if she's a girl?"

"It'll be a boy! I've got to go now; they're bringing the car around."

The call ended and Janice placed the cell phone down. She noticed he didn't answer when she asked if he minded having another girl. His mother was right; he desperately wanted a son.

JANICE LAY there with her baby daughter in her arms. She kissed her gently on her forehead and breathed in the scent of the newborn. As soon as Margaret had delivered Janice's baby, she'd headed to the other room to deliver another baby. Janice felt sympathy as she listened to the other woman groan and scream.

Tears ran down her cheeks. The birth should've been a celebration, but disappointment was all she felt. It wasn't right and she knew it. Her baby was beautiful and she was healthy, but as she was so hoping for a boy, she didn't feel the connection to this baby that she'd felt with her other two girls. It should've been a time for celebration, but it wasn't.

Soon the midwife came back into the room. "That's two births in one day."

"Two on Christmas day? I never really thought that I'd have her on Christmas day."

Margaret walked over to her. "I'll put her in the crib and help you to the bathroom. Then she can have her first feeding."

"Okay, but I'll be all right to walk by myself."

"Are you sure?"

"Yes. I'm feeling okay." Janice walked down the hall to the bathroom. When she came back, she heard the other baby crying and peeped into the room. The other woman looked up and saw her. She was alone too.

"Hello," she said smiling warmly.

"Hi." Janice moved closer and looked at the baby in her arms. "What did you have?"

The woman looked down at her baby. "He's a boy."

"Can I see him?"

"Yes. Come in."

Janice sat down on the chair next to the bed, staring at the beautiful baby boy. If only she'd had a boy. "I had a girl. My husband desperately wanted a boy." She wondered whether her husband would be able to hide his disappointment.

The woman studied her for a moment. "Are you Janice Doyle?"

"Yes, I am." It was no surprise that the woman knew who she was. She and her husband were well known in the area.

"I recognize you from the magazines."

Janice burst out crying, covering her face with her hands.

"I'm sorry. Did I say something wrong?"

"No." She wiped her eyes. "It's just that my husband desperately wanted a boy. He's driving back here now and I have to tell him we had another girl and I don't want to go through it all again trying for a boy."

The woman looked at her sympathetically.

Janice sniffed, looked up at the ceiling and blinked rapidly. "I'm sorry. I don't know why I'm telling you all this."

"How badly do you want a boy?"

"Very badly, but it's too late now."

"Maybe not!"

Janice sniffed again. "What do you mean?"

"Would you consider swapping? I mean I might be enticed to do so."

"I couldn't. No. Not at all."

"Think about it. My husband's truck is stuck in the snow somewhere and he doesn't know if we had a boy or a girl."

Janice could scarcely believe what she was hearing, but it might work. "Well, the only person who knows is Margaret and she'll keep quiet if I ask her." Janice shook her head. "I can't believe I'm considering this."

"I won't do it for nothing at all. I know how rich you people are and if you want it to happen you can pay."

"Would you tell your husband?"

"As long as we have a child, it doesn't make a difference where she came from. And then there would be the money. We've never had anything. We've always had one struggle after another. If you take him, I know he'll have everything he ever wanted. We can't give him anything. We could never pay for college."

This was a solution. If this worked, everyone would win. Her heart pumped hard within her chest. "How much money? I could pay you a lump sum and then send you money every month. Enough money for your whole family to live on."

"Won't your husband notice that much money gone?"

"I have my own money. I don't need to use my husband's."

"Let me see your baby and make sure she's healthy."

Janice put her hand on her chest. "Should we do this?"

"Let me see your baby and I'll tell you."

Janice walked back into the room.

Margaret was with her baby and she looked over at Janice. "Where were you?"

"Talking to the woman in the next room. What do you know about her?"

"They don't have much money. I'm not charging them. She's

got a fear of hospitals, and a doctor friend of mine asked me if I'd look after her. They're some distant degree of relative to him."

"Are they good people?"

"Yes. I believe so."

"How poor are they?"

"Very." Margaret looked at the baby. "Are you ready to feed her now?"

"I'm just going to take her to show the woman next door. I was just looking at her baby and she wants to see mine."

Margaret eyed her suspiciously. "Have you called Lyle yet? He'll be anxious to know how you are and to hear that the baby arrived safely."

"No. And if he calls here, tell him I haven't had it yet."

Margaret recoiled. "Why?"

"You've got to trust me." Janice took her baby into her arms and walked her to the lady in the next room. "Here she is," Janice said showing the woman her baby.

"Can I hold her?"

Janice put the baby girl into her arms and looked at the boy now in the crib, wondering if she'd be able to love him as her own.

"Pick him up," the woman insisted.

Janice picked up the little boy and held him close. Yes, the plan could work.

"We'd still each have a baby to love."

"Would you look after her as though she was your own?" Janice asked.

"I would. And I'd know you could give him everything that Joseph and I never could give him."

"You'll love her, though, won't you?"

"I wanted a girl." The woman chuckled. "I'll love her and keep her safe. Now, how much money are we talking?"

Janice, holding the other woman's baby, negotiated a large

settlement and then ongoing monthly payments. The woman had to agree that she'd never tell anyone of the swap.

"I need money today or there's no deal. How will I know you won't change your mind?"

"I'll call and get one of my staff to bring money in from home. Can I carry him back to my room to use my cell phone?"

"Go ahead. I'll keep her here."

When she walked back into the room, Margaret looked at her. "Are you ready to feed her yet?" She jumped to her feet. "What are you doing, Janice? That's not your baby!"

"I need to tell you something. Sit down."

She sat Margaret down and explained her intentions.

"No, Janice! You can't be serious."

"I am and I'm going to do it."

"Why? Does it matter if you have a girl or a boy? You'll be found out!"

"No, I won't. If I'm found out, the payments to Lillian and her husband stop. I certainly won't tell anyone and neither will you."

"I can't believe you're serious. It's illegal. I'll lose my credibility. No one will use my services again and I've spent a fortune on this place." Margaret glared at her. "You'll regret this."

"I won't. I'll raise him as my own. No one will find out. You can't tell anyone."

"I can't let you do it, Janice. It's madness! You'll be found out!"

"Don't forget who loaned you the money for this place."

Margaret's eyes grew wide.

"What would happen if I called in the loan?"

"You wouldn't."

"I'm desperate. You've got to look the other way. Please?"

Deep lines appeared in Margaret's forehead as she placed both hands on her cheeks.

Janice put her hand lightly on her friend's arm. "Stay there and we'll talk more. I've just got to make a phone call."

Janice called home and had her housekeeper stop cooking the Christmas dinner and bring money in from the safe. Her housekeeper wouldn't ask what the money was for and she couldn't even let her sister, Jane, in on such a secret. Jane would pull the 'big sister card' and refuse to allow her to go through with it. She might even tell Lyle of her intentions. No—the fewer people who knew about this, the better.

When Janice had hung up from giving Magda her instructions, Margaret said, "You're serious? I can't believe it."

"Margaret, are you going to keep quiet about this? I need to know now because this is going ahead. Otherwise..."

"It seems I don't have a choice. I just hope this doesn't blow up in all our faces."

CHAPTER 3

I am not ashamed: for I know whom I have believed,
and am persuaded that he is able to keep
that which I have committed unto him against that day.
2 Timothy 1:12

ONCE THE DEAL was done and Margaret had been sworn to secrecy, Janice picked up her cell phone and called her husband. "Lyle, we have a boy!"

"I was so worried when I didn't hear from you. Is everything okay?"

"Everything went perfectly. The birth was a bit longer than the other two, but he's a boy, so he took a little more time." Janice bit her lip hoping her husband wouldn't detect the lie from over the phone. He was normally pretty good at reading her. "How far away are you?"

"Another hour, I'd say. I've been held up along the roads. I just called home and Jane said the girls are fine. She also said you called Magda to the birthing center. Are you sure everything's all right?"

"Yes. I just needed some things from home that I forgot."

"I'll see you soon."

"I can barely hear you."

"Don't be concerned if you call and can't reach me for the next several minutes. I can already hear crackling in the phone."

"Okay. Are you pleased that we finally had a boy?"

"I'm over the moon! I always wanted a boy and now we finally have one."

His last words faded away and then the phone went dead. Janice smiled, pleased that she had made her husband happy. As far as she was concerned, this was a win-win situation for all of them. Her daughter would be raised in a home with plenty of money and a lot of love, and the baby boy would be raised with the same.

She went back into the other woman's room with the baby boy, so each could say a final goodbye to her child.

WHEN LYLE BROUGHT Janice home the next morning after they had both stayed the night at the birthing center, Janice wanted nothing more than to see the look on her mother-in-law's face.

Lyle was delighted with his son and the Simpsons were happy with their daughter.

Lyle pushed the front door open and Janice walked into the sitting room where Charlotte was waiting.

"Well, let me see him," the old woman said in her usual demanding way.

Janice sat down next to her, so her mother-in-law could get a good look at him.

"He's much bigger than the girls were."

"That's because he's a boy."

"He doesn't have the Doyle ears."

Lyle laughed at his mother's comment. "He has his own ears, Mother, and they *are* Doyle ears." Lyle sat opposite them.

"When you were born, you looked like all your father's baby photos. I just don't see a resemblance."

Lyle laughed again, amused at his mother. "He'll grow up looking like the rest of us. Don't you worry."

Charlotte gave Janice a sidelong glance.

"I told you we'd have a boy, Charlotte."

Janice's sister, Jane, walked in just then with the two girls who were eager to see their new baby brother.

~

Eight years later.

JANICE'S DEAL with the Simpsons had gone according to plan for eight years, until the day Janice got a call from her bank.

"What do you mean the money's stopped going in? How can that happen? I made arrangements for the money to go in every week."

"I know, but the account has been closed."

Janice's heart froze. "When did that happen?"

"A few weeks ago."

"Why? Do you know why it closed? And why am I only finding out about this now?"

"I'm sorry, Mrs. Doyle. Sometimes money doesn't go through due to some glitch, but I checked when it bounced back and found that the account's been closed. I've got no way of knowing why it was closed because the Simpsons named on the account are with a different bank."

"I see."

"Perhaps you can make contact with the owner of the account

and they can give you an alternate account?"

"That's what I'll have to do. Thank you." Janice ended the call. The only thing had to be that the Simpsons were after more money. Pain gnawed at her stomach. She had an address for them. Since they hadn't made contact yet, she'd have to knock on their door, talk to them face-to-face and see how much they wanted. Mr. Simpson had learned of the swap at the birthing center, and had been fine with it after his wife had talked him around.

The next morning, when the three children were in school, Janice drove to the address she had for the Simpsons. When she stopped in front of the house, there was a for sale sign out front. She got out of the car and knocked on the door. When no one answered after several more knocks, Janice walked around the side of the house and stopped to peep in the windows. There was no furniture—the place was abandoned.

When she got back to the car, she picked up her cell and called the number on the sign. The agent refused to give any details about where the people had moved.

The next stop was the Simpsons' bank. She went to their branch and inquired as to whether they'd opened another account. Again, she was met with a dead end. The bank refused to give her details due to privacy reasons.

Janice drove home defeated. Then it occurred to her that if the Simpsons needed more money, they'd have to contact her soon.

After weeks had gone by with no word from the Simpsons, she wrote a letter to their old address hoping the letter might be forwarded to their new one.

Four weeks later, the letter was returned.

CHAPTER 4

The thief comes only to steal and kill and destroy;
I have come that they may have life,
and have it to the full.
John 10:10

The present day.

THE DAY TURNED to night and Elizabeth still hadn't shaken the overwhelming feeling of sorrow. Lying in her warm bed, she stared out the window and watched the snowflakes softly falling. It wasn't long before her thoughts turned to her parents. Deep down, she knew that they would not want her to wallow in grief to the point she could not enjoy the simple pleasures of life. She knew from being raised Amish for so many years that death was a part of life, but that didn't stop her from missing her parents. *God, please help me to be stronger, and help to ease the pain I feel inside.*

Her mind turned to the man she'd met earlier in the day. Elizabeth normally wouldn't have minded if someone had seen her cry, but something about crying in front of him made her uncomfortable. Closing her eyes, she pictured the young man before her, and soon when sleep overtook her, he moved into her dreams.

THE SUN SHONE brightly through the bedroom window as Elizabeth popped out of bed to get ready for work. Shaking the cobwebs out of her head, she rushed around her room unaware that she was humming.

Gretchen knocked on her bedroom door and entered carrying ice skates. "You left these in the way downstairs."

"I'm sorry."

"Don't put down, put away. Just remember that."

"I will."

Gretchen folded her arms and leaned against the door frame. "Are you going skating today?"

"No. Yesterday didn't go so well. I have work, and then Megan is meeting me before we go to the singing at the Yoders.'"

"Take the buggy today. *Onkel* William is hitching it up for you now."

"Are you sure?"

"*Jah*. I'll have him take Megan to the coffee shop this afternoon and then the two of you can go from there."

"Denke."

Gretchen nodded. "Have a good day, then. Be careful out there on the roads; go slow. And wear your coat; you don't want to catch a cold."

Elizabeth took the skates, deciding that she could throw them into the back of the buggy just in case they could skate somewhere tonight.

~

After her work that day, Elizabeth looked around the busy coffee shop and found a seat at the end of a large communal table and waited for Megan.

Being early and knowing that Megan was always late, Elizabeth ordered a cappuccino and waited. Her thoughts were a million miles away when someone sat across from her. She looked over to see that the person was not Megan; it was the man from the day before.

"Hi," he said.

She smiled "Hi."

"What were you deep in thought about?" Joseph asked.

"Hey, look, I'm really so..."

He raised his hand signaling her to stop. Smiling, he held out his hand, "My name's Joseph. What's yours?"

"Elizabeth."

"I don't know how many beginnings we have to have, but at least you didn't shiver that time. I must not be as scary as I was yesterday." Joseph removed his hat and ran his large hand through his hair.

"You're not scary. I didn't think that."

"*Jah,* you did. That's why you shivered. It's okay, you know. I'm not begging for you to help me up today."

"Elizabeth."

Elizabeth looked up to see Megan.

"There you are. Late as usual."

"I can't stay to go with you today. I'm sorry, I have to help *Mamm* with something."

Before Elizabeth could say anything or introduce Joseph, Megan was out the door and disappearing up the road. Megan wasn't comfortable around men; neither was Elizabeth, but Megan was painfully shy.

"I can stay and keep you company," Joseph said.

She had to laugh at him. It seemed he wasn't going to let up.

They spent the next hour talking and laughing. Joseph filled her in on all the details of how his family had just come to Lancaster County. Elizabeth felt more relaxed with him now that she knew he was a new member of her community.

The crowd around them came and went and neither noticed until Tara sat down in the seat next to her.

"I'm Tara," she said, her beady eyes fixed on Joseph.

Joseph shook her hand, his eyes scarcely leaving Elizabeth's. "Nice to meet you."

"So, I haven't seen you before. Are you one of the new *familye* who just moved into the community?" Tara inquired while staring intently at him.

"*Jah,* we've just moved here. I guess I'll meet everyone this Sunday at the gathering."

Tara raised her eyebrows. "Oh? Why did your *familye* move here and where have you come from?"

Elizabeth rolled her eyes. Up to this point, all that she had learned about Joseph was that he couldn't ice-skate, he was learning the building trade from his uncle, Kevin, and he'd just moved here.

"Excuse my friend, she's a little nosy," Elizabeth said in a teasing tone.

"Curious and inquisitive. Interested, but not nosy."

Tara didn't move despite the look Elizabeth gave her for asking so many questions.

"Well?" Tara said, turning back to face Joseph.

Joseph obliged and filled the girls in on the details surrounding his family. And more about himself.

"So, you're going to be a builder? Will you make a lot of money?" Tara asked.

Elizabeth nudged Tara, frowning at her. Tara and Megan were total opposites. Megan could barely speak to the man and had run out, whereas Tara was so bold she was asking far too many questions.

Joseph didn't have time to say more before a crowd swarmed in singing Christmas songs.

"Oh yeah, that reminds me," Tara said at the end of the first carol. "They're having a singing tonight at the Yoders' *haus* and they're starting early tonight. You going?" Talking a mile a minute, Tara continued, "Oh, Joseph, you will love this. The Yoders have a big Christmas tree on their property, and they have a big celebration with cider and hot chocolate. You have to go; every young person in the community will be there."

Looking at Elizabeth, Joseph asked, "Shall we go see?"

Shrugging, Elizabeth wondered if she should go home now that Megan had gone home. "I'm not ready for Christmas yet."

"You told Aunt Gretchen you were going." Tara ignored her excuse and grabbed Elizabeth by the arm, tugging her out of her seat, begging, "Let's go! We can't miss this. It's a tradition."

"Okay, okay. *Onkel* William loaned me the buggy today. I can take us all in that."

"Are you girls cousins?" He looked between the two of them.

"It's a long story," Tara said. "What do you say, Joseph?"

"I brought my buggy," he responded. "It's just outside."

Never short on ideas of how to organize people, Tara made a suggestion. "Elizabeth and I will follow you to your *haus*, then you leave your buggy there and come with us. At the end of the night, we'll take you home."

As they followed Joseph back to his house, Elizabeth had to listen to Tara tell her what a nice man Joseph was.

"And he likes you, Elizabeth. That cool and calm exterior is reeling him in just like a fish with a hook through it."

Elizabeth pulled a face, not liking the images that sprung to her mind. "I don't know about that. I barely know him. He seems okay."

"More than okay if you ask me. Now we'll be the first ones in the community to see where he lives."

Elizabeth giggled at her friend. Life was never boring when Tara was around.

"Wasn't Megan coming?"

"She met me at the coffee shop and then ran away when she saw Joseph."

Tara shook her head. "We really must do something with her, or she'll be living with Gretchen and William forever and a day."

"She'll be okay."

"I hope so."

CHAPTER 5

Trust in the Lord with all your heart
and lean not on your own understanding.
Proverbs 3:5

It was mostly the young people who had gathered at the Yoders' house.

The three of them joined the crowd in singing the lively hymns. Joseph bellowed out as many words of the songs as he could remember. Within a few seconds, Elizabeth did her best to shrug off her sadness and put the loss of her parents to one side.

When there was a break in the singing, Tara finally left them alone.

Joseph turned to Elizabeth. "Tell me about yourself."

"You already know everything. There's not much more to tell."

"Somehow, I don't believe that. Let's go for a walk away from all this noise."

As they walked, Elizabeth felt comfortable enough to tell him about how she came to be in the Amish community. "I wasn't born in the community. The Grabers took me in ten years ago. I was eight when my parents died."

"That's awful. I'm sorry."

Elizabeth nodded and kept talking. "Neither of my parents had any relatives, which I find really strange. Anyway, that's how I ended up in foster care. I was briefly at a couple of places before I came to the Grabers' home. I don't remember the other places much—just vague recollections."

"What did you mean about finding it strange that your family had no relatives?"

"I didn't think about it as a child, but often when parents die, their child would be taken in by a relation. Neither of them had one. Now that I'm in the community, it's hard to think that a married couple wouldn't have had at least one relation between the two of them."

"Have you looked into it? They could both have been orphans or something."

She shook her head. "I haven't, but I think I will. I barely remember what they looked like. My memories of them are so fuzzy. I remember how they made me feel and that's the clearest thing—the feelings."

"How did they make you feel?"

Elizabeth glanced up into Joseph's face. No one else had ever cared to ask her so many questions. "I guess I felt safe and I felt loved. They were my protectors, and my teachers. I remember my father teaching me how to tie my shoelaces and my mother telling me how to spell words."

"Maybe if you look them up and do some research you could find some relatives somewhere."

"Do you think so?"

"I do."

"I don't think the Grabers would like me doing that. They want me to stay in the community forever."

"What do you want to do?"

She shook her head. "I think I would feel better finding out more about my parents. All I know is that my father drove trucks and my mother stayed home." When Elizabeth heard Tara's loud laughter, she looked back and saw that they'd gone far. "We should start back." She turned around.

Joseph turned as well and together they walked back to the house.

"It looks so beautiful from here," Joseph said.

Elizabeth looked ahead to see the Yoders' yard lit up. Christmas candles hung in the trees and luminous colored lanterns were strung everywhere. The snow sparkled and the whole place glistened like a wonderland.

"It's so pretty at night."

Tara walked up to join them when they got back to the yard.

"Would you like a cup of cider?" Joseph asked Elizabeth, but both girls answered, "Yes," at the same time. With a hint of a smile on his face, he walked off.

Tara nudged Elizabeth, and asked, "What's wrong with you?"

Elizabeth had known Tara long enough to know what she was getting at. "I've only just met him."

"Have some fun for once! He's most likely a gift from *Gott;* he's following you around, and you're frowning. That's not the Elizabeth I used to know. Make her reappear before you ruin your chances with that man." Tara stopped talking as Joseph returned with the cider.

Suspicious of Elizabeth's blushing, he asked, "Were you talking about me?"

"*Nee.*" Elizabeth knew she answered too quickly.

Tara leaned in toward Joseph. "Hey, Joseph, you know, Elizabeth loves to ice-skate. Do you skate? I heard they were decorating around the pond, too, tonight. Maybe you two should walk over and have a look."

Rolling her eyes, Elizabeth quipped, "She's so subtle, isn't she?"

Joseph turned to face Elizabeth, his blue eyes shimmering under the lights, "That's actually a pretty good idea. Do you girls want to go see?"

Tara excused herself and Elizabeth was left alone again with Joseph.

"Sorry about that. She's very forthright. Tara lives with me and so does the girl at the coffee shop earlier today. We're all the foster children of the Grabers," Elizabeth said.

Joseph nodded.

"Did I mention I worked at the coffee shop? Did you come there today to see me?"

He laughed. *"Nee,* I had no idea. I just wanted *kaffe.* Is that where you work?"

"Jah. I'd finished working and was waiting for Megan. Now I feel like a fool. I'm an idiot to think you were trying to find me."

"I was hoping we could spend some more time together. It was a nice surprise to see you there. I thought I'd have to wait until one of the Sunday meetings."

Elizabeth blushed.

They walked toward the pond on the edge of the Yoders' property.

"You seem down, Elizabeth. I know it's wretched about your parents; is that why?"

"It's just this time of year that makes me sad. I'm sorry, I didn't know it showed so much."

"It does."

"Christmas Day is my birthday. More than any other time of the year, I think about my parents at this time."

"That's understandable."

Elizabeth told Joseph what she remembered about her parents.

Wisps of wavy hair sprang out from underneath her prayer *kapp* every time the wind picked up.

Joseph gently pushed the strands of hair away from her face.

Elizabeth stopped speaking long enough to take in the gentleness of his touch.

"*Denke,*" she said.

"For what?" Joseph asked.

"For listening. That was sweet of you."

The iced-over pond was only a couple of yards away from them. They stood still and watched the many rays of light from the lanterns dance on the ice.

"It's beautiful, isn't it?" Joseph asked.

A lone tear fell from Elizabeth's eye. "It's beautiful." As if on cue, small flakes of snow fell around them.

Elizabeth and Joseph couldn't help but giggle with delight as they stared up into the dark sky.

"This might be the craziest thing I've ever done, but do you have your skates with you?"

Elizabeth replied, "They're in my buggy. Why?"

"Can you teach me to skate?" Joseph asked.

Elizabeth laughed in surprise and then, looking at his large feet, she said, "My skates won't fit on your feet."

Joseph laughed. "I know that. Let's go back and have a word with the Yoders. They've got about nine children, some of them as big as me. I'll see if they've got some skates I can borrow."

"Okay, let's do it.

Just as Joseph had said, the Yoder boys all had skates and they were only too happy for him to borrow a pair.

Once Elizabeth had her skates under her arm, she tried to keep up with Joseph as he strode with determination back toward the pond.

"You really want to do this?" she asked him.

"*Jah,* I can't wait to glide across the ice," Joseph said.

"It's not that easy, you know. It takes a while before you stop falling over."

"Depends."

Laughter escaped Elizabeth's lips. "What do you mean? Depends on what?"

"Whether you're a *gut* teacher or not."

"That's not fair. If you're a bad skater are you going to blame me?"

Joseph leaned down at the edge of the pond and strapped on the skates. "If you're a good teacher, I won't be a bad skater."

OVER THE NEXT SEVERAL DAYS, Elizabeth and Joseph met every day. Sometimes they met after she finished work and other times they met at the ice to skate.

Elizabeth, standing at the edge of the ice, watched now as Joseph glided across the surface of the pond. He'd had a few falls and he still looked wobbly, but the fact that he had learned to skate relatively well in just a few short weeks either proved that he was a natural or that Elizabeth's father had taught her well.

Stopping near her, Joseph asked, "Well, we've officially been dating for almost two weeks now. So, with Christmas only a week away, what would you like for a Christmas present?"

"Dating? Is that what we've been doing?"

"Jah."

"Oh."

"What's the matter?" he asked.

"I thought there should've been some official time that we had a conversation about it. Were we dating, or are we just friends?"

He smiled at her. "Friends and more than friends. At least that's what I'm hoping."

She gave a little giggle and skated into the middle of the pond hearing the sounds of him close behind her. Stopping suddenly, she waited to see if he'd be able to stop just as fast. He did, and then she spun around to face him.

"Answer my question?" he said.

"About a gift?"

He nodded.

"I have everything I want." She stared into his eyes wondering if he might kiss her.

"And I'm pretty happy too. You came into my life, and you've taught me to skate. What more could a man want?"

Elizabeth could feel her cheeks burning as her heart pounded in anticipation. What she wanted for Christmas was simply to feel his lips upon hers, but she wasn't about to say so.

"You're no longer that sad girl I first saw, alone on the ice."

"I'm not sad."

"I so wanted to impress you that first time that I saw you, and I fell flat on my face."

Elizabeth laughed. "*Jah,* I was sad that day. Sometimes I get like that."

"Are you happy with the Grabers?"

"I am. I love them and I'm really close with Tara and Megan. We're a family."

"I know. I've seen that. Now, shall we skate?"

"Aren't you tired of skating yet?"

"Not when I can skate with you." He skated away. "First one to the edge of the ice is a winner."

He always said that and she always managed to overtake him.

CHAPTER 6

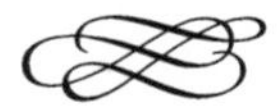

"For I know the plans I have for you," declares the Lord,
"plans to prosper you and not to harm you,
plans to give you hope and a future."
Jeremiah 29:11

"SLEEPY HEAD!"

Elizabeth woke up to a pillow being thrown on her head. She pushed it away and opened one eye to see Tara. "What are you doing?"

"Waking you up. Aren't you working today?"

"Yep." Elizabeth rolled over trying to grab another couple minutes of sleep.

"It's time to get up. You've got to take me to work today."

Tara had just gotten a job at one of the Amish quilt stores, not far from the coffee shop.

"What time is it?"

"A few minutes past seven."

"Okay. Just give me a few more minutes."

Then the blankets were ripped off her.

"Leave me alone!"

"Wake up now!"

Elizabeth sat up. There was no use arguing with Tara. "Okay. I'm up. Make me some *kaffe?"*

"Okay, as long as you don't go back to bed when I'm gone."

"I won't."

When Tara walked out of the room, Elizabeth rubbed her eyes. She'd been unable to sleep very much, her mind busy thinking about Joseph and the future they might share together. They'd get married soon so they could have children when they were still young, and they'd buy a little house and build on to it as their family grew. The idea of making a choice between the Amish community and the *Englisch* world was a dim memory. Joseph was her future, she was certain of it.

As she slowly changed out of her nightdress and into her dress and apron, she daydreamed some more about Joseph. Would he come into the coffee shop for a quick bite to eat as he did some days? She hoped he would.

She pulled on black stockings before she dragged a brush through her long hair, wishing she'd braided it the night before. It was always snarly if it wasn't braided overnight. When the tangles cleared and the brush finally went right through smoothly, she tossed her brush down on the chest of drawers. After she'd divided her hair evenly in two, she braided one side and then the other before winding the braids and pinning them against her head. Lastly, she placed her prayer *kapp* on her head.

"There you are," Gretchen said as Elizabeth entered the kitchen. "Tara tells me you're taking her to work?"

"*Jah.* That's our plan."

"And she's bringing me home too," Tara said.

"Okay. I can do that I guess, but I finish at three."

"I finish at four, so you'll have to wait."

Elizabeth yawned. "Okay. Where's that *kaffe?*"

Tara put a mug in front of her while Gretchen placed a plate of pancakes on the table for everyone to help themselves. William had already gone to work early that morning. As soon as Megan walked in and sat down, everyone dove for the pancakes.

JUST AS THE lunch crowd had died down and Elizabeth was wiping down tables in the coffee shop, a well-dressed man walked in. He sat down and looked at a menu. Elizabeth finished clearing a table and took the stack of plates back to the kitchen to give him time to make his selection.

When she came out, Cathy, a girl she worked with, nodded toward the man. "You serve him, I bet he'll give you a good tip."

"Why don't you?"

"I don't do well with those rich types."

Elizabeth walked over to him. "Hello, have you had enough time to look at the menu?"

He looked up at her and then his jaw dropped open.

She stepped back, not knowing what to do. It frightened her the way he was ogling her.

"Do you know what you want to order, or shall I come back in a few minutes?"

"I'm sorry I'm staring. You look exactly like my youngest daughter. It's uncanny."

"Oh, a few people say I look familiar. I guess I've got one of those faces. Did you want to have something to eat?"

He placed the menu on the table without taking his eyes from her. "I'll have a flat white on skim."

"Nothing to eat?"

He rubbed his forehead. "Just give me something. I don't know what. I can't think straight. Get me whatever you think is good."

She nodded and hurried away. She gave an order into the kitchen for a beef pie with salad, and began to make his coffee.

"What did he say?" Cathy whispered.

"He was weird. You take his food to him. He makes me uncomfortable."

"He likes you. You'll get a good tip."

"I don't want a tip that way."

Cathy dug her in the ribs, nearly causing Elizabeth to spill the milk she was pouring into the coffee. Because the rush hour was over, Cathy and she were the only waitresses left working.

"Please, Cathy? I'll return the favor."

"Okay, we'll go halves in the tip if he leaves one, which he will. He's rich. I can tell."

"Okay, we'll go halves, but I don't want to talk to him again."

Cathy gave a little giggle as Elizabeth passed her his coffee.

She watched from behind the coffee machine as Cathy made her way back to the man.

"Where's the other girl?" she heard the man say.

Elizabeth crouched down behind the counter.

"Working in the back," Cathy replied.

"What's her name?"

"Elizabeth Simpson."

Elizabeth covered her mouth wishing Cathy hadn't given out her name.

Cathy hurried back to the kitchen when the meal order was called out, and then she took the food back to the man. While Cathy wiped down more of the vacant tables, Elizabeth stayed in the background wishing the man would leave.

When he finished eating, he called for the bill and Cathy left it with him. He stood up and pulled some notes from his pocket, put them on the table, and placed a cup over the corner. Then he left but not without having another look around for Elizabeth. He caught her eye and stared at her intently before he left.

Cathy wasted no time running over to his table to see how big his tip was. She grabbed the notes and hurried back to Elizabeth.

"He's left a two hundred dollar tip."

"That must be an accident. Go after him."

"Are you insane? He's a rich man. He meant to give this tip to us. Well, to you, but you agreed to halves. I think the man's in love with you."

"Yeah, well, did you have to give him my name?"

"There's no harm in that. Don't you see yourself with a rich sugar daddy?"

"No! I like Joseph."

"Boring! You're not really Amish. What's to stop you having a better life?"

Elizabeth raised her eyebrows at Cathy. Cathy was born and raised Amish and was getting married in January.

"Don't you think I should stay in the community?"

"I suppose so."

"I'm just glad that man's gone. I didn't like the way he was staring at me. He said I looked like his daughter. That means he knows he's old enough to be my father."

Cathy passed her one hundred dollars, kept one hundred for herself, and placed the remainder in the till for the meal. "Not bad. One hundred dollars because he liked the look of you."

"Creepy." Elizabeth shook her head while wondering what to do with the hundred dollars. It would certainly come in handy for buying Christmas gifts.

CHAPTER 7

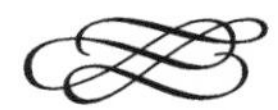

For in this hope we were saved.
Now hope that is seen is not hope. For who hopes for what he sees? But if we hope for what we do not see, we wait for it with patience.
Romans 8: 24-25

Across town.

JANICE RAN to meet her husband when he walked into the house.

She threw her arms around his neck and kissed him. "You're early."

"Where are Felicity and Georgia?"

"Georgia's just come home and Felicity is still at work." Their son, Lyle IV, was in college away from home.

Seeing the distracted look on his face, she asked, "Is something wrong?"

He shook his head. "I've just had the weirdest thing happen. I need a drink."

"I'll pour us some whiskey and you can tell me about it."

When they were seated with drinks in their hands, Lyle said, "I saw a young woman today and she looked the spitting image of Georgia."

Janice took a gulp of her whiskey. "Where was she?"

"She was at a coffee shop. She's an Amish woman."

Janice laughed and was suddenly relieved. The Simpsons weren't Amish.

"You should come back and see her."

"No. I couldn't do that. Did you talk to her?"

He gave a laugh. "I think I scared the poor girl. I was staring at her and I told her how much she looked like one of my daughters. If I'd seen her from a distance, I'd have been dead sure it was Georgia."

"Was she wearing Amish clothes?"

"Yes, she had on the whole garb. I should've taken a photo."

"What were you doing there?"

"I'd just finished a meeting with a lawyer. I heard your voice in my head going mad at me for continually forgetting lunch and that's when I saw the place."

Janice took a sip of scotch.

He shook his head. "I still can't believe it."

"Believe what?" Charlotte walked into the room and sat down with them.

"Hello, Mother. I was just telling Janice that I saw a young woman who looked almost exactly like Georgia."

"How old was she?"

"I didn't ask." He laughed. "I think my reaction scared the poor woman half to death. She was Amish, and I guess they're private people."

Charlotte glanced at Janice and then looked back at her son. "If you had to guess how old would you say?"

"A little younger than Georgia."

"Where did you see her?"

"Charlotte, it doesn't really matter. It's all a fuss about nothing. There are many people who look like others. They say everyone has a double somewhere in the world. Georgia's just happens to live close by," Janice said.

Georgia walked into the room. "Did I hear my name?"

Charlotte said, "Your father is just telling us that he met your double." The old woman turned to her daughter-in-law. "Oh, Janice, won't you be a dear and pour me a drink?"

Janice hid her irritation, and got up to pour her mother-in-law a drink.

"Really? I have a double—a doppelganger?"

"Your father saw her," Charlotte said.

Georgia sat down next to her grandmother. "Where did you see her, Dad?"

"In an Amish coffee shop of all places. She's a waitress."

"She's Amish?"

"Yes, and a waitress. She makes a good coffee, too, if she was the one who made it."

"You should take Georgia to see her tomorrow, Lyle," Charlotte suggested.

Janice scowled. "Charlotte, Lyle's too busy to do that. We never see him during the day."

"I've got the day off tomorrow. Would you take me, Dad?"

"I could juggle some things around and meet you there at eleven."

"Great, just text me the address and I'll put it into my GPS."

Janice passed her mother-in-law a drink as Georgia left the room.

This was all too close to home; her youngest daughter didn't need to go around looking at people who looked like her. When Janice sat back down on the couch, she wondered if this girl might be the baby she'd given to the Simpsons. She frowned as she tried to remember any clues that they might have joined the Amish. That would certainly explain them refusing the money and closing down that account. It would also explain them selling the house, because they would have had to move closer to other Amish people.

The only thing she could do was go to the coffee shop before Lyle and Georgia. They had mentioned eleven, so that meant that she had to get there before then. She'd know if that was her real daughter.

"Janice!"

She looked across at her husband.

"Where were you? You were a million miles away."

Charlotte had left the room and only Lyle remained.

"Just distracted, sorry. I'm hoping I gave Magda the right menu for dinner."

"She'll sort it out. How was your day?"

"Lyle got another speeding ticket, and they're threatening to throw him out of college again."

"It took me a while to settle into college. Don't worry about him."

"You said you'd take the car away from him if he got another ticket. Are you going to?"

"Okay, but that'll mean you'll have to drive him everywhere."

"Wait until the day after tomorrow, then, if that's okay. I've got some errands to run over the next couple of days. How's Felicity doing?"

Their oldest daughter had just joined the family firm.

"She's doing great. She's got real potential. I've always said that. I think she'll be the one who'll take over my company." He took another sip of his drink.

"What about Lyle?"

He wiggled his mouth. "Not everyone's cut out for it. He'll be successful at something."

"You've always told him he'll take over the company one day."

"No, I haven't. My mother has always told him that. I've been very careful not to say that to him or to anyone else. Anyway, it'll be up to the board of directors."

"How will they feel about a woman taking over, even if she's your daughter?"

"It's ability they'll be looking at. I still think that a woman has to be better than a man to make it in this world, but if anyone's going to do that, it'll be Felicity."

"I always thought you wanted a boy to take over the company. Isn't that why you wanted a son?"

"I never minded whether we had boys or girls."

Janice felt sick to the stomach and the room spun. "I remember you telling me you wanted a son. That's why we were so pleased when Lyle arrived. Lyle the Fourth, to carry on and take over."

"I guess it's nice to have a son but I'd have been just as happy with another girl."

The glass slid out of her fingers and it shattered on the hard marble floor.

"Are you all right?"

"Why are you saying that now? Both you and your mother said how badly you wanted a boy."

He stared at her, speechless at her sudden outburst.

She pulled her gaze away from him. "I have a headache. I need to lie down."

He put his drink down and rushed to her side. "I'll help you."

Once Lyle had helped her to bed, he covered her with blankets.

"Can I get you something?"

"No. It'll pass, it's just one of my migraines. Nothing really works on them."

He leaned down and kissed her softly on her forehead, and quietly left the room. As soon as he was gone, the tears fell down her cheeks. It'd all been for nothing. She loved her son, Lyle, as though he was her own flesh and blood, but that didn't stop her from thinking about her baby girl she gave away. Not a day went by when she wasn't plagued with feelings of guilt and regret. Margaret had been right. She regretted it. And now...was it all about to blow up in her face just as Margaret had predicted nearly eighteen years ago?

Every day it was clear to her that Lyle didn't fit in with the rest of the family, and if she saw it, what if others did? He was athletic and had a much larger build than the rest of the Doyle men.

If this girl was her daughter, the truth was going to come out and everyone would know the dreadful thing she'd done. How would the two children who'd been swapped react when they learned what had happened? How would her other two daughters react to knowing that the two mothers had deprived them of their sister? And what would they think of her as a mother for doing what she had done? Lyle would divorce her for sure, and she wouldn't be able to blame him.

She had to get a look at this girl before her husband and Georgia got there. When Lyle was in the shower the next morning, Janice would find the message he sent to Georgia regarding the address of the coffee shop and she'd get there to see her before they did.

CHAPTER 8

But the fruit of the Spirit is love, joy, peace, patience, kindness, goodness, faithfulness, gentleness, self-control; against such things there is no law.
Galatians 5:22-23

AT NINE O'CLOCK THE next morning, Janice parked her car across the road from the coffee shop. She was armed with a newspaper so it would look to passersby as though she was doing something. Squinting through the large glass windows, she saw three Amish girls working inside. She'd have to get closer.

The coffee shop was fairly crowded but from where she was, she could see a couple of empty tables. She left her car and walked across the road, pushed the door open, and sat at one of the empty tables.

After she'd been there a minute or two, a woman came to take her order. The woman looked nothing like her daughter. She ordered a coffee and kept looking around for the woman her husband had seen the day before. And then she saw her behind the coffee machine. She could've been Georgia's twin she looked so much like her. The age of the girl looked about right as well. When the girl looked up, Janice put her head down. Janice was suddenly dizzy. She stood up to go get some fresh air, but as soon as she stood she collapsed onto the floor.

Opening her eyes, Janice found herself on her back looking up at the ceiling with a sea of faces looking down at her. When she regained focus, she was looking right into the face of the girl she'd come to see.

"Are you alright?" the girl asked.

Janice couldn't speak. When she heard someone talking about calling 911, she made an effort to raise herself to a sitting position and, as she did so, the girl helped her.

"Are you alright, Ma'am?" the girl asked once more.

Putting her hand to her head, Janice forced herself to say, "Yes."

Someone passed a glass of water to the girl. She offered it to Janice. "Try a sip of water."

Janice took the glass from her and drank a little, sipping slowly. When she'd passed the glass back, she tried to stand.

"Please, Ma'am, stay there for a couple of minutes until you feel better. Do you want me to call someone for you?"

"No! Thank you. I just need a moment." She looked at the girl, seeing eyes that were the same as looking at Felicity and Georgia. This girl was her daughter. There wasn't a doubt in her mind about it. "You're very kind. What's your name?"

"Elizabeth."

"Such a pretty name."

Was her last name Simpson? How would she find out? She took the opportunity, even if the girl thought she was odd for asking. She'd just fainted and everyone had been staring at her so what did it matter if people thought she was odd? "Elizabeth what? What's your last name?"

She took a moment, and then said, "Simpson."

Janice dropped her head into her hands and sobbed. It made things worse when Elizabeth tried to comfort her.

"What can I do for you? Are you sure there's not someone I can call?"

"No." Janice summoned all her strength and pushed herself to her feet as more tears streamed down her face. She leaned over and grabbed her handbag from the table and then headed for the door.

Once she was out of the café, she heard someone behind her.

"Wait! Please, Ma'am, I think you should sit down for a while longer."

It was her daughter.

She whipped her head around. "I'm fine. I need to be somewhere." She walked up the street, not wanting Elizabeth to see what car she got into. When she'd reached the street corner, she turned to see that Elizabeth had gone back inside. Janice then crossed the road and hurried to her car.

ELIZABETH LOOKED out the window as she was placing an order onto a table. The lady who had fainted was now getting into a car. She hoped she was okay to drive, but she'd done all she could to help her.

The day wore on and all Elizabeth could think of was Joseph and whether he might come in on his lunch break. Even though she wasn't able to speak to him much when he had lunch at the café, it was still nice to see him during the day.

"He's back again!" her workmate, Cathy, told her.

"Who is?" She hoped she meant Joseph.

"The man who gave us that large tip, and he has someone with him. Take a look."

Elizabeth had taken over the coffee making and had been behind the coffee machine for the past hour.

"Let's swap. You go out and see him."

Curious, and wondering whether he'd brought his daughter who, he claimed, looked like her, she swapped with her friend and went to take their order.

When she approached the table, she saw a young woman who indeed bore a remarkable resemblance to herself.

The man looked up at her as she approached. "Here she is. I brought you my daughter I was telling you about."

"You do look like me," Elizabeth said, smiling at the young woman.

"Wow! I can't believe it. I really didn't think we'd look that much alike. Where are you from? Have you always lived around here?"

"I moved here when my parents died around ten years ago."

"Oh, I'm sorry to hear that. Were they Amish too?"

Elizabeth shook her head. "No. Do you live close?"

"Not that far. About an hour away," the man said.

"What can I get for you today?" Elizabeth asked, not at all comfortable talking about herself with strangers.

Once they placed their order, Elizabeth hurried away. She wondered if the girl might be some relation, maybe a distant relative. Perhaps she should look further into her parents' records to see if they had at least one living relative. Since she'd lived amongst the Amish with all the uncles, aunts, and cousins everyone was surrounded with, it was hard to believe that two people could have had no relations at all.

As she waited for the coffees to be made, she decided that she would see if they wanted to exchange addresses and phone numbers in case there was some connection that existed. She scribbled down her address and the Grabers' phone number on a nearby slip of paper. When the coffees were ready, she picked them up and headed back to the table with the slip of paper wedged between her fingers.

"Would you like to exchange addresses and phone numbers? I'm going to search and see if my parents had some relatives. We might be related somehow."

"I don't know if we are, but sure." The young woman looked into her bag. "Do you have a piece of paper?"

Elizabeth ripped the paper she'd given them in half. "You can use this. I'm Elizabeth by the way. Elizabeth Simpson."

The girl looked up from writing down her details. "And I'm Georgia Doyle, and this is my father, Lyle Doyle."

She nodded and smiled at the older man, now knowing that his story had been true and that he hadn't had any bad intentions.

When Mr. Doyle and his daughter finally left the coffee shop, Elizabeth couldn't help the weird sensation looming over her. They were obviously rich because the man had left another huge tip. The woman from earlier that morning had gotten into a very expensive car, not a type normally seen in that part of town, and she had asked her last name, becoming even more distressed at the Simpson name. Could there be a connection between that lady and these two people? It made her more determined to look into her family's history.

CHAPTER 9

The Lord is slow to anger and great in power,
and the Lord will by no means clear the guilty.
His way is in whirlwind and storm,
and the clouds are the dust of his feet.
Nahum 1:3

JANICE WENT STRAIGHT HOME and lay down in a darkened room with ice chips rolled into a towel and placed across her forehead. Her fainting spell had now developed into a bad headache. It was only two weeks away from Elizabeth's birthday, which was Christmas day, the same as young Lyle's, the day that she had chosen to swap her for a stranger's son. A wave of nausea swept over her and she leaned over the bed and heaved.

Her housekeeper walked into her room. "Are you okay?"

"No. I'm sick."

"Can I get you anything?"

"No."

She came closer and saw the vomit on the floor. "I'll clean that up."

Janice turned around and buried her head in the pillow. As much as she loved her son, Lyle, she wished she could turn back time. She never would've made the stupid swap. Tossing and turning for the next few hours, she couldn't help but wonder what would happen next. How did Elizabeth and her parents end up with the Amish?

She dozed off and the next thing she knew someone sat on the bed beside her. When she smelled her husband's aftershave, she closed her eyes and didn't turn around. If he thought she was asleep, he'd leave her be. Magda would've told him she wasn't feeling well. The last thing she wanted was for him to tell her about seeing Elizabeth again.

When she woke the next morning, she heard her husband's shower running. She pulled on a bathrobe and went downstairs. Their housekeeper was in the kitchen preparing breakfast.

"Coffee or tea, Mrs. Doyle?"

"Yes please."

"Which one this morning?"

"Oh, tea please."

"You feeling a lot better?"

"Yes." She sat down and pretended to be interested in the day's newspaper that was on the table in front of her.

ELIZABETH WOKE up pleased to have a day off. She'd arranged to meet Joseph briefly in town over his lunch break. She walked into the kitchen where Tara and Megan were already eating breakfast.

"Why are you looking so happy?" Tara asked as Elizabeth sat down.

"I'm seeing Joseph later today."

"I wish I had a man who made me smile like that."

Megan said, "You've got your choice of men, don't you?"

"I don't like any of them that much. I don't like any of them enough to marry them or anything." She gave a giggle and added, "Not like Elizabeth loves Joseph."

Elizabeth kept quiet, wanting to keep her feelings for him to herself, betrayed only by the small smile she couldn't keep from her lips.

Mrs. Graber put a pile of pancakes in the center of the table. "Don't you girls have anything to talk about other than men?"

"Nee," said Tara, causing the other two girls to giggle.

"I've got something else to talk about." Elizabeth placed two pancakes on her plate.

"What is it?" Mrs. Graber asked as she joined them.

"Yesterday I saw a girl who looked exactly like me. Well, not exactly but very much like me."

"Where was that?" Gretchen Graber asked.

"It was in the coffee shop. Her father had been in the day before and he told me that his daughter looked like me. I thought nothing of it until he brought his daughter back the next day."

"Who were these people?" Tara asked.

"I don't remember the last name, but her first name was Georgia and they said they live about an hour away."

Tara's eyes opened wide. "Are you related possibly?"

"I was told my parents had no relations." She looked at Gretchen. "Is that right?"

"That's what they told me, and that's all I know."

"How would I find out for certain?"

Aunt Gretchen shook her head. "I'm not certain. I could give you the phone number of the social worker."

"Okay. I'd like to find out if I do have some relations. It seems that everyone's got someone, unless my parents were both orphans or something."

"Oh, now I'm keen to know if this girl is related to you. Was she older or younger?" Tara asked.

"I don't know. Possibly the same age or maybe a little older; I don't think she was younger from what I could tell."

"Surely you could get your birth records and trace your parents that way."

"I guess so. I'll look into it. The girl and I exchanged phone numbers and addresses." Elizabeth cut a slice of pancake and placed it into her mouth.

JANICE FELT her body stiffen when her husband walked into the breakfast room.

He stared at her. "You better?"

"Yes. It was just another migraine."

"You should go back to the doctor about that. You get them too frequently."

"There's not much they can do about them."

"I'm not so sure about that." He sat down at the table without kissing her good morning as he normally would've.

"Have you finished with the paper?"

She pushed it over to him.

"Thanks."

Magda placed Lyle's usual mug of coffee in front of him. He took a mouthful while he read the paper. He'd never done that before. Normally they had a conversation which he'd start by asking her what she was going to do that day. Had Elizabeth told him something about herself? Did he know something he was keeping from her?

She had to know. After she took a deep breath, she asked, "How did your trip with Georgia go yesterday?"

He raised his eyebrows and looked over at her. "Good. Georgia saw the girl and they exchanged numbers. The girl is looking into her parents' family tree. Maybe she's some distant relation to us. She thinks she has no living relatives. Her parents died, and now she's living with an Amish family.

"They died?"

He frowned at her. "Yes. It's sad. She said they died some years ago."

"That's awful. How did they die?"

"She didn't say. I'm surprised she told us that much." He went back to reading his paper.

"Yes. That's true."

"Here's your tea, Mrs. Doyle. Can I get you anything besides toast? Anything for the headache?"

Every morning, Janice had two slices of toast with marmalade.

"Just the toast thanks. I'm fine. The headache's gone now. And thanks for cleaning up last night."

The housekeeper gave her a nod.

"We'll have all the children home again soon," Lyle said.

"What do you mean?" Janice asked.

"Lyle's coming back from college. We'll have the three of them here for a big family Christmas."

There was a weird tension between them. Janice could feel it. They'd always had their three children there for Christmas, so why had he said that? Was he suspicious? Lyle Junior had grown to six feet two, when all the Doyle men were no more than five eight. He was also not as good academically as the rest of their family.

She swallowed a mouthful of tea far too quickly and burned her mouth causing her to crash the cup back onto the saucer. Her fingertips flew to her mouth as the hot liquid scalded the back of her throat.

"Are you sure you're okay?"

"I might lie down again."

"That's it. I'm calling the doctor," Lyle said.

"No! Please don't. I'll be fine. I just need to rest. Magda, can you bring my toast up to me?"

"Yes, Mrs. Doyle."

Janice left the room quickly, unable to sit in the same room as her husband.

A few moments later, Magda brought her toast to her. "Mr. Doyle's left and he said he'd call you to check on you later."

"Thank you, Magda."

After her housekeeper left the room, Janice had to talk to someone. She called the only other person who knew about the swap, her midwife and good friend, Margaret.

CHAPTER 10

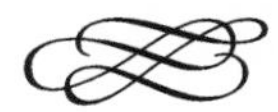

The Lord is slow to anger and abounding in steadfast love,
forgiving iniquity and transgression,
but he will by no means clear the guilty,
visiting the iniquity of the fathers on the children,
to the third and the fourth generation
Numbers 14:18

MARGARET ANSWERED the phone as though she was half asleep.

"Did I wake you?"

"Janice?"

"Yes."

"Is everything okay?"

"I don't know. Do you have time to talk?"

"I guess so. I'm awake now. I only got to sleep at two, I was working."

"I'm sorry."

"That's all right. What's going on?"

"I don't know where to start." She took a deep breath. "I think Lyle has found the baby I swapped."

"How? What do you mean?"

"He went to a coffee shop somewhere and came home and told me about this girl who looked like Georgia. I didn't think much of it, but then I got worried when he arranged for Georgia to go back with him to see the girl the next day."

"Do you think it's her?"

"I didn't at first. But I went there myself yesterday morning, before they went there. She looks very much like Georgia and a little like Felicity."

Margaret was silent.

"Lyle came back and told me that the girl said her parents died awhile back, and she has no relatives. She was taken in by an Amish family. She's wearing Amish clothes and she speaks differently than us." Janice fought back tears. When she was met with silence on the other end of the phone, she knew that Margaret was stopping herself from saying, *I told you this would blow up in our faces!* "Margaret, are you still there?"

"I don't know what to say."

"I think Lyle might know. He was acting weird this morning."

"He couldn't possibly know. It's just your guilty conscience making you feel that. He couldn't possibly have figured it out."

"You don't think so?"

"No. I don't!"

"What about how Lyle Junior looks so different?"

"That's not unusual. Your father was very tall, too, don't forget."

"I guess so. What am I going to do?"

"Nothing. There's nothing you can do. Just forget it. There's no way anyone can find out. Their birth certificates show that Lyle is yours and the other baby was the other couples. DNA tests are the only thing that would say otherwise. Don't worry. You can't lose your nerve—for both our sakes."

"Okay." Janice sniffed.

"Just keep away from the girl and it'll all blow over."

"Do you think so?"

"Yes."

"Thanks. I feel better."

"Good. Now pull yourself together and call me later."

When Janice ended her conversation with Margaret she felt much better. If it weren't Christmas time, she could've visited some friends and gotten away for a while. It just wasn't possible to be away from her family in the holidays. She'd have to keep it together, just as Margaret had said.

LATER THAT DAY, Janice drove past the same coffee shop. She wanted to get another glimpse of her daughter. There was no sign of her in the café, she realized after she'd driven past four times. When Janice headed home, she remembered how her daughter had been so kind to her; Janice was pleased that she'd grown into a kind and caring person. How desperately she hoped that her daughter was happy and had a good life.

AS SHE SAT down at the dinner table that night with her two daughters and her husband, Janice put on a brave face. Lyle had again been behaving strangely toward her since he'd arrived home.

Tonight she didn't mind that her older daughter and her husband discussed business.

When there was a lull in their conversation, Georgia said to her sister, "Did you hear about the girl we saw in the coffee shop yesterday?"

"Yes. Dad told me. You should've taken a photo with her."

"What girl?" their grandmother asked.

"A girl who looked exactly like me," Georgia explained. "You should've come with us, Granny."

"Oh, that girl. Well, I would've if I'd been asked. As usual, no one includes me in anything."

Georgia ignored her grandmother's comment. "She's an Amish girl."

"I don't know if she was properly Amish. She said she was taken in by them," Lyle said.

Georgia played with her food. "Well, she was wearing the clothing."

"How much did she look like you, Georgia?" Charlotte asked.

"They say everyone has a double," Janice said. "When I arrived at college many years ago, everyone told me there was another girl who looked exactly like me. When I eventually saw her, I didn't think she looked anything like me." Janice glanced up at her husband to see his eyes fixed on hers. She gave him a little smile before she looked back down at her food.

"I'd like to go and see her," Charlotte said.

Janice said, "Nonsense. The poor girl will feel like she's on display. Leave her be."

Charlotte glared at her daughter-in-law. "How are you feeling now, Janice?"

"Fine."

"I really think you should see a doctor about these constant headaches," Lyle said.

Felicity nodded in agreement. "Yeah, Mom. It could be something serious."

"It's fine. I've been tested for other things and they found nothing. They're just brought on by stress."

"What are you stressed about, dear?" Charlotte asked her. "You have everything you want. You don't have to lift a finger around this place."

Georgia answered, "Lyle of course, Granny. Everyone's stressed about him. Didn't you hear about the car accident he had yesterday? He totaled the car."

"He had an accident?" Janice asked. "Is he hurt?"

"He's fine, but the car isn't. Georgia, we were keeping that from your mother, remember?"

"What about all the other things he does? You'd never let Felicity or me get away with all the things he does. You should be stricter with him. You and Mom let him get away with everything."

"Where's the car now?" Janice asked.

Lyle shook his head. "Don't worry. It's all been taken care of. I think he needs to have some consequences for his behavior."

"Yes, well, think of a way to punish him," Janice said.

"Finally!" Felicity looked over at Georgia who nodded in agreement.

Janice was pleased that the conversation had gotten away from Elizabeth.

DAYS LATER, Janice's husband came home early and sat down in front of her when she was watching TV. Charlotte was in her bedroom having a nap, their daughters were out and, apart from their housekeeper, they had the place to themselves.

Janice stared at Lyle, wondering what was on his mind. "What is it?"

"You've been acting a little odd lately."

She frowned at him. "That's what I've been thinking about you. You've been distant."

He narrowed his eyes and tipped his head to one side. "Is there anything you want to tell me?"

"Like?"

"Anything at all?"

She shook her head. "I can't think of anything."

"I had someone check into a few things for me."

"Is that about buying Lyle that new car? Because I used my own money."

"It's not about the car," he said shaking his head. "There are far more important things going on."

"What is it? Just tell me."

"I had someone look into some things, as I said, and there was another child born in Margaret's birthing center on the same day. They had a girl, and that girl was Elizabeth—the girl who strikingly resembles Georgia."

He knows!

She opened her mouth, and no words came out. She wanted to make some kind of excuse to put his fears at rest, but she had no excuse.

"What I want to know is whether that girl is my daughter." He stared at her.

CHAPTER 11

Blessed is the man that walketh not in the counsel of the ungodly, nor standeth in the way of sinners, nor sitteth in the seat of the scornful.
Psalms 1:1

THE TRUTH WAS GOING to come out eventually. There was no use hiding it any longer.

She stared down at the soft colored patterns on the Persian carpet under her feet, unable to look him in his eyes. "We swapped babies."

When she heard him gasp, she looked up at him to see his head jerk backward and his eyes open wide in disbelief.

"You wanted a boy," she blurted in her defense.

He lifted his hand in the air. "Wait! You did what?"

"I thought you knew."

There was silence before he spoke again. "All I had were suspicions, but what you've just said... I don't believe you could do such a thing." He held both sides of his head. "I feel like I'm having a bad dream. This can't be real."

"Everyone wanted a boy. I couldn't take the pressure."

"There was never any pressure." He shook his head at her and then drew his eyes away as though he could no longer bear to look at her.

"Yes there was, horrible pressure from your mother. She's spiteful and always telling me I'm no good. I'm sorry. I've never said anything bad about her to you before, but you must see how she is."

"You gave our baby away, Janice! Our own baby! How could you do that?" He put both hands to his face and rubbed hard.

"I took in their baby and they took mine."

"Not yours, Janice, ours. You gave her away. How could you?" He jumped to his feet. Before long, he was pacing up and down in front of her with a hand on his forehead and his cheeks beet red, looking as though he would explode.

"I know it was a terrible thing to do and I can't live with the guilt anymore." Now that the truth had come out, it was a relief. Even if Lyle divorced her, she thought, she would've died if she'd had to keep the secret any longer. "You can divorce me. I won't fight it."

Once he finished pacing, he sat opposite her. "I don't know how you could possibly give away our child."

"I did it for us. I knew you'd divorce me if I didn't give you a son."

He scoffed. "We're not in the dark ages. I don't need a son. I don't have a throne and a kingdom."

In a small voice she said, "You wanted one, though. You said it a number of times."

"It didn't matter to me—boy or girl. Does Margaret know of this? I suppose she would've had to have been in on it."

"I made her keep quiet."

"Is that because she borrowed all that money from you for her birthing center?"

"I guess that helped."

He shook his head and leaned back in the couch. Suddenly, he sprang forward. "How did you get the other couple to agree with the madness?"

"They were poor. I gave them a large sum up front, and then monthly payments. Years ago, the automatic deposits suddenly stopped going through."

"Our daughter went into the foster care system. What do you think about that? Why didn't you look into things when the payments stopped?"

"I did. I tried. I went to their house, but it was sold. The realtor wouldn't give me any information and neither would their bank. What was I to do? I thought they might suddenly have decided not to take the money anymore. I didn't know they'd died. I didn't know!" When she thought of her small daughter all alone with strangers—the love of a mother and father gone—she put both hands up to her face and cried. "I didn't know she was in foster care. How could I know? Every time I thought of her it was with loving parents who cared for her."

"Stop it, Janice. What's done is done. We can't go back. All we can do is figure out how to make this messy situation work. The truth has to come out. That's the only way."

Sniffing back her tears, she asked him, "You're not going to divorce me?"

He frowned. "I don't know. No. I didn't marry to get a divorce. I married for life. I'll calm down. I can't believe what you've done, but this family needs you. We'll sort things out, and we'll make this work. The truth needs to come out."

"Does it?"

"There's no way around it."

"How will Lyle feel, and what about Georgia and Felicity? Oh, and I don't want your mother to know."

"I know mother is hard to get along with and she'll have a lot to say about it. Ignore her."

"What about Lyle?"

"What about Elizabeth? She's the one who's been the most damaged. She's been from one house to another. I found out the Amish family wasn't the first one she was placed with."

"Don't make me feel worse than I already do."

"We have to make this right."

She sighed. "How?"

"You and I will have to tell her, and tell the family she's living with."

Janice's stomach churned at the thought. Then her thoughts turned to Lyle. "Lyle's coming home for dinner tonight."

"Good. We'll tell him tonight and tomorrow we'll go to Elizabeth's house."

"You've got her address?"

"She gave Georgia her address. I had a private investigator look into things. That's how I found all this out. The first time I was at the coffee shop, I found out her name and…"

"You were suspicious back then?"

"I wasn't, not until I saw your reaction to hearing about her. I know you better than you realize."

It was true. When he was away on business trips and she tried to hide that she was ill, he always knew just by the sound of her voice.

"I'm sorry, Lyle. I've made a mess of things."

"Yes, there's no doubt you have. Whenever something goes wrong in the company, we focus on fixing it. That's what we have to do here."

She sniffled. "You're not going to divorce me?"

He shrugged. "Why do you keep saying that?"

"Most of our friends are divorced, and their wives wouldn't have done anything as horrible as this."

"I've already told you I've no intention of ever getting a divorce. Right now we have to sort this out the best we can. We have to visit Elizabeth and her foster family."

THAT NIGHT when they told Lyle Junior the truth of everything, he took the news well.

"That explains a lot."

"Lyle, can you ever forgive me?" Janice asked.

He stood up, leaned over and hugged his mother. "I must've been some handsome baby."

She gave a laugh. "You were. I'm so sorry, though, that you never got to meet your birth parents."

He stepped back. "There's nothing to forgive." He scratched his head. "It makes me feel a little odd, though. I thought I knew who I was and now I'm not one of you. It feels a little weird. It'll take some getting used to."

"You are one of us," his father said.

"You are my parents. You were the ones who raised me. I wouldn't mind finding out about the couple who gave birth to me. I wish they were still around. I wonder if my birth father was into sports. I can find all that out from Elizabeth."

Lyle Senior said, "We're going to have to break the news to your sisters tonight and then go and talk to Elizabeth and her family tomorrow."

"How do you think she'll take it?" Lyle Junior asked.

He shook his head. "I don't know."

Janice studied Lyle Junior's face. His words showed that he was taking the news well, but something like this would have to rock him to the core. "I think we should all go to family counseling about this."

"That won't be necessary, Mom."

"I think it's important that we all go; your sisters as well."

"Your mother's right, Lyle. The hard thing will be for us all to make the time to go."

"Does Granny know all this?"

"No, she doesn't. We're delaying telling her for as long as we can," Janice said knowing that her mother-in-law would be none too pleased.

"I'm happy you two raised me. I'm glad I'm here. I couldn't have had a better life."

Janice stepped forward and gave him a hug. Something told her not everyone else would take the news as well as he.

CHAPTER 12

Therefore I say unto you, What things soever ye desire,
when ye pray, believe that ye receive them,
and ye shall have them.
Mark 11:24

JANICE KNEW this was something she had to do. She'd made a mistake and now she had to go through the shame and embarrassment to repair what she'd done.

Lyle and Janice drove to Elizabeth's house in silence. Even though Elizabeth had given Georgia her phone number, Lyle chose not to call first. There was no way he could've explained over the phone what he wanted to speak with them about.

When they pulled up outside the white farmhouse, Janice grabbed her husband's arm. "Shouldn't we be doing this with the help of a social worker or something?"

"I don't see why. We're just telling them the truth."

Now there was no going back. A woman in her mid-fifties was looking out the window at them.

They walked to the front door and before they reached it, the woman opened the door. She was a plain looking woman with not a lick of make up. Her salt-and-pepper hair was severely pulled back off her face, most of it hidden under a white cap. Her ruddy cheeks grew wider as she smiled and her pale blue eyes crinkled at the corners.

"Hello," she said.

Lyle glanced at his wife and then back at the woman. "Hello, are you Mrs. Graber?"

"I am."

"We're here to talk with you and your husband about Elizabeth. Would she be home at the moment?"

"She's at work."

"Could we request a bit of your time?" Janice asked.

The woman stepped aside to allow them in.

Once they were seated, Janice confessed the whole story in between bouts of sobbing with her face buried in tissues. "Oh, I didn't want to cry."

Lyle put a comforting hand on Janice's shoulder.

Mr. Graber, a man with a long gray and brown beard, walked through the door and his wife conveyed the story to him. After that, Mr. Graber sat down with them.

Janice looked at the Amish couple seated on the couch in front of her. "I suppose you think I'm a dreadful person."

Mr. Graber shook his head. "We don't judge."

"God wanted Elizabeth here and that's why she's here," Mrs. Graber said matter-of-factly.

"Thank you for looking after her. You seem to be really nice people. We heard she was somewhere else before she came here. Was she okay there?"

Mrs. Graber answered, "She was briefly with two families, but they weren't able to give her a permanent home. I think she was okay. Nothing bad happened to her, if that's what you mean."

"Yes. Good. That's good." Janice glanced at her husband.

"Elizabeth will be home soon if you want to tell her yourselves. She's old enough to choose where she wants to go now that she's... Oh wait. She won't be eighteen until the twenty fifth."

"It's the other two girls who are over eighteen," Mr. Graber told his wife.

"You have other foster children?" Lyle asked.

"When we couldn't have our own, we knew God had a plan. We're all God's children, and now God has been able to use us to help in the broader community."

"You're wonderful people for giving them a home." Janice knew that they were loving as soon as she walked in; she could feel the peace and the love in the house. Her daughter had been fortunate, but things could have been very different and she'd only have herself to blame if Elizabeth had suffered in any way.

"We can't thank you enough for looking after her," Lyle said.

"So, will she stay on after her birthday? You said the other foster children are now older than eighteen," Janice asked.

"She can make her choice. Tara and Megan have chosen to live on here, but they're free to go at anytime."

"Have they become Amish?" Lyle asked.

"They haven't been baptized yet, but our job has been to care for them not to force them to join us."

Lyle rubbed his hands together. "Of course not. I didn't mean to imply that you were recruiting people into your faith or anything like that."

"God chooses people to come to us and then they are free to make their decision when they are older," Mrs. Graber said.

"How do you think Elizabeth will take the news?"

"I don't know," she said, turning to her husband. "What do you think?"

He shook his head. "She's a calm and pleasant girl with compassion and understanding."

His words gave Janice hope. Hope that Elizabeth would forgive her for the dreadful thing she'd done. Lyle Junior had appeared to take it well, but she was certain that he'd have questions as he processed the whole situation.

ELIZABETH FINISHED work and Joseph met her to give her a ride home.

"How was your day?" he asked when she climbed into the buggy beside him.

"Busy!"

He checked for cars behind him and then clicked his horse forward. "No more visits from people who look like you?"

She laughed. "No. That was weird."

"I've got my skates in the back if you want to go skating."

Elizabeth slapped him playfully on the arm. "Why didn't you tell me? I've left mine at home. I didn't think to bring them."

"I thought you'd bring them with you. Aren't you keen to give me more lessons?"

"I've gone as far as I can go with them. The rest is only practice."

"Where will we go? I can't take you home now."

"If I go home to get my skates, I can't really go out again. Aunt Gretchen will expect me to stay home and help her with dinner or something."

"You could watch me skate."

"Watching you fall over all the time is no fun. And you hurt my ears when you crash-land on the ice."

He laughed. "I'm not that bad am I?"

She nodded. "You know you are."

"You told me I was getting better."

"You are, but you were so bad before that it's not much of a compliment."

He frowned at her. "Well, I'm not taking you straight home. We'll go for a long drive."

She giggled.

After some time, Joseph stopped the buggy at the side of a quiet road.

"Have you done anything about finding relatives?"

"Not yet. I'm going to contact one of the social workers Gretchen knows and see if she can point me in the right direction. I think that's the simplest way to go."

"Good idea. Are you going to stay on in the community once you turn eighteen?"

"That's the thing I don't know. I've thought about leaving, but it's a little scary."

"You'd soon make friends and you don't strike me as someone who couldn't make her own way. You already have a job, so that's a good start."

"Joseph, are you trying to talk me into leaving?"

He smiled and took hold of her hand. "I want you to stay, and fall in love with me, and marry me."

She smiled and pulled her hand away. It was hard to know when he was being serious. Or maybe his joking manner gave him the courage to speak what was in his heart.

"I know you must make your own decision. I'm just saying that if you stay on, I'll be happy."

"You just want free skating lessons."

"Why wouldn't I? That's all I want you to stay for."

She slapped him on his shoulder and he tried to duck out of her way.

"Do you get two presents or one present for your birthday since it's on Christmas Day?"

She stared at him. "Where did that come from?"

His eyes sparkled as his lips turned upward. "It's a problem I've been thinking about."

"If it's that much of a problem, you should give me two."

He pulled away from her and frowned. "Who said I was getting you anything? All I said was, 'Do you get two presents or one?' I never said I was getting you anything. I didn't give you anything last year."

"We didn't know each other last year."

"See?"

She shook her head. "You always have to be right."

He wagged his finger at her. "I *am* always right. I'm glad you agree."

"You're impossible."

"Impossibly smart, and impossibly handsome."

She grunted at him and shook her head again. "Now that you're getting me a present, I suppose I'll have to get you a small something."

"Small? That doesn't sound very good."

Elizabeth laughed. "Depends what it is!"

"What do you have in mind?"

"Nothing yet. You'll have to wait and see."

"Does that mean we'll see each other on Christmas Day?"

"Would you like to?"

He nodded. "You know I would."

"Would your folks mind if you came over for the evening meal on Christmas Day?"

"I've got nine brothers, and seven of them will have their wives and families there, so I don't think they'll miss me."

"That's a big family."

"Yeah."

"Good. I'll let Aunt Gretchen know that you'll be there."

He fidgeted with the reins. "Are you sure it'll be okay?"

"Why wouldn't it be?"

"This is a serious step in our relationship."

"Christmas dinner is a serious step?"

He grinned cheekily. "Very serious."

She looked out of the buggy. "We should go. Aunt Gretchen will be wondering where I am. I don't want to worry her."

CHAPTER 13

But my God shall supply all your need
according to his riches in glory by Christ Jesus.
Philippians 4:19

ELIZABETH STEPPED out of Joseph's buggy when he stopped his horse outside her house. "Will I see you tomorrow?"

"You can count on it." He gave her a little wink before he turned the buggy around.

As she raced toward her front door, she noticed a car parked by the barn. She thought it must be one of the caseworkers the Grabers regularly saw.

She opened the front door and stepped into the warmth of the house. As she was taking off her coat, Aunt Gretchen hurried toward her.

"There are people here to see you."

"Who?"

"Come." Aunt Gretchen took hold of her arm and walked her into the living room.

There she saw the man from the coffee shop, and he was with the woman who had fainted at the shop. She stared curiously at the two of them, waiting for someone to speak.

"You should sit down."

When she heard Uncle William's voice, she noticed that he was also in the room. She sat down, took a deep breath, and waited to learn why they were there.

The woman cleared her throat. "I should be the one to tell her."

"Tell me what?" She hoped she wasn't in trouble for something.

The man nodded.

Elizabeth sat stiffly as she listened to the outrageous tale.

The woman told her that she'd been swapped at birth for a boy and they were her real parents and not the Simpsons who had raised her. They had raised the Simpsons' boy as their own. The man took over and explained that they hadn't known that the Simpsons had died. The woman had paid the Simpsons money, and then the deposits had just stopped going into the Simpsons account, with no explanation.

"I don't believe it! The Simpsons were my parents! This can't be true!"

"They were but they weren't, Elizabeth," the man insisted. "I'm afraid it's all true. Everything my wife has said."

"They pretended to be my parents… were my parents for money?"

"No, Elizabeth. It wasn't like that. They loved you and raised you as their own. I offered them money to help them out."

"It wasn't to help them. You wanted a boy and not a girl. You didn't want me!"

The woman bowed her head.

"You should be ashamed," Elizabeth spat out, finding anger

within that she'd never before experienced. "Where is my mother and father's real child—the boy?"

"We've raised him," the man explained.

"Does he know all this?"

"We told him yesterday," Mr. Doyle said.

"Don't blame your father. He's only just learned of this since he saw you in the coffee shop," Mrs. Doyle said.

Elizabeth sprang to her feet and yelled, "He is *not* my father!"

"I think you should listen to them, Elizabeth."

Calmed by Uncle William's words, she sat down again. She looked from Mr. Doyle to Mrs. Doyle, waiting for one of them to say something. Aunt Gretchen was now sitting beside her, speechless. She glanced at Aunt Gretchen to see a worry-lined face.

"We thought you should know the truth," Mr. Doyle said.

"Good. Great! Now I know that my parents weren't my parents and they raised me for money. I also know that my birth mother gave me away to strangers without a second thought, preferring some stranger's baby to me."

"It wasn't like that," Mrs. Doyle said in a small voice.

"Explain to me what it was like, then," Elizabeth demanded.

Mrs. Doyle shook her head and cried while her husband put his arm around her.

"This is the way she explained it to me, as weird as it's going to sound. My wife felt pressured to have a boy. She thought I'd only be happy with a boy and thought I'd divorce her and marry someone else and try for a boy if she couldn't give me one. I wasn't at your birth like I was at the births of our other daughters. I couldn't get back in time because of bad weather. The airports were closed. I had to wait and then hire a car and drive back home. She saw an opportunity when another couple had a boy. They were poor, and Elizabeth offered them money. The midwife knew they were good people otherwise my wife never would have swapped babies if she wasn't certain you'd have a good life, and that is the reason she sent them money to ensure you'd never go without."

"Well, I did go without. They died."

"I'm sorry," Mrs. Doyle said.

"All this time I thought they were my real parents. They lied to me every single day of my life."

"It wasn't a lie. You were their child just as Lyle is our child and always will be."

"There's truth in what the man says, Elizabeth," Mr. Graber said. "We love all our children and none of you were born to us."

Elizabeth closed her eyes and tried to absorb all that she'd been told. Her past, her whole past had been a lie. Events had led her to be with the Grabers who had been her mom and dad for the past ten years.

"This lady, and this man here, they are my real parents because they would never lie to me." Elizabeth pointed to the Grabers as she spoke.

"We're not trying to take anything away from anyone, Elizabeth. We've come here risking that you'll hate us, or not accept us. We just want you to finally know the truth of where you came from. We want the truth to be out once and for all," Mr. Doyle said.

She glanced over at Mrs. Doyle who was still hanging her head in shame. It couldn't have been easy for her to admit what she'd done.

"I can appreciate you coming forward with the truth. I guess it wouldn't have been an easy thing to do," Elizabeth said, now appreciating the life she had with the Grabers more deeply. They would never lie to her about anything.

"We should go, but we'd like to see you again, Elizabeth. And maybe you might like to meet the rest of your family. You have two sisters, and your brother, the Simpson's son. He's keen to ask you about his birth parents."

Elizabeth swallowed her words about them not being her

family. "I'd like to meet him and tell him about them. What I remember of them anyway." Now looking at her birth mother with tear-filled eyes, she asked, "Did you ever miss me?"

"Every day. I thought of you every day. I cried all the time at first; I missed you and wanted to hold you. I had another baby to love and care for. When I craved to hold you, I cuddled him. Your mother and I each had a baby to love and we did. All I can do is say that I'm truly, truly sorry for what I've done to you and to all of us."

Mr. Doyle tapped his wife on her shoulder as he stood up. She stood as well and so did the Grabers. Elizabeth stayed seated, fearing she'd fall if she stood. They said goodbye to her and she nodded when they said they'd leave all their phone numbers with the Grabers.

When they left, Mrs. Graber went to put the dinner on while Mr. Graber sat down with her.

"How are you feeling?"

"I'm in shock. My parents weren't my parents. I was sold."

"*Gott* has his hand on you. You've come to us for a reason. Don't take anger out on these people. They've admitted their wrongdoing and they've confessed everything. It took courage for them to tell you."

"I know. I saw the look on her face. It was hard for her. It was such a horrible thing to do."

"There's an old saying, Elizabeth, that you shouldn't judge others until you've walked a mile in their shoes. You don't know the woman's state in her head at the time. She's had to live with that mistake and keep it hidden for nearly eighteen years."

Elizabeth nodded in acknowledgment of the truth in what he was saying, but she was far more concerned about herself than how it had affected the woman who'd given her up.

"Don't forget, you're here because this is where *Gott* wanted you. If Mrs. Doyle hadn't made that choice, you wouldn't be here."

"I couldn't imagine not being here. I love it here. This is my home." Now more than she ever had before, Elizabeth knew she belonged with the Amish. They were gentle and caring people and they never would have made silly reckless choices like her birth mother had made. "I suppose I take after that woman. I hope I don't make bad choices."

"You won't. You're the most sensible girl I know."

She looked at the kind old man she'd resisted calling *Dat* in memory of the man she had thought was her father. The Simpsons who had raised her had looked after her well, but now she questioned their motivations. "Can I call you *Dat?*"

He laughed. "I told you when you first arrived here; you can call me whatever you like, just don't call me late for dinner."

Smiling at the old joke she'd heard so many times before, she moved next to him and gave him a hug. "Thanks, *Dat*."

CHAPTER 14

God is not a man, that he should lie;
neither the son of man, that he should repent:
hath he said, and shall he not do it?
or hath he spoken, and shall he not make it good?
Numbers 23:19

"THAT WENT BADLY," Janice said to her husband when they drove away.

"I expected it to. She was hardly going to welcome us with open arms. Let her get used to the idea and one day she might come around to not hating us."

"It's me she should hate, not you."

"At least we know she's been loved and cared for. They were such lovely people."

Janice remained silent while she dealt with feelings of jealousy that her daughter cared so much for the Grabers and was now calling them her real parents.

Lyle gripped the steering wheel so hard his knuckles were white. "It's all such a mess. I don't know how my mother will take it. It'll probably kill her."

"At least something good might come out of it, then." The words had slipped out of Janice's mouth before she could stop them.

Lyle took his eyes off the road to glare at his wife.

"I'm sorry, Lyle. I didn't mean it. I'm just stressed; I don't know what I'm saying."

He frowned and turned his concentration back to the road ahead.

Janice stared at her husband. "Is there a way around telling her?"

"No. Once the girls know, she'll find out; and you know Lyle's never been able to keep anything quiet."

"Is it true you didn't care whether you had a boy or a girl?"

"I told you. It didn't matter. It was nice to have a boy, but I would've loved a girl just as much. It never mattered. I'm sorry you felt so pressured." He glanced at her. "Don't be upset. This whole thing must've been so hard on you, keeping this buried all these years."

"It has. It's been dreadful. Every time I heard the doorbell buzz, I feared it would be the Simpsons exposing the secret. I thought about her every day."

"You did it all for me?"

"To be truthful, I did it because I wanted to keep you happy so you wouldn't divorce me."

He frowned at her. "I wouldn't divorce you. Mind you, it crossed my mind when all this first came out. I didn't get married to divorce; I meant my vows."

"You've always been faithful?"

"Of course, I have."

"What about all those business trips?"

He shook his head. "When I go away, I spend half the time at night on the phone to you. I'd hardly get the time. I've always been faithful to you. As faithful as a pair of old slippers." He chuckled. "It's me who should be fearful of you divorcing me."

"Why would I even think about it?"

"I'm old and cranky, and you always tell me I work too much. And I brought my mother to live with us."

"That's all true, but divorcing you never crossed my mind."

"Next year, I'm cutting back on my work. Now that the children are grown, we should spend more time together. We'll travel."

"Really?"

"Why not? Let's enjoy life."

"I'll only be able to enjoy life if Elizabeth forgives me. If one of our other children were angry with us, I'd bribe them with something like a car, but we can't do that with Elizabeth. Not now that she's been so many years with the Amish."

"This situation has forced us to take a good look at ourselves and our life."

She nodded and looked at the road ahead, hoping all their lives would change for the better.

WHEN ELIZABETH HEARD Tara and Megan come home, she said, "I must go and tell them what happened."

William nodded.

She hurried out the door pulling her shawl around her shoulders. When she got to the barn, Tara and Megan were climbing down from the buggy.

Tara immediately looked at her. "What's wrong?"

"I don't know where to start. Something's happened."

"Are *Mamm* and *Dat* okay?" Megan asked, rushing at her.

"Jah, it's not about them, it's about me. Remember I told you all about the man with the daughter who looked like me?"

"Jah."

"They were here—him and his wife. They say I'm their daughter. They swapped me at birth for a boy."

"But your parents died in the car accident," Megan said.

"They're saying that they are my real parents, and the people who died are the ones who took me when they gave up their son."

"Who would do such a thing?" Megan asked.

Elizabeth breathed out heavily feeling better now that she'd told her two best friends. "That girl was my sister and there's another sister, an older one. And they have the boy, who I guess is the exact same age as me. I wonder what he thinks about all this?"

"Are you sure it's true?" Tara asked. "What else did they say? Do they want you to live with them or something?"

"I don't know. I don't think so. The man said he only just learned of it. His wife kept it a secret all this time. If he hadn't seen me at the coffee shop, I never would've known that the Simpsons weren't my real parents." Elizabeth told them the whole conversation she'd had with the Doyles.

"How did they…?"

"I don't know anymore than I'm telling you, Tara. I'm not sure I want to know more. I feel my life has been taken away from me twice. Once when my parents died, and now finding out they weren't even really my parents. It's almost just as much of a shock."

Megan put her arms around her and Elizabeth rested her head on her shoulder.

Tara stepped forward and rubbed her arm. "You've got us. We'll always stick together no matter what."

Elizabeth felt a little comforted by her friends.

"Are you curious to meet your other sister and the Simpson boy?" Tara asked.

"Yes, Elizabeth, he'd be just as upset as you. I'm guessing he didn't know before now, either. They likely just told him, too, and his birth parents are now dead."

"That's true. I can tell him everything I remember about them." She sighed. "All I want to do right now is tell Joseph what's happened.

"When do you see him next?" Tara asked.

Elizabeth leaned forward and stared at Tara's lips. "Have you been wearing lipstick?"

She rubbed at her lips with the back of her hand. "Just a little bit. Don't tell."

"I won't."

"I'm seeing Joseph tomorrow at eleven. If you could take me to the pond by the Eshs' farm, Tara?"

"Okay. I don't start work until two, but I guess I'd be able to find something to do in town." Tara's eyes sparkled with mischief. "You'll feel better with his big strong arms around you. Make sure to cry a little; that always works."

"Tara!" Megan was shocked.

Tara laughed. "Elizabeth should make the best of every situation."

"Why? Joseph already likes her."

"I'm just saying what I would do. Now help me with this buggy."

Elizabeth helped them unhitch the buggy and rub the horse down. Finding out who her parents were caused her to question who she was. It seemed odd that the past could affect the present so dramatically.

THE NEXT MORNING when Tara and Elizabeth arrived at the pond, Joseph was sitting in his buggy waiting.

"Don't forget what I told you!" Tara whispered before Elizabeth left the buggy.

"Thanks, Tara. I'll see you tonight."

When Tara drove the buggy on, Elizabeth ran to Joseph and told him everything she'd learned about her past and about the Simpsons not being her birthparents.

He sat there staring at her. "That's awful, Elizabeth."

"In my mind, I'd already wondered if there was a connection between that woman who fainted and that man. She came there to the coffee shop to get a look at me."

"What are you going to do now?"

"I don't know. I think they're fake people with fake lives."

He rubbed his forehead. "They're your parents."

"She's a liar."

"Don't be so harsh."

"Easy for you to say."

"Nee, it's not. I know you're feeling awful that you were lied to, but maybe something drove your mother to it."

"Nothing's that drastic, not enough to give away your child. I'd never give mine away. I'd die for my children when I have them, and do anything to protect them."

He shrugged. "There's nothing you can do about it now. Did she say she was sorry?"

"She did."

"Did you forgive her?"

"Not yet. I forget what I said, but in my heart, I don't forgive her. And I don't know if I ever can. What made her do it?"

"What reason did she give? You told me she said she thought her husband wanted a boy."

"That can't have been the true reason."

"It probably was if she said so. She wouldn't have a reason to keep lying now that the truth has come out."

"Do you think so?"

Joseph nodded as he reached out and took hold of her hand. "This is the way I see it; you had parents who loved you that died. Then you came to the Grabers who love you as though you're their own. Now, you have another lot of parents who want to get to know you. So, in eighteen years, you have had three sets of parents who love you and want the best for you."

He pulled her hand to his lips and pressed his lips against the back of her hand while staring into her eyes. She didn't know whether it was the caress of his lips or his calming voice, but she started to feel a little more positive about her situation.

"That's true, but I don't know who I am now."

"You're the same person you were before you found out all this."

"You think so?"

He nodded. "Of course."

"Then why do I feel so murky inside and so betrayed?"

"I know it's not easy, but it's all in the way you look at things. You can look at it as though you've had three sets of parents who've loved you, or you can put all your attention on the lies and deceit part of it. Which do you prefer to think about?"

"The good part I guess, but how do I know I can trust these people again?"

"You could give them a chance. They might not be trustworthy and they might not be nice, but if you don't give them a chance you'll never know."

Elizabeth heaved a sigh. "They left their phone numbers with Gretchen."

"Gut! Call them when you're ready and go and meet the rest of the family."

"Come with me?"

"What?" Joseph laughed. "Why me?"

"See? You're just as nervous."

"Maybe so, but I'll go with you if you want me to."

"I do. I'll feel so much better if you're there with me." She put her head on his shoulder. "You're so clever and so wise."

He chuckled. "I'll remember that you said that here and now, so I can always remind you."

CHAPTER 15

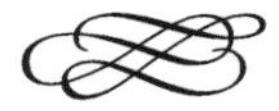

Let no corrupt communication proceed out of your mouth,
but that which is good to the use of edifying,
that it may minister grace unto the hearers.
Ephesians 4:29

"She has to know, Janice."

"Does she?"

"Elizabeth has called and we've arranged for her to come here on Christmas Eve. We can't keep it from my mother; we have to tell her now. I'm certain she already knows something's going on."

Janice sighed. "You know we don't get along. She'll use this as another reason to hate me."

"It doesn't matter; she has to be told."

"All right. I might as well get it over with."

That night before dinner was served, Janice went into the sitting room with her husband and found Charlotte reading a book.

She closed the book and placed it onto her lap and looked up at them. "Lyle, what are you doing home?" Charlotte looked between Lyle and Janice and watched them sit down on the couch opposite.

"We've got something to tell you," Lyle said.

"Go ahead. I'm listening."

Janice stared at Lyle, hoping he'd speak, and thankfully he broke the news.

"Lyle Junior is not really a Doyle."

Her beady eyes fixed on Janice. "I knew it! You faked that pregnancy. That boy never fitted in. He doesn't even look like a Doyle and as for his brain capacity..."

Lyle leaned forward and wagged a finger at his mother. "Mother! You best stop there. Lyle is our son in every way as far as I'm concerned, and he always will be."

Charlotte pouted and looked from her son to Janice. "Does he know he's adopted?"

"There's more to the story, Mother."

"Well, tell me. Out with it!"

Janice knew she'd have to take over. "You and Lyle, well, I thought Lyle wanted a boy—anyway, I swapped the girl I had with someone else's boy."

Charlotte's mouth fell open. "You gave your own child away?"

Janice nodded knowing that now Charlotte had a valid reason to detest her.

"Did you know about this, Lyle?"

"He only learned of it when he met Elizabeth, the daughter I gave away."

She frowned at Lyle. "Tell me what happened from the beginning and don't leave a single thing out."

They sat there and told Charlotte everything.

"We must bring this girl back into the family."

"It's not as easy as that. She's been eighteen years thinking her parents were other people and now she's been ten years living with the Amish family."

"Once she sees what we have to offer her, she'll stay with us. What's she like?"

Janice said, "She's a lovely girl and she looks very much like Georgia."

Charlotte could barely look at her when she was speaking. "Yes, Lyle already mentioned that when he said he saw her in that coffee shop." She looked across at Lyle. "We've got a lot to offer her, Lyle. You must see that Elizabeth comes back to us. Did you know that Elizabeth is a family name? It was your great grandmother's name."

"No. I didn't know that. Anyway, Elizabeth called us, and she's coming here to meet everyone on Christmas Eve. She's bringing a friend with her."

"An Amish friend?"

"Yes, a young man."

"We can't have that. If she marries an Amish man she'll stay there forever. You must do what you can do make certain that doesn't happen, Lyle. You must encourage her to end that relationship."

"I'll be back. I just have to make a few calls." Lyle left the room.

Janice stared after him not believing he could leave her alone with his mother.

"You of all people should know how one should make a good marriage, Janice. You've done well to marry my son. So many other women were after him and now you have everything you want."

"I've got my own money, Charlotte! I didn't marry Lyle for his money."

Charlotte turned up her nose. "All the same, you must make sure that Elizabeth does not marry someone Amish."

"Why not, if that's her choice?"

"Have you lost your senses, woman?"

"Charlotte, can you stop trying to control everyone? If Elizabeth chooses to stay with the Amish she can. If she chooses to marry someone, it's none of your business and it's certainly none of mine."

Charlotte's mouth dropped open. Janice was tempted to hurry out of the room to get away from the woman who'd continually caused her grief, but she stayed, standing her ground.

"I've never been spoken to like that by anyone in all my born days!"

"It's probably about time then."

"I'll have to tell Lyle how you spoke to me just now."

"I wouldn't."

"Why?"

"I told him how you harped on and on about him wanting a boy, so I'd be careful what you said if I were you. He might end up blaming you for this mess."

"Me? That's ridiculous."

"Is it? I remember you telling me that some women can only have girls."

"Yes, well that's true. Some women aren't capable of having boys."

"That's biologically unfounded, but you kept putting me down and hinting that Lyle would leave me if I didn't produce a son and an heir. When the reality was, he didn't care at all. You were the one who wanted a boy. So he could carry on the name."

"You're trying to turn this around, so it's my fault? You're unbelievable. I wish my son never got involved with you. I can't see what he sees in you."

"I know what you think of me and I no longer care. I'm admitting that I made a terrible mistake, and with Lyle's help, I'm trying to put it right for everyone's sake. You have to appreciate that it hasn't been easy for me to tell you this."

Lyle came back into the room and Charlotte changed her tune.

"Yes, dear. It must be awful for you."

Janice looked up at her husband to see a smile on his face at the idea that Charlotte and she were getting along.

"I'm okay. I feel better now that it's all out in the open," Janice said.

"How is Lyle taking it?" Charlotte asked. "And what do we know about his heritage?"

"Not much. We're hoping that Elizabeth can enlighten us about Lyle's family, the Simpsons."

Charlotte grimaced. "It's a waste giving him the same name. Lyle the Fourth. And he's not a Doyle at all. I always knew there was something odd about that boy."

"He is, Mother. Nothing's changed in our eyes. Lyle is still our son. He's still a Doyle and always will be a Doyle."

The old woman huffed. "But he's not really, so why should he have the same name as you, your father and his father before him?"

Janice butted in, "It's just a name. It's not really that important."

When Lyle put a hand on her knee, Janice realized she should've kept quiet.

"Not important! Not important to you maybe. You married into this family not appreciating our history—that's more than obvious to everyone."

Janice pressed her lips together and kept silent. Who was 'everyone?'

"I can't believe that a child with my blood running through her veins has been raised as a foster child." She scowled with her lips downturned.

Janice looked away, feeling bad for her daughter and hoping she hadn't had a bad life.

"I'll see how Magda's getting along with dinner."

Janice hurried out of the room, hoping her mother-in-law wouldn't say too many nasty things behind her back. Although, she expected she would.

CHAPTER 16

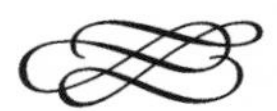

And thou shalt love the Lord thy God with all thine heart, and with all thy soul, and with all thy might.
Deuteronomy 6:5

Christmas Eve.

Mamm opened Elizabeth's bedroom door. "Can I come in?"

"*Jah,* of course."

Gretchen sat down on her bed while Elizabeth braided her hair.

"Are you nervous about meeting your family?"

"I am. What if I disappoint them?"

"You could never disappoint anyone. They'll be thinking the same of you." Gretchen gave a chuckle.

"I'm looking forward to meeting Lyle Junior and telling him what I remember of his parents. That feels funny, to say that they were *his* parents."

"They were yours, too."

"I guess. I just wish I'd known the truth earlier." She popped her prayer *kapp* on her head. "The only place that I can call home is right here with you and *Dat*." She sat down on the bed next to Gretchen and put her arm around her.

A giggle bubbled out of Gretchen. "We've been blessed to have you."

"How many children have you had over the years?" Elizabeth asked.

"Quite a few. You were our first and then we had those two girls when you were around eleven."

"Jah, they only stayed a few months."

"Then after that, there was little Tom."

Elizabeth giggled, remembering the chubby three-year-old. "So, with Tara and Megan, that's around... that's six."

Gretchen nodded. *"Gott* has a plan for each of us. *Gott* wanted you with us."

Placing her arm around Gretchen's shoulder again, she said, "I'm glad to be here with you. There's no place I would rather have been raised. I've felt safe here."

"You've been a blessing to us."

"Is it ever hard looking after children who aren't yours?"

"We're all *Gott's kinner.* It doesn't matter how each of you came to be with us. We had our struggles with Tara when she first came, but now she's settled down."

"That's right. I remember how she kept running away."

"Until she realized she had nowhere to run to and she was better off here."

Hoofbeats sounded outside the house.

"That'll be Joseph," *Mamm* said.

"I'm so glad he agreed to come with me."

"How are you getting there?"

"Mr. Doyle said he'd send a car for us at six."

"Mr. Doyle? Is that what you're going to call him?"

"That's all I can call him. I know none of it was his fault, but I can't call the man Dad. I barely know him."

Gretchen nodded. "Don't put any pressure on yourself. You'll get to know them all in time. Give them a chance to get to know you, too. You can be a little too quiet sometimes. Speak your mind. Otherwise, they won't get to know the real you."

Elizabeth breathed out heavily. "Okay. Thanks for the advice. I'll do my best."

When they heard a knock on the front door, Elizabeth said, "I'll go down and let him in."

On the ride to the Doyles' house, Elizabeth clutched Joseph's hand. There was no way she could've done this alone. Gretchen's words ran through her head; she'd have to be bold and speak up to let these people get to know her. Too often she'd hold back and let others talk around her. Tara was the one who usually took the lead when they were in a crowd of people. What she needed was a good dollop of Tara's confidence.

The car drove through double iron gates and headed to a grand two-story home.

"Wow! Look at it," Joseph said.

"I think they have a lot of money," Elizabeth whispered.

Once they got to the front door, it opened and Mr. and Mrs. Doyle stood before them. Elizabeth introduced Joseph and then they were walked through the house to meet the others. The house opened into a huge foyer with a glass framed ceiling. From the center hung a huge crystal chandelier. Once Elizabeth pulled her eyes from that, they were drawn to a sweeping staircase leading to the next level. As they walked alongside the Doyles, Elizabeth couldn't help noticing the six-foot-high portraits of people in old-fashioned clothing. Were they her ancestors? It seemed odd to know almost nothing of the Simpsons, and here there was a wealth of family history to be learned. By learning more about the Doyles, she'd surely learn more about herself.

They were shown to a sitting room where the rest of the family waited for them. There was her grandmother, Charlotte, her two sisters, Georgia and Felicity, and Lyle, the biological son of the people who'd raised her until she was eight.

Lyle was the first to speak after the introductions were done. "Tell me about my parents."

Elizabeth smiled as she remembered them. "Mom was always teaching me things. She taught me how to read and write before I went to school. Dad loved ice-skating. I think he was some kind of champion. There were trophies with little figures on top—gold and silver trophies."

"I knew he'd be athletic."

"You look a little like him, I think. I can't remember their faces now."

"Do you have any photos? Do you still have those trophies?"

"I had a box of things, but they were lost. I remember I had them at my second foster home, but I arrived at the Grabers' with nothing but my clothes. The Grabers asked about my things for me, but the caseworker said the other family didn't have anything of mine."

Lyle Junior nodded and smiled at her. He seemed nice, like the rest of them.

"I was told that both of my parents, Joseph and Lillian didn't have any relatives at all and I was going to check into that, but I haven't yet."

"I'll look into it," Lyle said. "Or, we could both do it."

"They did have a relative," Janice said.

All eyes gravitated to Janice.

"I remember that Margaret told me that Lillian was scared of hospitals and that's why she had her baby at her birthing center rather than a hospital. The recommendation to go to Margaret came from a doctor friend of Margaret's who was a distant relative to Lillian."

"A doctor relative. That's interesting," Lyle said. "I might go into medicine. I think I'd like that."

Charlotte frowned at him. "You're not capable of getting grades good enough."

"I could start over. I only got bad grades because I've not really seen where I'm headed, so nothing makes sense, but if I have a goal like being a doctor that'll be a different thing."

Charlotte sighed. "Well, we'll just have to wait and see how that turns out, won't we? It'll be more of your father's money you'll be burning through why you try to find something you're good at."

"I'll pay him back when I'm a famous surgeon. I might even go into research and find cures for diseases."

The oldest daughter, Felicity, nodded. "You can do anything, once you put your mind to it, Lyle."

"Thanks, sis."

"I'll ask Margaret who that doctor was and I'll look into things," Janice said.

"We shall see," Charlotte said. "Tell us about yourself, Elizabeth."

Everything left Elizabeth's head once all eyes were turned her way. She'd never been good at speaking in front of people. She recalled what Gretchen said to her; she must speak, so they get to know her. "I like to ice-skate. That's my favorite thing to do. I work in a coffee shop." She giggled. "That's right. You already know that. That's about all really. After the accident, I went to live with a foster family for a few weeks, and then another family for a short time before I was placed with the Grabers when I was a young girl of around seven or eight. I've been with them ever since."

"Are you going to stay with the Amish?" Georgia asked.

With Joseph sitting right beside her it was a difficult thing to answer. Part of her wanted to get to know about her roots, and the other part of her wanted to stay where she felt safe. "I'm not certain." She could sense Joseph's disappointment in her answer.

"Do you think you'll stay at the coffee shop forever?" Charlotte asked.

"I don't know. It's good to have a job to bring money in."

"You can live with us and you wouldn't have to work," Charlotte said. "What's another one for my son to support?"

"Forgive my mother, Elizabeth. We don't want to put pressure on you, but we want you to know that you've always got a home here. You're welcome here at anytime and I was going to tell you once you got a little comfortable with us that you're welcome here whether you want to visit or indeed live with us."

"Thank you. That's nice to know."

"Well, would you consider it? We have to find a way to make up for what Janice has done," Charlotte said.

Elizabeth noticed that Janice opened her mouth in shock while Lyle Senior and everyone else seemed equally disturbed at what Charlotte had said.

"Thank you for the offer. I'm getting used to the idea. It would be too soon to make any decisions."

The old woman leaned forward. "So, you will consider it, dear?"

"Yes." Elizabeth couldn't see herself moving there anytime soon, but felt pressured to say she'd think about it.

"Will you both come and have Christmas with us tomorrow?" Janice asked.

"Yes, that would be wonderful. We'd really like to get to know you," Felicity said while her other sister nodded, looking equally as excited.

"I don't know that we'd be able to," Elizabeth said giving Joseph a sideways glance. After he had looked at her blankly, she said, "Thank you, but I don't think we can."

"It's our birthdays, Elizabeth. It would be nice if you could make it. Could you spare us just a couple of hours? Maybe have lunch here? No pressure."

Elizabeth smiled at Lyle. He was relaxed and friendly and was a link to the parents she'd lost so long ago. "Okay. I think we could. What do you think, Joseph?"

Joseph nodded.

"Excellent!" the grandmother said.

"As long as that's okay with everyone." Elizabeth looked at Janice and Lyle Senior.

"We couldn't think of anything better," Lyle Senior said.

"We'd love it," Janice added.

CHAPTER 17

Commit thy works unto the Lord,
and thy thoughts shall be established.
Proverbs 16:3

AT THE END of a tense night, Elizabeth and Joseph were driven back to the Grabers' house.

They walked inside and, since everyone was asleep and they were away from the ears of the driver, they were free to talk about the evening.

Elizabeth slumped into the couch and Joseph sat next to her.

"How are you feeling after all that?"

"I feel like everything is spinning out of control. Everything's moving so fast lately."

"I sensed a lot of tension in the house. Most of it coming from the granny."

Elizabeth laughed. *"Jah,* she's one used to getting her own way over things, and I don't think she likes Janice."

"No love lost between the pair, it seems. Did you really mean you'd think about living with them?"

"Nee, but what could I say?"

"Why did you agree to go back there tomorrow? Don't you want to spend Christmas day here with William and Gretchen?"

"I said we'd go for lunch. I'll be back here before the evening meal. You will go with me, won't you?"

He grimaced. "I'd rather not, but if you want me to go with you, I will."

Elizabeth heaved a relieved sigh. *"Denke.* I'm trying to like them, but all I do is stare at Janice and wonder how she could give me away. Then I look at Lyle Junior and wonder why she chose him over me."

"It was simply because she was desperate for a boy. She explained that."

"Words don't help take the hurt away. She can explain whatever she wants, but I can't help feeling hurt that another baby was chosen over me. How could she have done it?'

"I don't know."

"I have confusion over everything. What if I took one year to live with them and learn more about them? Then I'd learn more about myself." She wondered what it would be like to live in that home that was like a palace. There she could have everything she'd ever wanted.

Joseph pulled back. "You'd actually do that? Leave the community?"

"I never said I'd stay."

"I thought… I thought that you would. What would happen to us if you left?"

"I don't know. I haven't thought everything through."

"Perhaps it's best you go there by yourself tomorrow."

"Nee, I can't do this without you."

"I didn't say anything tonight. I barely uttered a word. You'd be more free to be yourself without me there."

She knew his feelings were hurt. He wanted to marry her; he'd made that known. If she married him, then her life would be set on a course with no turning back. They would set up house, and together they'd raise a family. With Joseph, she knew how life would turn out. There was another road she could take. The road was unknown and her future uncertain if she went to live with the Doyles. Her insides felt hollow when she realized she couldn't marry Joseph without first exploring the other side of herself. The side of the person she might have become if she'd been raised as a Doyle.

"Tell me what you're thinking, Elizabeth. You've gone quiet again."

"There's a lot going on in my head. I've been thinking so much lately I feel like my head's going to burst. Lyle really wanted to know about his parents and I didn't have anything much to tell him. I don't even remember their faces, just vague impressions. I wish I still had that box of their belongings and photos. They were most likely thrown out."

"I'm not concerned about him; I'm concerned about you. As much as I want to protect you and be by your side, I think it's better if you go alone tomorrow. I'll come here in the morning to see you for Christmas and your birthday."

She nodded. "If you think that's best."

"I do. You've got some big decisions to make. I'll be around if you need to talk anything over with me."

She smiled at him. "You're the best."

"Don't forget it," he said with a cheeky wink. "Now, I better get home."

"Denke for coming with me today."

"You're welcome. Don't get up." He leaned over and kissed her softly on her forehead. "I'll see you tomorrow morning."

He walked out the door and then she was left alone, but not for long because as soon as she heard Joseph's buggy horse clip-clopping down the driveway, Tara rushed out of the kitchen toward her.

"What happened?" Tara asked as she sat down next to Elizabeth with her legs tucked under her.

"Were you hiding in the kitchen?"

"I had started to get myself some tea before you got home. I didn't mean to hide, but you didn't know I was there, so I didn't want to interrupt the two of you."

"What did you hear?"

"You're going back there tomorrow?"

"Just for lunch. You should've seen their grand home. They had ceilings that were so high I don't know how they got up there to clean them and I would hate to have to clean that huge staircase. I'm sure the floors were made out of marble. I've never seen anything like it. Their house was like a museum."

"Elizabeth, you have all the luck. Why couldn't it have been me?" She leaned toward her. "I'd leave here in a heartbeat and make the most of being one of them. I'd love having them try to make up to me for all those lost years." Tara chuckled.

"Yeah, but if it really happened to you, you'd feel differently."

"I doubt it. Did they ask you to live there?"

"They said I was welcome to if I wanted."

"I know what I'd be doing. Want to swap?"

Elizabeth frowned at her.

"Oh, I'm sorry, bad choice of words."

"Yeah. Already been done. Why don't you come with me?"

"For real?"

"I'd feel so much better if I had you there. They think that Joseph is coming and so I'm sure they wouldn't mind."

"What about Megan?"

Elizabeth sighed. "Oh. She'd feel left out. I can't take the two of you."

"Best I don't go. Megan would feel left out."

"That's so nice of you, Tara. I wouldn't like Megan to feel bad. She's so sweet."

"I'm a nice person."

Elizabeth giggled. "I know you are."

"I hope you do."

"Would you ever leave?"

"I guess so. I don't know. I'm hesitant to leave the same as you are. We'll all have to make that decision now that we're all eighteen."

"That's true. It kind of crept up on me. I can't believe I'll be eighteen tomorrow."

"If I were you I'd see what their life is like. It's the life you should've had, Elizabeth."

"What concerns me is that I didn't have it. What if I didn't have it for a reason? William and Gretchen are always saying we're here for a reason. I believe that's true. This is where God wants me to be. But does He still want me here, or is it time for me to be somewhere else? What if He want's me with the Doyles?"

Tara shook her head. "I don't know."

"How do I find out?"

"That's a hard question. I don't know. Do you think you have to try and see? Maybe talk to Gretchen."

"I'll talk with her before I go there tomorrow. It'll be weird going there by myself."

"You'll be okay."

Elizabeth nodded. "I guess. They're sending a car for me at eleven."

Elizabeth had so many questions, but deep down, she didn't think anyone had the answers. She hoped that she'd get some direction tomorrow. As for now, the only thing she wanted was to crawl into her warm bed, pull the covers over her head and sleep.

CHAPTER 18

This book of the law shall not depart out of thy mouth;
but thou shalt meditate therein day and night,
that thou mayest observe to do according to all
that is written therein:
for then thou shalt make thy way prosperous,
and then thou shalt have good success.
Joshua 1:8

On Christmas morning, Janice and Lyle had just woken when Lyle presented Janice with a gift.

Sitting in bed, she stared at the carefully wrapped gift in her hands. "I don't deserve anything after what I did."

"We all have to make an effort to put the past behind us."

She stared into her husband's eyes. "Does that mean you forgive me?"

"I do forgive you. That doesn't mean I'm not still shocked and trying to get my head around it. I know women have all kinds of hormones going on when they're pregnant, so maybe that was a good part of it."

"I don't know."

"Open it."

She pulled on one end of the red ribbon and the bow unraveled. Then she unwrapped it. It was a jewelry box. Janice opened it to see the diamond earrings she'd been admiring. "How did you know?"

"Travis told me."

Travis was their jeweler.

She picked up the delicate platinum and diamond drop earrings and held them up to the light. The sun shining in through the window broke into reflections of every color of the rainbow. "They're so pretty." She leaned over and kissed him. "Now you can open yours. I hope you like it. You're so hard to buy for."

"I told you, I don't need anything." He opened the present by his bedside. It was the latest designer watch by his favorite watchmaker. "Thank you." He clipped it onto his wrist. "I love it." He kissed her on her cheek.

She knew he was trying hard, but a wedge had developed between them. They'd grown distant, and finding out what she'd done had only caused more distance between them. Janice knew the only thing that would heal their relationship would be time and effort. He could've divorced her and never wanted to talk to her again, so she was grateful that he hadn't done that. That had to mean he was serious about their marriage.

"Are you going to put them on?"

She stared at him.

He frowned at her. "What were you thinking about? You go so quiet sometimes."

"Oh, I was just thinking about us. I just want things to go back to being the way they were when we first married."

"So many things have changed. We didn't have children when

we were first married. We were on our own and more carefree. That's why I said we should travel. Then we wouldn't have so many day-to-day worries."

She smiled. "I'd like that."

"Are you going to put them on?" he asked again.

"I will." One after the other, she pushed them through the holes in her ears. "How do they look?"

"Stunning!"

She gave a little laugh.

"We've got a big day ahead. I hope Elizabeth doesn't change her mind. She seemed a little timid."

Janice gasped. "No. She won't change her mind, will she? That would be dreadful."

"I shouldn't have said anything. I hope not. It'll be good if she gets to know all of us."

"I hope she likes us. It must be like coming into a different world from the one she's been living in. I don't know how they all live in that dark little home."

"Whatever it is, that's the only home she's known for a long time. The one she's lived in most of her life. Did you call Margaret about finding out if the Simpsons have relatives? You mentioned that you thought they might have a doctor who's a relation?"

"I haven't talked to her, but I will."

"I thought you spoke to her nearly every day."

"I do, but there have been so many other things going on that I forgot to ask her. I'll find out today."

"Is she coming to the house?"

"No. She's visiting relatives in Connecticut for the holidays, but she's always got her mobile with her. I forgot to tell you something else; I've given Magda some time off from working today."

"Who's going to be cooking today?"

"We've got a chef coming in as well as other staff. Don't worry. It's been organized."

. . .

ELIZABETH WAS SHAKEN awake by Megan and Tara.

"What? What are you doing?" Elizabeth had never liked the early morning starts.

"Happy birthday," they chorused.

"Thank you. Now I need some more sleep." She rolled over hoping they'd leave her alone.

"You don't have a lot of time. Aren't they sending a car for you mid-morning?"

Elizabeth sat up. "What time is it?"

"Eight."

She flopped back into the pillow. "I suppose I should get up. Joseph is coming at eight thirty. The car isn't coming until eleven."

Right at eight thirty, Joseph arrived. She ran out to meet him.

"Have you changed your mind about coming with me today?"

He shook his head. "This is something you should do alone." He stepped closer and pulled her to him. "Happy birthday."

She pushed him away. "Stop. Someone will see."

"Come behind the buggy, then, so I can give you a birthday kiss."

She giggled. She'd never been kissed before and it would be perfect to be kissed on her eighteenth birthday by the man she wanted to marry.

"Do I have to beg?" he asked.

"Maybe?"

He pulled a sad face, so she stepped closer to him and pointed to her cheek. "You can kiss me there."

He stepped in and gently pressed his lips against her cheek.

When he finished, he stepped back. "I have a present I want to give you before we go inside."

"What is it?"

"You have to close your eyes."

She closed her eyes, and then peeked a little.

"Stop it! I saw that. No looking."

She closed her eyes again. "I'm not looking."

"Put out your arms."

Soon she felt something in her arms and she opened her eyes.

"Open it," he said.

She ripped the paper open to reveal a new set of skates. "They're beautiful." She looked them over. "And they're my size. How did you know?"

"It wasn't too hard. I just had a look at your old ones."

"I don't think I've ever had brand new skates like these. Thank you." She stepped closer and kissed him on his cheek.

"That's for your birthday, and not for Christmas. I'll take you shopping when the stores open again. I'm afraid I'm hopeless where gifts are concerned. I couldn't think what else you'd like."

"That's not necessary."

"It is. And it's a way I can spend more time with you."

She ran her hands across the white skates. "They're so lovely. I wish you could come with me today."

He placed both his hands on her shoulders. "Look at me."

Staring into her eyes, he said, "I've told you how I feel about you, but I don't want to influence your decisions about this family. You might want to live with them and leave the community."

"I know, you've explained it to me before, but I can still wish. Now come inside so I can give you your present."

"You got me a present?"

She giggled. "Of course I did. And I hope you like it." She led him back to the house thinking it funny that she'd also bought him skates.

When he got inside and opened them, he laughed. "Great minds think alike, they say."

"Well, I was hoping they would improve your skating because nothing could make it any worse."

. . .

ELEVEN O'CLOCK CAME and the car arrived. She said goodbye to everyone she loved and headed to the house of her newly discovered family.

On the way in the car she cried, and then she wiped her eyes the best she could so the driver wouldn't see. She was upset over Joseph. If he really loved her, he would've come with her and helped her through it. He'd said he didn't want to distract her, but didn't he love her enough to encourage her to stay within the community?

He'd never proposed to her, he just talked of marriage in a joking manner. If he had ever asked her properly to marry him, she would've said yes.

CHAPTER 19

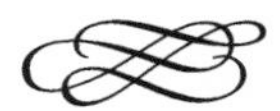

Study to shew thyself approved unto God,
a workman that needeth not to be ashamed,
rightly dividing the word of truth.
2 Timothy 2:15

IT WAS hard for Elizabeth to walk up to the front door alone. Just as she reached it, it was flung open and once again Mr. and Mrs. Doyle stood there.

"Welcome," Mr. Doyle said as Mrs. Doyle leaned over and kissed her on her cheek.

"Isn't Joseph coming?" Mrs. Doyle said.

"He's, err. No."

"Well thank you for coming," Mr. Doyle said, ushering her inside. "We're all anxious to get to know you better."

She sat in the sitting room and talked with her sisters and Lyle Junior while the old grandmother eyed her from a distance and made her feel uneasy. As nice as her sisters and Lyle were, she still felt as though she didn't belong.

Lyle asked his questions about his birth parents, and she answered them as best she could.

Then a bell sounded and it was announced that the meal was ready.

Elizabeth walked with the others into a grand dining room. A long narrow table was filled with cut glass, silverware and fine china. After they sat, a waiter brought in a large turkey and then more food was brought out.

Mr. Doyle said a prayer of thanks while everyone closed their eyes.

Although Elizabeth was in glamorous and beautiful surroundings, her heart longed to be back in the small dark Amish farmhouse with mismatched plates and the plain wooden table surrounded by people she loved.

When she opened her eyes, Joseph was being shown into the room.

All eyes turned to him.

"I'm sorry I'm late," he said looking directly at Elizabeth and then looking at Mr. and Mrs. Doyle

Lyle and Janice stood up.

"That's no trouble at all. We'll seat you next to Elizabeth," Janice said.

Mr. Doyle pulled another chair from the corner of the room and placed it between Elizabeth and Felicity.

"I thought you weren't coming," Elizabeth whispered to him when he sat down.

"It didn't feel right without you. I got back home and all I wanted to do was spend the rest of the day with you."

One of the staff placed a table setting in front of him.

"I hope I haven't put anyone out by being late," Joseph said.

"Of course not. We're glad you were able to make it," Mr. Doyle said.

Joseph gave him an appreciative nod and then slid his hand under the table toward Elizabeth. She reached out and placed her hand in his.

She could get through anything with him beside her.

They ate a traditional Christmas dinner, with turkey and roasted vegetables and ham—all the foods she would've eaten at Gretchen's house, although there was a lot more of everything. Their dessert was traditional Christmas plum pudding, with ice cream, cream and brandy sauce. Afterward, liquor chocolates and coffee were served.

The Doyles knew already that Elizabeth was expected elsewhere so when the meal was over, they knew she had to go and they said their goodbyes.

When Elizabeth and Joseph got back to the Grabers' house, snow was lightly falling. Elizabeth watched the car that drove them there get smaller and smaller on the road. It was just at dusk.

"Don't go inside yet, Elizabeth."

"We have to; it's freezing."

"No more than usual." He grabbed her hand and ran with her to the barn where his horse and buggy were waiting. "I didn't come with you because I wanted you to make up your mind and feel no ties to the community, not to have you stay in the community out of guilt or out of your fondness for the Grabers." He looked upward. "I didn't think this would be so hard."

"What?"

"I want to marry you, Elizabeth. What do you think about that?" He shook his head. "Oh boy. That wasn't good."

She giggled. "Start again. Like how you started over when we first met."

"Elizabeth, will you marry me? I just need to let you know how I feel so you have all the facts and everything will be out in the open. I always want to…"

"Shh."

He stopped talking.

"Kiss me?"

"Is that a yes?" he asked.

"I wouldn't let you kiss me if it weren't."

He smiled, and stepped toward her and gently lowered his lips until they met hers. She closed her eyes, enjoying his soft lips against her own. When he lifted his head she looked into his blue eyes.

"When I saw you walk into the house tonight, I was so happy I felt I would burst. That was the best gift I've ever had. It meant the world."

He smiled. "I'm glad. I honestly never thought I'd meet a girl like you. I don't want to keep you from your family; that would be selfish."

"You're not. Janice gave birth to me, but other people raised me. You're my family now and so is the community. William and Gretchen always said that *Gott* wanted all the children who came through their *haus* to be there. I know that now, and I'm no longer angry with Janice. How could I be? If it weren't for what she did, I would never have met any of the people who are so dear to me now. And I wouldn't have met you."

Joseph took hold of her hand and brought it up to his lips and kissed it. "I knew I'd marry you the very first time I saw you."

For the first time since she learned the dreadful news, she felt whole. It was true what she'd said to Joseph, she no longer felt anger or resentment because it had all been God's will.

CHAPTER 20

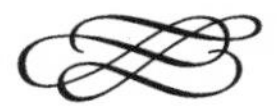

Commit thy way unto the Lord;
trust also in him; and he shall bring it to pass.
Psalm 37:5

That night across town.

"How do you think tonight went? Do you think Elizabeth will ever want to come and live with us?"

Lyle Senior and Janice were sitting alone in one of their sitting rooms after everyone had gone to bed.

Lyle pressed his lips together and shook his head. "I strongly doubt it. She seems very fond of that young man."

"He seems nice. He's very polite."

"It was nice for Lyle to learn a little about his birth parents."

"I feel better about things now that they're out in the open. I thought you'd divorce me for certain."

"Janice, you have to forgive yourself."

She nodded.

"We have to look into the legalities of Lyle and Elizabeth's birth certificates and get them changed. I didn't want to raise that subject tonight. It wasn't the right time."

"Yes. That'll have to be made right. I didn't even think of that."

"It certainly makes me see that the two of us have suffered from a lack of communication. I've been too focused on work and you must say what's on your mind instead of worrying all the time. That's what causes some of your headaches."

"I'll try."

"Never mind trying, just do it."

Janice sighed. "Okay."

"It's been a big day, but I believe a successful one."

"Yes, another Christmas day is over and it was one like no other. I hope Elizabeth always keeps in touch with us. In a way, I feel that we owe it to the Simpsons to watch over both of them, Lyle Junior and Elizabeth."

"Of course, they're both ours. We'll have to take things at her pace, though."

"Did you see she hugged me when she was leaving tonight?"

He smiled. "I did. She relaxed by the end of the night. Janice, I guess I don't say it often enough, but I love you."

Tears stung at the back of her eyes. He'd not told her that for years. "I love you too."

"Let's make these last years count."

She laughed. "We've not gotten that old yet."

"I know, but this whole business has made me realize that I've been taking everything for granted—you and the children. I want to make things right."

"All I ever wanted was to make you happy and be a good wife."

He pulled her close and put his arm around her. "You have made me happy and I'm going to spend the next years making you know it." Lyle kissed her on her forehead and she rested her head against him.

~

SHALL we tell them we're going to get married?" Joseph looked at the Grabers' house.

"*Nee,* we'll keep it to ourselves for a little while."

"I want the world to know."

Elizabeth giggled, and then whispered, "Keep quiet! You're too noisy."

"You're not going to change your mind, are you?"

"Is that why you want to tell everyone?"

"Uh huh. That way, you'll be locked in."

She giggled again. "I'm locked in now."

"We better go inside, then or I'll have to kiss you again."

She ducked away from him and ran to the house. "Last one's last."

He ran after her and got to the door at the same time as she.

"Let's tell them tonight if you want to," she said.

"We'll get married at the end of January and my *bruder* will help me build us a *haus.*"

"You've got it all figured out."

"That's all I've thought about these past weeks. I started planning everything when I met you. I couldn't risk losing you to the Doyles."

"I'll see them again, but you'll never lose me to anyone."

Elizabeth's thoughts went to the Simpsons who'd raised her and given her love. They had to be with God; she was certain of it. Now looking through the window at the Christmas tree and the soft light from the candles in the windows, she knew her life was full, and her future was with Joseph. Everything had come together on her birthday, Christmas Day. Eighteen years ago, a decision changed her life and put it on a different course.

Just as Joseph put his hand on the door handle, she said a silent prayer of thanks to God for her life turning out exactly how it had.

The End of Book 1

AMISH FOSTER GIRL

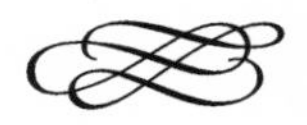

BOOK 2 AMISH FOSTER GIRLS (AMISH ROMANCE)

CHAPTER 1

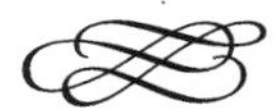

Be of good courage, and he shall strengthen your heart, all ye that hope in the Lord.
Psalm 31:24

STEPPING through the door of the café, Tara spotted Elizabeth waving at her from a table at the back.

Tara hurried over to her and slid into the chair opposite. "Sorry I'm late. You've finished your shift?"

"Jah. What kept you?" Elizabeth sipped her drink through a straw.

"Gretchen said William told her the horse was lame. I had to change over to Sox."

"Sox isn't good in traffic."

"He's a bit flighty. I'm glad Gretchen didn't know that, or I would've been stuck at home. This is my only day off this week apart from Sunday." Tara sighed and placed her bag down on the edge of the table. "I'm going to miss you so much when you get married. It'll only be me and Megan left at home."

"Gretchen and William might take in some more foster children."

"Really? Did they say that?"

Elizabeth laughed. "I don't know; it's not likely. They've only had the three of us for years."

"And with you gone, there'll be a spare room."

"True."

A young *Englisch* man came to take their order. Tara looked him up and down.

After he had taken their order and left, Tara leaned forward and whispered, "What's going on with that? Why did they hire a man? He's not even Amish."

Elizabeth shrugged her shoulders. "I don't know. I think they're going to make him a shift manager or something."

"What about you?"

"I don't care. I'm only here for the money. I'm not here to make a career out of it."

"Yeah, I guess so. Especially when you're getting married."

When the young man returned with Tara's tea, he picked up her bag and placed it on a chair before walking away.

Tara's mouth opened in shock at the man. "Did you see that?"

"What?"

"He touched my bag without even asking me."

"It's not a big deal. He just wanted to make more room on the table."

"I reckon it was weird. Would you have picked up someone's bag and moved it like that without asking?"

"Nee. I wouldn't. He didn't mean anything by it. Don't worry."

Tara poured her tea from the small teapot, filling the cup just as the man brought Elizabeth her coffee.

When he left, Tara leaned forward. "He doesn't have nice manners, either. He doesn't even smile."

Elizabeth groaned. "Stop being hung up about little things all the time."

"Well, don't you think that it was a weird thing to do—the thing about my bag?"

"Not especially. Don't over think things." Elizabeth ripped open a packet of sugar and poured it into her coffee. "Now, the reason I wanted you to meet me here was to talk about you minding the *haus* for me and Joseph."

"Oh, and I thought it was because you'd miss me so much when you're both away for a month."

Elizabeth smiled. "You know I will. I'll miss everyone."

"I'm still willing to mind your *haus*. I'm actually looking forward to being by myself."

"*Jah,* I remember you saying..."

"You've written down all the instructions, so I don't forget anything, haven't you?" Maybe looking after Elizabeth's *haus* would pull her out of the doldrums.

"*Jah,* I've left a list on the kitchen table. I can't wait to move into it. Joseph's lived in it for three weeks and said there's a fair bit to do, but we can do things as we go, while we're living in it."

Tara frowned. "What things need doing?"

"Don't worry; the roof isn't going to fall in. There's nothing structural going on."

Tara watched her friend speak with excitement about her new life. It was still hard to believe that Elizabeth was getting married. She'd be someone's wife and have her own house just like a grown up.

Tara took a sip of tea. "Have you noticed how everything goes right for you, Elizabeth?"

"What do you mean?"

"Your birth family is rich and they want you to live with them and then there's Joseph. Your life is pretty much perfect. When you said you'd marry Joseph—boom, out of the blue, his family gets left a *haus* and they give it to Joseph."

Elizabeth laughed. "I guess so. *Gott* is watching over me."

"When you marry, I hope we can still meet up like this and do the simple things we used to do. You'll come back to the *haus* and visit us won't you?"

"*Jah,* that's where I grew up; it'll always be home."

Elizabeth had been with her foster parents, the Grabers, since she was eight, and then Tara and Megan had joined them later. In the early years, there were various children coming for short stays, but none had stayed as long as the three girls.

Tara sighed. "I always thought I'd get married first, then you, and then Megan."

"I never really thought about it." Elizabeth brought the coffee cup up to her mouth, placed her perfect bow-shaped lips onto the rim of the cup and took a delicate sip.

"See? That's the difference between you and me. You never have to think about things; they just fall into place."

Elizabeth frowned and placed her cup back onto the saucer. "Tara, you have more attention from men than any other woman in the community. You've got nothing to grumble about."

"Yes, but the only man I want is Mark and he took off."

"You should've told him how you felt."

Tara raised her eyebrows. "If he'd loved me, he wouldn't have gone. Anyway, we told each other how we felt and I think that's what scared him off. I think if he'd stayed then things would've been different."

"He'll be back."

"We'll see. Anyway, enough about him. I'm trying to forget him."

"Okay."

"I'm looking forward to staying in your *haus.* It'll be a good distraction."

"Have you been pining after Mark?"

Shaking her head, she said, *"Nee.* Well, maybe a little, but don't you tell anyone."

"Who would I tell?"

"Aunt Gretchen, or Megan."

"I won't."

"It doesn't matter, I guess. Megan knows anyway and I'm sure she's sick of hearing me talk about him."

"I thought you were sneaking away to see someone for the last few months. I didn't know if it was one man or different men."

Tara giggled. "It was only Mark. We wanted to keep things quiet and I thought the relationship was going somewhere—heading toward marriage."

"I thought you might have been thinking of leaving the community. You told me I should move into the Doyles' home and not look back."

"Only because they're your family—your birth family—not because they're rich. It wouldn't have hurt to stay with them and get to know them."

"Their place wasn't my home. *Gott* had planned for me to be with the Grabers. They're always telling us we were sent to them for a reason and it's true." She stared into Tara's eyes. "Don't worry; he'll be back."

"I asked you not to talk about him. Can we change the subject?"

"Okay. What do you think of Joseph's *bruder,* Caleb?"

Tara shrugged her shoulders. "He's nice, I guess. I don't know him that well."

"I know that he likes you."

"How? Did Joseph tell you?"

Elizabeth smirked. "I can't say more."

Tara's attention was taken by a couple who sat down at the

table next to them. She looked back at Elizabeth. "That's not fair. You've said that much, so you have to tell me more."

"Everything will work out for you just as things have worked out for me." Elizabeth wagged a finger. "Just you wait and see."

Tara nodded, not wanting to argue with her friend. The fact was that things had never worked out for her without her putting in a huge effort. Elizabeth had been the first of the three of them to get a job, and Tara had gotten one rejection after another until finally, she got the part time job at the quilting store. Megan had applied at a couple of places but, being painfully shy, she hadn't made a good impression in any of the job interviews.

"You've always been a good friend to me, Tara."

"Oh no. You're getting deep and meaningful on me."

Elizabeth laughed. "I'm going to miss everyone, that's all. My life's going to be so different once I'm married."

"I'm glad the three of us were together for the last few years. We're all different and none of that matters. In real families, people can be different too."

"Tara, I've never heard you talk like this."

Tara gave a sideways glance at the new waiter as he served the newcomers at the table next to them. Again with no smile, she noticed. She looked back at Elizabeth. "You're like my *schweschder,* and so is Megan. You just understand me a little better than she does."

Elizabeth narrowed her eyes. "You seem a little down. Where's the happy bubbly Tara?"

Tara inhaled deeply. "I've just been thinking about things that's all."

"About Mark?"

"You're not going to stop talking about him are you?"

"Well, is *he* the problem?"

Tara cringed. "Is it that obvious?"

"Jah. At least to me."

"I don't think I'll ever feel about anyone the way I felt about him." She glanced at Elizabeth and didn't want to ruin her happiness. "That's why I'm so excited to be looking after your *haus* until you get back." Tara felt better when the smile returned to Elizabeth's lips. She'd have to forget about her problems until after Elizabeth's wedding. Then, when she was by herself for that month, she could figure out what to do with the rest of her life.

"Are the Doyles coming to the wedding?"

"*Jah.* I've invited all of them."

"I can't wait to see them. You've described them all so well. I want to see how closely the pictures in my head match up to how they look in real life."

"I hope they all come. I'm not so sure they will."

"Your birth mother and father will at least come, won't they?"

"They said they would."

"How do you feel about them now?"

Elizabeth shrugged her shoulders. "It still feels weird. I'm getting used to them being my family and Lyle Junior being the Simpson's real child. I'm used to thinking of *Mamm* Gretchen, *Dat* William, Megan, and you as my family."

"I'm sorry. I shouldn't have asked. I don't want to make you sad."

"I'm not sad. It's weird; that's all."

Tara didn't know anything about her birth parents, even whether they were alive or dead.

Tara said, "I guess it would feel weird to grow up thinking your parents were the people who raised you, and then find out they were someone else."

Elizabeth stared into her coffee. "Let's move on."

Tara laughed to ease the tension about the subjects that they wanted to avoid. It was clear that Elizabeth's wounds were still there, like her own.

"What would you like to talk about?" Tara asked.

"Caleb."

Tara tipped her head to one side. "I'm sensing some kind of a set-up."

Elizabeth raised her eyebrows and smirked again, causing Tara to sigh.

"Who put you up to talking to me about him?" Tara asked.

"You're not supposed to know."

"Of course I'm not. I'm not about to blab, so tell me."

"Joseph asked me to find out if you're interested in Caleb. Because Caleb likes you."

"I don't know how I feel about him. I don't know him very well."

"My wedding will be the perfect place to get to know him. He might make you forget all about the person I'm not allowed to mention."

"I hope so."

"Caleb is quiet, but he's worth taking the time to get to know."

"Well, forgetting about that certain person would be good. That's something I need to do, but I don't know if I should use another man to do it."

"Don't be silly. That's not what I meant. Wait a minute, though, it's not a bad idea."

Tara frowned until Elizabeth reached over and tickled her ribs, and then Tara had to join with Elizabeth's giggles.

CHAPTER 2

Be thou my strong habitation, whereunto I may continually resort: thou hast given commandment to save me; for thou art my rock and my fortress.
Psalm 71:3

ELIZABETH AND JOSEPH'S wedding was to be held at the Grabers' house and the girls had spent the last week scrubbing the house from top to bottom in readiness. Because the house wasn't large, an annex had been set up outside the kitchen to manage the food preparation for the hundreds of guests. There were no formal invitations sent out. The wedding was announced and written up in the Amish newspapers, as was customary, and people always showed up—usually in the hundreds. Weddings were major social events for the Amish and, for the young people, one of the best places to meet their future spouses.

On the morning of Elizabeth's wedding, Tara woke early. As

soon as she had dressed, she bounded into Elizabeth's room and jumped on her bed.

"Wake up, sleepy head. This is the last morning you're going to be here. You'll be an old married woman by the end of the day."

Elizabeth opened one eye and then rolled over the other way, burying her face in the pillow. She'd never been an early riser.

"How come you're not excited?" Tara pulled the blankets off her friend and Elizabeth tried her best to grab them back.

Elizabeth sat up. "How early is it?"

"It's not early; it's time to get up. Aunt Gretchen is already awake. I can hear her downstairs."

Groaning, Elizabeth wiped her eyes. "I guess I should get out of bed."

"Jah, we've got so much to do yet today before people arrive. Starting with putting clean sheets on this bed, since it won't be yours after today."

The wedding was at nine o'clock. And now it was five thirty, only a few short hours before everyone arrived.

Tara leaped off the bed, and the two of them quickly remade it with clean linens. Then Tara unhooked Elizabeth's blue wedding dress from the peg behind the door.

"I'll put that on at the last minute, so I don't get it dirty."

"Good idea." Tara spread it over the bed.

All the women in their family, Aunt Gretchen, Megan, Elizabeth and Tara, had sewed the dresses for the attendants and the wedding dress for Tara. They'd also sewed the suits for Joseph and his two attendants.

Lastly, Tara placed the white organza prayer *kapp* and apron alongside the blue dress.

"Let's go and have breakfast before Aunt Gretchen finds a million things for us to do."

Elizabeth giggled while she changed into an everyday dress.

Before they left the bedroom, Elizabeth wound her hair on her head and placed a prayer *kapp* on top.

When they reached the kitchen, they found a frazzled-looking Aunt Gretchen, and Megan making the breakfast.

"What's the matter?" Elizabeth said striding toward Gretchen.

"I've got a crowd coming and I'm feeling a little daunted." She pulled out a handkerchief and dabbed at her eyes.

Tara knew the truth of it was that she was sad that Elizabeth was leaving her. Elizabeth glanced up at Tara and, from the look on her face, Elizabeth also knew what the real problem was.

Elizabeth placed her arm around Gretchen. "We'll handle it, *Mamm* Gretchen. Many of the ladies always help."

Gretchen nodded as Tara sat down at the table. "I know the real reason you're upset is that I'll be gone for a month looking after Elizabeth's *haus.*"

That made Gretchen giggle. "It might be a *gut* rest for me."

Tara gave an exaggerated gasp. "Aunt Gretchen! I'm offended."

The four of them laughed.

Tara called her foster mother either Aunt Gretchen or *Mamm* Gretchen depending what mood she was in.

"We'll be alone for a whole month, *Mamm.* Just you me and *Dat.*"

Gretchen nodded at Megan's words. Megan was a homebody who was quite content to stay at home, cooking and sewing. She was also the only one out of the three of them to start right out calling William and Gretchen Graber, "*Mamm*" and "*Dat.*"

"You were such a sweet girl when you came to us, Elizabeth," Gretchen said, confirming Tara's thoughts of what she was upset about.

"Aren't I still sweet?"

Gretchen patted her hand. "You are. We'll miss you. It won't be the same with you gone."

"But we know how happy you'll be with Joseph. And you'll have lots of babies and bring them here for their *Gossmammi* Gretchen to babysit," Tara said.

"Jah, please," Gretchen said.

"That's a little too far in the distance. Let me think about getting married first before you start seeing me with babies," Elizabeth said.

"Everyone want pancakes?" Megan asked.

"Jah!" the women chorused.

"A man can't sleep in with women cackling," William said with a grin as he walked into the kitchen.

"You can't sleep in today," Tara said.

"We've still got so many things to do before people get here," Gretchen added.

William sat down next to Tara.

"Pancakes, *Dat?"* Megan asked.

"Jah, please." He turned to his wife. "I've got the men coming with the wagon at seven to move the furniture out to the barn and the benches into the house."

There was excitement in the air and Tara couldn't help feeling envious of Elizabeth. Everything always went her way. She was beautiful, her birth family was rich and they had wanted her to live with them. Now, she had a wonderful man who'd fallen deeply in love with her.

The next few hours past by in a blur as people rushed around inside the house. Finally it was time for Megan and Tara to go and help Elizabeth get dressed.

Elizabeth sat down on her old bed after pulling on her wedding dress.

She put her hand on her stomach. "I'm nervous."

Megan said, "You'll remember this day for the rest of your life, Elizabeth."

Elizabeth nodded.

Tara ran to the window to see more people arriving. The row of buggies was now so long it nearly reached the front gates. She looked down at a crowd of men, hoping Mark would be amongst them. Surely if he'd ever had real feelings for her, he'd be at her best friend's wedding. He knew how close she was to Elizabeth, and besides that, Joseph was one of his good friends.

Tara pushed him out of her mind and turned around to Elizabeth. "You look beautiful."

"Do I?"

"Jah, you always look beautiful, but especially today."

"Denke, Tara. Can you see any cars out there? What if they don't come?" Elizabeth asked, referring to her birth family.

"They'll come. They said they would."

Elizabeth pushed her bottom lip out slightly. "Can you look outside again?"

Tara moved back toward the window and looked down the driveway. "There are two cars coming through the gates now. That has to be them." Tara whipped her head around in time to see Elizabeth's smile.

"I'm glad they're here."

It amazed Tara that Elizabeth had been so quick to forgive her mother after what she'd done. Her birth mother had swapped her for a boy and had paid the boy's birth mother a lot of money. No one had known about her deception until Elizabeth's birth father saw her at the café where she worked. After her birth father had done some digging into the past, the secret came out.

"I hope they brought the old granny with them after all you told me about her," Tara said.

Elizabeth and Megan giggled.

"Jah, we'll see if she's as unfriendly as you've told us," Megan said.

"If she's here, you'll see I wasn't exaggerating. She looks at me as though I've got a secret and she's trying to uncover it."

Megan giggled. "Maybe she thinks you're not really her granddaughter."

"I'm sure that's it, but they're the ones who found me. I didn't go looking for them."

"That's only because you didn't know they existed," Tara pointed out.

"Yeah. That's what I mean. It's all so complicated in that family. I prefer to have a simple life like the one Joseph and I will have, and just have visits with them once in awhile."

Tara sighed. "You'll have a *wunderbaar* life, Elizabeth."

"You're perfectly suited to Joseph. I hope I meet a nice man one day," Megan said.

"You have to talk with people, Megan. Get over your shyness," Elizabeth said.

Megan pouted. "I wish I was more like you, Tara. You're so brave. You could talk to anyone."

"And why not? Everyone is just flesh and blood, deep down. There's no one who's better than anyone else. You've just got to think more confidently about yourself and stop hiding away in this *haus."*

Megan nodded.

"She will in time," Elizabeth said fiddling with the *kapp* in her hands. "You must take her out with you, Tara."

"Jah, I will, if she'll go with me."

Elizabeth whipped her head around to look at Megan.

"Okay. I will get out more," Megan said.

Elizabeth smiled. "Good."

Tara stared at Megan, not so sure about what she'd said. Today Tara would try to find a man to suit Megan and then she'd introduce the pair. Maybe a quiet man would suit her, as long as he wasn't also shy.

Megan sat on the bed behind Elizabeth and brushed her wavy hair until it was silky smooth. Elizabeth's hair fell way past her waist. It hadn't been cut in the ten years she'd been with the Amish. Megan braided it and pinned it up, and then Elizabeth put on the organza prayer *kapp*.

Once Elizabeth was fully dressed, Megan and Tara hugged her and then they went downstairs first. Megan and Tara took seats next to Gretchen, and they watched as Elizabeth walked down the stairs and greeted Joseph who was waiting for her at the bottom. It brought a tear to Tara's eye the way they looked at one another. The couple then walked to the front of the room where the bishop stood.

The deacon opened with prayer and then Gabe Hostetler sang a hymn in High German. After that, the bishop preached a lengthy sermon. It was the same kind of preaching that Tara had heard so many times before. She scanned the seated crowd and the people who were standing, and still there was no Mark. Before she looked back to the front, she felt someone looking at her. Focusing her gaze as she quickly scanned the crowd, she saw that it was Caleb.

She gave him a little smile when she recalled that Elizabeth had said that he liked her. Caleb wasn't handsome like his younger brother, Joseph. He had a pleasant face, but that was marred by a large scar down one side of his face. Mark was the only one who'd made her heart pitter-patter.

Everyone stood when the bishop pronounced the couple husband and wife. Since the late January day was cold, they couldn't eat in the yard and the benches had to be taken out and tables brought inside for the wedding feast.

As attendants, Megan and Tara sat with Elizabeth at the head wedding-table. Tara let Megan sit next to Elizabeth knowing it would make her feel that little bit more special. There was no use looking around for Mark any longer; if he were coming, he would've been here by now.

Instead of thinking about Mark, Tara concentrated on enjoying the food in front of her. There was no better food than could be found at an Amish wedding. Her gaze traveled over the various roasted and simmered meats, coleslaws and other salads, and all sorts of roasted vegetables. Tara took her plate and started helping herself to her favorites, creamed celery, and bologna.

CHAPTER 3

Yea, though I walk through the valley of the shadow of death, I will fear no evil: for thou art with me; thy rod and thy staff they comfort me.
Psalm 23:4

JUST BEFORE JOSEPH and Elizabeth left the Grabers' place after the wedding celebration, Joseph handed Tara the key to the old house. Elizabeth and Joseph were going to spend their wedding night at Joseph's parents' house, and would leave in the early morning to begin their four weeks' travels to visit many of Joseph's relatives.

Tara was looking forward to staying in the old house and she'd make sure that they arrived home to a spic and span home. She would've loved to start on a vegetable garden for them, but it was the wrong time of year to plant.

"Caleb said he'd be happy to take you there tomorrow morning if that suits. Or, are you going to borrow one of William's buggies for the month?"

"Nee, I haven't asked him about that. To tell you the truth, I didn't even think about a buggy." Tara bit down on the inside of her lip, but relaxed a little when she remembered there was a telephone in a nearby shanty and she could get a taxi to and from work. *"Jah,* I'd appreciate it if Caleb could take me there tomorrow. Would it be in the morning?"

"If that suits," Joseph said.

"The earlier, the better."

"How about I have him collect you around nine?"

"That would be perfect." Tara could've had William or Gretchen take her, but figured there was no harm in getting to know Caleb a little better. Besides, Mark might be getting to know some other girl somewhere—wherever he was, so why shouldn't she see who else might be out there?

The rest of the night was filled with cleaning, after the hundreds of guests left. Some of the women had stayed on to help, but after they left there was still a mountain of work to do.

"You go to bed, *Mamm.* Tara and I can finish this," Megan said.

Gretchen frowned. *"Nee,* it's too much for just the two of you."

"We're fine. You go," Tara said.

"Are you certain?"

"Jah!" both Tara and Megan said firmly.

"Denke. I need to put my feet up, they're aching."

When she left the room, Tara sat down.

"Are you going to leave this all for me?" Megan asked.

"I just need a five minute break. You do, too. Let's sit down for a bit."

Megan took her hands out of the dishwater, shook off the suds and wiped her hands on a nearby hand towel before she too slumped into a chair.

"That was such a long day. And I thought the bishop would never finish that sermon. That's got to be his longest ever."

Megan giggled. "It was long."

"Why don't you come and stay at Elizabeth's *haus* with me?"

"I couldn't. *Mamm* would be alone."

"She'll have *Onkel* William."

"Nee, I couldn't." Megan stared at the table.

"It's getting so that you're hardly ever leaving the *haus.* You don't go to any of the singings, so how do you think you'll meet a man?"

"There were plenty of men here today."

"Did you talk to any of them?"

"I didn't see any that I liked the look of that much."

"I didn't like the look of Mark until I got talking to him. I mean I thought he was handsome, but I didn't think he was for me. There was just something about him that put me off him at first."

"Was Mark here? I thought he'd gone away."

Tara slumped further into her chair wishing she'd never brought up his name.

TARA HAD her bags packed the next morning, ready and waiting for Caleb to fetch her. She'd already said goodbye to William before he'd left for work.

As soon as Caleb's buggy appeared at the bottom of the drive, she ran to the kitchen. "He's here." She wrapped her arms around Gretchen and gave her a tight hug, and then did the same with Megan.

"You're not going across to the other side of the world, Tara," Gretchen said.

"I might as well be. I've never lived on my own before."

"Well, if you get hungry, we've always got plenty of food here."

"Denke, but I've got everything organized." She walked out the door to meet the buggy.

"Hello, Caleb." She climbed into the buggy.

"Those yours?" His head nodded toward the house.

She looked back and saw her bags. "Oh, sorry, I completely forgot them."

"Stay there." He leaped from the buggy, collected her bags and placed them in the back.

"Denke." She looked back at the house to see that Megan and Gretchen were now standing at the front door. When Caleb got back into the driver's seat, she waved to them. Gretchen was smiling, but Tara knew it wouldn't be long before the older woman shed a tear.

Now sitting beside Caleb, she could see his scars close up. One side of his face had a huge scar, and she'd just noticed that his hands had some long scars, too, that looked like they'd come from deep scratches. Perhaps having that deep scar on his face had made him keep away from people.

Noticing that Caleb had barely said a word, she thought she should strike up a conversation. "It was a good wedding yesterday."

"*Jah,* it was."

"Why didn't you want to stay in Joseph's *haus?"*

He glanced over at her and then looked back to the road. "I wasn't asked."

"Oh. Would you have wanted to if you had been asked?"

"Dunno."

It didn't seem that he liked her, despite what she'd been told. He wasn't making much of an effort to converse, at any rate. So much for her hopes of him taking her mind off Mark.

Deciding it was his turn to talk about something, she put everything out of her mind and looked at the partially melting snow. The sun seemed unusually strong for the early part of a January day.

For the first time in months, Tara found herself smiling for no particular reason. The winter sun and the fresh air flowed over her face in waves. The once-green fields were now covered with snow and the beauty of the wildflowers was replaced with the shimmering sparkles of snow as the sun danced on the surface.

She found comfort in the sound of Caleb's graceful black gelding clip-clopping his way down the road back to the old homestead. Maybe it was the prospect of having a whole month to herself and finally having a little independence from her foster family that had altered her mood.

A good twenty minutes passed in silence before they came to the house.

"Here we are," he said as he pulled the buggy up.

"Ah good."

"You got the key?" he asked, seeming to use as few words as possible.

"I do. Joseph gave it to me yesterday."

He gave a grunt from the back of his throat. It was becoming clear to her why he wasn't married. He needed a good lesson on how to relate to women. Her opinion of him improved slightly when he took her bags out of the back and placed them at the front door. At least he was polite.

Before he got back into the buggy, Tara fumbled with the key. "Are you going to come inside with me?" she called out.

"Do I need to?"

"Um. No. It's just that… no, don't worry." She glanced at the old house behind her and tried to stop her imagination from running away with her. It was just an old house, but if hauntings were real, then this place would've been perfect for one. It wasn't at all like the usual Amish farmhouse.

"Bye," he said just before he clicked his horse onward.

Tara looked down at the large black key in her hand, and then ambled to the front door. She pushed it into the keyhole and with one turn to the right the door creaked open. She waited a moment before she stepped inside. A waft of stale air met her nostrils and she wondered why she'd agreed to stay in the house. As she took small, reluctant steps further inside, the stale air was mixed with a definite smell of damp—perhaps even mold.

The first thing to do was get rid of the old stale air. After she'd gone around opening all the windows for some much needed fresh air, she pulled her bags into the house.

The old *haus* would have been grand in its day. The ceilings were high and the staircase was wider than the average, with a beautifully carved wooden bannister—quite unlike any Amish *haus* would have. From the decorative iron ceiling roses and cornices, it was clear that this *haus* was not built to be a home for an Amish person. Amish homes were much plainer, practical, with no fancy features.

As she walked around inspecting the house, she wondered what parts Elizabeth and Joseph would keep and what ones they'd replace.

When Tara walked toward the kitchen, she realized she would have to do something about buying food. There was only one thing for it; she'd have to walk down to the phone and call a taxi to take her to the nearest market.

It was nearing midday, and knowing the coming night would be cold, Tara went into the kitchen to see if it might have a wood stove or some other heating system so she would not have to light the huge fire in the living room. Tara knew better than to light a fire in an unknown fireplace; it could have a blocked or un-working chimney and the place could very well fill with dirty and dangerous black smoke. To her delight, there was a woodburning stove in the kitchen, rather than a gas stove.

"I may as well do it sooner rather than later," Tara said to herself aloud, regarding going to the store.

A quick look around in the kitchen told her she only needed to buy food, as pots and pans, utensils and plates were all there.

Everything would need scrubbing, but she could do that when she came back.

Tara had so much work to do in the *haus* before Joseph and Elizabeth got back that she felt a little guilty doing something that was not in her tight schedule. She knew she could not work every waking hour of the day, but she'd factored that in as well. She'd brought her needlework and she would work on that for an hour or so every night. Tara smiled to herself; she was glad to have the project of working on Elizabeth and Joseph's place.

Driving back in a taxi from the brief visit to the food store Tara was pleased it hadn't taken long. That was only because she'd hidden from old Mrs. Yoder, the local gossip. Tara had been about to head down an aisle in the store when she saw her and turned on her heel to get away from her. Thankfully, Mrs. Yoder hadn't see her, or they'd still be talking now.

As the taxi drove her back to the house, a buggy came into view. She didn't know who it could be and she didn't recognize the horse.

When the taxi came closer, she suddenly did recognize the tall bay horse with his broad blaze. He was named Big and the owner, although he was nowhere in sight, was none other than Mark Young—the same Mark Young who'd run out on her.

"What the heck is he doing here?" she said under her breath.

"That'll be eight fifty, Ma'am."

She handed the driver a ten dollar bill. From her backseat position, she glanced at her reflection in the rear view mirror. Thankfully, she had no dark circles under her eyes from lack of sleep; she pinched her cheeks to give them color.

"There you go." The driver handed her the change.

After she had straightened her prayer *kapp* and tied up the loose strings, she grabbed hold of her two bags of groceries and stepped out of the taxi.

She knew that Mark and Joseph were friends, but wouldn't

Mark know that Joseph wasn't here? And why hadn't he bothered to go to his good friend's wedding?

Tara walked around Mark's buggy and even looked inside it, but he wasn't there. Then she realized what was very wrong with this scene. The front door of the house was ajar, when she clearly remembered locking the doors and the windows before she left.

Now angry with him, firstly for leaving and secondly for arriving there the day after her best friend's wedding, she marched toward the house. With her arms full of shopping bags, she shoved the door wide open with her foot and walked through.

"Watch it!" The voice belonged to Mark.

Tara looked behind the door. "Mark Young!"

Mark stared at her and then raised himself from his crouched position, with hammer in hand. "Oh, it's you."

Suddenly feeling the weight of the bags, she set them by her feet. "Well?" She folded her arms and despite her feelings of rage for what he'd done to her, she wanted to reach out and touch him.

He flicked his dark hair away from his face and stared at her with his even darker eyes. Was he more muscled and a little taller, maybe?

"I could ask you the same question." His eyes ran up and down her in an instant and then their gaze locked in an intense stare.

Lifting her chin high, she announced, "I'm staying here while Joseph and Elizabeth are visiting." Tara unfolded her arms and clasped her hands in front of her.

"Joseph asked me to do some work on the place while he was away." He mirrored her earlier stance with arms folded across his chest.

"*Nee,* he wouldn't have. Not without telling me, and how did you get a key – do you even have one?"

He reached down to the floor and picked up a key. It was identical to the one Joseph had placed in her care.

Tara pouted. "I don't know why they wouldn't have told me that *you* would be coming here."

Mark shrugged his shoulders. "Looks like you'll have to put up with me coming and going all the time. Unless—"

CHAPTER 4

Be thou exalted, Lord, in thine own strength:
so will we sing and praise thy power.
Psalm 21:13

"Unless what?" Tara snapped back.

"I stay in the *haus* as well to save me the dr—"

"You'll do no such thing!"

Mark threw his head back and laughed. "You haven't changed."

"Neither have you!" It was lame, but that was all she could think to say. He had given her no apology and no reason why he'd left. He was acting like she was a total stranger instead of someone with whom he'd once talked of marriage. Didn't he feel he owed her a reason for leaving? Or was she so unimportant in his life that she was of no consequence to him?

"Well, we'll have to find some way of getting along together while I work on the *haus*."

She couldn't take it any longer; she had to know. "Why did you leave?"

He frowned at her. "What do you mean?"

"Forget it!" She picked up her two bags of groceries and stomped into the kitchen.

Tara was ashamed of herself. Ashamed that he could bring her to anger so quickly, and that he still had a place in her heart.

"Where are you off to now?" He followed her into the kitchen.

Annoyed at him shadowing her, she yelled over her shoulder, "You don't have to come with me. I'm just putting the groceries away."

"*Nee*. I'll do it for you." Mark hurried, overtaking her.

She ran in front of him. "I can do it."

He leaped in front of her again and stopped.

She had no choice but to stop and listen to him, as he said, "I'm here to help you."

"It's my food and I'm not cooking for *you.*" She glared at him wanting him to leave her alone. He'd hurt her enough.

"I'll get the supplies in from the buggy."

"What supplies? You're not staying here! They said I could stay here and it's all been arranged."

"Relax! I'm not staying here, but I brought some food to eat while I'm here during the day working. I'll bring the things in when I put the horse away."

Horse away? How long is he staying for?

She turned to fill the teakettle with water and put it on the stove. A cup of hot tea would calm her jangled nerves and make her feel better.

SHE STOOD by the kitchen window, took a sip of freshly brewed peppermint tea and wondered whether it was any use her being there at all. Perhaps she should go home and let Mark keep an eye on the place. That would be better than seeing him all the time.

Tara cast her mind back over the past weeks since Mark had left.

When he came back into the kitchen with his food supplies, he looked at her groceries. "How long are you staying here? This doesn't look like four week's supply of food to me." He put his things on an open shelf.

She poured more boiling water into the teapot.

"I'll go to the store again. I'm not stranded here. I'll get a taxi like I did today." Mark stared at her without saying a word, so Tara continued, "I'm planning to be here until they get back. While we're on the subject, what work are you doing on the *haus*?"

"There are various things that need to be done."

Tara pulled out one of the wooden chairs from under the table and sat down. She poured herself a second cup of tea. "Help yourself to tea, if you wish." She would have him get his own tea if he wanted any.

"*Denke*, don't mind if I do."

While Mark poured tea, Tara took large sips from her cup, wishing she had added cold water to it. She would not make small talk with this man since he'd given her no apology for what he'd done. As soon as he sat at the table, Tara stood and poured the contents of her cup down the sink.

"Well, I don't have time to sit around all day; I've got things to do." Tara set about putting her groceries away in the utility room.

"I need to speak with you about something, Tara. Will you sit down?"

A large knot formed in Tara's stomach. Was she finally going to hear why he up and left her? Or was he just going to make suitable arrangements for the days ahead? Still in the utility room, she looked over her shoulder at him.

"What do you want to speak to me about?" By the way he sat

rigidly looking at his cup; she could tell that he was in a serious mood.

"Just sit, will you?"

Tara let out a deep breath and decided she might as well get it over with. Whatever excuse he had, there was no way she'd ever forgive him for leaving without telling her. What he'd done brought back too many memories of the past. The right man for her would be a man who'd always be there for her no matter what. Her perfect man would make her feel safe, protected and loved.

"I want to speak to you about why I left suddenly."

She huffed. "Why does it have anything to do with me?"

"Don't be like that."

She stared into his dark eyes, wondering how they could be so cold and cruel when once he had been so tender and loving. "What makes you think I even care?"

"Because you did, and not so long ago. Before we left, you said—"

"Things have changed."

"All I want to do is talk."

She sighed noisily and sat down clasping her hands in front of her on the table. "I'm sitting."

He fixed his dark eyes on hers. "I was swept away with it all happening too quickly. My feelings for you have never changed. It was just that it was—well, I didn't know if marriage was for me."

She didn't buy his excuse. "Every Amish person wants to get married."

"You see? That's what everyone keeps saying, but what if it's not for me and I found that out later after we had married? I didn't want us both to be miserable."

"Now we don't have to worry about that." She bounded to her feet. "Like I said, I've got things to do." She hurried back to the utility room to unpack her shopping bags.

He stuck his head around the doorway. "I'll get back to work since you don't want to talk."

She didn't answer or turn around and when she heard him walk away, she glanced over her shoulder to make sure he'd gone. What he'd said was lame. If he'd been scared, why hadn't he discussed it with her at the time? He was the one who'd brought up marriage. Now she had to be stuck with him hanging around the house when she wanted nothing more than to be by herself.

Once she'd finished unpacking the food onto the shelves, she headed upstairs to the bedrooms. She decided on a small bedroom that overlooked the road so she could see who was coming and going.

"This will do nicely," she murmured to herself. She pulled off the older sheets on the single bed and replaced them with new clean sheets that she had brought with her. Once the bed was made, she opened the window to allow the chilly fresh air in.

She headed back downstairs to get Elizabeth's list. If she could get through everything as soon as possible, she could get back home.

Seeing Mark hammering something by the front door, she walked up to him and stopped in front of him, so he couldn't avoid seeing her. "How long will it take you to do these repairs?" She tapped the toe of her black boot impatiently.

He stopped what he was doing and looked up at her. "It's hard to say."

"Give me a rough estimate."

"Two weeks, maybe three."

She rolled her eyes and walked away. With Elizabeth's list in her hand, she sat down at the kitchen table.

She had to laugh when she read her friend's list.

Relax

Have a good time

Don't worry about anything

Enjoy some time alone

Don't do any work

Try not to miss me too much

Love,

Elizabeth

She'd been fooled into thinking she was there to help Elizabeth. She threw the list down on the table. Now she had a decision to make. And that was, should she stay there and ignore Mark the best she could, or go back home?

The repairs had to be done because that's what Joseph wanted, and she would stay there and clean the place so Elizabeth and Joseph would have a clean place to come home to. Mark Young would not ruin her plans. Tomorrow she had work at the quilting store, but as for the rest of the day, she'd clean the kitchen.

Hours later, she heard Mark call out, "I'm heading off now."

"Okay."

He stuck his head around the door. "Do you want me to bring anything back with me tomorrow?"

"I won't be here."

"Why not?"

"I work. Remember?" Immediately, she regretted her harsh tone.

"I've got the fire ready for you. The chimney's okay and all you have to do is light it."

"Denke." She cleared her throat and looked away from him. When she looked back around, he was gone.

Moving to the window, she watched as he hitched his buggy, and kept watching as Big trotted away from the house.

That night, she cooked herself an easy dinner and after that, she settled in front of the fire with her needlework. As far as she could, she put all thoughts of Mark out of her mind.

CHAPTER 5

While the earth remaineth, seedtime and harvest, and cold and heat, and summer and winter, and day and night shall not cease.
Genesis 8:22

In a different part of town.

IT WAS three weeks after he'd buried his wife, and Redmond O'Donnell decided it was time to sort out her belongings. He could no longer bear to look at his wife's clothes and her bits and bobs. The loss was difficult enough without these constant reminders. He didn't want to do it alone, but neither did he want to put his son or his daughter through the task.

His wife had suffered from heart disease and had been sick for some time. It was the pneumonia she'd caught in her last days that escalated her illness to the point she could no longer continue. They'd all three been there with Marjorie when she passed away—

their thirteen year old daughter, Avalon, and his son from his first marriage, Brandon. Marjorie had clutched his hands and mumbled something about being sorry and the rest of her words made no sense. Those words had been her last.

He walked into their once-shared wardrobe to start packing her clothing. Everything was to go except for her jewelry and a few keepsakes to pass on to Avalon. He took armfuls of her clothes and placed them on the bed for Goodwill.

Blinking back tears, he recalled when he'd had to do the exact same thing when Brandon's mother had died. It didn't seem fair that he'd had two wives and they'd both died before him.

A rare shade of turquoise blue caught his eye as it peeped through the black that had become Marjorie's main color choice for clothing. He pulled on the material and out came Marjorie's favorite dress she wore on vacations. Pushing his face into the dress he breathed in Marjorie's favorite scent that lingered in the fabric.

Reminding himself to be practical, he placed the dress back on the pile with the rest of her clothes. There was no point keeping her outfits even if they held memories.

Redmond continued the task, amazed how women thought they needed so many clothes. He had less than a tenth of the clothing Marjorie had. Many of these items were unworn, with their price tags still attached. It seemed wasteful to him, but Marjorie and he had different views on most things. Theirs had been an attraction of opposites.

Once all the clothing items that had been on hangers were on the bed to be packed in boxes, he turned his attention upward to Marjorie's shelves. Seeing a large box, he walked over and pulled it down. After he'd placed it on the bed, he blew off a fine layer of dust, and then opened the lid. Inside was Marjorie's fine lace wedding dress that she'd worn a good twenty years ago. He replaced the lid quickly. The decision was simple. Avalon might like to wear her mother's dress on her wedding day.

He put the box on the far side of the room, which he'd designated as the 'keeper side.'

The next task was her shoes, and dozens upon dozens of pairs went into large boxes. He scratched his head, knowing that he'd set himself a task that would take days, not hours, and he was going to need a lot more boxes.

Noticing a red box at the back of the shelf Marjorie's wedding dress box had been on, he took it down and saw that it was full of jewelry. Avalon could have the task of going through this box. She'd know the pieces of value and the ones that were merely costume jewelry since she'd always gone shopping with her mother. The box was placed beside the wedding dress.

He stood on tiptoes, and then headed back near the door so he could see if there was anything else on the top shelf. On tiptoes again, he saw that there was something else; another box. Reaching up, he could just get hold of it and he tried to keep it steady. He overbalanced and the box tipped to one side and out scattered a mass of papers. Looking at the mess on the floor, he recognized them as important documents and receipts. Most of them looked aged. Sitting down with his legs in front of him, he took hold of his glasses that he'd folded over the top edge of his shirt and placed them on the bridge of his nose. Stubbornly, he refused to wear his glasses unless it was absolutely necessary, but knowing official documents were never in large print, it was a fitting occasion to wear them.

The box had contained their certificate of marriage and the birth certificates of Avalon and Brandon. There were also receipts for the major purchases they'd made over the years. He reached out for the next one and adjusted the distance from his face, so he could read the small print with his bifocals. His heart pounded as he read, and then re-read the document.

"How can this be true? It can't be!"

Sadness mixed with regret pained his heart as though he'd been stabbed repeatedly with a dagger. The paper fell from his hands and he doubled over closing his eyes. Marjorie's last words echoed in his head. Her words finally made sense.

CHAPTER 6

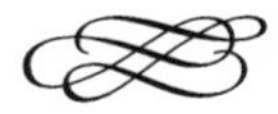

And we know that in all things God works for the good of those who love him, who have been called according to his purpose.
Romans 8:28

At eight the next morning, Tara was hurrying up the road to get a taxi. She noticed a buggy coming toward her and recognized it as belonging to Caleb. He gave her a wave and then pulled his buggy over.

"Where are you headed?"

She walked right up to him. "I've got work today."

"And you're walking there?" His eyebrows drew together.

"*Nee.* I'm heading to call the taxi."

"Don't you work at the quilting store in town?"

She smiled at him. "That's right."

"I can drive you there."

"Really?"

He offered a friendly smile. "Yeah, jump in."

Once she was sitting next to him, she asked, "What are you doing out this way?"

"Joseph asked me to keep an eye on you."

"Did he?"

Caleb nodded.

"I wonder why."

Caleb laughed.

"What's funny?" she asked.

"Nothing."

He was much friendlier than he'd been the previous day.

"Tell me."

He glanced at her. "It's nothing. I'm laughing at myself for asking you dumb questions."

"Oh. What questions?"

He glanced at her with a twinkle in his eyes. "When I asked if you were walking to work."

"Well, I could've been."

He looked back at the road. "Not in this weather."

"I'm just trying to make you feel better," Tara said with a giggle.

He glanced at her again, smiling. "I'm too far gone for that."

"What kind of work do you do?"

"I work on the family farm, but I'd rather be a builder like Joseph."

"Can't you do that? Joseph is younger, isn't he?" Joseph had so many brothers it was hard to know who was older than whom.

"The older sons work on the farm, the younger ones get to do whatever they want, it seems."

"You're not working on the farm now?"

He frowned at her. "Harvest is finished."

"Oh, silly me. You're not alone in the 'dumb question' department!"

He gave a quick laugh. "We're repairing the barn and fixing the wagons, and things like that. At this time of year, there's not much else to do."

Soon they were in town and as she stepped out of his buggy, she said, "*Denke,* Caleb."

"Will you be okay to get home? I can come and get you."

"*Nee,* that's fine. I'm not sure what time I'm finishing today anyway."

"I'll need to check on you every couple of days to keep Joseph happy. I hope you don't mind."

Tara smiled. "Okay. I don't mind at all."

When he drove away, she headed toward the quilt store. She glanced back to see how far Caleb's buggy had gotten when she saw Mark's buggy heading toward her. She whipped her head away, so he wouldn't know she'd seen him. In the reflection from a nearby window, she saw a young woman beside him. Jealousy mixed with rage inside her. Had he been trying to get back in her good books while also dating someone else? Is that why he'd wanted to keep their relationship quiet from the start? A dozen scenarios flashed through her head before she pushed the door of the quilt store open.

WHEN TARA WAS SITTING down to eat dinner that night, she heard a buggy. She jumped out of her chair and rushed to the window. It was William and Gretchen. After she had pushed her plate in the oven to keep it warm, she headed out to meet them, hoping nothing was wrong.

Gretchen walked over to her when she climbed out of the buggy and Tara searched her face to see what her mood was.

"Is everything alright?"

"*Jah,* but we've got some news."

Tara frowned. "Good or bad?" In her experience, news coming out of nowhere was normally bad.

"Let's sit down and we'll tell you."

When they were all seated in the living room, Gretchen began, "Carol came around earlier today."

The only 'Carol' Tara knew was Carol Booth, her caseworker. "Why? She said she's finished with the visits because I'm over eighteen."

"There's someone who's tracked you down."

"A relative?"

Gretchen nodded. "Your mother's brother."

"Oh. Where's he been?"

"I don't know the full story. He wants to meet you. She didn't tell us too much."

William added, "Now that you're eighteen you're in charge of yourself, it seems."

"Jah, I'm an adult. Well, I'll call her and find out about him." If she'd had an uncle why hadn't he taken her in? She still didn't know anything about her parents, not even whether they were alive or dead. All she knew was that she was adopted as an infant; when she was around eight, she was relinquished by her adoptive parents; and then she was adopted again only to have the same thing happen. It seemed the only people who never gave up on her were Gretchen and William.

"You don't have to unless you want to," Gretchen said. "Anyway, you can learn more about him from Carol."

"It worked out well for Elizabeth. She's pleased to know who her real parents were."

Tara wondered if her uncle was rich, like Elizabeth's family who had appeared out of the blue. Somehow, she doubted it. Elizabeth was the one who had all the luck.

"You can learn something about your parents."

Tara shrugged. "I'm not sure I want to know." She didn't want to shock William and Gretchen by saying what was really on her mind. Her parents hadn't wanted her, so why would she want to know about them? "I wonder why after all this time he's come forward. Why now?"

"Most likely he didn't want to interrupt your childhood," Gretchen said.

"I guess. That could be a reason."

"There's one way to find out," William said.

"I'll call her tomorrow. I'm curious now. Have you seen the house yet?"

"Nee," Gretchen said looking around.

"Let's start in the kitchen."

Tara tried to remain herself while her foster parents were at the house, while inside she was struggling with the information they'd come with.

Fifteen minutes later, she was waving goodbye to Gretchen and William. Feeling a little strange being all alone again, she pulled her dinner out of the oven and sat down in front of it. After a few minutes of pushing her food around the plate with a fork she covered it over and put it away for later.

What if her uncle came with the offer of a new life just as Elizabeth's relatives had? Would she leave the Amish looking for a better life? If Mark had been a more reliable person they would've married and her choice would've been easy. Now, she had to keep her mind open.

She slumped into the couch and picked up her needlework. Looking over at the fire, which needed more logs, she wondered why Mark hadn't been there that day.

THE NEXT MORNING, she was more anxious than ever to find out more about her uncle. Before she called for her taxi, she made a call from the shanty to Carol.

After the exchange of pleasantries, Carol delivered some news.

"Tara, it's not your uncle. I told Gretchen and William it was an elderly male family member and they immediately started referring to him as your uncle. I just didn't correct them. Now that you're eighteen, I need to give such information directly to you."

"If it's not my uncle, who is it?"

"Your father. I was contacted by your birth father."

"He's alive?"

"Yes, very much alive. It's a long story, but he's anxious to meet you. He's only just learned of your existence."

"Oh." That was all Tara could say for a few moments.

"Tara, are you still there?"

"Yes. I'm trying to take it all in."

"I know this is a surprise. Would you like to meet him?"

"Does he want to meet me?"

"He's very anxious to meet you."

"What's he like?"

"I've only talked with him over the phone. He seems very nice."

"I'd like to meet him."

"I'll set up a meeting for the two of you. Call me back later this afternoon. By that time I should have something set up."

"Thank you, Carol."

Tara hung up the phone and wished she didn't have to go to work that day. An orphan was what she'd always assumed she was. It was easier to think she was an orphan rather than having people out there somewhere who hadn't wanted her.

She turned around when she heard the sounds of a buggy coming toward her. It was Caleb.

He pulled up next to her. "Want me to drive you to work?"

"Jah, denke." She climbed up beside him and he flicked the reins and the horse moved on.

He glanced over at her. "Are you alright?"

"I've just had the most bizarre news from my caseworker. I suppose you don't know what a caseworker is?"

"Of course, I do. What did they say?"

She shook her head, still not believing that she had a real live father after all this time. "She told me that my father is still alive and that he only just learned about me."

"How does that work?

Tara shrugged. "I've got no idea, but I'm going to find out soon because, Carol, my caseworker, is setting up a time when we can meet each other."

"That's good. You can finally get some answers to the questions you've had."

"How do you know I had questions?"

"If I were in your position, I'd have a lot of questions. It's only natural."

"I hope he's not expecting someone perfect. He's probably built up an image of someone wonderful." Tara sighed.

"Tara, you *are* wonderful."

She narrowed her eyes at him thinking he might be joking. His face showed no hint of a smile.

He was too shy to talk much, and yet not too shy to say something so lovely to her. "You don't know a lot about me."

"If I found out I had a daughter, I'd be happy if she was exactly like you."

She could sense he was being genuine. "But you don't know anything about me."

"I've been watching you for some time." He laughed. "That came across as a bit creepy. I've kind of been observing you. I couldn't get to know you because you were close with someone else. I thought he'd gone, but it seems now he's back."

She didn't say anything, but she knew that he meant Mark.

"Well, that's over."

"Is it?"

He glanced over at her and she nodded. "It is."

"Why's he back? I'm sorry; it's none of my business. I'm always saying the wrong thing."

"I don't think you are. You don't say enough."

He laughed. "That's because whenever I say something I usually end up regretting it. It's better if I keep quiet."

"I don't think that's true. You should speak up all the time. Anyway, Mark's doing work on the house. He says Joseph asked him to do repairs before they got back."

"I see. That explains a few things." When he stopped the buggy, she saw that they had already reached the quilting store.

"There you are."

"Thanks for talking to me about my father. You made me feel much better."

He smiled at her. "Glad to be of help. Can I take you home tonight?"

"I finish at three."

"Then I'll be here at three."

"I'd like that." She stepped out of the buggy and hurried to her work.

During her lunch break, Tara called Carol. All morning long she'd been unable to get her father off her mind.

"I know you told me to ring later today, but I was wondering if you'd set up a time with him yet?"

"I did. I spoke to him right after our conversation this morning. He's very keen to meet you."

"When?" Tara asked.

"It's up to you. He said for you to name the time and the place and he'd be there."

"I think I'd like to meet him at home."

"At the Grabers'?"

"Yes. I think tomorrow night at seven."

"Okay. Are you sure things aren't moving too fast for you? You could write him a letter first."

"No. I want to meet him and hear from his own lips how I came to be adopted and fostered, and who my mother is."

"Okay. I'll arrange it."

"Thanks for everything, Carol."

"I'm glad to help out."

For the rest of the day, Tara tried to concentrate on her job but all she could think about was her father and what he would be like and what he would look like. She had so many questions. With his sudden appearance in her life and his curious claim about only recently learning about her, all of that gave her more questions.

When Caleb came at three o'clock, she was anxious to share her news.

"Caleb, I'm going to meet my father tomorrow night."

"Things are moving quickly."

"I know. Would it be too much trouble for you to drive me to Gretchen's, so I can ask her if it's okay to meet there tomorrow night? I arranged it for seven o'clock."

"That's fine. I can drive you there now."

"Thank you. And then wait for me and then take me back to Joseph and Elizabeth's?"

He nodded. "Okay. It's probably a good idea to meet him at the place where you feel most comfortable."

"That's what I thought. My whole life I didn't know anything about my parents, not even whether they were living or not. Now I found out my father is alive, and tomorrow I'll find out about my mother."

"Do you know anything about her at all?"

She shook her head. "I still don't even know whether she's alive or dead. The main thing I want to know is why she gave me away."

They drove for awhile in silence. When they arrived, she invited him into the *haus,* but Caleb told her he'd prefer to wait in the buggy.

After she'd told Gretchen that she'd arranged to meet her birth father, Gretchen agreed for the meeting to take place in their home. Because Caleb was waiting in the buggy, she took some cookies that Megan had just baked and headed back out to him.

"How did it go?" Caleb asked.

Climbing up next to him, she said, "Good, and I scored us some cookies." Once she was seated, she handed him two and kept two for herself.

He smiled as he took them from her. "Are these chocolate chip?"

"Looks like it. "

"They're my favorite. I love chocolate." He took a bite and smiled his approval before he turned the buggy around and headed back to the road.

CHAPTER 7

And be not conformed to this world: but be ye transformed by the renewing of your mind, that ye may prove what is that good, and acceptable, and perfect, will of God.
Romans 12:2

TARA JUMPED down from Caleb's buggy when they arrived back at the house. "*Denke,* Caleb. "

"I can do the same again tomorrow."

"That won't be necessary, *denke.* I have the day off tomorrow."

"Okay. I hope all goes well with meeting your father. "

"So do I."

"I'll see you later, Tara. If you need anything, just give me a yell."

"I will." She headed to the house, more impressed by Caleb every moment she spent with him. He had a quiet self-confidence hidden beneath his initial shy exterior.

She wasn't home long when she heard a buggy. Looking out the window, she saw Mark's tall bay horse, Big, heading toward the house.

"Aargh! Why couldn't he have done his work when I was out today?" She poured herself a cup of tea, disappointed that her peace would now be ruined by Mark's loud hammering.

He knocked on the door and when she opened it, all she could see was a bunch of flowers. He lowered them and a smile lit up his handsome face.

She hid her delight at being given flowers. "What are those for?"

"Don't you mean 'Who are these for?' instead?"

She put one hand on her hip. *"Nee,* I meant, 'Why?'"

"A peace offering."

"For me?"

He held them out toward her. *"Jah."*

She reached out and took the flowers. "Peace is a good thing. Are you coming inside?"

"I can't do the repairs on the house from the outside."

She stepped aside, allowing him to pass, and remembering her manners, added, *"Denke* for the flowers."

"I'm glad you like them. They're not easy to find at this time of year."

She was confused by his comment. The mixture of roses, daisies and lilies were obviously store-bought flowers and not ones picked by the roadside. If she mentioned her thoughts, however, he would accuse her of being argumentative. She kept quiet.

"How about a cup of tea?"

"Okay."

She placed the flowers down beside the sink and poured him a cup of tea.

She'd made a full pot, planning on having more than one while she planned out the rest of her day. Once she placed his cup on the table, she set about finding a vase for the flowers. All she could find was a large preserving jar. She'd have to look for a nice vase in town to leave as a gift to Elizabeth.

When she'd arranged them nicely, she pushed the flowers into the center of the table.

"They look pretty."

"They do." She sat down to drink her hot tea.

"How was work today?"

"It was fine."

"I know you hate me for leaving when I did, without a word, and I know I was wrong, but if we can't go back to being how we were, can we at least be friends?"

"I don't know if we can be friends. I need to be able to trust all my friends."

"I figured out that it's your past making you act like this."

"Forget my past. This has nothing to do with people letting me down before. And it's not an excuse for you to let me down."

"Now come on, Tara. That's going a bit too far."

She bit her lip. Too often she said what was on her mind without thinking her words through. "What I mean is that you were talking of marriage and we were imagining a future together. We were even talking about names for our *kinner,* and the next thing I know, you just run off without a word. You deserted me. And then you come back as if nothing has happened." Glaring at him, she added, "It's not okay."

"You didn't let me explain."

"There's nothing to explain."

"It's not all about you all the time, Tara. I'm a real person and I have feelings too. And I know you're spending time with Caleb just to get back at me. That's your way of punishing me and it's a juvenile thing to do. You can't build the man's hopes up like that."

Tara laughed. "That's the silliest thing I've ever heard."

"That's the only reason I can think that you even talk to him.

He never says two words, so I doubt that the two of you could find anything in common."

"We talk about many things. He says a lot to me."

"I don't want to argue with you, Tara."

"It appears you do. You say silly things and when I set you straight you don't listen, you say you don't want to argue." Tara shook her head and then took a sip of tea.

"I realized when I came back and you were so mean to me that you have a fear of people leaving you just like your parents left you. I've a friend studying psychology and I discussed it with him. You have a fear of abandonment."

She screwed up her face. "You don't know anything about my feelings or my fears. Or my parents and what happened with them, so leave that topic alone."

He sighed. "Can't things go back to the way they used to be? I just want you to know that I was scared to make the next move—marriage—but I'm over that now."

"The moment has past."

"You can't mean that."

"I thought you were reliable and a strong-minded man. On the outside, you're handsome and strong, but on the inside you're a five-year-old boy."

"They say every man needs a woman to help him mature."

"Who says that?"

He shrugged. "You know—'they,' whoever that is."

"I want someone who knows me and knows himself. Maybe I won't marry; maybe after tomorrow night I'll have a new life and I'll leave the community for good."

"What do you mean after tomorrow night?"

"If you must know, I'm meeting my birth father."

Delight spread over his face. "Tara, that's fantastic. Have you spoken to him on the phone?"

"I'm meeting him for the first time tomorrow and we haven't

spoken before at all." She shook her head. "I don't know what he'll say, or whether it will be good or bad. Maybe he'll want me to move in with him and his family, just like Elizabeth's parents wanted. Maybe once we meet, he'll want to have no more to do with me. I won't know until after tomorrow night."

"It's possible, either way." He drank the rest of his tea in silence. "*Denke* for the tea. I had better go do some jobs while I'm here."

CHAPTER 8

If we confess our sins, he is faithful and just to forgive us our sins, and to cleanse us from all unrighteousness.
1 John 1:9

REDMOND O'DONNELL KEPT the news to himself that Marjorie and he'd had another child, saying nothing to Avalon or Brandon. He had no idea how this young woman would take the news he had to tell her. He only hoped that she wouldn't hate him and his late wife. The worst thing would be to find out that she'd had a miserable life. Wiping a tear from his eye, he wished things would've been different. Long ago, he'd learned that life takes twists and turns, and he had to cope with whatever was thrown at him. With his first wife dying and now losing his second wife, Marjorie, he'd had his share of sorrow.

Brandon lived away from home and had done so for some time. He called a sitter to watch Avalon while he was out. She was kind of old for that, but he hated to leave her home by herself at night.

He told Avalon he had a business appointment after dinner, knowing she wouldn't ask questions.

Picking up his wife's photo on the nightstand, he wrestled with feelings of guilt. Surely there had been signs that he'd missed. If he'd been a more sensitive and caring person, he would've picked up on those signs.

"We're both to blame," he said as he put the photo back where it had been.

He took hold of his car keys, a small photo of Marjorie, along with the birth certificate, and headed off to the address that the social worker had given him.

"WHERE DO you want us to go?" William asked Tara.

"I guess I'll talk to him myself in the living room if you want to stay in the kitchen. If all goes well, I'll call you out to meet him."

"Oh, I hope it goes well," Megan said.

"We all do. Just don't leave us," Gretchen said, now giving Tara a hug.

Tara said, "I'm not going anywhere."

WHEN THEY HEARD a car's engine outside, Gretchen said, "That's gotta be him. We'll be praying for you, Tara."

And then Tara was alone in the living room. Her heart was pounding. This was unquestionably the most nervous she'd been in her life. She was anxious to hear what the man had to say but at the same time, she hoped he wasn't expecting someone wonderful. She peeked out the window to see a tall man who easily had to be as old as her foster father.

He had gray hair, was clean-shaven and wore a brown suit—a business suit.

When he knocked on the door, Tara took a deep breath and then opened it. The man smiled when he saw her and then his mouth turned down at the corners and his lips quivered a little, as though he was about to cry.

Should she hug him, kiss him, or shake his hand? What was appropriate? She offered her hand, thinking that was the safest option at this point. "I'm Tara."

"And I'm Redmond O'Donnell."

"Come in. We can sit over here." He followed her to the couch and they sat down.

"Thank you for meeting me."

"Can I call you Redmond?"

"Yes. Please do."

"Carol said you didn't know anything about me. How did you find out about me and when did you find out about me?"

"My wife and your birth mother, Marjorie, died recently."

Tara's fingertips flew to her throat. Her mother was dead! Now that she knew that for certain, she was filled with sorrow for the lost opportunities. She'd never meet her. Tears filled her eyes.

"I'm sorry. I don't mean to make you sad," he said.

"I don't think there's any avoiding it. Please go on. I have to know."

"It wasn't until I was clearing out my wife's things that I came across your adoption papers." He stopped, closed his eyes and pinched the bridge of his nose. "I should start at the beginning. My wife and I were total opposites, which led to frequent clashes particularly when we were first married. We disagreed on almost every subject. Finally, when she thought she couldn't take any more of me, she left me and Brandon, my young son from my first marriage. I was already a widower when I met Marjorie. For the first few days after Marjorie left, I was angry, but then I tried to find her. A year later, I found her and convinced her to come home."

"And she'd had me within that year?"

Redmond nodded.

"Why didn't she contact you and tell you about me?"

He shook his head. "The only clue I have about that is the last words she uttered from her hospital bed. Her words didn't make sense then, but when I found your adoption papers, they clicked."

Tara leaned forward wanting to know everything.

"She said, *Tell her I'm sorry, but it was too late. It had already been done and there was nothing I could do.* Then she took her last breath."

"Was she talking about me?" Tara blinked back more tears that filled her eyes. Her mother *had* cared about her.

"There was nothing else she could've been talking about. She knew I'd find those papers. She would've known I'd stop at nothing to find you. Going by the date of your birth, you'd been adopted. Keeping quiet would've been Marjorie's way to save everyone pain."

"I had no idea. I never knew anything."

"I can only assume she didn't want me to have the pain of knowing that our first-born child wasn't with us." He wiped away a tear. "We went on to have a daughter."

"You did? So, she'd be my—"

"Sister. And you have a half brother, Brandon. Your sister's name is Avalon. She's just turned thirteen."

Tara sat there, stunned. She had a sister and a half brother. "Do they want to meet me?"

"I wanted to meet you first before I mention you to them. I didn't know if you'd want to meet them and I didn't want you to be overwhelmed. I don't know how they'll take it when they find out their mother kept this secret from all of us."

"I grew up not even knowing if my parents were alive or dead and what the circumstances were. I'm just grateful to know how I came to be born and to know that I'm not alive under bad circumstances. I would like to meet Avalon and Brandon as long as they want to meet me."

His face lit up. "You would?"

"Yes. Did Carol tell you anything about me or my past?"

"She didn't."

Tara went on to tell him about the two families she'd been in, and finishing by telling him about the happy ending, that she'd landed on her feet with the Grabers. "Do you want to meet them?"

"I'd love to."

Tara sprang to her feet and ran into the kitchen. Seeing their faces staring at her awaiting instructions, she waved them forward.

"Come on. He wants to meet you guys."

Tara led them out to Redmond and made the introductions.

After an awkward beginning, William told Redmond some stories about Tara when she'd first come to them.

"She was a lovely girl," Gretchen insisted frowning at her husband.

"She's always been lovely," William said, "but she's always had a strong mind to do things her way. There were a few times she tested us."

"Both my wife and I were strong minded people. Sometimes to our detriment, I'm afraid. I was just telling Tara about our rocky marriage in the beginning years before we learned to compromise and take the time to understand each other."

"I have a sister and a half brother," Tara announced proudly. "I hope they'll want to meet me."

"I'm sure they will." Redmond glanced at his wristwatch. "I should be going."

Tara jumped to her feet. "We didn't give you tea or anything!"

"Yes, will you stay for some hot tea?" Gretchen asked.

He shook his head. "I should go." He looked over at Tara. "Perhaps after I tell my children, you might be able to come to my house? Maybe come for dinner with us?"

"I'd like that."

"Good." He handed her a card. "All my phone numbers are on that. We'll talk soon."

"I hope so."

Tara stood up to walk him to the door.

After Redmond had driven away, she turned back to look at the Grabers and Megan. They were all staring at her. She walked back and sat down with them.

"I never thought this day would come. I honestly thought my birth parents were dead. Now I know a little about my mother, and my father is alive, and I'm someone's sister. I even have a half brother."

"Don't forget us," Megan said.

"I won't! You're my family, silly. All of you are."

William and Gretchen smiled and looked lovingly at each other. Tara noticed that they hadn't felt threatened in the slightest by her father's appearance in her life. They were so full of love and so giving, they were happy because she was happy.

"Stay here tonight?" Megan asked.

"Nee. I've got all my things over there at the *haus."*

"I'll take you back whenever you're ready," William said.

"Denke. I should go now before it gets too late."

"Come into the kitchen first," Megan said pulling Tara by the arm.

As soon as they were in the kitchen, Megan whispered, "What's going on with you and Mark?"

"Nothing."

"Have you seen him since he's been back?"

"Joseph has given him jobs to do at the *haus.* I can't tell you how annoyed I was about that. No one told me that was going to happen."

"I know how you feel about him, but—"

"Felt about him," Tara corrected her.

Megan nodded. "I saw him with Mary Lou."

Tara frowned at the news. Could it have been Mary Lou she'd seen in the buggy with him in town? "Where did you see them?"

"Yesterday at the markets. I went there with *Mamm.*"

"It might mean nothing."

Megan shook her head. "Okay, I didn't want to tell you this today, but Mary Lou's *scheweschder,* Sue Anne, told me that they're secretly dating. I thought you should know. I'm sorry if it upsets you."

"That's hard to believe. He told me he wants to make things right between us and he's sorry for leaving the way he did." Tara held her head. So many things were happening.

"I don't know. What if he's lying?" Megan asked.

"Maybe Sue Anne was mistaken. Maybe Mary Lou just *wants* to be dating Mark."

"I guess it's possible."

"Denke for telling me, Megan."

"I thought you should know. Are you working tomorrow?"

"Nee. I've got a free day tomorrow."

"Can I come over and see you?"

"Jah! I'd love that." Tara giggled.

"Are you ready, Tara?" William called out.

Tara hugged Megan goodbye. "Come around anytime. I'll be home all day."

CHAPTER 9

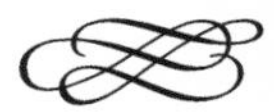

Whoever loves instruction loves knowledge, But he who hates correction is stupid.
Proverbs 12:1

TARA GOT INTO BED, reached over to the bedside table, and turned off the lantern. Elizabeth would be the only one who would understand what she was going through right now, since her family had found her recently, but Tara couldn't talk to her because she didn't know exactly where she was. Elizabeth and Joseph were staying at a different family's house every night.

As her head sank into the pillow, her thoughts turned to Mark and the disturbing news she'd heard about Mary Lou. It troubled her more than it normally would've because she was pretty sure she herself had seen the two of them together.

Maybe when Elizabeth got back, she could find out about Mark and Mary Lou, or could get Joseph to find out some things. Sue Anne had most likely gotten things wrong and it was quite possible that they'd only been out together once in his buggy and that was the same time she'd seen them.

TARA WOKE the next morning to the sound of a buggy outside her window. She opened her eyes and it took her a moment to gather where she was. The sunlight streaming in from the window told her she'd slept longer than she'd intended.

She jumped out of bed and looked out the window. It was Mark outside.

What is he doing here at this time of morning?

The last thing she wanted was for him to think he could enter without knocking just because he had a key, so she dressed fast and ran down to the front door.

He had his hand up, apparently about to knock when she opened the door.

"In time for *kaffe,* am I?" he asked with his usual smirk hinting around his lips.

"I suppose I can put some on for you."

He nodded.

"Denke?" She stared at him waiting for a response.

"Oh. Yeah, *denke.*" He looked her up and down. "You're not going to work today?"

"I've got the day off."

He scoffed as he followed her into the kitchen, "You seem to have a lot of those."

"That's because I work part time. You don't seem to be doing much work yourself."

"It's a quiet time of year. I'm starting back at the beginning of February. I saw you in town with Caleb yesterday."

He *had* seen her. *"Jah,* he was good enough to take me to work."

"That was very *nice* of him."

"He's a nice person."

"He's not for you."

She raised her eyebrows and glared at him. He couldn't run away from her and then come back and boss her about as if he owned her. "Says who?"

"Are you going to act like nothing ever happened between us? Is the past going to be swept under the rug?"

"You're the one who chose… chose to leave. I was here all the time. I didn't go anywhere."

"I explained everything to you. I thought you would have some compassion and understanding when I opened my heart and..."

"I'm low on compassion and understanding at the moment. Anyway, I've got far more important things to think about than you running away like a scared rabbit."

"Yeah? Like what?"

"Oh, that's right. You don't know."

"Know what?"

Tara's first instinct was to keep her news from him, but the way news traveled through the community, he'd find out soon anyway. "I met my birth father last night."

"Jah! You told me you were meeting him. How did it go?"

She told him what her father had told her.

"I'm happy for you, Tara. It must make you feel different about yourself."

"It probably should, but it doesn't. It feels good to know that he cares and would've cared back then if he'd known about me. I could've grown up in that family. *My* family. I guess she gave me away because she thought she was going to be a single parent. Things were more difficult back then—Gretchen explained that to me. These days there are more single-parent families than there were back then. Less stigma about it."

"Gott wanted you here in the community that's why. So you could meet me, your husband."

She was certain now that there was nothing between him and Mary Lou.

"I know. That's what William and Gretchen said. Not about marrying, you—the bit about *Gott* wanting me here. They say that all the time, and I guess it's true."

"Now that you know something about your past, how about thinking about your future—with me?"

Her heart was saying yes, but her head was saying no. Before she gave in to her heart again, there were some things she had to know.

"Why didn't you tell me you needed some time alone to think? I would've understood—tried to understand."

He slowly nodded, then said, "I don't know. I guess I didn't want to hurt you."

She leaned forward; she had to be truthful. "You hurt me more by remaining silent and then vanishing."

His gaze lowered. "I needed some space, some time to think. I felt as though I was losing myself in my love for you and trying to become someone I wasn't."

Tara did not understand the nonsense he was carrying on with; it all sounded like gobbledygook to her. "Well, you've got yourself back now and all is well with the world." He looked up at her with raised eyebrows and an open mouth. She continued, "I'm glad you've got that off your chest." She stood up and went to walk away.

He bounded to his feet causing the chair to fall back, and then reached out and grabbed her arm. "Tara wait; I've just told you that I love you."

Tara pulled her arm away. *"Jah,* Mark, I heard, but that's in the past."

"Nee, Tara. It doesn't have to be in the past."

"If you will excuse me, Mark, I've got things to do."

"Wait!" She swung around to see him picking up the chair.

"What else is there to say? Finish your *kaffe* and then do whatever it is you have to do around here. I'll be upstairs out of your way."

The corners of his lips turned upward and he laughed.

"What's funny?" she asked.

"Life's so funny."

"There's nothing funny about you leaving me just when we were getting closer. Why would you do that to me, as though I'm some game that you put away when you're bored, and pick up again later when you feel like it?"

His face flushed and his voice rose. "It's not a game. I had to be sure that marriage was right for me, and not just because it's expected for everyone else in the community. What if I wasn't the same as everyone else? I did *not* want to disappoint you. Is that so hard to understand? We were moving too fast."

Tara was silent for a moment while she tried to understand his reasoning. "Why didn't you tell me?"

His face softened and his voice lowered. "Would you have understood?"

She dropped her eyes to the floor and shook her head. "*Nee*, and I don't understand now. What if you suddenly disappear again?"

He took two steps toward her. "That's exactly why I didn't explain my actions to anyone, not even you. No one would have understood. But, I never stopped loving you. It wasn't about love, or about you, it was about me."

She took a step backward.

He swiftly moved in front of her, as close as he could be. "Want to know a secret?"

"Aha," she said softly as she looked up into his dark eyes.

"Joseph never asked me to do anything here. I heard you were staying in the *haus* and I took the opportunity to be alone with you to explain myself. Joseph gave me a spare key for emergencies."

Tara opened her mouth in shock at his audacity. He took his chance and swiftly lowered his mouth to kiss her. She ducked out of his way.

He drew his head back and took both her hands in his. "Say you'll marry me, but for real this time?"

She shook her head. *"Nee."* Seeing his tools by the door, she said, "Don't forget to take all your tools with you." She walked to the front door and held it open.

"I won't give up," he said as he walked over to his wooden tool box, grabbed it, and then walked out the door.

She closed the door and leaned against it. When she gave her heart, it would be to someone who she'd feel safe with. He didn't have to be the most desirable man in the community, or the best looking, as long as he was a man she could trust.

Closing her eyes, she heard Mark's buggy horse clip-clop away from the house. When relief washed over her like a warm shower on a cold night, she knew she'd done the right thing.

She shook her head, trying to shake away all remnants of the man she'd once thought so highly of.

CHAPTER 10

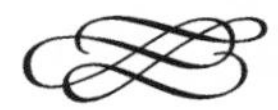

Charm is deceitful and beauty is passing,
But a woman who fears the Lord,
she shall be praised.
Proverbs 31:30

WHEN REDMOND ARRIVED back home after visiting Tara, he paid the babysitter and then got Brandon on the phone and asked him to come to the house. Redmond was anxious to relieve himself of his wife's long-held secret.

"What's this about, Dad?" Brandon said as he came through the front door.

"It's something very important." Redmond sat his son and daughter down in the living room and started right from the beginning, starting at the tumultuous relationship that he'd had with Avalon's mother. And then he went on to explain that they'd separated for over a year and then gotten back together. Brandon had been a toddler at the time of their separation.

Brandon and Avalon sat in silence as they listened to the whole story.

"We have a sister?" Avalon asked, her eyes bulging.

Redmond nodded.

"I can't believe Mom kept that from us," Brandon said about the only woman he remembered as his mother.

"She thought it best. Tara had been adopted before we reunited, and she wouldn't have wanted to disrupt her life."

"And you've met her?"

"Yes. I've just come back from meeting her at her foster family's house."

"Does she know about us?"

"She does now, and she wants to meet you if you want to meet her."

"Of course we do," Brandon said while Avalon nodded enthusiastically.

"What do you think about it, Avalon?"

"Weird. Why didn't you and Mom try to get her back?"

"Dad already said he didn't know anything about her. Weren't you listening?" Brandon said.

"Yeah, well, Mom should've done something. What if that had happened to you or me?"

"It did. She's one of us. Just the same."

"When can we meet her?" Avalon asked her father.

"She'll call me soon."

"Call her and tell her we want to meet her as soon as possible," Brandon suggested.

"She doesn't have a cell phone. She's been raised Amish for the past few years."

"Oh, man!" Brandon hit his head. "Are you serious?"

"No electricity, no Playstation, and all that? No car?" Avalon asked.

Redmond nodded. "I met the foster family and they're very nice people. Tara had been adopted twice and both times it didn't work out."

"Why?" Brandon asked.

"I don't know really. I suppose she'll share more when she feels more comfortable."

"Does she look like me?" Avalon asked.

"There's a resemblance. She looks a lot like my mother did as a girl."

Brandon frowned. "So, we just wait for her to call you?"

Redmond nodded. "If she hasn't called in a week or so, I can always pay her another visit."

"What was the family like?"

"Very quiet, and humble, softly spoken."

"What about their house?" Avalon asked.

"Smallish, neat and clean. They had gas overhead lighting, so it was a little dark."

"Are you sure it was dark, or maybe you just didn't have your glasses on," Brandon joked.

"Yeah, Dad. You're supposed to wear your glasses all the time."

He scratched the bridge of his nose. "I think if I wear them too much my eyes will become dependant on them."

"You're vain, that's what it is," Brandon said with a laugh.

"Yeah," Avalon agreed.

Ignoring their teasing, Redmond continued, "I thought we should have Tara join us for dinner one night and I want you both to be on your best behavior. Keep in mind that she might be a little standoffish and shy."

"Yeah, we're not stupid, Dad. We'll try not to scare her away."

"Brandon would scare her away," Avalon said.

Brandon picked up a cushion and hit his sister with it. Then she did the same to him.

"Stop it! And don't do things like that while she's here, whatever you do."

"We won't." Avalon giggled.

"Now I've got another sister to boss me about," Brandon said.

Redmond was pleased that his children had taken the news well. If only his wife were still alive.

CHAPTER 11

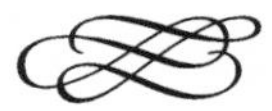

To every thing there is a season, and a time to every purpose under the heaven: A time to be born, and a time to die; a time to plant, and a time to pluck up that which is planted;
Ecclesiastes 3:1

TARA WAS WASHING up her breakfast dishes when she saw William's buggy heading toward the house. It had to be Megan driving it. Looking forward to having someone to talk to, she came to the quick conclusion that living alone wasn't for her.

She dried her hands on a tea towel and went to open the door. As soon as Megan had tied up the horse, she hurried over to Tara.

"I came as soon as I could. Let's go out somewhere. I haven't been out for a long time."

"I'm glad to hear that you want to go out. We can go to a coffee shop in town. I've got lots to tell you," Tara said.

"Lots? Since last night?"

Tara nodded.

"Okay let's go now. We'll go to the one where Elizabeth works."

"Do you want to have a look around the house first?" Tara asked.

"Nee. I've seen it before with Elizabeth before the wedding. Let's just go."

"Sounds good to me. I've just eaten, though, but I could do with another cup of coffee."

Tara grabbed her coat, found her key and was careful to lock the door, wishing that Joseph had never given Mark a key.

As they traveled down the winding roads, Megan asked, "What is it you want to tell me?"

"I'm going to call Redmond today and tell him that I want to meet my sister and my brother."

"That's good. I'm sure they'll be happy to meet you."

"I hope so."

"What else? You look like you've got something else on your mind."

"Do I?" Tara breathed out heavily. "Mark was here this morning."

"Did you ask him about Mary Lou?"

"Nee, I didn't. He said he wants to marry me, so I don't think it's true about Mary Lou."

Megan gasped. "What did you say?"

"I said, 'No.' I can't marry him if I can't trust him."

"You should've asked him about Mary Lou."

"I don't know. Anyway, it doesn't matter."

"Do you still love him?"

Tara swallowed hard. She couldn't help the feelings in her heart. "I guess I do."

"Why didn't you say you'd marry him? You're not making sense."

"I am so. He vanished and no one knew where he was, or if they did, no one told me. We were talking about marriage before he disappeared. And now he comes back and when he feels ready, he expects me to be ready."

"What does that matter? It sounds to me like you want the upper hand."

"He hurt me. I don't want to feel like that anymore. I get a hollow feeling in my stomach. Mark says it's because I was adopted that I fear being left alone and that's why I was upset that he went away so suddenly."

"Maybe."

"Well, then that's his excuse for doing anything he wants. I just can't see that I should be okay with him hurting me like that. He would've known I'd be upset about it and he didn't care enough about me. He cared more about himself."

"You want someone who'll put you first?"

Tara nodded. *"Jah,* exactly. That's how it's supposed to be."

"That's how it's supposed to be, but everyone's human, don't forget. People make mistakes and we're supposed to forgive them."

"Yeah, I can forgive him. That doesn't mean I have to marry him."

Megan giggled. "That's true."

"Anyway, since when are you Mark's biggest fan?"

Megan whipped her eyes away from the road to glance at her. "I'm not. I told you what I heard about him. I believe what Sue Anne said. You're the one who said you loved him."

"Yeah, well I'm working on talking myself out of that."

Megan giggled again. "You're so strong, Tara. I don't think I could ever be as strong as you."

"I don't think you'll ever have to be. You'll be just like Elizabeth, and everything will fall into place for you. The perfect man will come along at the perfect time and you'll be the most perfect *fraa."*

"You think so?"

"Yeah."

. . .

Megan and Tara sat down at a table in the back of the coffee shop. There was one menu on the table. Tara passed it to Megan.

"See what you want."

"I'm not hungry," Megan said pushing the menu back to Tara.

"Me either. I think I'll just have a coffee."

"Me too."

A waiter came up to their table. Tara recognized him from when she had met Elizabeth there before the wedding. She placed her hand on her bag, which she'd placed where she always did, on the side of the table. "Just a coffee for me."

"Black?" he asked.

"Yes, thanks."

"I'll have a white coffee thanks," Megan said, smiling up at him.

"Nothing to eat?" he said. Tara noticed he didn't return the smile.

"No."

He grabbed the menu and walked away.

"He's a weird one," Tara said before she could stop herself.

"Do you know him?"

Tara shook her head. "No. Don't worry."

"Are you working tomorrow?"

"*Jah,* until three."

"Have you forgotten about Connie and Devon's wedding?"

"I did. I would've completely forgotten if you hadn't mentioned it. I don't finish work until three. I could go after that. I'll have to miss most of it."

"I can come and get you from work when you finish."

"Would you?"

"Of course."

"*Denke.*"

"No one ever thought Connie would marry. Just as well Devon came along when he did."

"*Jah.* He came to his aunt's funeral didn't he?" Tara asked.

"That's right. Then they fell in love before they got back to his *onkel's haus."*

Tara stuck her nose in the air. "See? It's easy for some."

Megan giggled.

"Megan, why don't you come with me when I meet my sister and brother?"

The waiter brought their coffees to the table. Tara grabbed her bag and put it in her lap. After he'd placed their drinks on the table, he walked away.

"Well?" Tara asked as she perched her bag back on the edge of the table.

"Nee, I couldn't. I'm no good at meeting new people. I wouldn't know what to say."

"Just be there next to me. You don't have to say a thing if you don't want to."

Megan pulled a face. "I will if you want me to."

"Really?"

Megan nodded. "Okay."

"Denke. I feel a lot better now."

"You were nervous?"

"Jah. You're not the only one who gets scared."

"I'm shy. I'm not scared." Megan ripped open a packet of sugar and poured it into her coffee.

"You don't have to be shy."

"That's just the way I've always been. You've never been that way; you wouldn't understand. You've always been good with people. That's why you work in a store and talk to strangers every day."

Tara took a sip of her hot coffee. "Other people are just like you and me."

"When are you meeting your family?"

"Sometime soon. Maybe next week, I guess. I'm calling Redmond later today."

"Let me know and I'll be ready."

When they heard a loud knock on the window of the café, they turned to see the Tomkin brothers who were waving at them as they walked past. Tara and Megan smiled and waved back at them.

"Do you like one of them? They're handsome and they're our age," Tara asked.

"Nee. I'm hoping there might be someone new at Connie's wedding."

Suddenly Megan grabbed Tara's hand. "Look over there, across the road, Tara."

Tara looked through the large window of the coffee shop to see Mary Lou and Mark walking together. Close together.

"That must've been her I saw in his buggy the other day. I thought it was, but I wasn't all that certain."

"See? I told you he's been seeing a lot of her."

Tara nodded. "Why did he ask me to marry him when he's spending time with her?"

They stared at him.

"They both seem to be enjoying each other's company," Megan said.

"Yeah, a little too much if you ask me. I think Sue Anne was right."

"I told you."

"Yeah, yeah."

"Don't worry, Tara, Elizabeth told me that Caleb likes you."

"Caleb?" Tara acted like Elizabeth had never mentioned him to her.

"Jah. Caleb, Joseph's *bruder."*

"I know who he is. He drove me to work and back the other day."

"And to the *haus* the other day," Megan reminded her.

"Oh, yeah. I forgot about that."

Megan lowered her head keeping her eyes fixed onto Tara. "Is there anything you'd like to share with me, Tara?"

Tara giggled. "Just that he's talking a little more."

"Ah, so that's why you refused Mark's proposal."

She looked out the window, and the couple they'd been studying had moved on.

"Nee, Megan. I don't think so."

"Hmmm."

Tara giggled. "You sound just like Aunt Gretchen."

"That's where I learned to say 'hmmm.'"

"And you've got the same look on your face as she gets when she's suspicious about something, or she doesn't believe us."

Megan laughed and then wagged her finger just like William often did. "I'll be keeping an eye on you and Caleb at the wedding tomorrow."

The two of them laughed.

MEGAN COLLECTED Tara from work at three o'clock. The ceremony had taken place at one o'clock, but people would still be socializing and eating. And those two things were Tara's favorite pastimes.

"How was the wedding?" Tara asked.

"Really good."

Tara wanted to learn about Mark and find out if he was hanging around close to Mary Lou, but she didn't like to ask.

"Was anybody interesting there—anybody new?" Tara asked knowing that Megan had been hoping that there would be.

"I saw two men who looked nice. One of them smiled at me. I think they were brothers; they looked similar."

"Point them out to me when we get there."

"Nee. Not if you're going to do something embarrassing."

"Embarrassing like what?"

"Like being obvious and dragging me over to introduce me to them."

"Well, how are you going to meet them if I don't do that?"

Megan rolled her eyes. "Just forget it."

"I mean it. Tell me, how are you going to do that?"

"Do what?" Megan asked.

Tara's head was elsewhere; she was trying to talk with Megan and thinking about Mark, and also Caleb, all at the same time.

"What I meant to say is, how are you going to talk to them if you don't make an effort?"

"They can come and talk to me."

Tara stared at Megan, blinking rapidly. "They haven't yet, have they?"

"Nee, so that means they can't be interested."

"They might be ridiculously shy like you."

Megan's mouth fell open. "I am not."

"You are so."

"I am not."

"I'm already making my plans to go over and talk to them," Tara said.

"If you go over and talk to them, I'll go and tell Mark that you're going to marry him."

Tara laughed. "It's hardly the same thing."

Megan giggled. "Well, just don't you dare do it."

CHAPTER 12

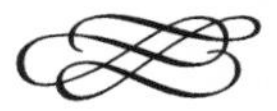

Be careful for nothing; but in every thing by prayer and supplication with thanksgiving let your requests be made known unto God.
Philippians 4:6

WHEN THEY PULLED into the driveway of Connie's parents' house where the wedding was held, they had to park their buggy a long way away due to the seemingly hundreds of buggies that were there.

"This is a popular wedding,"

"I think there are a lot of relatives on both sides."

"It seems like it," Megan said.

"Now show me where those boys are," Tara said.

"Nee, Tara. Don't be embarrassing."

"I won't say anything if you really don't want me to, you have my word on it. Just point them out to me."

"Are you certain you won't embarrass me?"

"Not over that. But I might embarrass you over something else."

"Good."

"But first I need food. I'm starving. I didn't eat lunch just so I could make more room."

Megan secured the horse and the two girls walked quickly into Connie's house.

Tara couldn't help looking around for Mark and Caleb. She was a little disappointed that Caleb hadn't visited to find out what happened when she met her father.

After taking a plate, Tara helped herself to food from one of the many tables that ran down the length of the house.

Glancing at Megan standing beside her, she asked, "Have you already eaten?"

"Jah. I couldn't fit another thing in if I tried. Except until the dessert comes out, and I'm hoping that's soon."

Tara giggled and then her attention turned to filling her plate with more of her favorite foods.

"Where are we sitting?" Tara asked when she couldn't fit any more on her plate.

"Follow me."

They sat down where they had a good view of two handsome young men Tara had never met before. She leaned over to Megan, and whispered, "Is that them?"

"Please be quiet; they'll hear you."

"Nee, they won't."

Megan rolled her eyes.

"I agree with you. I mean, what you said about them before."

Megan smiled.

Tara could see the boys glancing in Megan's direction. She hoped it wouldn't be long before one of them came over to say hello. That was the only hope Megan had, because there was no way Megan would get to talk with them if they didn't make the move.

When Tara was halfway through her food, someone sat down next to her. She turned to see that it was Caleb.

"Hello, Tara."

"Hello."

"Have you just finished work?"

Tara nodded.

"I came to visit you yesterday, but there was no one home. "

"Did you? Oh, I must've been out with Megan. We went into town. What did you come to see me about?"

He smiled. "To see how things went with your father?"

"Really good. He explained everything to me, and I have a sister and a half brother."

"A half brother and a sister?"

"Jah, it's a long story."

"I've got a lot of time."

Tara was pleased he was interested. She told him all that Redmond O'Donnell had told her.

"That's an interesting story."

"I know. And he would've wanted me if he'd known about me."

"It's good that you know your past and how you came to be adopted. It puts an end to you not knowing and having to wonder."

"I feel different inside. I don't know why. I guess it shouldn't make any difference. But it's answered all the questions that I've had. Well, not all of the questions. I've still got a million questions I want to ask him."

"Can I take you home when the wedding's over, Tara?"

Tara smiled. "I'd like that."

A smile brightened his face. "Good. I see someone I need to say hello to. I'll meet up with you a bit later."

"Okay."

When he was gone, Tara turned around to look for Megan,

expecting her to have gone to visit with some of the other guests. "Oh. Were you sitting there all that time?"

"What was I supposed to do?"

"I'm sorry, I was too caught up with Caleb to think that I had my back to you."

"It's okay. You were obviously focused on Caleb."

"He's driving me home."

"I know. I heard."

"Well, what do you think about him?"

"I like him. You're relaxed with him."

"I like him too. I used to think he was a bit strange because he was so quiet."

"Same as me?"

Tara pulled a face. "Yeah well, you can't get to know someone when they don't talk. It's like they think that I don't like them or something."

"What are you talking about?"

"I thought Caleb didn't like me because he never talked when he was around me. And now that we're seeing more of each other, he's starting to talk more. That's why you should stop being so quiet; no one can get to know you."

"It's just hard for me. I'm not as confident as you."

"Just try. Come over with me now and we'll talk to those two." She nodded toward the two men Megan had been talking about.

Megan giggled. "We can't do that."

Tara noticed that Megan's gaze had locked onto something.

"What is it?"

"It's Mark and he's walking this way. I'll leave you two alone to talk."

"*Nee.* Don't leave me." It was too late. Megan was already out of her chair and Mark was getting ready to sit on it.

"I was wondering where you were. I was nearly going to go to the house to find you."

"I was working."

"I'm sorry how things were between us the other day. I don't want us to fight. You know how I want things to be."

"I know how you *tell* me you want things to be, but I should let you know that there are rumors about you and Mary Lou."

When he gulped noticeably, she knew that it must've been true. She stared at him, waiting for an answer. When none came, she continued, "I saw you in town with her the other day and I've heard a lot of talk since then, so I guess it's true."

"She's just a friend."

"That's what we used to tell people. Or, more accurately, that's what you told me to tell everyone."

"*Nee.* She *is* just a friend."

"I think she's more than that. What were you going to do if I'd said yes? How do you think Mary Lou would feel about that?"

"It's not like that. We're just friends. I keep telling you that. Why are you giving me such a hard time?" He hunched his shoulders and pulled the neck of his coat up.

"I know you well enough to know that what you're telling me is not quite right."

He was lying, but she didn't like to flat out accuse him of lying.

"Don't you want to get married, Tara?"

"*Jah,* I do, but I will only marry someone I can trust."

He leaned forward and traced his finger along her hand as it rested on the table. She pulled her hand away from him and placed it in her lap.

"You're being silly, Tara. You can trust me."

"Time will tell."

"What does that mean?"

"Exactly what I said."

"So, you're going to make me wait, and then what?"

"Mark, I'm not doing anything to you. I'm certainly not making you wait for me or anything else."

"What if I asked Mary Lou to marry me—would you be jealous?"

She stared into his eyes. She'd be upset if he married someone else. He wouldn't, would he?

"I've got too much going on at the moment."

He leaned in and whispered, "I'm not going to wait around for you because you might still reject me and then I would've missed my chance with Mary Lou." He stood up and walked away.

It was true! She stared at the nearly empty plate in front of her and stopped herself from picking it up and throwing at the back of his head.

"They're bringing the desserts out now, Tara."

She looked up to see Megan. "Good. Just in time."

CHAPTER 13

But that no man is justified by the law in the sight of God, it is evident: for, The just shall live by faith.
Galatians 3:11

TARA WAS PLEASED when the wedding was over so she could escape and be with Caleb. Looking around for him, she saw Mark and Mary Lou standing close to each other, talking with barely an inch between them. She was upset to see them together, but more than that, she was upset about the way Mark had treated her. She was glad she hadn't gotten sucked into his flattery.

"Are you ready?"

She turned around and looked into Caleb's pleasant face.

"Yeah, I'm ready. I'll just say goodbye to Megan."

After she said goodbye to her and a few more people, she hurried to the buggy with Caleb without bothering to look over at Mark. Caleb and Tara walked past the bishop and his wife and they exchanged nods. Tara had never had much to do with them.

Mark wasn't interested in her as an individual it seemed, he just wanted to get married to somebody. Now, that somebody was most likely Mary Lou.

"It seems to be getting colder," Caleb said as soon as they were both in the buggy.

Tara pulled her shawl tighter around her. "Certainly does."

"I've been thinking about getting one of those heaters to put in the buggy, but I don't drive it enough to make it worthwhile."

"It's okay. It's not that far to Elizabeth's house."

As they drove down the winding roads, Tara was pleased that she'd gotten to know Caleb. Maybe he was the man God had intended for her to be with. A loud crash coming from nowhere coincided with the buggy coming to a halt.

"What's wrong?" Tara looked over at Caleb who looked worried.

"I don't know. I'll get out and take a look."

Caleb jumped out of the buggy and Tara leaped out after him. She joined him as he was looking at the rear wheel.

He looked up at her. "Tara, get back in the buggy. It's too cold out here."

"Is the wheel broken?"

"Nee, it's not broken. I can fix it."

"Well, what's happened to it?"

"Tara, get back in the buggy!"

She looked at him, surprised that he could be so forceful. He took her by the arm and marched her back into the buggy. Then he pulled a blanket out of the back and covered her with it.

Wagging, his finger at her, he said, "Sit there until I fix it."

She gave no response and neither did he wait for one. He strode back to attend to the wheel. Tara pulled the blanket around her shoulders. She felt safe and protected around Caleb. He was turning out to be a real man.

The next thing she knew he was by the side of the road dragging a fence post that had fallen over, pulling it back toward the buggy. Then he appeared beside her.

"I might need you out of the buggy for one moment. I need the buggy as light as possible."

She got out of the buggy and the freezing air bit into her cheeks.

He rubbed her on the back. "Are you okay?"

Shivering, she nodded. He pulled off his coat and placed it gently around her shoulders even though she still had the blanket on.

"You'll need your coat, or you'll freeze."

"Nee. I'm getting too hot," he said heading back to the rear of the buggy.

With the help of the large post, the buggy tipped over to one side while he tended to the wheel.

"Okay, Tara, you can get back in now."

As she climbed back into the buggy, she saw him discard the old fence post.

She wanted to get out and see if she could help, but she knew he would only tell her off again, so she waited patiently, which wasn't easy for her.

He retrieved the toolbox from the back of the buggy and several minutes later, after some hammering, they were ready to go.

"Are you okay?"

She could see that the concern on his face was real. He was more attentive and caring than Mark had ever been.

She nodded. "I'm fine. What about you?"

"I'm okay. Sorry about that."

"You couldn't help it."

"Well, it's ruined our buggy ride."

It was then that she realized that he was looking on this as a date, and not merely driving her home for convenience sake. She wondered what the bishop had thought about her going in a buggy with Caleb.

Now looking at the snow-covered view, she said, "I don't recognize this road."

He glanced over at her and smiled. "I'm taking you on a nicer drive home."

She giggled. "That explains it. I don't know all these back roads."

When they neared the house, Tara was amazed to see that Mark's buggy was there.

"That's Mark!" Caleb said.

"Why's he here? I was only just talking to him at the wedding and he mentioned nothing of coming here."

"Strange."

Once they pulled up, they both got out to meet Mark. He was on the porch leaning against the front door with his arms folded.

As they approached, he stepped forward. "Where have the two of you been?"

"I just drove her home from the wedding," Caleb said.

"Why are you even here, Caleb?"

"Don't be rude, Mark. He was kind enough to drive me home."

"Where have you two been?" he asked again.

"We had a bit of trouble with the buggy and that's why it took us some time to get here."

He dipped his head and his dark eyes were looking straight at Caleb. "I came straight here from the wedding and I didn't pass you."

"Well..." Tara started to explain and was cut off by Mark.

"What's going on here, Caleb? Tara and I are in a relationship and you're coming in between us."

Tara gasped at his lie. A few weeks ago it would've been true, but he as good as said if she wouldn't marry him he'd ask Mary Lou.

"I'm sorry, I didn't realize," Caleb said softly taking a step back.

"You don't have to go, Caleb."

Caleb turned around. "I'll talk to you later, Tara."

When he kept walking, Tara glared at Mark. "Are you happy now?"

"What do you think you were doing just now?"

"What are you doing with Mary Lou?"

"I told you we're just friends."

"You said if I didn't marry you…." she looked around at Caleb to see him leaving. "Now that Caleb is gone, you had better go too."

"Why? Worried about your reputation?"

"My reputation is fine. Now please leave."

He stood still with his hands on his hips for a few moments before he walked over to his buggy. He turned to face her. "I don't know what you're playing at."

"Goodbye, Mark." She walked inside and slammed the door behind her. She waited until she heard his buggy leave and then she collapsed onto the couch.

She felt awful that Caleb would think there was something still going on between her and Mark. If she'd only spoken up and said there was nothing going on, but surely Caleb knew that.

Why did Caleb take her the long way home? It had to be because he liked her and wanted to spend more time with her. Now she had to convince Caleb that Mark and she were over for good.

CHAPTER 14

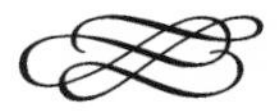

But seek ye first the kingdom of God, and his righteousness; and all these things shall be added unto you.
Matthew 6:33

WHEN TARA WALKED outside the quilting store for her lunch break, Megan was right outside waiting for her.

"What are you doing here?" Tara asked.

"Waiting for you."

"Why didn't you come inside? It's freezing out here."

"I didn't want you to get into trouble. You know how Mrs. Thomas complained about you having so many friends calling in to see you."

"*Jah,* that's true. Come to the coffee shop with me."

They linked arms and walked up the street.

"I came here to tell you that the bishop wants to see you this afternoon."

"Wants to see me?"

"Jah."

"Why?"

"I don't know. Did you do something?"

"Not that I'm aware of."

"William and Gretchen arranged for me to drive you there when you finish work. Did you get a taxi this morning?"

Tara nodded, disturbed by the bishop wanting to see her. It had to be because she'd unknowingly done something bad.

"What does he want to see me about?"

"He didn't say."

"Well, what do Gretchen and William think it's about?"

"They don't know either. I guess you'll just have to wait and see."

"I hope I haven't done anything wrong."

Megan laughed. "Wouldn't you know if you had?"

Tara pulled a face. "I guess so. I don't think I have."

"He's probably just asking if you want to stay on in the community, or if you're going to get baptized, things like that."

"He didn't ask Elizabeth any of those things and she's younger than both of us. Has he asked you?"

Megan shook her head.

They sat and had something to eat in the coffee shop while Tara told Megan what had happened when she arrived home the night before.

"Mark must've seen you go home with Caleb and it made him really jealous."

"It seems like it. It makes me wonder about a few things."

"And how do you feel about Caleb?"

"I like him; he seems really nice. I don't think he's had a girlfriend before. Do you know if he has?"

"I wouldn't know if he has or hasn't. You're asking the wrong person."

Tara took a bite of her bacon pie. There had been no sign of

Caleb this morning and she had hoped that he would come by to drive her to work.

"Have you called your father yet to arrange that meeting?"

"No. I'll do that before I go back to work. I hope his children want to meet me."

"They will. Don't worry."

"I hope you're right."

SEVERAL MINUTES later when they'd finished eating, Tara had Megan stand next to her while she called Redmond, her birth father. They arranged to meet for dinner next week. Tara hung up the phone.

"He said he'll pick us up from Grabers' house on Tuesday evening."

"Okay, that sounds good. So, that means they all want to meet you?"

"Yeah, he said so."

"That's great. I knew they would."

Tara nodded, glad that Megan had so much confidence about her siblings wanting to meet her.

"I better let you get back to work. How are you getting home?"

"It's okay. I'll get a taxi. I'll just have a look around the shops first before I go home."

"Are you sure?"

"Yes. Oh, wait. Didn't I have to go to the bishop's this afternoon?"

Megan hit her head. "That's right."

Both girls laughed at their forgetfulness.

WHEN THE GIRLS arrived at the bishop's house, the bishop's wife had Megan wait in a sitting room while Tara was taken into another room. There were two couches in the room and Tara sat down on the one opposite Bishop John. The bishop's wife, Ruth, sat next to him.

"How about some hot tea, Ruth?" the bishop asked.

"The pot is boiling," she answered.

The Bishop nodded and then looked at Tara. "It's a rather delicate subject I'd like to discuss with you, Tara."

"Have I done something wrong?"

"Nee, but some things have come to my attention and there has been talk. I wanted to caution you to be aware."

"I'll just go and check on that tea," the Bishop's wife said before she headed out of the room.

"Be aware of what?"

"Perhaps I'll wait until Ruth comes back into the room. She's good at helping me explain things."

Tara nodded.

"William tells me you're working at a quilting store in town?"

"I work there a few days a week. It's only a part-time job, but I really enjoy it."

The bishop nodded. "That's good. And Gretchen tells me that your father has contacted you recently?"

"That's right." Tara glanced at the bishop's large Bible that was next to him on the couch. She wondered if he was going to preach out of it to her. If she hadn't done anything wrong, it certainly made her feel like she had.

The bishop's wife came back in with a tray of tea, cookies and cake.

"This looks lovely," Tara said, feeling slightly hungry.

"It's an apple cake. It's my mother's recipe. My family had an orchard and that's probably why I always cook with so many apples. It's a habit really."

"Tara is *not* here to speak about apples, Ruth!"

Ruth stopped pouring the tea and handed a cup to Tara. *"Jah,*

I'm sorry, Tara. Once I get started talking about apples, sometimes I just can't stop. It's because I grew up amongst them and have a fondness for them."

"That's alright. I like hearing what people did when they were growing up. I'm going to meet my family soon. I've met my father, and soon I'll meet my sister and my half-brother."

"William told us that your father came to the house."

"Yes. It was quite a surprise when he made contact. Especially after Elizabeth was just found by her family."

Ruth offered her a cookie and she took one while balancing the tea cup and saucer on her knees. Her eyes were drawn to the cake, but since no one else had taken a piece, she didn't want to be the first to do so. She politely sipped her tea, avoiding looking at the cake that was silently calling to her.

"Ruth, I was waiting for you to get back before I continued telling Tara why I wanted her here."

Ruth nodded. "Go ahead."

"Tara, I just want you to be aware that, just because some men belong to the community, it does not mean that they are completely trustworthy and will not take advantage if you let them."

Tara's eyes grew wide. Was he talking about one person in particular? "*Denke* for the warning."

"Have you heard about a wolf in sheep's clothing?"

"I think so. That means someone in disguise, I'd say."

"*Jah.* There might be some men who are thinking of leaving our community and are not totally abiding by the *Ordnung.*"

"I see. That's a good point. I'd never thought of things like that."

"You should," Ruth blurted out.

"Are you talking about one man in particular?"

"It would be wrong of me to call someone by name. But I can say this to you, sometimes it's the quietest of men that you have to watch out for."

"I understand, but can't you give me a hint?"

The bishop glanced at his wife and then his bushy eyebrows drew together as he looked back at Tara. "This person might have an interest in leaving us and working on cars. Now, that's all I can say in my position."

"You must be strong to stay on the narrow path, Tara," Ruth said. "Wide is the road that leads to destruction and narrow's the way."

"Got it. Narrow path." Tara nodded recalling the subject of the bishop's favorite sermon.

"I hope you'll stay with us after you meet your *familye,* as Elizabeth did," Ruth said.

The bishop turned to his wife. "Now that I've said what I have to say, you can invite Megan to have tea with us."

Ruth sprang to her feet and obeyed her husband.

Megan walked into the room with Ruth and sat down beside Tara. They had a lovely talk with the bishop and to Tara's surprise, Megan was bold enough to take the first piece of cake. Tara happily followed her lead.

On the way home from the bishop's house, Tara told Megan everything that the bishop and his wife had said to her.

"He was giving you a warning."

"Obviously. I was right not to have anything to do with Mark when he came back. I should never have trusted him—ever."

"Mark?"

"*Jah.* Don't you think the bishop was talking about Mark?" Tara asked.

"*Nee.* I don't. Didn't he say a sheep in wolf's clothing?"

Tara giggled. "It was the other way 'round. Wait a minute… a wolf in sheep's clothing. That's right." She looked over at Megan to see she wasn't laughing. "What do you mean and why are you looking so worried?"

"Well, doesn't that describe Caleb?"

Tara gasped. "*Jah.* And the bishop did talk about someone appearing quiet. He said it's the quiet ones I have to watch."

"I thought right away, as soon as you told me what he'd said, that he was talking about Caleb."

Tara's tummy squirmed. "And at the wedding, the bishop saw me leaving with Caleb, so that fits too."

"He must know things about Caleb that we don't know."

"I've got a bad history with men already and I'm not even nineteen years old."

"Things could've been worse. If the bishop hadn't warned you, who knows what might have happened?"

Tara put a hand over her tummy. "And I was really starting to like him."

"He seemed nice. What if he'd tried to attack a woman and she fought back and that's how he got those scars?"

"*Nee.* Elizabeth said he's had them for a long time. But, you know what else?"

"What?"

"When he took me home last night, he went the long way and then something happened to the buggy wheel. We were alone for some time in the middle of nowhere."

"Did he try anything?"

"*Nee,* but he might have intended to and then changed his mind. When we got back to the *haus,* Mark was there."

"Mark has probably heard about Caleb and was trying to protect you."

"That doesn't excuse him for being too friendly with Mary Lou."

"What did he say when you asked about Mary Lou?"

Tara shook her head. "He told me at the wedding if I didn't

marry him, he'd marry Mary Lou. Other times he insists that they're just friends."

"When you're not ready to announce a relationship, you have to say you're just friends. I don't know, Tara. It seems you can't trust either of them."

Tara nodded. "I feel like such a fool for starting to like Caleb. He just seemed so trustworthy."

CHAPTER 15

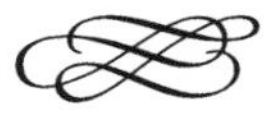

While the earth remaineth, seedtime and harvest, and cold and heat, and summer and winter, and day and night shall not cease.
Genesis 8:22

TARA WAS glad that both Caleb and Mark kept away from her for the next few days. She had time to think about meeting her siblings.

On Tuesday afternoon, Tara took a taxi from work straight to William and Gretchen's house to wait for Redmond to collect her and Megan.

Tara sat in the kitchen watching Megan help Gretchen with making dinner.

"Just be yourself. They'll be more worried about whether you like them," Aunt Gretchen said.

"I think I'm more scared than she is," Megan said with a giggle.

"You just have to be yourself too, Megan. Stop concentrating on how you feel and start thinking how the other people feel. Don't be nervous. Concentrate on putting them at ease."

"Thanks for the advice, *Mamm.* I will," Megan said.

"I AM SO glad you called me, Tara," Redmond said.

"Didn't you think I was going to?"

"I was a little concerned that you might not. Your brother and sister are looking forward to meeting you. Avalon can't stop asking questions about you. Brandon just takes things as they come."

"How did they take the news when you told them about me?"

"They were shocked naturally, but they're very eager to meet you."

"Good. I'm looking forward to meeting them too."

"If you don't mind me asking, how did it come about that you were adopted twice? The social worker didn't tell me too much."

"I don't mind you asking at all. The first time—I don't remember much, but I learned later that the wife died. I probably was with them since I was born virtually until I was about eight—"

"I heard it was younger," Megan said.

"It could've been. Gretchen knows it all. When I was adopted with the first people, the wife died and I was relinquished. I think that's the term used. Then I was adopted again, but I wasn't well behaved. I don't know why. I had a lot of anger, I guess, and I just didn't want to do anything I was told."

"And how long have you been with the Grabers? I'm sure you told me the other night, but there was a lot to take in."

"I've been with the Grabers for a few years."

"I'm sorry things worked out the way they did."

"There's no need to be sorry; things work out how they were supposed to work out."

"Well, I wish it had been supposed to work out differently."

"We've met now, so that's a good thing."

"It is."

THEY EVENTUALLY PULLED up at Redmond's house.

"Is this where you live?"

"It is."

"It's very big."

"Yes, Marjorie liked spacious houses. Now, Brandon and Avalon have been in charge of the dinner, so I hope it works out well. Brandon tells me he's a pretty good cook. He's lived away from home for two years, and he enjoys cooking."

"Oh, he's here tonight just to see me?"

"He is."

Redmond parked in the driveway and then they walked to the front door.

When Redmond opened the door, Brandon and Avalon were there to meet her. Brandon was as tall as Redmond, handsome, with light brown hair and a wide smile. Avalon was tall for her age, with the same dark hair as Tara, and she wore jeans and a T-shirt.

Redmond introduced everybody. Then Avalon started talking at a mile a minute and Tara had to smile. Avalon's personality was similar to her own. Redmond walked everybody through to the living room and they sat down for a while.

Tara took a minute to glance over at Megan to make sure she wasn't feeling too awkward. Megan was looking relaxed, engrossed in a conversation with Brandon.

Avalon got right down to asking all the nitty-gritty questions.

When Tara was in the middle of answering one of her questions, Avalon suddenly jumped to her feet. "I found something; I'll just go get it and show you."

She ran out of the room and came back a moment later holding a photograph. She placed it in Tara's hands.

"I think this is you," Avalon said.

Tara stared at the small photo of a woman with a newborn in her arms. The woman was smiling and looked proud, so it had to be her baby. She looked up at Redmond. "Is this me and my mother?"

"It could well be. It's Marjorie for certain. I haven't seen that photo before. The baby's not Brandon or Avalon," Redmond said.

"I found it in Mom's box one day. I asked her who it was. I expected her to say Brandon, or me, but she slapped my hand and told me I had no right going through her things. She acted really strange and now I know why."

Tara stared back at the photo. If her mother had kept a photo of her all those years, surely that meant that she cared about her.

"Can I keep this?" Tara asked.

"Yes. Would you like to see more photos of Mom and us?"

"I sure would."

"How about we leave that until after dinner?" Redmond looked over at Brandon who was conversing with Megan.

"Brandon, how's the dinner coming along?"

"Should we have it now? It's all ready to go."

Redmond nodded. "We might as well have it now."

Brandon headed out of the room. A moment later, he yelled for Avalon to help him.

Megan jumped to her feet and said to Avalon, "I can help him if you want to stay talking with Tara."

"You're a guest."

"You'd be doing Megan a favor; she loves being in the kitchen," Tara said.

Avalon giggled. "I don't."

Megan hurried to the kitchen and Tara was pleased that Megan was finally coming out of her shell. It was a big step for her to offer to help in the kitchen and especially to be alone with a man. With Brandon, Megan didn't seem awkward or shy at all.

"Dinner smells amazing. What is it?" Tara asked.

"It's roast lamb and vegetables. Brandon wanted to do something fancier, but Dad said he should have something more plain."

"It sounds like he's a good cook."

"He is. And now that he's left home, I'm stuck with Dad's cooking."

Tara laughed.

"Dad said you work in a quilting store. What do you do there?"

"I'm a sales assistant. We sell Amish quilts, and everything someone would need for quilting."

"Do you like sewing?" Avalon asked.

"Yes, I do. How about yourself?"

"Mom and I used to do needlework, embroidery. It was years ago and then we stopped. I can't remember why."

"That sounds nice. It's always more fun to do it with somebody else."

Tara and the others heard Megan's faint giggles.

"Sounds like they're having fun," Redmond said.

"Yes, it sounds like it."

"I hope they're not gonna take too much longer because I'm starving," Avalon said.

Tara giggled because that was exactly what she was thinking.

When Megan and Brandon brought the food out, Megan explained that she was just showing Brandon a different way to make gravy.

"And if no one likes it, it's not my fault," Brandon said as he placed a large platter of lamb and vegetables in the center of the table. He continued, "I was going to put these onto individual plates, but Megan said this is the Amish way, so this is the way we're doing it tonight."

"We say grace before we eat," Redmond said.

"We do too, so just do what you normally do." Tara closed her eyes.

Redmond said a prayer of thanks for the food. Tara was a little surprised and pleased. The *Englisch* families she'd been in hadn't said thanks to God before they ate.

When everyone started to eat, Tara answered a lot of Avalon's questions about the Amish.

When the meal was over, Brandon stood up. "Megan, would you be kind enough to help me with the dessert?"

"I'd be glad to."

Megan and Brandon carried the serving platter and the plates to the kitchen.

"I hope you like dessert, Tara," Avalon said.

"What is it? I like most desserts. No, I'll correct that, I like all of them."

Avalon giggled. "It's fruit salad, chocolate mousse and ice cream.

"I love all those things."

"Brandon made the ice cream and he made the chocolate mousse. I cut up the fruit salad."

"It sounds delicious."

Tara didn't feel as awkward as she had thought she might. These people were friendly and lovely and nothing like the family she thought she might have come from.

CHAPTER 16

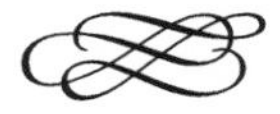

Ask, and it shall be given you; seek, and ye shall find;
knock, and it shall be opened unto you:
Matthew 7:7

REDMOND HAD BEEN WAITING all night to ask Tara some important questions and now he was nearing the Grabers' house, taking Tara and Megan back home. Time was running out.

"I hope you've both had a good night."

"We have. I'm so glad to have met Brandon and Avalon."

"I hope you'll stay in our lives."

Tara nodded.

He pulled into the Grabers' driveway. When he stopped the car, he said, "Do you mind if I have a word with you in private?"

Megan opened the car door. "I'll leave the two of you to talk. Thanks for tonight and thanks for the ride home, Redmond."

"You're most welcome, Megan."

When they were alone, Tara said, "Do you want to talk here or do you want to come inside the house?"

"Here will be fine. Tara, I own a printing company and if you'd like, I could train you. You could come and work in the family business."

"Really?"

"Yes. You're welcome to come and live at the house too. I just didn't want to overwhelm you, but I want you to know that our home is your home. That's the way it should've been."

"Thank you. What would I do if I worked for you? I don't know anything about printing."

"There are a lot of different jobs you could do and you could be trained for any one of them."

"Really?"

He looked into her eyes and was reminded again of an old photo of his mother. He'd have to find it to show Tara. "Yes, really."

"I don't know what to say."

"It's a big decision. It would bring you closer into our family, but it has to be what's right for you. I've been reading up on the Amish and I'm guessing you consider them to be your family."

Tara nodded. "Can I think about it?"

"Take all the time you need."

"I like having this photo of my mother, and seeing what she looked like from all the other photos."

"I hope you're not mad at her for putting you up for adoption. Knowing Marjorie as I did, I know it couldn't have been an easy thing for her to do. She was the kind of woman who always put herself last even though she was a spitfire on other occasions."

"I'm not mad at her. I'm glad I found out the truth and got to meet you, and Brandon, and Avalon. Avalon is a lot like me."

"Yes. You two got along well. Would you consider coming to dinner once a week?"

Tara nodded. "I think that would be okay. Yes, I'd like that. Can you drive me somewhere else? I'm staying at a friend's house while she's away. It's not far from here."

"Yes, of course."

"Good. Can you give me a minute and I'll just let the Grabers know you're driving me back there tonight?"

"Yes. I'll wait here." Redmond watched Tara walk into the house. He hoped he wasn't rushing the relationship or moving too fast. It was hard to know what to do. There was no guidebook for something like this—no set of rules or unspoken etiquette. He couldn't make up for her past, but he hoped with his support and friendship he could make Tara's future the best it could be. Realizing that the best thing for her might be for him to fade into the background so she could continue with her Amish life, he had to let her take the lead.

She opened the door and got back into the front seat. "Okay."

"All set?"

"Yes." After Tara had given him directions, she explained that she was staying at Elizabeth's house.

"And I understand that Amish people marry young?"

"Compared to other people, I guess. I don't really consider myself Amish. Well, I do in a sense because that's the way I was raised for the last few years. To be officially Amish, you need to be baptized and young people normally do that just before they marry. Before that, young people can go in and out of the community, but not too much."

"Yes, I've read about the *rumspringa.* Do you have a young man you're fond of?"

"I did once. Not so long ago. It's kind of complicated."

He laughed. "Many relationships are. Marjorie and I disagreed on most things, and once we realized we were never going to agree on anything, we worked around it in our own way."

"I want a relationship I don't have to work on."

Redmond laughed. "I hope you get that."

"Me too, or I shall not get married."

Redmond gave Tara a sideways glance. She reminded him so much of himself and at other times, his wife.

"Take a left here."

He took the left fork in the road and then Tara directed him up a driveway to an old house. "It's in darkness. Do you want me to come in with you?"

"*Nee.* I'll be fine. I've got a lantern right inside the doorway."

"I'll leave my headlights on for you until I see some light in the house."

"Okay. Goodbye, and thanks for tonight."

"Thank you, Tara. And don't forget next Tuesday night. I'll collect you from the Grabers, and Megan too if she wants to come back."

"I'll be waiting. I think Megan will, too." She leaned over and gave him a quick hug before she left the car.

He wiped a tear from his eye as he watched her walk to the front door of the house. That was his daughter, and other people had raised her.

I can't do anything about that now. I must look to the future and not the past, or I'll drive myself mad.

When a light beamed from within the house, he turned the car around and headed down the driveway.

CHAPTER 17

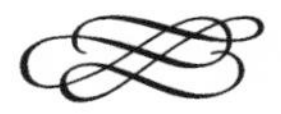

I am not ashamed: for I know whom I have believed, and am persuaded that he is able to keep that which I have committed unto him against that day.
2 Timothy 1:12

TARA WAS IN BED, but hadn't been home long when she heard hoofbeats. Looking out the window, she saw nothing but darkness. She lit the lantern by her bed and carried it as she walked downstairs to see who it was.

As soon as she opened the door, she heard Elizabeth's voice.

"What are you doing home? I thought you'd be at least another two weeks away."

"We got homesick."

"I could go back to Gretchen's if you want to stay here by yourselves tonight."

Elizabeth shook her head. "*Nee.* We can all stay tonight. I need to catch up with what's been happening since I've been gone."

"I'll put on a pot of tea," Tara said, pulling Elizabeth toward the kitchen.

While Joseph unloaded the buggy, the two girls sat in the kitchen drinking tea.

"So much has happened, and all I wanted to do was to talk to you about it."

"Tell me."

"My father—my actual real father—came looking for me. I've met him. I have a younger sister and an older half brother. Megan came with me to meet them just tonight. I've only just got back from his place."

"I can't believe it. I wish I'd been here."

"Me too, and days before that, my father, I just call him Redmond, came to the house and that's where I met him for the very first time with William, Gretchen and Megan." Tara told Elizabeth everything about her family, how her mother had given her away and then gotten back with her father.

"That's amazing. And he never knew about you?"

"No, not until he found the adoption papers after my mother died." Tara jumped up then and got the photo that she'd been given. "This is my mother holding me as a baby. She'd kept it all that time."

"She never forgot you."

"She didn't."

"I'm so happy for you, Tara."

"I've got more news. Mark's back. Did you know?"

"Nee. How would I?"

Tara sniggered. "Well, he made up a story about Joseph giving him work to do in the *haus.* Then he confessed it was a lie and he just wanted to spend time with me."

"You're back together with him?"

"Nee. Everything is messed up. There are rumors about him."

"There are rumors about everyone. That's not unusual."

"Yeah. Tell me about your visiting?"

"I've been visiting all of Joseph's relations. And staying not more than a night at each place. It's been exhausting; I'm glad I'm home."

"I'm glad you're home, too. We've all missed you."

"There's nothing else to tell. We visit the homes of people, and then we can't relax because we're not in our own home. I felt tense the whole time. That's why we cut it short."

Tara blurted out everything about Mark and what had happened between them. She kept quiet about Caleb, as he was now Elizabeth's brand new brother-in-law.

WHEN JOSEPH WALKED into the kitchen, he said, "Do I get a cup of tea?"

Tara sprang to her feet. "Yeah. Take a seat."

He pulled out a chair and sat down. "That's everything out of the buggy. I've just left the boxes in the living room by the door."

"That'll give me plenty to do tomorrow," Elizabeth said. "Tara's had some exciting news." Elizabeth told Joseph about how Tara's father had found her.

"That's good news, Tara."

"I know. It's answered questions I've always had. Now, about those boxes, Elizabeth. I can help you with your unpacking after work, and then can you drive me back home, Joseph?"

"Sure, but don't feel you have to rush off. We said you could stay here for a while. We don't want to ruin your plans."

Tara could scarcely keep the smile from her face. As newlyweds, they'd surely want their new home to themselves. "I have had a good time being on my own. *Denke.* Now I'm ready to go home."

"Okay."

"Tara, I'm going to have a big dinner here and invite everyone."

"When?"

"In about a week."

"Sounds like fun."

"I hope so. All our friends can come take a look at our new place. We won't have everything done by then, though."

"It'll take some time to get it into the shape we want."

"I'll help you with the dinner."

"Denke. I was hoping you would."

"I don't see a buggy here, Tara, has Caleb been driving you?"

Tara frowned as she placed a cup of hot tea in front of Joseph. "Caleb?"

"He drove you here, didn't he?"

"Jah, he did. He drove me to work and back a couple of times."

"That's good."

"Did you ask him to?"

"Nee."

"Did you know Mark is back?" Elizabeth asked Joseph.

"Nee." He looked at Tara. "Back to stay?"

Tara shrugged her shoulders. "He can do whatever he wants. It makes no difference to me."

Joseph looked at Elizabeth with raised eyebrows as he picked up his teacup.

Tara guessed that Elizabeth would tell Joseph everything when they were alone. How nice it would be to have someone to confide in.

"You two must be tired."

"Jah," Elizabeth said.

"We're exhausted," Joseph agreed.

"I'll be gone early in the morning. I start early and finish early tomorrow."

"Can I drive you to work?" Joseph asked.

"Nee. I'll get a taxi. It's no trouble."

"Are you sure?"

"Quite sure."

"If I'm awake I'll drive you."

"Forget it. You have a good sleep-in. And then I'll come back and help Elizabeth unpack and then you can drive me back home. Okay?"

He nodded. "Okay."

Tara drank her tea quickly and went to bed feeling like she was an intruder. The least she could do was give them time alone. The first night as a married couple in their new home, and they had Tara under their roof. It wasn't ideal for them and if she'd had her own buggy, she would've gone back home right then.

"GRETCHEN, can I talk to you about something in private?"

"Of course come with me to the barn. I'm getting the chicken food."

Gretchen walked out the door with Tara. "What's on your mind?"

It wasn't easy for Tara to talk to Gretchen about men. They'd had so few talks about them, and any conversations that Gretchen had with the girls about men were in general and not about any man or any relationship in particular. "I'm confused. At first, I liked Mark and, I didn't tell you, but we had discussed marriage and then he disappeared and I don't know where he went."

"Yoder or Hostetler?"

"What?"

"Mark Yoder or Mark Hostetler?"

"Mark Young."

Gretchen raised her eyebrows and said nothing.

"And then he came back with an attitude that it was my problem that he disappeared. And..."

"Did you say that?"

"*Nee,* but whenever we discuss anything, I always end up feeling that it's my problem. He said he wanted to get back together and I said no because I can't trust him and he said it's because I was given away as a child and I have a fear of abandonment or something like that."

"Are you having a problem forgiving him for going away?"

Tara shrugged her shoulders. "I guess he can do whatever he wants, but I just think he's untrustworthy now."

"Well, it might be a good thing that he disappeared when he did."

Tara was suddenly glad that she was talking to Gretchen; things just seem to make sense when they came out of Gretchen's mouth.

"But there is someone else I like."

"That's good."

"I thought it was good to start with, but now I hear that he might not be very trustworthy."

"You don't want to go on what you hear. You need to take people as you find them. There's far too much talk that goes on in the community. Some people have nothing better to do than to gossip."

"It wasn't like that, though, Aunt Gretchen. This person who warned me about him was a very reliable person."

"The bishop?"

Tara nodded. "And that's not all. There are rumors about Mark and Mary Lou. So even if I forgave him for that… I don't know; it just seems that he's far too friendly with Mary Lou for my liking."

"It's interesting that you're so upset about Mark being friendly with Mary Lou. It sounds like you haven't gotten over him."

"I still like him, but I can't trust him."

"Sensible girl. You're choosing a man with your head and your heart. And—"

"So far I'm not choosing one, I'm just unchoosing them, it seems."

Gretchen giggled. "How can I help you?"

"This other boy I like—well, how do I know if the things I've heard about him are true?"

"Why don't you ask him?"

Tara stared into Gretchen's wise face. "Aunt Gretchen, you're a genius. I never thought of that. I just hope I don't offend him when I ask him."

"You might, but at least then you'll be closer to the truth. You've always been bold and forthright—some might say strong minded —in the past. That's got you into a lot of trouble, but now I see that you are using those emotions and your personality in a good way."

Tara brightened up. "Do you think so?"

"Just ask the young man if what you've heard is true."

Tara looked into Gretchen's kindly face, and wondered if she would have ever had a conversation like that with her birth mother, had things been different.

CHAPTER 18

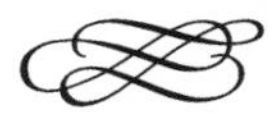

Knowing that whatsoever good thing any man doeth, the same shall he receive of the Lord, whether he be bond or free.
Ephesians 6:8

TARA WAS at Elizabeth's big dinner at her house when she next came into contact with Caleb. It was after the dinner was over, and Caleb was getting a breath of fresh air on the porch. She came up behind him as he was staring into the darkness of the night.

"Caleb, can I ask you a question?"

He jumped slightly and then turned to face her. "You can ask me whatever you want."

Tara licked her lips. "If I ask you a question will you answer me truthfully?"

He frowned. "Of course I will."

"When you drove me home from the wedding the other day, why did you take me the long way?"

He looked away from her. "I just wanted to spend more time with you."

"And you didn't know that the wheel would come off and we could've been stuck on a deserted road?"

His mouth opened in shock. *"Nee!* How would I know that?"

She could tell by the way he looked into her eyes he was telling the truth. Caleb hadn't plotted for them to be alone and stranded.

"Tara, what's this about?"

"I don't know." She shrugged her shoulders. "Someone just told me to be wary of wolves in sheep's clothing and I guess I'm anxious about everybody around me now."

"You don't have to worry about me. Whoever told you that... I'm sure they had somebody else in mind. Or, did they mention me by name?"

"Nee, they didn't. I'm sorry I said anything."

"I know you don't know me very well, but I hope you'll come to trust me in time."

"It's hard sometimes to trust." She stepped closer to him.

"It can't have been easy for you going from house-to-house like you did when you were younger."

"It wasn't easy at all. I suppose that's how I came to be mistrusting of people."

"You don't have to mistrust me. I only want the best for you and I have no bad intentions toward you. It was a silly thing for me to do—to go the long way. I should've told you, or I should've asked you if you wanted to go that way home." His voice trailed away.

She wanted to get to know him better. The more layers she peeled away, the better she liked this man. He was like a mystery package.

Feeling that she now knew him well enough, she asked, "How did you get that scar on your face and the scars on your hands?"

His hand flew to his temple where the scar ran down past his eye. It was clear that whatever had caused the deep cut, it had narrowly missed his eye. "These scars are ugly. I wish no one had to look at them."

"Nee, they're not ugly. They give you character."

He laughed.

"Will you tell me how you got them?"

He swallowed noticeably. "I had a disagreement with a barbed wire fence."

Tara frowned. "How did it come about?"

"It's a long story."

"I'd like to hear it. I'm intrigued now."

"It happened when I was around eight. It was a Sunday and I wasn't feeling well, so I stayed home with my *grossmammi* while the rest of the family went to the meeting. When we were alone, she started gasping and was having trouble breathing."

"You said you were eight?"

"Thereabouts. I knew I had to go for help, but my family had filled two buggies to go to the meeting, so there was only one horse in the paddock. I was to find out later he wasn't broken under saddle. I slipped a bridle on him and he was fine—didn't flinch or anything. Then I leaped on his back as I often did with our other two horses, and he was sidestepping and wouldn't move forward. Then we hit the fence and he bucked me off into it."

"Oh no." Tara cringed.

"Yeah, and I hung on to him for everything I was worth and was dragged a few paces."

"Ouch."

He looked down at the back of his hands.

"What happened to your grandmother?"

"I'm getting to that. I told you it was a long story. The horse stopped and I got back on him and was able to ride him to the doctor's house."

"How could you get on his back if you were only eight?"

"We used to ride our other horses and learned to vault onto

them somehow. We'd take a handful of mane and jump just right and up we'd go. Anyway, when I arrived at the doctor's house, I had blood all over me and he thought I'd come there for myself. I told him about my *grossmammi* and then he drove me back and found she was having an asthma attack. He was able to treat her."

"You saved her life."

He sniggered. "I think that's an exaggeration."

"I don't. Did you need stitches for your cuts?"

"*Nee.* I was bandaged up and that was that. Apart from some injections for tetanus and probably some kind of antibiotic."

"What about your face?"

"Believe it or not, I had it bandaged too." He laughed. "I wasn't allowed to move for days. I had large cotton swathes out to here." He motioned with his hand. "I can laugh about it now, but it was pretty awful."

Tara grimaced imagining the pain. "That was so brave of you to go for help, and you were so young."

"Anyone would do it."

With a loud guttural clearing of his throat, Mark stepped onto the porch.

They both turned around and looked at him.

"Tara, could I have a private word with you?" He looked over at Caleb. "I'm sorry Caleb, but I need to speak with Tara."

"Okay." He stepped down the porch steps and walked into the dark yard.

Mark walked over and stood next to her. "I thought I'd do you a favor and save you from him. You looked bored."

"That's clever of you to be able to see that from the back of my head."

"Don't be sarcastic. It doesn't suit you. Anyone would be bored with Caleb."

"I don't think you know him very well."

"Does anyone?"

Tara blew out a deep breath. "What did you want to speak with me about?"

"Marry me?"

"We've talked about this."

"We'll have to keep talking about it until you say yes."

"What will Mary Lou think if you marry me?"

"She'll think that you're very blessed to have a man like me as your future husband."

"I'll ask her and see if that's true."

His face instantly went stiff. "Why would you talk to her about me?"

"I've heard a lot about you and Mary Lou lately and I've seen you talking with her on a number of occasions." It was only two, but that didn't sound as good.

"I don't like the way you're talking now, Tara. What's gotten into you? I liked you better the way you were before."

"I could leave and go away, too, all of a sudden."

"Where would you go?"

From the look on his face, he thought she was serious. Tara had to think fast. "I've just met my family. I could leave the community and go to live with them. They've invited me."

"Would you?"

"I might."

"That would work out perfectly for both us. Now I can tell you that when I was away, I was looking into becoming a mechanic and working on cars. We could build a life away from the community."

Tara jerked her head back and stared at him. The bishop had been giving her hints to be wary of Mark and not Caleb.

CHAPTER 19

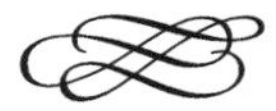

For we wrestle not against flesh and blood, but against principalities,
against powers, against the rulers of the darkness of this world,
against spiritual wickedness in high places.
Ephesians 6:12

"My place is not with you, Mark. I thought it might have been, once."

"You won't do better than me, Tara. I could have any woman I want and I'm not saying that because I'm being prideful."

"Then you must not waste your time on me." Tara walked down the lightly snow-covered porch steps.

"Tara, where are you going?"

Tara hurried off into the darkness hoping Mark wouldn't follow. When she walked around the barn, she looked around for Caleb, convinced that was the direction he'd gone. Just when she was about to turn back, there was movement to the left of her.

"Caleb?"

He strode toward her. "What are you doing out in the dark like this?"

"Looking for you."

He glanced back at the house. "You finished with Mark?"

"Yes, finally, all finished with him. I was through with him days ago, but I've finally convinced him we're never getting back together."

"I meant finished speaking with him just now," Caleb said smiling.

"Oh." She shook her head and looked down. "I'm such an idiot, I thought… never mind."

"What did you think? That I'd like to know you and Mark were over with and your secret relationship no longer exists?"

"Something like that. I guess it wasn't so secret, though." She looked into his eyes. "You're happy it's over with Mark?"

"It's the best news I've heard since I can't remember when."

She laughed and wasn't certain what to say, which was unusual for her.

"If you were my girlfriend, I wouldn't keep something like that a secret. I couldn't. I'd have to tell everyone."

"You would?"

"Jah. I'd want everyone to know."

"And what else?"

"I would ask you to marry me, and then marry you real quick if you said yes, before you could change your mind."

Just as Tara laughed, the wind picked up and a chilly gust of wind smacked the ends of her prayer *kapp* strings across her face.

Gently, he pulled them away from her face and tucked them into the sides of her prayer *kapp.* Her heart pounded at his closeness and his soft touch.

"Tara," he breathed. "Would you like to do something together, just the two of us?"

Nodding, she replied, "I'd like that."

"You would?"

"Jah."

"Okay. How about I come to collect you at six tomorrow night and we'll have dinner somewhere?"

"Perfect." Tara glanced back at the house and saw Elizabeth standing on the porch and guessed she was looking for the two of them. "I guess we should get back."

"I suppose we should, although I'd much rather stand here talking to you in the moonlight."

She looked up into his face and wanted to kiss him right there, right then. He took hold of her hand and gently brought it to his lips and kissed it. Waves of happiness tingled through her body and she knew that this was the man she'd someday marry.

"Let's go inside and not leave each other's side until the night is over. We'll let the gossips say what they will," he said. "We can ignore the whispers and the raised eyebrows."

"All right. Let's do it, but if Mark tells you to leave again, I won't let you go."

He chuckled. "Okay. I'll stay by you."

They walked back to the house side by side.

Throughout the night, Tara could see that Mark was fuming. He wasn't a fool, and he knew that something was happening between her and Caleb. Thankfully, Mark didn't have anything to say, and he left with the others when it was time to go home.

Tara said goodnight to Elizabeth and Joseph before she walked outside with Megan. Tara hurried over to Caleb who was just about to leave.

"I'll see you tomorrow night, Caleb."

"I'm looking forward to it."

When he drove away, she walked back to the porch to wait with Megan for Aunt Gretchen and Uncle William.

"So, it's Caleb now?"

"Is it so obvious?"

"Jah."

Tara giggled. "He's so honest and he's got nothing to hide."

"Jah, he's nice. I like him. What about what the bishop said?"

"I found out tonight that he wasn't talking about Caleb."

"That's good. Maybe you can take Caleb to dinner with your family on Tuesday night next week?"

"Well, maybe not that soon, but I'd reckon he'll be going there with me shortly." Tara stared at his buggy lights as they disappeared into the darkness. She wished the night had gone on longer so she could have spent more time with him.

Megan waved a hand in front of Tara's face, causing Tara to look at her.

Megan laughed. "You're a goner."

"A goner?"

"You've fallen hard for him. I can see it on your face. You were never like this when you were secretly dating Mark."

"Speaking of that, what about you and Brandon?"

"What do you mean?"

Tara nudged Megan with her elbow. "Aw c'mon. I've never seen you talk like that with any man. I'm surprised you don't want to keep going there every Tuesday with me."

Megan's lips twisted upward at the corners. "We've been talking other than Tuesday nights. He gave me his phone number. He's not Amish, but I wasn't born Amish either."

Tara resisted giving Megan any cautions. It was up to her to decide her own future.

IT WAS four weeks later that Caleb went with Tara to meet her birth family. After Redmond drove them back to the Grabers after dinner, William, Gretchen and Megan had made themselves scarce, giving Tara and Caleb some time alone.

"We must be late getting back," Caleb said when he saw that no one was around.

Tara whispered, "I think they're leaving us alone."

"Oh. Good idea."

"Sit with me," Tara sat on the couch and Caleb sat right beside her.

"Denke for taking me there with you tonight. I'm glad you're letting me into your world."

Tara giggled and took hold of his hand. "You let me into yours."

"My life has an open door and yours is closed."

"You weren't so easy to get to know."

He pulled back and stared at her. "What do you mean?"

"That first time you drove me out to Elizabeth and Joseph's house you didn't say a word."

"I did too."

"Barely. Maybe you grunted once or twice."

Caleb laughed. "I guess you're right. I don't feel comfortable with a lot of people, which leads me to my next suggestion."

"What's that?"

"That we marry."

Tara smiled and looked into his eyes. "I want to marry you, but not right now. Can we wait?"

"For what?"

"I'm adjusting to what I found out about my past and who I am." She waved her hand around her head. "My head's in a muddle."

He grabbed her hand in mid air and lowered it and kept a hold of it. "I don't care if it's next week or next year just give me a proper answer, and you must mean it with all your heart." Caleb looked into her eyes, "Tara, will you marry me?"

"Depends."

"On what?"

"Do you have any interest in cars?"

Frowning, he asked, "Cars?"

She nodded.

He grimaced. *"Nee.* I don't."

"Would you ever leave the community?"

After a silent moment, he answered, "Only if you wanted to leave."

"Really? You'd leave with me?"

"I'd leave reluctantly, but someone has to look after you. Are you thinking of leaving?"

"Nee."

He swallowed hard. "Tara, we've spoken of these things before."

"I know. I'm just making sure I can give you an honest answer to your question."

With a slight squeeze of her hand, he said, "Don't keep a man waiting."

"Come closer and let me whisper my answer." He leaned his head closer to hers, and she whispered, "Yes. I will marry you, Caleb."

Tara now had everything she wanted. She'd learned about and come to terms with her past. Her past had brought her two siblings and a father. Her future came with a man she could trust. Caleb wasn't the best looking man in the community, but he possessed all the qualities that were important to her in a man and more. He'd stand by her, never leave her, and he was open and honest.

A smile spread across Caleb's face after he'd heard the words he'd longed for Tara to say. He turned to face her and their lips met in their very first kiss.

Blessed is the man that endureth temptation: for when he is tried, he shall receive the crown of life, which the Lord hath promised to them that love him.

James 1:12

The End of Book 2

THE NEW AMISH GIRL

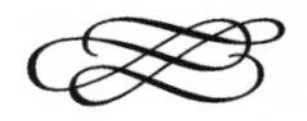

AMISH FOSTER GIRLS BOOK 3

CHAPTER 1

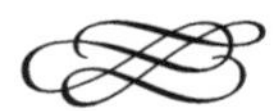

Be strong and of a good courage,
fear not, nor be afraid of them: for the LORD thy God,
he it is that doth go with thee; he will not fail thee, nor forsake thee.
Deuteronomy 31:6

"MY NIECE STEPHANIE is coming to stay with us for a few months."

That was the first time Megan had heard of *Mamm* Gretchen's *Englisch* niece in over two years and that was most likely because Stephanie's father was an outcast. Her father was Gretchen's brother, who had left the Amish when he was a teenager and had never returned.

"Why is she coming?" It was a perfectly simple question and Megan expected the answer to be just as simple.

"Just because," was the answer her foster mother, Gretchen Graber, gave her.

Simple, Megan thought, *but entirely uninformative.*

Megan was one of the two remaining foster children at the Grabers, since the third, Elizabeth, had recently gotten married.

"Well, when's she coming?" Surely *Mamm* Gretchen would tell her that much.

"Today."

"So soon?"

Her foster mother nodded and her lips remained closed.

"Aren't you going to tell me why she's coming here?"

Momentarily ignoring Megan's question, Gretchen looked around the corner of the kitchen into the living room. When Megan peeped around too, she saw that Gretchen was looking at her husband who was reading The Bulletin, an Amish newspaper.

Gretchen ushered Megan to the back of the kitchen and whispered in her ear, "She's gotten into a lot of trouble and Tom thinks she needs time with the community to sort her life out."

Megan searched Gretchen's face. "What kind of trouble?"

Gretchen shook her head so hard that her bottom lip wobbled. "Never mind about that."

"I won't tell anyone." Megan knew, with just a little encouragement Gretchen would reveal all.

"Well, you'll have to pretend you don't know." Gretchen eyed her skeptically.

"Of course. I won't tell anyone anything. I'll pretend I don't know a thing—not one thing."

"She was involved in stealing a large sum of money. The court let her go since it was her first offense, and it helped that Tom told the officials he would have her come here for a time."

Megan tapped a finger on her chin. She figured Gretchen's brother, Tom, did not think that the stay in the Amish community would do her good, but rather, the court might have enforced her stay. As always, Megan's thoughts wandered to Brandon. Megan wondered what Stephanie might steal of hers. It didn't really matter as long as she did not take Brandon. Megan smiled knowing no one would be able to steal him. Anyway, he wasn't even hers—not yet.

"Why are you smiling? Are you looking forward to having another girl in the *haus* since Elizabeth's gone?"

"*Jah,* that's it. It'll be nice having another girl around especially with Tara at work most days and spending the rest of her time with Caleb."

"You must be on your best behavior while she's here. Understood?"

Megan nodded, a little offended at *Mamm* Gretchen thinking that she was ever on anything less than her best behavior.

That afternoon a car pulled up outside the house and then Tom and Stephanie stepped out. Megan watched them out the kitchen window. Stephanie was still beautiful; it didn't take Megan long to notice that. She was fancy and wore fancy clothes and makeup. Megan had to wonder if she'd still look that good with the makeup scrubbed off and dressed in plain Amish clothing.

Mamm Gretchen walked into the house carrying Stephanie's small suitcase while *Dat* William and Tom spoke to each other at Tom's car.

"Stephanie." Megan walked over to Stephanie and gave her a hug, as soon as she walked into the house.

"Hi, Megan."

Stephanie seemed much quieter than Megan remembered. Maybe she was embarrassed at being shuffled away somewhere, hidden amongst their Amish community. Or, maybe she was ashamed over her wrongdoing and humiliated that she'd been arrested.

William came inside after Tom had driven away. "Nice to have you here, Stephanie. You can stay as long as you like."

"Thank you, Uncle William."

Stephanie sounded so sweet that Megan wondered if she was

innocent of the crime she'd been accused of. She couldn't wait to get Stephanie alone to find out exactly what had gone on.

William said to Gretchen, "I've just got a few errands to run and then I've got work waiting down the end of the farm."

Gretchen nodded, not saying a word to her husband, and as William walked out the door, her attention turned to Stephanie's clothes. "We'll have to find you something suitable to wear."

By 'we' Megan knew that Gretchen meant that she'd have to do it. "Come with me, Stephanie," Megan said before Gretchen had the time to ask. "We've plenty of dresses upstairs." Megan picked up Stephanie's suitcase and Stephanie followed her up the stairs.

Megan walked into Elizabeth's old room. "You'll be staying in this room."

"I stayed in this room with Elizabeth last time I was here. I heard she got married just recently."

"She did." Megan pointed to some dresses hanging on the clothes pegs. "They're freshly washed and they should fit you."

Stephanie pulled a face. "Do I really have to wear one of them?"

Megan smiled. "I would if I were you. You know how strict Gretchen and William are. If they ask you to do something, it's a lot easier to do it the first time 'round. They'll always win in the end." Megan passed a yellow dress to Stephanie.

Stephanie took it and held it out at arm's length. "You've got to be kidding me."

Megan giggled. "You'll have to get used to it. Don't worry; everyone wears the same, so it doesn't really matter." Megan studied Stephanie's heavily made up face. "And, sooner or later, Gretchen will ask you to wash your face."

"Oh yeah, the makeup?"

Megan nodded.

"It just gets worse." Stephanie rubbed her head.

Megan sat on the bed. "So what did you do that was so bad?"

With dress in hand, Stephanie sat next to her. "I guess I just got mixed up with some bad people. I thought they were my friends, but when they got questioned it seemed they all blamed me, or one of them did at least."

Megan wondered if anyone was really 'bad.' Now it appeared that Stephanie carried that label just because of one mistake. "Is Gretchen supposed to straighten you out?"

"I guess so." Stephanie threw herself back on the bed and stared up at the ceiling. "What's there to do around here?"

"Chores. Nothing's changed since you were here last."

"I thought so."

Megan was glad that Stephanie was easy to speak with. She'd have a friend while she was staying there.

"Megan, why are you here? How did you come to be here?"

"Well..."

"You don't have to tell me if you don't want to."

"It's okay. I don't mind talking about it. My father died when I was a baby and my mother got very sick and had to give me up. There was no one to look after either of us. No family at all. I don't know what became of my mother after that, but she never came looking for me. My best guess is that she died."

"I'm sorry, Megan. Where did you go when you were a baby? I know you've only been with Gretchen and William for a few years."

"I went from foster home to foster home. I was a sickly child. I don't remember that part, but that's what I've been told. Some of the places I lived in weren't the best. I love it here. This is the only home I've ever truly had."

"I guess I should be grateful for my parents. Mostly I'm just annoyed with them. Now down to the important things. Are there any men around?"

"There are a few who have started visiting recently, but none that I really like. They mostly end up talking to Gretchen. I find it hard to know what to say to them."

"I was talking about for myself." Stephanie giggled. "Anyway, why do you let them talk to Gretchen when they come here?"

"I just don't know what to say."

"I get like that too sometimes. Where can we go to find some men?"

"You want to see Amish men?"

Stephanie nodded.

"Amish men wouldn't be allowed to date *Englisch* girls."

Stephanie smiled widely and tossed the dress in the air. "Well, they won't know because I'll be wearing this." She caught the dress and held it toward Megan who ignored her comments.

On the one hand, she did not want Stephanie to lead any Amish boys astray. On the other, it might be good for her to have an Amish boyfriend to steer her in the right direction. "I'll find you some boots that should fit you."

When Megan came back into Stephanie's room, she had two pairs of boots in her hands. "Here, I've found these. They're slightly different sizes, so one pair should fit. I'll go down and see if *Mamm* needs any help with dinner. Come to the kitchen when you're ready."

"Thanks, Megan."

Here I am, stuck in this place as if I'm in a time warp, Stephanie thought. *I don't even have my cell or my computer.*

Looking around at the bleak room, she pulled a face. Apart from the blue and green quilt on the bed, the room was entirely a bland shade of gray. Nothing was in the room that didn't have a purpose. There were no ornaments, no paintings or posters on the walls—nothing, not so much as a mirror. A bed, a dresser, and a nightstand were all the furniture in the room. She flung herself back and looked up at the ceiling again.

Okay. The bed's comfortable. I suppose that's something.

Stephanie got off the bed and when she pulled the plain gray curtains apart to look out the window, she saw nothing but farmland for miles. The snow had melted away and the low afternoon sun shining through the leafless branches of the trees created shafts of light beyond the barn. It was a pretty sight, but Stephanie would've preferred to be closer to the action. And that meant near a coffee shop.

Looking out to nothingness in the faraway fields, she thought, *Where am I going to get my double caramel lattes from?* She was a city girl at heart.

There wasn't a coffee shop within miles. At home where she lived with her parents, the local coffee shop was a short walk. There she'd meet up with her friends every day. When she'd been living away from home recently, she'd been living above a store in the middle of town and had her choice of cafés.

"Now I'm here in the middle of nowhere!" she mumbled to herself.

She wondered what kind of coffee they served in jail. *Most likely instant coffee. Yuck!* Her mood worsened when she suddenly realized tomorrow was Sunday.

With my luck, it'll be the second Sunday, the Sunday that their church gathering falls.

Stephanie had attended a Sunday meeting when she had stayed with them last time. What stood out in her mind was that the wooden bench seats were hard, and that the men and women sat on different sides of the room. Perhaps she might see Jared Weaver again, unless he'd moved away, or worse, she might learn that he had gotten married.

The only good thing about the Amish church meetings was all the food there was when the service was over. Now that she was watching her figure, she was trying to be less interested in food, but who would notice a few more pounds under the horrid dresses she'd be wearing for the next few months?

Stephanie let go of the curtains and they fell closed, causing the room to once again become gloomy and darkened. She slipped off her jeans and tee shirt and pulled on the purple Amish dress instead of the yellow one Megan had handed to her, and then the traditional black stockings. Lastly, she pushed her feet into one of the pairs of black lace-up boots that Megan had brought to her. She hoped that they would not make her wear a prayer *kapp* like all the other women did since she wasn't really Amish. Stephanie went down to join her aunt and Megan in the kitchen.

As Stephanie helped Megan and Aunt Gretchen in the kitchen, Gretchen handed her cutlery to set the table. As she laid it out, she said, "I thought you said Tara wasn't coming home for dinner?"

"She's not," Megan answered.

"So, I only set… Let me see. There's us three and Uncle William, so that's four of us for dinner and you've given me five of everything."

"That's right. We've got a farm hand who eats with us. He sleeps in a room off from the barn," Megan said.

"He's a nice young man. His name's Jared Weaver," Gretchen said as she got the dinner plates out of the cupboard.

Stephanie froze, clutching the cutlery in her hand. "Jared Weaver?"

Gretchen looked up. "*Jah.* Do you know him?"

"Um. I might remember him from last time I was here. Or maybe not, maybe the name just sounded familiar." She carried on with setting the table, trying to stop herself from smiling too much. Maybe her stay here wouldn't be so bad after all. *He can't be married, not if he's staying in a room off from the barn. There was no mention of a wife.*

Darkness fell and William and Jared came home. William

walked in the door first and then Jared walked into the kitchen. He was every bit as nice-looking as Stephanie remembered him. His hair was thick and dark, with eyes an unusual shade of dark hazel.

"Hello, Stephanie."

He remembered my name! "Hello, Jared."

"You two know each other?" Uncle William asked looking directly at Stephanie.

"We met a couple of years ago," Jared said, smiling at Stephanie.

After they'd taken their seats around the dining table, they closed their eyes to give their silent thanks for the food set before them.

Megan opened one eye and saw that Stephanie had her eyes closed too.

Once they were finished with their prayers, William said, "So we've got the gathering tomorrow, Stephanie."

Stephanie nodded smiling all the while. Megan noticed Stephanie's gaze kept veering toward Jared.

William continued, "You don't have to go if you'd rather stay here."

Megan could not believe what he'd just said, and she stared at him in disbelief. Why was he letting Stephanie off going to the meeting? Didn't she have to live as one of them while she was there? Otherwise, what was the point? Last time she was there Stephanie had to go to all their Amish events including the meetings.

"No that's all right. I'd like to go," Stephanie said.

Megan then transferred her open-mouthed stare toward Stephanie until her foster mother tapped her foot under the table.

"You would really like to go?" Megan asked Stephanie, figuring it might have something to do with Jared.

Stephanie nodded while she spooned food onto her plate from one of the bowls in the center of the table.

The dinner was spent in awkward silence. No one could ask

Stephanie what she'd been up to, or about school because she'd dropped out.

"We've got bees now, Stephanie." Megan interrupted the silence with her statement.

Jared laughed. "You and your bees, Megan."

"Don't laugh, Jared. They're very interesting."

"As long as they keep away from me and don't bite me, I suppose they're okay," Jared said.

"They've never stung you yet, have they?"

"*Nee*, they must be friendly bees."

"You won't mind so much when you're putting their honey on your bread."

"That's true," Jared said.

Stephanie turned to Megan. "So you keep bees, with a queen bee, a hive and everything?"

Megan nodded enthusiastically. "I've got a few hives, in fact, and in the summertime, the man who gave them to me said I'd get enough honey to sell. We'll have more than we can eat. I can show you the hives tomorrow."

William coughed loudly.

Glancing at William's stern face, Megan corrected herself. "Well, tomorrow after the meeting we might have some time. That is if we don't stay on for the young people's singing."

"I'd like that. I've never seen bees' hives before." Stephanie shoveled mashed potato onto her fork.

That night, Megan sat up sewing and wondering what man in the community would be a suitable match for Stephanie. Surely if Stephanie became a part of their community, she'd keep out of trouble. And what better way of doing that than to find her a suitable man? She would keep close to Stephanie tomorrow, and then she would test her matchmaking skills.

CHAPTER 2

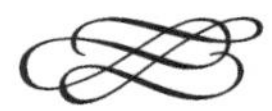

But they that wait upon the LORD shall renew their strength;
they shall mount up with wings as eagles;
they shall run, and not be weary;
and they shall walk, and not faint.
Isaiah 40:31

STEPHANIE DID NOT KNOW whether it was being away from her family and friends or being with her Amish aunt and uncle, but she was thinking about God for the first time in ages.

Even though her father had left the Amish, he believed in God. Her parents had sent her to Sunday School when she was younger, and, despite Stephanie seldom joining them anymore, they regularly attended church together. Stephanie knew that she should pray a prayer of forgiveness. Staying with her aunt and uncle, there seemed no getting away from God.

Dear God, forgive me for all the bad things I've done and all the people who I've hurt. Please lead me and guide me to have a good life. I don't want to make any mistakes anymore. I want to lead a good and happy life. Amen.

Stephanie wasn't sure what she should have prayed, but she remembered that someone once said that if you're pure in your heart, God hears your prayer. She closed her eyes and for the first time in a long time fell asleep quickly, peacefully.

WHEN TARA CAME HOME from spending time with Caleb, Megan waved her over as she stepped in the door.

Tara flopped on the couch next to her.

"Stephanie's here. *Mamm's* niece."

"Already? I thought she wasn't coming until Monday."

"You knew she was coming?"

"Jah."

"*Mamm* didn't tell me until this morning just before she arrived."

"She told me over breakfast just before I left this morning. I wasn't listening properly. Obviously, she must have said she was coming today."

"Oh."

"How much do you know about her?" Tara asked.

Megan said, "All *Mamm* told me was that she'd gotten into trouble and Tom asked the courts if she could come here."

"Yeah, that's what I heard."

"You remember her from a couple of years ago, don't you?" Megan asked.

"I do, but what's she like now?"

"Pretty much the same. I thought she might be interested in Jared since they seemed to get on so well over dinner, but she didn't ask me one thing about him. She did ask me where all the men are, so she's interested in men."

Tara giggled. "Aren't we all?"

Megan pulled a face.

"Except you of course."

"I guess."

"You only like Brandon."

Megan frowned. She wasn't sure that she should be talking to Brandon's half sister about her feelings for him.

"Why don't you come with me on Tuesday night? Brandon will be there."

Every Tuesday night, Tara had dinner with her newfound birth family — her father, her younger sister, and her half-brother, Brandon. Megan had been with Tara at the first dinner and had met Brandon and they'd hit it off right away. Megan was painfully shy with other men, but with Brandon, it was somehow different.

"What about Caleb?" Megan asked. "Doesn't he want to go with you this time?"

"He doesn't have to. He's been the last few times."

"Yeah, I know."

Tara leaned in towards her. "Well?"

"Jah, I'd like to go. *Denke."*

"Good! That's settled, then."

Megan hushed Tara. "You don't want to wake anyone up. How are things with Caleb?"

"What do you mean?"

"Are you sure he doesn't mind waiting to marry you?"

"He agreed to it, and I'm not ready yet."

"Hmmm." Megan frowned at her.

"What was that for? You sound like Gretchen when you do that," Tara said.

"Are you sure you're over Mark?"

"Do you think that's why I'm not rushing into marrying Caleb?"

"Don't get angry, but I thought it might have something to do with it."

Tara shook her head. "I'm not angry. I just don't see how you could think I would still have any feelings for Mark at all after what he's been like."

Megan shrugged. "You liked him once."

"*Jah,* well that was a big mistake. And now he's already marrying Mary Lou after telling me, I don't know how many times, that they were only friends. He was stringing Mary Lou and me along, probably seeing which one would say yes to him first."

"You can't say that for certain."

Tara shrugged. "It's pretty obvious."

"When are they getting married? Have you heard?"

"It'll be at the end of the year. I think someone said November."

"That's a long time to wait."

"I just hope Mark doesn't change his mind. It would break Mary Lou's heart, but that's what type of person he is."

"Yeah, I'd hate to see that happen. I think she's a nice girl."

CHAPTER 3

And now abideth faith, hope,
charity, these three;
but the greatest of these is charity.
1 Corinthians 13:13

"WAKE UP, STEPHANIE."

The next thing Stephanie knew, Megan was shaking her awake.

"We have to leave in fifteen minutes."

Stephanie sat up in bed and rubbed her eyes. "Are you kidding me? It's so early. Far too early."

"Nee, I'm not kidding you. We have to leave soon."

Stephanie groaned. "It feels like I've only just gone to sleep."

Megan didn't answer. She had already left her room. Stephanie got out of bed and pulled on the same dress she had worn briefly the day before. She splashed water on her face from the large bowl on the dresser, trying to wake herself up. There was something freeing about not spending half an hour applying makeup. She was showing the world what she really looked like—flaws and all.

Minutes later, she was downstairs and ready to go. When she looked into the kitchen to see where everyone was, she saw Tara and Gretchen.

"Hello, Tara."

"Hi, Stephanie. I hear you're staying here for awhile."

"I am. You weren't here last night. I started to wait up until you got home, but then I got too tired."

"I got in late. I was out with Caleb."

"You don't have a curfew?"

"Nee, and don't give *Mamm* Gretchen ideas." Tara giggled.

"We only have a quick breakfast on Sundays," Gretchen explained, pretending to ignore the girls' chatter. She pointed at a bowl of cereal and mug of coffee on the table in front of her.

"Thank you." After Stephanie poured a bit of milk into the bowl and ate a couple of spoonfuls of cereal, she drank as much coffee as she could. She was hoping Jared would appear, but he was nowhere to be seen.

"Let's go," William called from the front door.

Stephanie listened to Megan's footsteps running down the stairs, and then heard Gretchen calling her name from the other room.

"I'm coming!" Stephanie yelled back before she filled her mouth with cereal.

"William hates to be kept waiting," Tara whispered to Stephanie before she made her way out of the kitchen.

Once she got to the front door of the house, she looked up at the horse and buggy waiting directly outside.

Megan said, "Oh, I nearly forgot the cookies I made yesterday. Come and help me with them, Tara please?"

As Megan and Tara hurried back to the house to get the cookies, Jared drove past in a buggy pulled by a fine looking gray horse with long silvery mane and tail.

Stephanie leaned across and watched the buggy disappear up the driveway. "Where's he going?" she asked William.

"He's going the same place as us. He likes to take his own buggy when he goes places, even if we're going too."

Megan and Tara returned with two large trays covered with white tea towels. They passed them to Gretchen and Stephanie to hold while they climbed into the buggy.

"Everyone usually brings something to eat," Megan explained when she'd settled into the buggy with the tray on her lap.

Once they were all in the buggy, William instructed the horse to move forward.

"Whose place is the meeting at today?" Stephanie knew that the meetings were held at different people's houses. There was no actual building where the services were held.

"It's at the Zooks' *haus,*" Megan said. "They're an older couple with five grown *kinner* and a heap of *grosskin."*

"Jah." Megan realized that Jeremiah Zook, one of the Zooks' *grosskinner,* might be a match for Stephanie. He was tall and handsome, too boisterous and loud for her, but he might be nice for Stephanie. He'd just come back from his *rumspringa,* so he'd be used to *Englisch* girls and because he had returned to the community, it meant that he was in the community to stay.

Not many of Megan's friend's had been on a *rumspringa*. She would never want to go and sample the *Englisch* world even though she'd not been born Amish. Besides, if she went on *rumspringa* now, what would become of her bees?

CHAPTER 4

For we are saved by hope:
but hope that is seen is not hope:
for what a man seeth, why doth he yet hope for?
Romans 8:24

IT WAS WEIRD, almost otherworldly, to see all the Amish people arriving in their buggies. Stephanie felt like she was on a movie set. There were no cars in sight, just green fields, clear blue skies, horses and buggies, and Amish folk. Since it was a warm day, all the wooden benches were set up in rows outside the *haus*, rather than inside, as they'd been the last time Stephanie was at one of the Amish meetings.

Stephanie was ushered to a seat between Megan and Tara.

During the service, Stephanie's attention was diverted to the young men. From where she sat, she could see two nice looking ones. She'd have to wait until the meeting was over to get a closer look at them.

When Stephanie heard the bishop say the word 'mistake' amongst his ramblings, she listened to what he had to say. The bishop said that mistakes were simply a form of lesson to learn from. In essence, genuine mistakes were learning opportunities. Stephanie found that very useful to her own situation. She could learn from what had happened to her. She had gotten caught for keeping quiet about what she knew. It wasn't fair. In hindsight, if she hadn't been arrested, she might have gotten roped into something bad if she'd seen her friends getting away with what they'd been doing.

When the bishop stopped speaking, the singing started. All the songs were sung in German and Stephanie knew it was useless to attempt to mouth the words to look like she was singing the songs.

Stephanie had to stop herself from giggling as she listened to many of the people singing off key. With no musical instruments accompanying them, the singing sounded dreadful. In contrast to the bulk of the congregation, Megan's voice was a delight. Her voice rang out clear and true like a beautiful bell resounding—every note in perfect pitch.

She looked at Megan and smiled while thinking her voice was such a waste. With a voice like that, she could go far in the normal world.

When the singing finished, Stephanie whispered to Megan, "You have such a beautiful voice."

"*Denke*," Megan said, with a polite nod of her head.

When everyone rose to their feet, Stephanie whispered to Megan again, "Do you like anyone here?"

Megan giggled. "I don't, but I've already picked one out for you. His name is Jeremiah Zook." Megan looked across to the men. "There he is, over there."

Stephanie followed her gaze. "Oh, I know him. He was a friend of one of my friends. I didn't expect to see him again." Stephanie thought it best to admit that she knew him, but not disclose the closeness of their relationship.

"It's funny that you know him. I'd heard he'd just come back from being on *rumspringa*. Is that when you met him?"

"Yes."

"Do you remember him from last time you were here?"

"Not at all." It was the truth. She'd met Jeremiah while he'd been on *rumspringa,* and had no memory of him from her visits to the community over the years.

Megan glanced back over at Jeremiah. "Do you like him?"

"Well, I don't dislike him."

"I was right. I thought you two would like each other." Megan took hold of Stephanie's arm and despite her protests, led Stephanie to Jeremiah.

JEREMIAH WAS NOTICEABLY SHAKEN by her appearance there amongst the Amish. "Stephanie! What are you doing here?"

"Gretchen and William Graber are my aunt and uncle. Anyway, I'm staying with them for a few weeks, possibly months."

He looked up and down at her borrowed Amish clothing. "It's nice to see you again."

Megan interrupted, "Excuse me. I'll leave you two alone; I have someone I must talk to."

Jeremiah turned around to make sure that Megan had gone.

"I told you that Gretchen and William were my aunt and uncle."

"You need to get that money back to me," he hissed.

"I don't have it." Stephanie laughed as she spoke, to make Jeremiah even more upset than he appeared to be.

"Where did it go, then? You were the only one who knew where it was."

Stephanie shrugged her shoulders. "I have no idea. Didn't the police find it?"

Jeremiah stepped in close and, with his bottom jaw jutting out, said, "What are you really doing here?"

Stephanie stood her ground and stared back into his eyes. "I'm visiting and I think I'll stay around a little longer." She walked away. It disappointed her that Jeremiah was only interested in the money. He acted like he didn't care about her one little bit.

When Stephanie reached the drinks table, she took a cup of soda and casually turned to see what Jeremiah was doing. He was leaning against a fence post, still looking directly at her with his hands casually folded across his chest. She turned away. It wasn't the reunion she'd hoped for.

What would he do with thousands of dollars anyway? It's not as if anyone actually needs money in the community. The other Amish don't seem to be driven by greed or money; I wonder why Jeremiah is.

"Stephanie, this is Benny. He's a friend of Jeremiah's," Megan said.

Stephanie jumped in fright, so lost she'd been in her thoughts. She hadn't seen Megan and the young man approach.

"Pleased to meet you, Stephanie." Benny held out his hand.

Stephanie and Benny shook hands. Benny seemed nice, but Stephanie wondered why anyone nice could be a good friend of Jeremiah's.

When evening came, the older folk went home and the young people stayed on for the 'singing.'

The young people sang songs far more lively than the ones sung during the service.

When it was close to over, Megan tugged at Stephanie's arm. "Do you mind if Jeremiah takes you home?"

Her face fell. Tara would've been going home with Caleb and that left her with no options. "Why can't we go together?"

"Benny wants to take me home. Jeremiah said he'd take you home."

By the urgent look in Megan's eyes, Stephanie could see that the buggy ride with Benny meant a great deal. If she did Megan a favor, Megan would owe her one.

Stephanie nodded, yet she did not feel safe being driven home by Jeremiah. It was clear from their earlier conversation he was annoyed with her.

When Megan left, Stephanie was worried.

"Do you want me to take you home?"

Stephanie turned to see that the kind-sounding soft voice belonged to Jared Weaver. "Thanks, Jared, but Megan already arranged for Jeremiah Zook to take me home."

Jared raised his eyebrows. "Are you sure?"

"Yes, it'll be fine." Part of her was afraid of Jeremiah and part of her still craved his approval. Maybe time alone with him would help resolve her feelings for him.

Jeremiah walked up to them and stood between them, almost elbowing Jared out of the way.

Jared did not speak to him, and simply said, "I'll see you later, Stephanie."

"Yes, I'll see you later." Stephanie could sense the tension between the two men.

As they set out for the Grabers' house, it did not take long for Jeremiah to bring up the subject of the money again.

"Tell me where it is."

"What would you do with that money anyway?" Stephanie was annoyed that he looked even more handsome to her in his Amish clothes—the white shirt and black pants— than he had in jeans.

"I could help a lot of people with that money."

She didn't believe a word of what he said. "Phooey. Those dollars are ill-gotten gains. I'm sure that's not what your God would want for you."

He shot her a quick look and then stared back at the road. "That's my business. You don't run my life, so you can't tell me what to do. I had the money and I was responsible for it. You're the only one who could've taken it. I owe other people out of that money."

"I don't know where it's gone. The police got me, and I was in jail for days until the court agreed to send me to stay with my aunt and uncle."

Jeremiah shook his head.

"Anyway, you only care about money." Stephanie tried to contain her anger.

"That's not so. You're the one who ran out on me. I didn't know where you were. I tried to find you," Jeremiah said.

"I went back to live with my parents. You obviously didn't try very hard if you tried at all. Did you confess your sins to God and the bishop for what you did—the robbery?"

Jeremiah shot her a look of disdain. "None of your business."

Stephanie hoped she was getting under his skin a little. "Well, I'm sure God wouldn't be very happy with what you've been up to."

"That's not for you to concern yourself with, Stephanie."

Stephanie looked out at the road. "This isn't the way to Megan's *haus*, is it?"

"*Nee*, I'm taking you somewhere else."

A cold shaft of fear ran down Stephanie's spine. Was he going to kill her? *Nee, of course, he won't hurt me,* she reassured herself, even though she was too scared to look at his face.

Once they were on a quiet, dark road, Jeremiah pulled the buggy off to the side. "Stephanie, I came back to the Amish because the *Englisch* way of life isn't for me. I know I got mixed in with a bad crowd, but from what I saw of the rest of it, I don't like it at all." He lowered his head. "No one really cares about each other in the *Englisch* world. In the community, everyone cares about each other and everyone helps each other out."

Which one was the real Jeremiah? The one who only cared about his money, or the one who sat next to her now talking about helping people and caring for others? She wanted the caring Jeremiah to be the real person, not the one who stole the money. Was he playing her again? Was this just another route he was taking simply to find out about the money?

Unless Jeremiah had some kind of condition which led to sudden mood swings and changes of opinion, he had to be telling her what he thought she wanted to hear. The best thing to do, she figured, was to play along with him.

CHAPTER 5

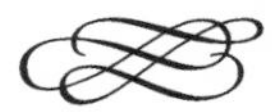

Blessed is the man that trusteth in the LORD,
and whose hope the LORD is.
Jeremiah 17:7

"CAN'T you see the difference, Stephanie?" Jeremiah asked now staring at her more intently.

"In the community?"

Jeremiah nodded.

"It's hard to say. I've only been here a little more than a day. And I've only visited Gretchen and William every few years, and only for a couple of days at a time."

He turned his whole body to face her directly; his soft brown eyes looked intently into hers. "I've been a fool, Stephanie. I don't care about the money. When I saw you again, I was shocked and said the first silly thing that came into my head. Can we go back to how things were between us?"

Stephanie laughed. If he was pretending that he was interested in her to find out where the money was, he was certainly doing a very good job of it. "Of course, things can't go back to how they were. We were living together for months; that certainly wouldn't be accepted amongst the Amish, would it?"

"*Nee,* but I didn't mean that. I want you to be my girl if you decide to stay in the community."

Stephanie looked ahead onto the blackened road that was lit partially from the moonlight and partially from a distant street lamp. "It's too early to tell."

Yes, she wanted to be held in his strong arms once more, but only if she could trust him and now she knew she couldn't.

"Take all the time you need; I'm not going anywhere." He clicked the horse forward.

It was a romantic scene, clip-clopping down the deserted dark road under the moonlight, but Stephanie was not going to be sidetracked by emotion. Her head had to be clear. It hadn't been clear when she'd fallen in love with him; she had to stay focused.

A test – ahh that's it, she thought. She would find a way to prove that he loved her and was not simply after the money that he thought she still had.

When he pulled up at Gretchen's house, he tried to prolong their goodbye. To save herself from falling back under his spell, she thanked him for the ride and leaped from the buggy and hurried to the house.

After she was safely inside, she waited until she heard his buggy leave. Then she went up to Megan's room hoping she'd be home. Megan was sitting up in bed doing some needlework by the gaslight on her nightstand.

"There you are," Megan said.

"Yeah. Here I am."

"Did you enjoy your drive with Jeremiah? You took a while to get here."

"I know. It was okay." She slumped onto the edge of Megan's bed. "What's Benny's story?"

Megan smiled. "He's a friend. He's nice enough, but I like someone else."

"Were you trying to set me up with Jeremiah? Is that why you went home with Benny?"

Megan covered her mouth with her fingertips and gave a small giggle. "I thought you two might like each other. He looked at you as though he was fond of you. I could see it in his eyes."

"How would you know if someone is truly in love with you?"

"You would feel it in your stomach, or he might tell you that he loves you."

Stephanie was silent while she considered what Megan said, since Megan was a little older. "What if someone has shown he can't be trusted? How would you believe someone like that again?"

"Stephanie, are you talking of a real person?"

Stephanie was distracted by sounds of a horse outside. "Is that a buggy?"

"It's just Jared coming home."

"Megan, if I tell you something will you keep it quiet?"

Megan frowned. "I don't like knowing secrets in case someone is in danger and I have to tell."

"It's nothing like that, but I can't keep it to myself any longer and Aunt Gretchen wouldn't understand."

"Okay. What is it?"

Stephanie considered it would not matter if she told Megan all about her situation. She told her the whole story, but left out some minor details of the robbery.

"You two were in love and living together? The same Jeremiah Zook who drove you home tonight?"

Stephanie nodded. "Yeah, but now that he's back in the community, I'm guessing he wants to keep that part quiet."

"Well, I see. You think he might think you still have the money, so he's pretending to still like you and hoping you'll give it to him?"

Stephanie pouted. "When you say it like that it does sound far fetched. But, I was wondering if I might be able to test his love in some way."

Megan was quiet for a moment. "I can't see that it can possibly be done."

"Oh, I was hoping you might be able to think of something."

Megan unraveled her braids. "*Nee,* I don't think you can test someone's love."

"Well, what should I do? He says that he wants me to be his girl, but what if it's just for the money?"

"It doesn't sound right to me," Megan said, as she ran her fingers through her long hair.

"What do you mean?"

"You'd have to become Amish to be his girl now that he's back in the community. Did he mention that?"

She shook her head. "He didn't. If he did, I don't recall it. Well, he sort of implied it when he said he wanted me to be his girl if I stayed here. And another thing, he didn't come to find me and if he really loved me, he would've looked for me, wouldn't he? Even when he thought I'd taken the money, he still didn't come looking for me."

"Just wait, then. Take things slowly and let him prove himself. If it's an act, he can't play the part forever."

"You're very wise, Megan, very wise. I'm sorry we didn't get to see your bees today."

"We can see them tomorrow."

Stephanie nodded and left Megan alone and went back to her own room. Maybe it was a silly idea, making a test to see if he really loved her. Megan was right; she should just give it time and see what happens. She knew that she had been too spontaneous, too impetuous, in the past. From now on, she would wait and take her time with important decisions. If she'd taken her time back then, she most likely wouldn't have gotten mixed up with Jeremiah and his friends, and now she knew she should've left him as soon as he told her about the robbery.

CHAPTER 6

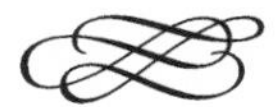

He that loveth not knoweth not God;
for God is love.
1 John 4:8

"DON'T you have to wear some special kind of equipment? Like a net over you and a big helmet thing?"

"I never do. They know me. I used to help the man who gave them to me." They continued walking to the beehives with the melting snow causing moisture to seep through their boots.

"Yeah, well they don't know me and I don't fancy getting bitten by any of them. Bitten, or stung, or whatever you call it. With my luck, I'll be allergic and then I'll swell up and die."

Megan laughed when Stephanie puffed out her cheeks and staggered crookedly.

"I've been stung a couple of times." Megan laughed again. "Maybe I shouldn't have told you that. You just pull the stinger out."

"Yuck! Seriously? I'm not gonna get close to them, then."

"I was joking just now. I have all the equipment to wear and enough for you too. There they are." Megan pointed to her beehives.

"I'll just watch from over here and hope they don't swarm me."

"They won't do that unless you roll around in honey first."

"All the same, I'll stay over here."

Megan waved Stephanie to come along. "They won't come out; it's too cold. They'd die if they all came out."

"Seriously?" Stephanie asked taking a step forward.

"Yes. They have to stay in the hive throughout the cold weather. Don't worry; you can come closer. If I opened it now, they'd all die because all the heat would go out of the hive."

Stephanie walked over and had a look at the hive closest to Megan.

"I've packed all the hay around the hives to insulate them and help keep them warm and keep the cold out."

"They stay there right through the winter?"

"*Jah.* The main job for them is to keep the Queen bee alive. Every hive has a queen bee. And the job of the worker bees is to surround the Queen flapping their wings to keep her warm and keep the temperature up. They live on the honey in there while they're doing that."

"Oh, that's interesting."

"*Jah,* they are interesting. I told you that. A few of them at a time will come out and fly around on a warm day, because they need to eliminate their waste, but then they'll go right back in and a few others will come out. But they won't all come out at once in the freezing cold. They are highly organized."

"What else do you have to do with them, or for them?"

"I have to give them syrup before the flowers are blooming when winter ends, when the weather warms up. If I don't do that, they could die if they didn't get enough food."

"You're brave being around them."

"They give me something to do."

"Will we come back on a warmer day and see if any come out?"

"Okay. If you want to."

"Yeah, but I'm going to keep my distance, don't you worry about that."

On the way back to the house, Stephanie thought she could see Jared in a distant field. "Is that Jared?"

Megan squinted into the distance. *"Jah."*

"What's he doing?"

"Looks like he's fixing fences."

"Let's go over and see."

Megan shook her head. *"Nee.* I'm too cold. I need to warm myself by the stove. You go if you want."

"You don't mind?"

"Nee. Go on."

Stephanie stood still on the cold ground while Megan marched back to the house, then she hurried to Jared, so she could get there before he finished the fence repair. Though not too quickly. Otherwise, he might look up and think she was overly keen to speak with him. Even though she was, she didn't want him to know that.

He looked up when she was around twenty paces away, and waved.

"Hello." She waved back.

"What are you doing out here?"

"I was taking a tour of Megan's bees."

He laughed and wiped his hands on his pants. "I don't know why she likes those bees so much."

"Yeah, me either. It's an unusual hobby to have."

"I suppose they do give her an interest and they produce honey that can be sold."

"Ah, spoken like a practical Amish man."

His hazel eyes twinkled and he grinned. "That's what I am. Being practical is a good thing."

"Sometimes it is, I guess. Anyway, what are you doing?"

"*Ach*. Fences always need repairing. When you finish one spot, there's always another."

"What do you do here exactly? Why did you come to live here?"

"I have no family anymore. A family in the community raised me after my parents died. They took me in." Jared chuckled. "They had five *kin*, so I guess they figured one more wouldn't make a difference. Then, as I got older, I started having a difference of opinion with some of the children. Not the parents mind you. The Zooks gave me a good life and they were caring and kind. I'm still close to them."

"That's so sad that your parents died."

Jared nodded. "I'll see 'em again some day."

"You came to live here because you were having disagreements?"

"That's about it. William must've come to hear of it because he offered me my board and keep, with a salary in exchange for farm work. He never needed a farm hand before."

"He's getting older."

"*Jah*, maybe that's it. Or, maybe he was rescuing me and giving me a place where I could be myself."

"Uncle William is kind. I can see him doing that."

He leaned against the fence post. "I remember you from a couple of years ago."

She stepped closer. "I remember you, too."

"*Jah*, It was at a singing and it was one of the hottest days I can remember."

"I was overheated and my head was aching. You noticed there was something wrong and you found out I was sick from the heat and you brought me ice wrapped in a cloth to put on my head."

"You've got a good memory."

"You were my hero."

He chuckled and his gaze fell to the ground as though he was embarrassed. "I don't think I've been called anyone's hero before." Looking back up at her, he said, "I saw a girl in distress and I was just doing what anyone would do."

"No one else did it, though. It was only you. I never forgot that, or you."

"Me too." He stared at her for a moment before he looked back at his tools.

Stephanie could tell that he liked her from the way he looked at her, with just the hint of a smile around the corners of his lips.

With his head, he nodded toward the fence. "Want to learn how to mend a fence?"

Stephanie laughed. *I probably need to mend a few fences, but not fences like these.* "Yeah, I'd like to watch."

She stayed with him until he mended one stretch of fence, and then he had to leave to meet Uncle William somewhere, so Stephanie headed back to the house.

CHAPTER 7

Greater love hath no man than this,
that a man lay down his life for his friends.
John 15:3

The next day.

"STEPHANIE, would you like to come with me while I take Tara into work in town?" Megan asked over breakfast.

"I'd love that."

Aunt Gretchen said, "And I've got a list of things I want you girls to get me from the farmers market. No need to hurry right back."

Stephanie's face beamed. "Thank you, Aunt Gretchen."

Stephanie looked down at the bacon dish her aunt had prepared. She wasn't certain what it was, and ate it all the same.

After breakfast, Stephanie went to the barn with Megan to hitch the buggy. While she was there, she looked around for Jared.

She hadn't seen the place where he stayed, but she knew it was close by the barn.

"He's not here."

"What do you mean?"

"Jared's not here. He goes to work early with William."

"Oh, I didn't know I was being that obvious."

Megan said, "You weren't, but I've noticed the two of you seem to have a thing together. The way you talk to each other."

"Really? You noticed that?"

"Oh *jah*. I saw it last night at the evening meal. Now, do you know how to hitch a buggy?"

"No. Is it hard?"

"Not when you know what you're doing."

"You do it and talk me through what you're doing, and I'll watch and learn."

When the buggy was hitched to the horse, Megan asked Stephanie to go and fetch Tara who was still getting ready for work.

When Tara came out, they all got into the buggy. Megan was in the driver's seat and she headed the horse down the driveway.

Stephanie leaned over from the back seat. "Can I have a go at driving the buggy?"

Tara asked, "Have you ever driven one before?"

"No, but it looks easy enough."

"You'd have to learn all the road rules for buggies," Megan said.

"Just let me have a go down one of the back roads."

Tara turned around and looked at her. "We couldn't let you do that without asking *Onkel* William first."

"And, he'd want to teach you properly first," Megan added.

"Come on; he'll never know. I won't tell anyone."

Megan said, "*Nee.* You have to ask *Onkel* William if he'd teach you."

Stephanie slumped back into the seat and crossed her arms in front of her. These girls were no fun at all.

The rest of the trip, Stephanie remained silent while she listened to Megan and Tara talk about the dinner they were going to that night. When they arrived in town, Tara got out and then, after they'd said goodbye to her, Stephanie got into the front seat.

"Where to now?" Stephanie asked, hoping to do something fun.

"*Mamm* wants us to go to the farmers market."

"I know that, but isn't there something else we could do before that? Something more fun? Aunt Gretchen said we needn't hurry back."

"Like what?"

"I don't know. What do you usually do for fun?"

"I look after the bees, go to the singings, and sometimes in the summer we have volleyball games."

Stephanie folded her arms in front of her. *You've got to be kidding!*

"We could go to the café where Elizabeth works," Megan suggested.

Stephanie's face lit up. "I'd like that. Do they have caramel lattes?"

"I'm sure they would."

"Okay let's go. My father heard from Aunt Gretchen that Elizabeth just got married."

"That's right, and she married Joseph. And Tara's boyfriend is Joseph's older brother, Caleb."

Stephanie rolled her eyes. "And now you like Tara's half brother, Brandon?"

Megan giggled. "I do. I don't know if anything will ever come of it with him not being Amish."

"You're not really Amish, so what does it matter?"

"I'm not baptized yet, but I always want to stay in the community. I don't want to leave."

"I can see how that would be a problem for you. It would be

easier for you to leave, though, than to expect him to come into the community. That would be a hard thing for him to do."

"I know. Maybe I'd be better off keeping away from him and not going to Tara's family dinner tonight."

"No, you must go. You might regret it if you don't. He might be your soulmate."

"I don't know if I believe in that kind of thing."

"That doesn't mean they're not real."

"Brandon's so easy to talk with. I'm not nervous around him at all, not like I am with most men. He saw right into me, like he knew who I was right away. We connected."

"That's a lovely story. I hope I find someone like that one day."

When Megan had stopped the buggy, Stephanie looked around. "Are we close by the café?"

"It's just around the corner."

Together they walked up the street, and strolled around the corner to the café.

Megan stepped back to allow Stephanie through the door first. Finding an empty table near the window, Stephanie sat down in the seat furthest from the door.

After Megan caught sight of Elizabeth and gave her a wave, she sat opposite Stephanie.

"I guess you know Elizabeth quite well since she's been with Gretchen and William for the longest?" Megan asked.

"We've met a few times over the years. I wouldn't say I know her any better than you or Tara."

Elizabeth hurried over to them and greeted them while she passed them each a menu. "What are you doing in town?"

Megan answered, "We drove Tara into work and *Mamm* wants us to get some things from the markets for her."

"Do you have caramel lattes?" Stephanie asked.

"*Jah,* we do."

"Goodie. I'll have a double caramel latte, please. And can I have that in a glass, not a mug?"

"Sure. What about you, Megan?"

"I'll have a lemon cheesecake and just a black coffee, thanks."

"Oh, that sounds good. Can I have a lemon cheesecake too, please?"

"Of course." Elizabeth nodded and hurried away.

Stephanie looked around at the crowded coffee shop. It was nine o'clock and it seemed they'd made it in time for the breakfast rush. "I wonder what it's like working in a place like this."

"Have you ever had a job?" Megan asked.

"No, have you?"

"Nee. But I guess I'll have to get a job soon, unless I get married."

"Elizabeth is married and she's got a job."

"A lot of women are married and have a job. Maybe my husband will want me to have a job to bring in more money."

"What kind of thing would you do?"

Megan sighed. "I wish I could just have babies and sell honey. I'd need a lot more bee hives to make enough money to matter, though."

"That sounds better than a regular job to me."

"What about you?" Megan asked.

"That's what my father's always asking me. He's sick of giving me money all the time. *You need a job,* is what he says all the time." She'd lowered her voice to imitate him, which made both girls laugh.

"You're not going to college?"

"No. I don't know what I'll do. I'm not interested in anything, so I'll just have to get some boring old job I guess."

Elizabeth brought their lemon cheesecakes to the table and set them down. "The drinks are just coming out now."

A waiter soon followed with their drinks.

After Stephanie arranged her cake and latte on the table in just the right place, she happened to look out the window to see an

Amish man waiting outside the post office. "Who's that? I didn't notice him at the meeting. Is he Amish, or a Mennonite?"

Megan made a sound in the back of her throat. "That's Mark. He used to be Tara's secret boyfriend. He's not exactly trustworthy. Just when she thought they were about to get engaged, he disappeared. When he came back, he said he wanted to marry her, but then everyone kept seeing him around with another woman—Mary Lou. Now he's getting married to her."

Not liking the sound of that, Stephanie took another look at him. "Why is it always the handsome ones who are like that?"

"I don't know."

Stephanie put her fork into her lemon cheesecake and broke off a bit to taste. It melted in her mouth and the tang of the lemon perfectly complemented the smooth texture. "Wow! This is really delicious."

"I know. They make the best cheesecakes here."

"I wouldn't mind learning a bit of cooking while I'm staying at Aunt Gretchen's."

"That'll make her happy. She loves to show people how to cook."

"Yeah, but I only want to make the desserts and the sweet things."

Megan laughed. "That's a start."

Stephanie looked back out the window, now seeing a woman with Mark. She asked Megan, "Is that the woman he's going to marry?"

"Yeah, that's Mary Lou."

"They look well-suited."

"Don't say that around Tara. I think she's still angry with him."

Stephanie raised her eyebrows. "Okay. I won't even mention his name." She took a long drink of her latte. When she finished, she asked, "What's Elizabeth's husband like? I didn't see him at the meeting."

"He's lovely. He matches with Elizabeth just beautifully. His family moved here recently and I guess it was love at first sight for the both of them."

"Kind of like you and Brandon?"

Megan giggled. "Maybe. Who knows?"

"I'm going to wait up for you tonight so you can tell me all about him, and what happened."

"Would you?"

Stephanie nodded, as she now had a mouthful of cheesecake.

"Thank you. It would be nice to have someone to talk things over with. I can't talk to Gretchen about it because I told her I was going to stay in the community and then she might think I'm going to leave. I don't see much of Elizabeth now that she's married, and I can't really talk to Tara about him too much, with him being her half brother and all."

"Well then, it's a good thing I came when I did." Stephanie sipped on her latte. It had just the right amount of caramel. If only the coffee shop were closer to Aunt Gretchen's.

"I'm glad you came, Stephanie."

Stephanie liked Megan's soft and gentle nature. The downside of being so easygoing was that she might easily be taken advantage of. Maybe she could teach Megan a thing or two to protect herself.

Elizabeth appeared and pulled a chair up to the table, a glass of orange juice in her hand. "I've got a ten minute break. What are you doing today after you go to the markets?"

"Most likely chores, chores and then some more chores," Stephanie said while rolling her eyes, which made Elizabeth and Megan giggle.

ON THE WAY home later in the day after they'd been to the market, Stephanie asked, "Can we go past Jeremiah's house?"

"Why would you want to do that?"

Stephanie pouted. "Just because."

"Okay. It's not too much out of the way."

"Thank you, Megan."

Megan chuckled. "I won't even ask."

The house was set well back from the road, so there wasn't much to see.

"Looks like no one's at home," Stephanie said, gazing at the house as Megan slowed the horse to a walk. "Okay, thanks, Megan. Have you been to his house before?"

"Once or twice. Aunt Gretchen goes visiting every once in awhile and I go with her. She's a friend of Jeremiah's mother."

"That's interesting."

"Why? Are you going to ask Aunt Gretchen something about Jeremiah?"

Stephanie laughed. "No. There's nothing I want to know about him. I know all I want to know about him already." Once they were well past the house, Stephanie asked, "And you're going to see Tara's family tonight?"

"Yes. I've been there a couple of times before. Tara has dinner with them every Tuesday. Either her father or Brandon will come and collect her and bring her home. Caleb's gone with her a couple of times, too."

"I'm excited for you."

Megan giggled. "Me too."

"Would you leave the community for him?"

"I don't even want to think about it. It probably won't come to anything."

A buggy appeared at the end of the road.

"Who's that, Megan?"

Megan squinted hard. "I think it's Jeremiah."

"Oh no. Is this the road we'd normally take?"

"No, it's not, but he won't know where we've come from."

"Don't slow down, go faster."

"If he slows, we'll have to slow too and then stop and talk. That's the way things are done on these quiet back roads."

Stephanie breathed out heavily and slumped down further in her seat. It had been a dumb idea to have Megan drive past his house.

She closed her eyes and wasn't happy when she felt the buggy slow. Opening her eyes when the buggy came to a halt, she looked over to see Jeremiah alone in his buggy.

He leaned over. "What are you two doing out this way?"

"I'm taking Stephanie out for a drive. It's such a nice day today."

Stephanie looked at him and he gave her a smile. She gave him a small smile before she looked away.

"Why don't you come inside and have something to eat?"

"Nee, denke. We've got Aunt Gretchen waiting on things we've got from the markets."

He dipped his head down keeping his gaze focused on Megan. "You're coming back from the markets?"

Megan nodded. *"Jah,* and I thought I'd show Stephanie around on the way back."

"Call in sometime. You know how *Mamm* likes to get visitors."

"I will. Err... we will," Megan gave Stephanie a sideways glance.

They said their goodbyes, and then Megan lightly slapped the reins against the horse, telling him to move.

"That was a piece of bad luck," Stephanie whispered.

"Jah, I should've realized it was around the time of the midday meal."

"He seemed suspicious. Like he knew we'd gone past his house deliberately." Stephanie shrugged her shoulders. "Too bad. I don't know how I ever liked him. Now I just feel as though someone else had taken over my body."

"And your mind," Megan added with a grin.

"Especially that," Stephanie said with a laugh. Megan joined in, and they giggled together as the horse clip-clopped down the road.

CHAPTER 8

He delivereth me from mine enemies:
yea, thou liftest me up above those that rise up against me:
thou hast delivered me from the violent man.
Psalm 18: 48

When five o'clock came, Megan rushed upstairs to get ready for dinner with Tara's family. Stephanie followed close behind.

"When's Tara's father coming?" Stephanie asked.

"He'll be here soon."

"Well, I guess you'll have to wear one of these horrible dresses." She touched the dresses that hung near the door.

"Yes. I'm just going to wear what I normally do. There's nothing wrong with them. I made them all myself with *Mamm's* help."

"That won't attract him."

"I don't think he thinks like that, Stephanie."

"Trust me. All men think of things like that."

"Brandon is different."

"I hope so, if you're going to wear something like that. It might be okay to wear things like that around Amish men but normal men... Well, I just don't think you should wear it."

"I have to. I've got nothing else anyway. If he's not interested in me for myself, then he's not the right man for me."

Stephanie sat on Megan's bed. "You're so confidant in who you are, Megan."

"Really?"

"You're quiet, but you know how you want things to be."

"I guess I do. I never thought of myself as confident before."

Stephanie picked up Megan's pillow and hugged it. "I think you are," Stephanie said, while thinking, *Wearing that dress you'd have to be confident.* "And what do you want to happen there with Brandon tonight?"

"What do you mean?"

"What outcome are you hoping for?"

"I'm hoping we get to have a nice talk like we do every time I go there."

Stephanie's face soured. "Talk? Is that all?"

"Well, what else could happen? I'm not sure what you mean."

"I thought you'd want him to ask you out or something, like on a date."

Megan stopped brushing her hair. "That would really complicate things."

Stephanie threw the pillow back to the top of the bed and then crossed her legs under her. "What's the point in going, then?"

"I thought you said it was a good idea."

"Yes, because you like him, but what's the point of liking him if you can't get closer to him? And the only way to do that is to go on a date with him."

Megan started braiding her hair. "I just thought I had to get to know him more."

"What's the point of that if you can't date him? I think you have to decide if you want to stay in the community or leave it."

"*Nee.* I wouldn't want to leave. I couldn't."

"I can tell you right now, and I don't even know the man, but he won't join the community."

"What makes you so sure?"

"It's not likely that he will. Only old people have ever joined the community, as far as I know, and they join with their family."

"I have to trust in *Gott.* If it's *Gott's* will that Brandon joins the community, then he will."

"Have you told Tara about this?"

"She knows I like him, but I don't think she knows how much. It's awkward to talk to her about him because of him being her half brother."

"I just don't want to see you being disappointed."

"That's nice of you. Don't worry; I won't be."

Stephanie kept quiet while Megan finished braiding her hair.

"You have such pretty hair and no one ever gets to see it."

"You know why we wear the *kapps,* don't you?"

"Yes, I do. I just reckon that Brandon would like to see your pretty hair."

"The man I marry will see my hair."

Stephanie had nothing to say. Megan's views were so different from her own.

"Now, what color dress should I wear?" Megan pointed to three dresses, dark green, a purple grape-color, and a brown color.

"Are they the only choices?"

"Yes."

"Oh. Well, hold them up against you."

In turn, Megan held the dresses against her.

"I'd say the purple one. The others are too dark and depressing."

"Okay."

Megan gave a little giggle and while she got changed, Stephanie looked away from the sight of Megan's boring plain white underwear.

On hearing a car, Stephanie jumped off the bed and ran to the window.

"That must be Tara's father. Wow! That's some expensive car."

"Is it? I didn't know."

Tara called out from downstairs, "Are you ready, Megan?"

Megan yelled back that she was coming. Looking back at Stephanie, she said, "I'll see you tonight and don't forget to wait up for me. I'll tell you everything."

"I will."

Stephanie followed Megan downstairs, and when Tara and Megan left the house, she walked into the kitchen to find Gretchen.

"Not many for dinner tonight," Gretchen said when she looked up to see Stephanie.

"Can I do something to help?"

"Everything's done. We're having an easy dinner tonight. We're having leftovers from what we've had the last couple of nights."

"I'll set the table, then."

"Denke. Onkel William and Jared will be here soon."

While Stephanie set the table, she said, "Jared tells me he used to live with the Zooks."

"That's right. He hasn't been here long. He'd been living with the Zooks since his parents died."

"Were his parents Amish?"

"Jah, they were. His *mudder,* Prudence, was a *gut* friend."

"I wonder why he didn't stay with the Zooks?" Stephanie was fishing to find out if Jared leaving the Zooks had something to do with Jeremiah.

"That's not your business and it's not my business."

Stephanie whipped her head around to stare at Gretchen. From the irritation in her voice, Stephanie guessed that something had gone on between Jared and the Zooks. Her best guess was a falling out with Jeremiah.

"Perhaps they'd had some kind of falling out?"

“Don't stare at me with those big brown eyes, Stephanie. I'm not gonna tell you.”

OVER DINNER, Gretchen and William talked about the farm while Jared and Stephanie talked about what had changed in the community since Stephanie's last visit. This was not what Stephanie wanted to talk about, but there was nothing else she could say to Jared within earshot of her aunt and uncle.

CHAPTER 9

O Lord, thou hast brought up my soul from the grave:
thou hast kept me alive, that I should not go down to the pit.
Psalm 30:3

It was Brandon who'd come to collect Tara and Megan. Megan noticed that his face lit up when he learned that she was coming to dinner as well as Tara.

When they got to Tara's birth father's house, Megan was given a warm welcome from Tara's father and her younger sister, Avalon.

"Has Brandon told you about his volunteer work?" Avalon asked Megan.

"No. He hasn't mentioned it." She looked back at him. "What kind of volunteer work do you do?"

"I help out two nights a week with a van that goes around feeding the homeless."

"That's a good idea."

Redmond, Tara's birth father, explained, "It's a program our church has started."

"Before that, he worked at a helpline," Avalon said with a twinkle in her eyes.

Brandon laughed. "I much prefer the van work."

"Why? What's the helpline?" Megan asked.

"People call in if they're having a problem; mostly they're stressed about some situation that's going on in their lives. It's a big responsibility to be on the other end of those calls. Now, we've got trained professionals on the helpline. I had some training, but I'm not qualified properly in counseling. That's best left to the experts."

Megan couldn't take her eyes from Brandon. "I think it's wonderful that you give your time like that."

"It's not much really. Care to help me in the kitchen, Megan?"

"Yes, sure." Megan jumped to her feet, not needing to be asked twice.

When they reached the kitchen, he leaned over and looked into the oven briefly and then leaned against the counter. "I've made lasagna tonight and we're having it with salad."

"It smells lovely."

"I hope you like it. It's got five different cheeses and two sauces in it, and five different levels. My mother used to make it and she showed me how to make it."

"That's nice."

"I know you've told me you never knew much about your mother, but have you ever tried to find her?"

"No. I've thought about it because of Elizabeth and now Tara knowing about their parents and meeting them."

"Aren't you curious?"

"No. I guess I should be, but I'm not. I'm happy where I am now and I don't want to upset the apple cart."

"I can understand that."

"Can you?"

"Yes."

"Not many people understand me. I keep thinking that it might not turn out well for me if I met her. It's been good for Tara and Elizabeth. I just think, I'm happy now, so I figure, why going digging in the past? If she wants to find me, she can. It wouldn't be that hard for her. The other thing is, I'd be sad to learn that she died, if she has passed away. My father died when I was just a baby and she was too sick to look after me. If I found out she died..."

"I see."

Megan shrugged. "It doesn't bother me only because I do my best not to think about it. Gretchen is my mother now. She's the only foster mother who made me feel loved and like I belonged somewhere." Megan blinked back tears. There had been so many lonely days in her past.

"We certainly got a surprise to learn about Tara."

"I guess you would've."

"It makes me see my mother in a different light. She wasn't perfect after all." He gave a chuckle.

"Is that what she seemed to be—perfect?"

"She was always telling us what to do. Nothing was quite good enough. Maybe that had something to do with her missing the child she gave away."

"She was your stepmother wasn't she, Brandon?"

"Yes, but she never made me feel I was anything other than her own child. I don't remember her disappearing when I was two, when she separated from my father and had Tara. All my memories are after she came back, it seems."

"Did she have high expectations of you?"

He chuckled again. "If I got ninety eight in a test she'd ask me where I lost those two marks. Getting second was never good enough, I had to be first."

"That doesn't sound encouraging."

"It made me strive to do my best in everything, whether it was sports or school. But, it also made me feel I was never quite good enough."

"It sounds like she was doing her best to encourage you."

"I guess she was. That was her way. That might have been how she was raised."

"I notice your father says grace before every meal. Is that because you all go to church?"

"We've always gone to church. That's where Mom and Dad met."

"I didn't know that. Is church an important part of your life?"

"Very much. I put God first in everything. Would you like to come with me in the van this Friday night?"

"I'd like that very much."

"Good." He rubbed his hands together. "I'll pick you up from your house at five, and then you can come and see where we cook the food and what we do from there."

"I'd love that."

When Megan heard footsteps heading toward them, she was disappointed they were about to be interrupted. It was Avalon.

"Can't you two talk after dinner? We're all starving."

Brandon frowned at his sister. "I'm waiting for the rolls to warm."

"Sure you are," Avalon said with a cheeky smile, glancing over at Megan.

Brandon picked up a piece of celery out of the salad bowl and threw it at her. Avalon ducked out of the way just in time.

He rolled his eyes. "Teenagers."

Megan kept it quiet that she was still a teenager, although at eighteen she wasn't so very young. Perhaps he thought she might be older?

. . .

MEGAN LEFT that night more impressed than ever with Brandon. He believed in God and even did charitable works. He was definitely a man that she could see herself with, but would someone like him want her?

WHEN TARA and Megan arrived home, Tara went straight to bed because she had to get up for work the next morning. Megan was pleased to see that Stephanie had waited up for her, and now they headed into the kitchen.

"Well, what happened?" Stephanie asked.

"You won't believe it. He goes to church and he does things for charity. He helps the homeless."

"You've got to be kidding!"

"I'm not."

"He's like your perfect man."

"I know."

"I'm boiling water for tea."

Megan nibbled on the end of her fingernail while she followed Stephanie into the kitchen.

"So, what are you looking so worried about?"

Sitting down at the kitchen table, Megan said, "He's asked me to go with him in the van when they give the food out."

"That's good, isn't it?"

"Yes, but I'm nervous. Does that mean he likes me?"

Stephanie laughed. "Of course it does. He wouldn't bother taking you if he didn't like you."

"I guess that's right. He's collecting me from here and that's a long way out of his way. What worries me is Tara knows I'm going with him and hasn't said anything to me." Megan sighed. "What if she doesn't want me to like him? She might want someone better for him."

Stephanie raised her hands in the air. "Wait and see. Anyway, she's the one who invited you there tonight. You're just looking for things to worry about."

"Thanks. I'll trust in God and see what happens."

"Okay."

When the water boiled, Stephanie stood to make the tea.

Stephanie knew it was time to keep quiet and stop asking questions about Brandon. "Anyway, didn't you say you often had men calling 'round to see you?"

"Jah, you asked me that before. It seems they've stopped coming. Two came just before you got here and two others the week before that."

"Just my luck. I probably scared them away," Stephanie said as she poured the boiling water into the teapot.

CHAPTER 10

For his anger endureth but a moment;
in his favour is life: weeping may endure for a night,
but joy cometh in the morning.
Psalm 30:5

WHEN THEY WERE at another singing on that week's Thursday night, Stephanie was glad she had kept her distance from her old boyfriend, Jeremiah. He was giving attention to another girl. Was he trying to make her jealous? If so, that was a cruel way to gain her attention. It did nothing to make her want to be with him; in fact, it made her feel more distant. She pushed him out of her mind and walked over to Jared, who was heading to the food table.

He glanced over at her. "How are you enjoying your Amish vacation, Stephanie?"

"Different from what I'm used to."

Jared laughed. "I imagine it would be."

"Have you ever been on *rumspringa,* Jared?"

"Who me? *Nee,* never. I'm happy here in the community and I'd never want to be anywhere else."

"Where's your *familye?*"

Jared frowned at her. "I told you that my parents died and the Zooks took me in when I was twelve. I grew up with Jeremiah and his *bruders.*"

"Yeah, I know. I'm sorry to ask again." Stephanie glanced at Jeremiah, only to see him still speaking to the same girl. "You don't seem to care for Jeremiah too much."

Jared laughed. "Is it that obvious?"

Stephanie nodded.

"I don't like to speak ill of anyone, so I won't say anything further."

"Has he done something to you?"

"Not so much. All I'll say is that some people say one thing and do another."

Stephanie knew exactly what Jared meant. She wondered what had happened to Jared's folks, but she didn't like to ask. As Jared rolled a small sausage into a slice of bread, Stephanie took another look at him. He had a calm and assertive air about him and a confidence beyond his years, which she found appealing. Leaning over the table, Stephanie took hold of a strawberry and popped it into her mouth.

"Will the court allow you to work?"

Stephanie was a little taken aback that Jared spoke so openly about court until she realized that the Grabers had spoken of it at home, in Jared's presence. Besides, there was no one around to hear them. "I think so; there was never anything said that I couldn't work. Why do you ask?"

"No particular reason. Just wondering whether you're seeing your stay as a long one or a short one."

A smile tugged at Stephanie's lips. She looked into Jared's deep hazel eyes and knew that he was kind and trustworthy. Stephanie wondered why Megan had not thought of him as a match for her, rather than Jeremiah Zook. She would have to ask her at the very next opportunity. "Maybe long, I might stay on."

Jared smiled at her, making her feel weak at the knees.

"If you did stay, what would you miss?"

"I'd miss my caramel lattes."

He laughed. "We're allowed to drink lattes."

"I know, but Amish people live in such isolated places. At home, I'm just walking distance to a café."

"So that's it?"

"That's the main thing."

He shook his head. "You're so funny. You know you can make your own lattes."

"They never taste the same. I have two shots of caramel in the coffee and I like it in a glass instead of a mug."

"And it's better in a glass?"

"Much better. I'd better go and find Megan." Stephanie hurried away; she did not want to like anyone too much. It seemed it only led to disappointment.

As Stephanie walked through the young people to find Megan, she could feel Jeremiah's eyes were fastened upon her from wherever he was lurking. He had to have seen her speaking with Jared. She walked a few more steps and felt a warm hand on her shoulder. Turning, she saw Jeremiah.

"What were you speaking to that idiot for?"

"That's a very rude thing to say. I didn't know that the Amish were rude; I thought they were holy and nice."

"Cut the charade. You were trying to make me jealous just now."

Stephanie smiled, and said, "Think whatever you like."

"You know we're going to end up together, don't you? Tell me where the money is, and we can have a great life together. We can go anywhere, you and I."

"You're a joke." Stephanie turned on her heel and walked away as fast as she could. He wasn't serious about being back in the community. It seemed he was hiding out in the Amish community so the police wouldn't arrest him. Perhaps he'd even given the police her name to get himself off the hook.

He caught up with her. "There are things I know about you, and I can tell Jared or anyone else you might fancy. Don't think any Amish man will have anything to do with a woman with loose morals like you."

Stephanie's jaw dropped, and she covered her mouth with both hands. No one had ever said anything so horrible to her. As tears formed in her eyes, she ran into the field, away from the lively crowd.

While Stephanie walked alone in the darkness, she wondered if there was any truth in what Jeremiah had said. She had lived with him for five months as though man and wife, so wouldn't that make him just as much to blame? Hadn't he sinned to the same degree as she? She knew, from speaking with Megan, that a lot of Amish girls save their first kiss for their wedding day. She had given away a lot more than her first kiss.

She'd been too young to think of a relationship before she'd met Jeremiah. The closeness she'd had with him, the feeling of being half of a couple, was something she wanted to have again, but not with him. At least she knew now that Jeremiah was definitely not the one for her. Megan had been right when she said to wait and things would become clear over time.

Stephanie took a deep breath and wiped the last of the tears from her eyes. It had been a good thing that Jeremiah revealed his true intentions and character. Stephanie followed the noise back to the crowd she'd run away from. She hoped that no one had seen her run away crying. What a fool she was.

A familiar figure walked toward her.

"Are you alright, Stephanie?"

It was Jared.

She sniffed, and then took a deep breath. "Yes, I'm okay."

"Did Jeremiah say something to upset you?" Jared's eyes narrowed.

Stephanie dabbed at her face with the back of her hand to make sure no more tears were on her face. "Yes, he did, but I'm okay."

"Do you want me to speak with him?"

Stephanie managed a little laugh. "No, I think he's best off ignored."

"That's the same conclusion I came to a long time ago. Would you allow me to take you home?"

She looked up into Jared's kind eyes. "I'd like that."

CHAPTER 11

Thou hast turned for me my mourning into dancing:
thou hast put off my sackcloth,
and girded me with gladness;
Psalm 30:11

ONCE STEPHANIE WAS SAFELY home in her bedroom, Megan crept into her room. "Stephanie, did you go home with Jared?"

Stephanie nodded. "Yeah."

"Why? Is everything okay?"

"I kind of like him."

"Jared?"

"Yeah. Is that so unbelievable?"

"Nee. I suppose not. I've just always thought of him like a *bruder,* but I don't know why I didn't think of him for you before. I could see by the way he was talking to you tonight at the singing that he likes you."

"You think so?"

Megan nodded enthusiastically.

"But what about me living with a man before? Has that tainted me?"

"*Nee,* of course not. Everyone does wrong; you weren't raised in the community and haven't been baptized. What do you think people who go on *rumspringa* do?"

"I suppose so."

"They get to try everything the world has to offer before they make their choice."

"I know."

"If you want to stay on in the community, confess your sins to the bishop and get baptized. *Gott* covers all your sin, and you are born anew. Now, if you were to do something like that after you were baptized, you'd be shunned."

"I see how it works. I never really knew before. Everyone seems so happy and contented in the community." *Except Jeremiah,* she thought.

"That's what the young people say when they return from *rumspringa*. No one out there cares about them like the community does."

"It's a big decision." Stephanie pursed her lips.

Megan leaned forward and touched her on the shoulder. "You don't have to make it now; you've plenty of time."

As Megan left for her own room, Stephanie knew that Megan was right, as usual.

Peace and calm floated across Stephanie as she slipped between the sheets breathing in the fresh scent of the sun-dried linen. Closing her eyes, Jared came to mind. He was nothing like Jeremiah; he would never behave toward her as Jeremiah had.

She decided if she wanted to do things correctly, she'd have to get the money back to the rightful owners since she was the only one who knew where it was hidden. To do that, she had to be careful not to get into even more trouble.

There was only one thing for it. She'd need to get Megan on board to help her since she couldn't do it on her own.

THE NEXT MORNING, she went with Megan to take Tara to work. On the way home, she broached the subject with Megan.

"You know how I told you that I got into trouble, Megan?"

"Jah."

"Well, some money was taken from someone and I need to get it back to them."

"Okay."

This was going to be tougher than she'd thought. "I was involved with a group of people who stole the money."

"Yeah, you told me. Did they give it back?"

"No. That's where I need your help."

Megan glanced over at Tara. "My help? What can I do?"

"I'm the only one who knows where the money is, but if anyone finds out I know, I'll be in much bigger trouble than I'm in now. I might even end up in the slammer."

"Can't you just tell the police?"

"No, Megan. You're not listening. I'll get into big trouble. It's a huge amount of money. I figure if I can get it back to the person it was stolen from, I won't need to do anything else. The pressure will be off me."

"But then the person will think you stole it and not your friends."

"I kept quiet about it and anyway, I'll give it back anonymously and no one will know who got it back to them."

"I'm not understanding everything you're saying. You weren't the actual person who stole it, but you're the only one who knows where the money is hidden?"

"Exactly. You've finally got it."

"I'm not used to hearing about crimes. It's not my fault."

When she saw Megan pouting, she knew she'd offended her. "I'm sorry, Megan. I didn't mean to be rude. Would you help me?"

"It depends. What would I have to do? Nothing bad I hope."

"No. Well, a little bad if you call trespassing bad."

Megan frowned. "Where's the money?"

"It's at the Zooks' house."

"Jeremiah's house?"

"Yes."

"What's it doing there?"

"I can't tell you that."

Megan shook her head. "I can take a pretty good guess that Jeremiah was involved somehow when he was on *rumspringa.* What's he doing with the money?"

"I told you he was. Anyway, he doesn't know he's got the money. I hid it in the house."

Megan glanced over at her again. "When were you there?"

"A while ago when Jeremiah was still on *rumspringa.* We didn't have anything to eat and it was a Sunday and he knew his parents were at the meeting. He drove over there and we took some food."

"Why didn't you just spend some of the money you had?"

"We hadn't divided it up yet, so we couldn't touch it. I didn't trust any of them and I thought they'd blame it all on me, which they did in the end. Anyway, without the money, the cops had no proof we did anything. I mean, *they* did it."

"They?"

"The other people who were involved."

"And the group trusted *you* with the money?"

"Not me. They trusted Jeremiah."

Megan shook her head. "It's hard to believe all this."

"You must, Megan because I need your help to go to the Zooks' house and get the money back."

Megan's mouth dropped open in shock. "I can't. I can't do

anything dishonest. If *Mamm* and *Dat* found out, they'd be so disappointed."

"You mean Aunt Gretchen and Uncle William?"

"Jah."

"No one will find out. Won't you please help me, Megan? I'm trying to do the right thing. I'll take the money back to the rightful owner and everything will be sweet. Don't you want everything to work out well for everyone?"

Megan sighed. "I do."

"You'll be helping me if you do this."

"Okay. How do we do it?"

"We visit them and then you keep 'em busy while I go and get the money."

"Where is it hidden exactly? Wait! Don't tell me."

Stephanie laughed.

Megan shook her head. "I can't believe I'm actually considering this."

"No one will find out. Besides, you're not doing anything wrong. You're helping me to right a wrong."

Megan groaned.

WHEN THEY GOT BACK HOME, Megan knew she'd have to find a good excuse to get away from the house and to the Zooks' house. She walked into the kitchen where Gretchen was washing up.

"Mamm, I thought Stephanie and I might go and visit some people." She leaned in and whispered, "It might help Stephanie if she got to know some folk around here."

"Jah. Okay. Where were you thinking of going?"

"We thought we'd start at the Zooks' house. Mrs. Zook is so nice."

Stephanie walked into the room. "Did you say we're visiting Mrs. Zook? Why don't we make her a cake or something?"

"That's a marvelous idea. Both of you start on the cake while I go outside and hang the washing out. I'll tell you what, I might as well come with you." Gretchen walked out the back door.

Stephanie rushed to Megan's side. "She can't come. She'll ruin everything."

"No, Stephanie. This might be good. She can help me keep Mrs. Zook occupied while you go off and get the money."

"We can't tell her."

"Nee! We don't have to."

Breathing out heavily Stephanie wiped her dark hair away from her face. "I dunno. This doesn't feel good."

"It'll all work out. We'll just have to hide the money somewhere once you get it. Is it big?"

"Yes! It's a lot of money." She motioned with her hands how big the bundle was.

"Well, wear something baggy and hide it in your clothes and smuggle it out that way."

Stephanie looked down at the Amish dress she was wearing. "You don't call this baggy?"

"Wear a big coat over it as well. There's a spare one hanging by the back door."

"Okay."

"Let's get started on the cake."

CHAPTER 12

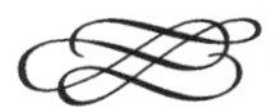

Blessed is that man that maketh the Lord his trust,
and respecteth not the proud, nor such as turn aside to lies.
Psalm 40:4

All the way to the Zooks' Megan was worried about what Stephanie had asked her to do. It was possible that she'd get into trouble too, just by helping her. The other issue was that if she didn't help Stephanie, someone would find the money and Jeremiah and Stephanie could get into a whole heap of trouble. After weighing everything up, Megan decided she had no alternative but to help her friend.

At the Zooks', Mrs. Zook and Gretchen were busy talking while eating chocolate cake, and Megan gave Stephanie a nod indicating it was a good time for her to go and get the money from wherever she'd hidden it.

"Excuse me, Mrs. Zook, where's the bathroom?" Stephanie asked.

"It's just out to the living room and through to the end on your left. You'll see it."

Stephanie left the table, and while she was gone, a buggy pulled up at the house. It was bad timing. Mrs. Zook stood up and looked out the window. "That's Jeremiah home. I didn't expect him home today."

Megan's heart pumped hard against her chest worried that Jeremiah might walk in and catch Megan with the stolen money.

"I might go out and say hello," Megan said standing up.

"Megan, you haven't finished your hot tea yet," Mrs. Zook said frowning.

"I don't like it too hot." And with that, Megan hurried out the front door before anyone could stop her.

Jeremiah looked over and saw her. "Hi, Megan."

"Hi there." She kept walking to him trying to think of something to say. If she engaged him in conversation, she could keep him outside long enough for Stephanie to do what she had to do. "Nice horse."

Jeremiah smiled and patted his horse. "Yeah, I like him." He looked back at her. "Since when do you like horses? I thought you only liked bees."

"Ah, you've heard about my bees?" Good! She could talk about her bees for hours.

"*Jah.* Jared told me you keep bees."

"I got the hives from Mr. Palmer. His wife made him stop looking after the bees and Gretchen thought it would be a good thing for me. I'm glad she did because I love them. I helped Mr. Palmer with them often." A mixture of boredom and confusion covered his face. He clearly wasn't a bee lover, but Megan didn't let that stop her. "Did you know that bees don't come out of their hive all winter? Except for a fly-around on a nice warm day. They keep the queen warm by flapping their wings—"

"That's really interesting, but maybe you can tell me about it another time? I've just stopped home to get something to eat and then I've got to go out again."

He started walking toward the house and seeing no sign of Stephanie, she had to stop him. "Wait!"

He turned around frowning. "What is it?"

"Why don't you come and see them sometime?"

Still frowning, he asked, "The bees?"

"Jah." She nodded enthusiastically hoping to make it seem exciting.

"What's to see? You just said they don't come out of their hive all winter."

"That's true. But you can see how I've arranged things to help keep the hive warm."

He frowned. "You want me to go and look at your beehives with you?"

"Only if you want to."

He went from frowning to smiling as he took a step closer. "How about we do something else instead?"

She hadn't planned on this. Now he thought that she liked him and had been throwing herself at him. In desperation, she looked back at the house and saw Stephanie signal to her from the doorway. "Oh look. There's Stephanie."

He swung around. "Stephanie's here?"

"Jah. We came visiting with Gretchen."

He eyed her suspiciously and then turned and strode toward the house.

By the time Megan got inside, Stephanie was sitting back at the kitchen table wearing a black bulky coat.

Jeremiah greeted everyone.

"Are you cold, Megan?" Mrs. Zook asked.

"Just a little. The tea will warm me up."

Mrs. Zook looked over at Jeremiah. "I didn't know you were coming home today. I didn't cook anything for lunch."

Jeremiah pulled out a kitchen chair and sat down. "That's all right. Just give me whatever you've got."

Mrs. Zook stood up. "I can heat up some soup."

"Fine." Jeremiah folded his arms and glared at Stephanie.

"Would anyone else like some soup?"

"Nee denke. We should go now," Gretchen said.

"Denke for stopping by. I'll come to your *haus* next time."

"That'd be *gut.* Come on, girls."

The girls stood and after they'd said goodbye to Jeremiah and Mrs. Zook, they walked out the door.

Megan knew from Stephanie wearing the coat that she'd retrieved the money.

As the horse trotted up the road back to the house, Gretchen yawned. "Sitting for that long made me tired. That's why I prefer to keep doing things during the day."

"Doing things should make you tired," Stephanie said, and that set Gretchen off talking about the virtues of not being idle.

"Well, that was a nice visit. *Denke* for coming with us *Mamm."*

Gretchen smiled over at Megan who was sitting next to her.

"We'll put the buggy away and tend to the horse," Megan said.

"Denke. I should get that washing inside. It looks as though it could rain soon." Gretchen climbed down from the buggy and made her way to the house.

When she was out of earshot, Megan asked, "Did you get it?"

"Jah. I'll have to keep it somewhere until I can get it back to the owner."

"Hide it in the barn somewhere. Make sure you hide it where no one will find it. *Dat* and Jared go in there all the time. Do that while I unhitch the buggy."

Stephanie glanced back at the house. "Okay. Any particular place you can recommend?"

"Where it won't be found."

"Obviously."

"No. I don't have a need to hide things. Just use your brain."

Stephanie said, "Or, should I hide it inside? Maybe keep it with me?"

"No. The barn's much better. Gretchen might go into your room to clean it. She's fanatical about not having any dust in the house. How are you going to get it back to the owner, anyway?"

"It's from a store in town."

"I won't be able to take you into town for a couple of days. Gretchen doesn't like me going into town every day. I could find some excuse."

"Okay. See what you can do."

"Quick. Go in and hide it now while you can, before Jared and *Dat* William get home."

Stephanie chuckled. *"Dat* William," she said under her breath.

Megan heard her, but she wasn't going to let Stephanie's amusement bother her. That's what she called William, and mostly she just called him *Dat.*

While Megan busied herself unhitching the buggy, Stephanie was in the barn.

"All done." Stephanie came out of the barn pulling the black coat off.

"Good. Now, I'll rub the horse down and we can have a rest."

"Yeah, but not for long if Aunt Gretchen's got anything to do with it. Idle hands are the work of the devil, or whatever she said when we were coming home."

Megan laughed. "She said, 'The devil's workshop.' We'll have a cup of hot tea first. How does that sound?"

"At least that's something to look forward to, if I can't have a latte."

"Then tonight I've got Brandon coming to take me to deliver food to the homeless."

CHAPTER 13

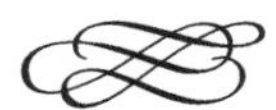

Let all those that seek thee rejoice and be glad in thee:
let such as love thy salvation say continually,
The Lord be magnified.
Psalm 40:16

MEGAN GOT ready for her night with Brandon while listening to Stephanie's advice. Firstly, on how to wear her *kapp* and dress, and then advice on what to say to Brandon, and when to laugh. Although Megan listened and took it all in, she wasn't so sure about taking her well-intentioned advice.

"Aunt Gretchen doesn't seem to mind you going out with an *Englischer.*"

"That's because we're going to a Mission where they do charitable works. And she knows him, which helps. If he was just someone she didn't know anything about and an *Englischer* and I was going on a date with him, that would be an entirely different thing."

"Okay."

"How do I look?" Megan asked once she was fully dressed. She spun around in a circle.

"You look a bit pale. I think you need some blush."

Megan giggled. "I couldn't."

Stephanie pouted. "I don't see why not."

"He'll like me without blush, if he's going to like me in that way."

"It doesn't hurt to look as good as you can."

"This is as good as I can look," Megan said as she walked to the window. "Here he is. I can see his car."

Stephanie jumped off the bed and stood beside her and looked out the window. "Okay, well, you have a good time."

"I will."

"I'll wait up so you can tell me all about it."

"Are you sure? I might be late."

"Megan, there's no TV, no radio, no books—none that I want to read, anyway—I need my drama fix."

Megan laughed. "Okay. I'll do my best to keep you entertained when I come home."

"Good. Thank you!"

Once she was in the car and they'd greeted each other, Megan asked, "Where are we going? What town, I mean." She glanced over to see that he was wearing dark jeans and a checkered blue shirt with rolled up sleeves revealing his tanned, strong arms.

"Allentown. That's where the Mission is. It's a little over an hour away."

"I thought you would've lived closer to your father."

"He's about half an hour's drive away in the other direction. That's not too far to go for the Tuesday night dinners. We've only had these once-a-week family dinners since we discovered Tara."

"It's a nice idea to all get together."

He turned the car around. "Yeah. I know Dad misses Mom a lot. It's got to be hard for him. I think the dinners help."

"Tara said your father told her that he and your stepmother were opposites."

"Yes, and opposites attract sometimes. Not all the time, of course."

"It must be so odd for you that you never knew about Tara."

"It's taken some adjusting. Mom was always so active in the church that it's alarming that she could've kept a big secret like that. Not that I'm judging mind you. No one knows what they'd do in certain circumstances. She would've done what she thought best."

"I'm sure she did. Just as my mother did. She had no other choice."

He glanced over at her.

"I've been doing some thinking after our talk the other day and I still think I'm comfortable with not trying to find my mother. Gretchen and William are the only mother and father I've really had."

"It's hard to believe that you were never permanently adopted."

"I was sick a lot as a young child and I was told that's why I was never permanently adopted."

"What was wrong with you?"

"I had a lot of ear infections. Gretchen saw my health records and she said I got one ear infection after another. They're incredibly painful, so I cried a lot, and I was almost permanently on antibiotics. No one wants the burden of a sick child."

"It all helped to land you where you are now."

"You believe that?"

"I do."

"That's what Gretchen and William always say."

"It's fate—God's hand on you."

"Yes, but I'd use the word "grace" instead. I'm where I'm supposed to be."

He put his hand up to the air that blew out from the air conditioner. "Is it warm enough for you?"

"It's lovely and warm in the car. Warmer than the buggies."

He laughed. "I suppose it would be."

"William has a heater in his buggy, but not all of them have one."

"You seem quite happy where you are in your Amish community. Do you want to stay there forever? I'm guessing you've had to give it some thought."

"I've never seriously considered leaving because that's the only place where I've ever truly felt at home."

"That makes sense. They seem to be a private people. Closed off, almost."

"They don't want to associate with the outside world because they don't want to be tempted by things that would pull them away from God." When he didn't ask anything else, she considered that a change of subject was in order. "How long have you been helping out at the Mission?"

"My mother always used to help out at Christmas and other holidays, and when I got older, I just took on more responsibility there. I arranged the fund raising for the three vans that we deliver the food in."

"That must've been a lot of work."

He chuckled. "When I say I arranged it, I should've said that I was in charge of the committee that did the fund raising."

"Avalon said it was all your idea."

"It was, but it took an enormous amount of work from volunteers to pull it all together."

"I wouldn't have thought there would be that many homeless people around."

"I think you'd be surprised. We had a lady who lost her job and a month later she was homeless living in her car. You'd never know it to look at her. When people hear the word homeless, they think of old people wheeling a shopping trolley of their belongings around the street and when they're hungry they sift through trash —it's not always like that."

"I'm sorry to say I've never given it too much thought at all. It must feel good to help them."

"It does. We feed people on low incomes, too, and others who are confined to their homes for one reason or another. Often ill health will prevent them from working and then their standard of living rapidly slides south."

"Listening to you makes me grateful that I have a roof over my head."

"It's grounding, that's for sure. You come away knowing what's important in life."

After several minutes, he pulled into the parking lot of a large flat-roofed building that looked like some kind of a factory. "This is the Mission here. People can come here for a hot meal three nights a week."

When Megan got out of the car, he walked around to meet her. He touched her lightly on the shoulder to turn her to face where he pointed. "Those are our vans."

She nodded. "They're new."

"They are. This way." He strode toward the back of the building and she hurried to catch up.

He opened the door and immediately turned right into another room. He held the door open for her and Megan saw a commercial kitchen.

"Wow. It's huge."

"I'll show you around."

He led her around, past the deep fryer, three large ovens and a row of hotplates.

"That pizza oven over there was donated by a local man. It's worth a ton of money."

Megan nodded as they walked past several workers in aprons and hairnets who were busily preparing the food. They all happily greeted him and he introduced them to Megan. None of them took too much notice of her, but she figured it was polite of him to take the time to introduce her.

"They'll prepare meals on those trays." He pointed to segmented cardboard food trays. "Then we'll load them in cartons into the truck."

"Will I help with that?"

"Yes. You can help me pack them once the cooks fill them."

"Okay. Good."

"All the trays are recyclable, so they're not harmful to the environment. We've got a dietician who's a member of the Mission, and she's worked out the menu."

"You've thought of everything."

"I hope so. There's always room for improvement."

Brandon showed her around the rest of the building. While they were waiting for the food trays to be filled, a woman walked up to them.

"Brandon."

"Hi, Debbie." He leaned forward and kissed the woman on the cheek. "Megan, this is the dietician I was telling you about." Brandon introduced the two of them.

As Megan nodded politely at the woman, she couldn't help noticing how nice she looked in her slim-fitted jeans and figure hugging pale pink blouse. Was Brandon attracted to her? The woman was certainly smiling a lot at him.

"Megan's coming on the run with me tonight."

"Oh, in the van?"

"Yes. She'll be a good help to me since Marco is still on vacation."

"Do you need an extra pair of hands? I'm free tonight."

Megan held her breath. She didn't want to share any of her precious alone time with Brandon tonight.

"Thanks, but the two of us will manage just fine."

"Perhaps I could help you next time? Unless Megan's going to become a regular here."

"She lives too far away for that."

"Okay. It's a date then," the woman said.

He chuckled. "Thanks, Debbie, it's kind of you."

"Anytime." She flashed him a smile, and then turned and gave Megan a nod before she walked away.

"When you mentioned a dietician, I pictured an old man with gray hair. She's very attractive."

"Really? I suppose so. I hadn't really noticed."

His response pleased Megan immensely. He didn't seem like a person who would lie, and if he wasn't interested in women for their looks, he must be someone who looked deeper than surface appearances.

"Brandon, we're all done."

They turned to see one of the cooks in a white apron and black hair net waving at them.

"Good. We're coming."

Brandon and she packed the food into plastic crates that were then loaded onto trolleys. The trolleys were then wheeled to the vans. The process was repeated several times until the three vans were filled. Brandon then sent texts from his phone and four people arrived. Two to drive the other vans, and an extra helper for each van.

"You've got your list?" Brandon asked each driver who confirmed that they had.

When the two vans drove past them, Megan said, "That was impressive. Everything is highly organized."

"When we're dealing with a lot of people and hot food, it has to be. Are you all set?"

Megan nodded.

While they drove, Brandon told her more about the Mission. It was there not only to meet the physical needs of people, but also their spiritual and mental needs. They used the services of other agencies when people had specific requirements.

As Megan watched Brandon interact with all kinds of people, she grew more impressed with him.

Four hours later, they were in the van heading back to the Mission.

"One night's work, over and done. What did you think?"

"It's just a great idea. You're doing such wonderful work. It's not just about feeding people it's about being a friend. You really connected with those people."

He glanced over at her. "Exactly. That's exactly right. For some of them shut in their homes, I'm a link to the outside world."

"Everyone needs someone to talk to."

When they pulled into the parking lot, he said, "Normally, I clean the truck and unload everything from the back, but tonight I've got someone else doing that while I drive you home."

"Thank you for everything. It's been such an inspiring experience."

"It was my pleasure. I really enjoyed the night."

They climbed out of the van and he unlocked his car. "You get comfortable and I'll just drop the keys off inside."

Megan waited in the car, watching him walk into the building. She'd have another hour of him all to herself. Once he was sitting back beside her, she wanted to find out even more about him.

He started the engine and soon they were back on the main road.

"Do you live in a house or an apartment?" Megan asked.

"I live in a house. It's pretty small and it needs a lot of work. I moved into it two years ago intending to renovate, and I haven't done a thing."

"You're too busy to do anything like that, what with your job and then your work with the Mission."

"When I bought it, I thought it would be a good place to raise a family. It's got a big backyard and it's all perfectly flat. There's a huge tree that would be great to hang a swing from. There's even room for chickens and a vegetable garden."

"It sounds lovely."

"Would you like to see it sometime?"

"Yes. I would."

"I'll arrange something. Are you generally free on Saturdays?"

"I am." Since she didn't have a job, she was unoccupied most of the time apart from household chores, which were somewhat flexible, and except for the meetings.

They chatted about a lot of different things and the time passed far too quickly for Megan. He pulled up at Gretchen and William's house.

"There you go," he said.

"Thank you, again. I had a lovely time."

"It was my pleasure. I'll be in touch with you. If I don't see you, I'll send a message through Tara." He got his phone out of his pocket and scrolled through it. "Yep, I've got Tara's number which is the same as yours."

The Grabers' family phone was in the barn as they were not permitted to have one in their house.

She opened the car door. "Okay. Good night. Oh, would you like to come in?"

"No thanks. It's late. I should be getting home. Good night."

Megan closed the car door and headed to the house. She was in love, deeply in love with Brandon.

CHAPTER 14

I cried unto the Lord with my voice,
and he heard me out of his holy hill. Selah.
Psalm 3:4

Earlier that same evening.

AFTER DINNER THAT SAME NIGHT, Stephanie was washing dishes when Jared came into the kitchen.

"Can I talk to you about something in private, Stephanie?"

"Sure, when?" She couldn't keep the smile from her face. Jared liked her.

"Whenever you finish with what you're doing."

"Okay. I'll only be another few minutes."

He leaned in closer and said in a low voice that William and Gretchen wouldn't hear from the living room, "I'll wait on the porch."

Stephanie nodded. As soon as he left the room, she hurried to finish the washing up as quickly as she could. Aunt Gretchen was coming back in to finish the drying, so she drained the water from the sink, wiped her hands, and hurried to see what Jared wanted.

She managed to slip outside without her aunt and uncle seeing her.

Jared was sitting on a porch chair, so she sat herself down in the chair next to him.

"It's a nice night," she said smiling up at the sky.

"Stephanie, I need to talk to you about something kind of troubling."

Looking at his worried face, she thought he might ask her if she'd been involved with Jeremiah. He wouldn't want to ask her on a date if he thought there was something between her and Jeremiah Zook.

"What's the problem?"

"I don't know how to say this, except just to say it. I found a great deal of money in the barn this afternoon."

Stephanie gasped. "You didn't tell anyone, did you?"

He frowned. "You know about it?"

"Yes. I hid it there only today. How did you find it?"

"It wasn't hard. You didn't hide it well at all. I put my hand up to steady myself when I finished rubbing the horse down and I saw a large stone. I knew it hadn't been there before and when I moved it, I saw the bundle of notes."

Stephanie sighed. "I'm giving it back to the store it was taken from."

"So this is the money you've gotten into trouble over?"

Stephanie nodded. "I had it hidden in a different place, and I just brought it back here today. If the police know I've got it, I could be in serious trouble. I was already arrested and they only let me go because they couldn't prove I'd done anything, without the money as evidence."

"What are your plans?"

"I've got to get it back to the store it was stolen from."

"How? And why did they have thirty eight thousand dollars lying around waiting to be stolen?"

"It was a store's Christmas takings. One of my friends knew someone who worked there. They keep all the money they make for the week in a safe, and then at the end of the week they put it in the bank."

Jared raised his eyebrows. "Sounds dumb. I bet they're sorry they didn't take it to the bank at the end of every day. I would guess they've been forced to change that system now."

"Someone grabbed the bag with the money in it and then ran, and then threw it to someone who was waiting in a getaway car."

"What part did you play in it? Were you one of those 'someones.'"

"I had a boyfriend and he was the one who drove the car. I didn't know anything about any of it until he came home with the money. He told me the whole story and then said he had to split it between four people. The one who thought the plan up, the one who snatched the bag, and the one who told him about the money in the first place."

"Some boyfriend that was, to get you into trouble like that."

"Yeah. I'm starting to think he told the police I had some involvement so he could get himself off the hook, too. When it had nothing to do with me. I should've just given the police all their names to start with."

"Well, I hope you're not having any more to do with him."

"No. I'm not. We've broken up."

"Good! What are your plans?" Jared asked again.

"For what?"

"You just said you need to get the money back to the store where it belongs."

Shaking her head, she said, "I haven't come up with a plan. I just thought I'd… I don't know what to do."

He grimaced.

Stephanie continued, "I guess I could leave it somewhere and call the police and tell them where it is."

"That sounds risky too. And leave it where? Someone might get it before the police get there."

"Well, what am I to do?"

He rubbed his chin. "What kind of a store is it?"

"It's a general store in town."

"I'll give it some thought and help you figure something out."

"You'll help me?"

"Yeah. I'll see what I can do. I'll take it back for you."

"No! You can't! You might get into trouble."

Jared put his finger to his mouth. "Shh. They'll hear you. I'll get into less trouble than you would if they catch you."

"Would you really do that for me?"

"Of course. We're friends, aren't we?"

Stephanie nodded. "That's why I don't want you to do it."

"I'll be okay. Trust me. I'll organize some free time at around midday, hopefully, by then we can come up with a plan." He locked eyes with her. "Meet me here tomorrow morning at six."

"Okay."

Jared nodded toward the front door. "You better get back inside."

She rose to her feet. "Are you coming in?"

"*Nah.* I'm more of a loner. Talking over the dinner table was enough for me."

"Okay. Good night."

He stood and pointed to the floor of the porch. "Stephanie, I'll see you here at six."

"I'll be here."

CHAPTER 15

And the Lord God said, It is not good that the man should be alone;
I will make him an help meet for him.
Genesis 2:18

STEPHANIE WOKE up and immediately jumped out of bed to look for her watch. She thought she'd left it on the nightstand and it wasn't there. She climbed out of bed and searched around the floor. Jared said to meet her downstairs on the porch at six and since he was doing her a favor, it would be awful to stand him up. Then something caught her eye from under the bed. It was her watch. She snatched it and saw that it was fifteen minutes until six. Heaving out a relieved sigh, she stood up and changed out of her nightdress and into one of the Amish dresses that Gretchen made her wear while she was visiting.

Once she'd dressed, she looked out the window to see that Jared was steadily making his way toward the house from his sleeping quarters by the barn. As quietly as she could, she ran down the stairs to meet him.

Seeing no one in the living room, she turned the handle of the front door and stepped onto the porch closing the door softly behind her. A chilly gust of wind bit into her cheeks causing her to shiver. She hadn't stopped to put on a coat or a shawl.

"Well, what's the plan?" she asked him breathlessly.

"I've been thinking about it all night. The only thing that I can think of is if I leave it in the store somewhere and then I'll make a call to them and tell them where it is. If I made an anonymous call to the police station, they'd most likely get a recording of my voice."

"Let me do it, Jared. It's not your problem. It should be me who does it."

He shook his head. "I'll do it. I'll slip away in the middle of the day and tell William I've got an errand to run in town. It'll raise suspicion if I come and take you somewhere."

Stephanie took a deep breath. "You don't have to do this."

"Friends help each other. And you're doing something good by returning the money."

"Thank you. I feel bad for getting you involved."

"You didn't get me involved. I found the money in the barn, remember?"

"Yeah."

"Don't worry, Stephanie. It'll all work out. Give me the name of the store."

"You've got the money?"

"I've got the money hidden in the buggy already."

After she gave him the name of the store, she said, "Thank you so much. I'm so grateful."

He chuckled. "You're welcome." He wagged his finger at her. "Make sure you don't do anything like this again."

"I won't get involved with anyone crooked again, don't worry about that."

"I'm very glad to hear it."

"Be careful."

"I will. If I get caught and go to jail, just bake me a cake with a file in it." Jared chuckled as he left her there on the porch.

After she watched him disappear into the barn, she walked inside to make herself a cup of coffee to wake herself up. She hadn't had the best night's sleep, worried about what she might have to do to get the money back. It was such a relief that Jared had taken control and was looking after everything for her.

"You're up bright and early."

She swung around from the stove to see her aunt. "Yeah. I couldn't sleep, so I figured I should get up early today."

"Good. It might help if you went to bed earlier."

"I'll try that. Coffee?"

"Jah. I'll put *Onkel* William's breakfast on. Do you want some pancakes?"

"Yes please."

After Stephanie had made the coffee, she sat down at the kitchen table. Soon her uncle and Tara joined her, talking together as they came in.

"I'll take you to work this morning, Tara. I think Megan had a late night," William said.

"Jah, she was with Brandon at the Mission."

"It's nice to see your half brother involved in charity," Aunt Gretchen said.

"The whole family is involved in their church."

Tara looked at Stephanie. "What are you doing today?"

"I'm sure Aunt Gretchen will find a lot for me to do. And in between times, Megan is going to show me her beehives again." Stephanie took a mouthful of coffee, and then asked Tara, "How do you like working at the quilt store?"

Tara nodded. "It's good. I get to meet a lot of different people. They've got a Saturday morning job going to be available. You should apply."

"Oh no. I don't know anything about that kind of thing. Don't I have to be Amish?"

"No. The store's owned by an *Englischer,* and her two daughters sometimes work there. One of them is going off to college soon."

"What kind of work did you do when you lived away from home?" William asked her.

"I just did odd jobs here and there. Sales jobs mostly and a lot of them were cash in hand. I don't have any real experience for anything."

"Let me know if you change your mind. I could put a good word in for you. They haven't advertised the job yet and I can teach you what I know."

"Yeah, I'll definitely think about it. I guess I have to do something sooner or later."

"We should leave soon, Tara," Uncle William said, standing up from the table.

"Okay. I'm ready now." Tara stood and drained the coffee in her mug before she headed off with Uncle William.

Aunt Gretchen gathered the dishes and filled the sink to wash them. Stephanie grabbed a tea towel to dry them.

"You seem fairly friendly with Jared."

"Yes. He's very nice."

"Hmm."

"Well, you think he's nice too don't you?"

"I consider him one of the people *Gott* gave me to look after, just the same as you."

Stephanie giggled. "Yeah, well, Jared might not like to hear that you think you're looking after him. He's a grown man."

"We all need to have people we consider family. He's part of mine and I hope we're part of his. Perhaps that's a better way of putting it."

"Morning."

They turned around to see Megan yawning and stretching her hands above her head.

"Morning, sleepyhead," Stephanie said.

"Sit at the table and I'll make you some pancakes," Gretchen said. "And it's just as well you came down when you did. I was just about to wash the pan."

"Denke." Megan slumped into a chair.

While Gretchen mixed up some more pancake batter, Stephanie took over the washing up.

IT WAS mid morning when Megan and Stephanie went for a walk in the fields.

"How did your night go with Brandon? I didn't want to ask in front of Aunt Gretchen at breakfast."

"It was wonderful. Just to see him interact with people was just so touching."

"The homeless people?"

"Yes. And everyone, really, the cooks and all."

Megan talked and talked about Brandon and how wonderful he was. As much as Stephanie tried to listen and be interested, she couldn't help being nervous about Jared taking the money back.

"You're not listening."

"Yes, I am."

Megan stared into her face. "You're not. You're commenting with the wrong things in the wrong places."

"Oh, I'm sorry. I'm happy that you like Brandon so much, but I've got a lot of worrying things on my mind."

Megan stopped walking and grabbed her arm. "What?"

Stephanie licked her lips, and decided it wouldn't hurt to tell

Megan what was going on. She already knew most of it anyway. "Jared found the money in the barn."

"Stephanie! That's dreadful! Did he tell *Dat?*"

"No. He asked me about it. He had heard about the trouble I'd gotten into and figured the money had something to do with it."

"What did you say to him?"

Stephanie told her everything.

"He's going back there today?" Megan asked.

"Yes."

Megan blew out a deep breath. "That's good of him."

"I know. I feel so much better. I would've been too nervous to do anything with the money. I mean I would've done something to get it back to the owner, but I'm glad I didn't have to."

"Does he know about Jeremiah's involvement?"

"No! He doesn't get along too well with Jeremiah and I didn't want him to know that Jeremiah and I were once in a relationship. I just said it was my former boyfriend."

"Yeah. He wouldn't be too happy about that, since he likes you."

"I know."

"You'll have to tell him if things get serious between the two of you," Megan's eyebrows drew together.

"No, I won't."

"Stephanie, it'll be better if you tell him before he finds out himself. And, he will find out."

Stephanie agreed, but decided she'd delay telling him for as long as possible. "I guess you're right."

"Now I'm nervous, too. I hope he gets it back there with no trouble."

"It'll be okay. He was confident he knew what he was doing. He had it all planned out."

"Good."

"Are we checking on the bees?" Stephanie asked.

"We're just going to walk past them to see how they are."

Stephanie sighed. "Most people have a dog, do you realize that?"

"Gretchen doesn't like dogs. She was attacked by one when she was a girl."

"I didn't know."

"Yeah."

"I guess that leaves you stuck with your bees."

"It does, and I'm happy to have them."

Stephanie laughed. "I don't think I'll ever understand the attraction."

"The life of a bee is something so fascinating. Have you ever looked at the honeycomb and wondered how they get them so perfect?"

"Yeah, I admit that's pretty amazing. But it turns me off that they can sting you."

Megan started talking about how wonderful bees were while Stephanie pretended to listen, all the while worried about Jared. *He'd be at the store about now.*

Megan suddenly asked, "Exactly where did you hide the money in the barn?"

"Somewhere I'd thought no one would ever find it. I'll show you when we go back."

When they walked into the barn, Stephanie pointed to where she'd hidden the money. "I put it up there."

The phone ringing distracted them.

Megan hurried over and picked it up.

Stephanie listened in.

"You're where? Oh no! Okay."

"What is it, Megan?"

"Jared's at the police station."

Stephanie grabbed the phone from her. "Jared?"

"Yeah. Things didn't go as planned. I got caught with the money. I'm just calling to let everyone know where I am. I could be here for awhile. They allowed me a phone call."

"I'll come right down there."

"No! Stay put. There's nothing that can be done. You don't need to involve yourself further. I have to go."

The phone clicked in her ear. "Jared!" She hung up the receiver and looked over at Megan. "He's got caught taking the money back. I have to help him, and I'll have to tell Aunt Gretchen everything."

CHAPTER 16

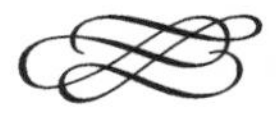

I will say of the Lord, He is my refuge and my fortress:
my God; in him will I trust.
Psalm 91:2

STEPHANIE RAN into the house and found her aunt. "Jared's at the police station and it's all my fault."

"Did you say Jared's at the police station?"

"Yes!"

Gretchen put her hands on Stephanie's shoulders. "Slow down, and tell me everything."

Stephanie opened her mouth to speak, and Gretchen ordered her to sit down. When she was seated, she told Gretchen that Jared had offered to take the money back for her and in doing so, was caught with the money. Now he was at the police station being questioned. "So you see I have to go and tell them everything. Jared's innocent. He was only trying to help me make things better."

"How did Jared get ahold of the money?" Gretchen asked.

Stephanie cast her gaze downward.

Gretchen folded her arms in front of her chest. "It's time you told me everything. Let's go to the living room and you can tell me the whole thing and leave nothing out."

"Can we do that later? I've got to go and help Jared."

"He's not going anywhere for the moment."

They moved from the kitchen to the living room.

Stephanie sat down on the couch with Gretchen and told her aunt all about the robbery, and also told her of her involvement with Jeremiah. "You won't say anything to Jeremiah, or his parents, will you?"

"Right now, we should do what we can for Jared."

"I'll have to tell the police everything I know."

"Are you prepared to do that? They could charge you. Even though you say you didn't know about it and Jeremiah set the whole thing up, they mightn't believe you."

Stephanie wrung her hands. "I have to. It's not right that Jared is in trouble over this."

Gretchen called out for Megan to hitch the buggy.

"I'm sorry to involve you with all this, Aunt Gretchen. I've brought a big mess to your house and involved everyone."

"As long as you've learned from your mistakes. That's all we can ask for."

"Yeah, but there must be something wrong with me. Megan wouldn't have gotten into trouble like this."

"Comparing yourself with others will only lead to disappointment. Someone else could look at your good qualities and feel they fall short."

"I hope I become wise like you someday."

Gretchen raised her eyebrows. "Come on. We'll see if we can help Jared. And then we'll have to find *Onkel* William, so we can tell him where Jared is."

"Jared said that Uncle William is at the Thompsons' house today. Do you know them?"

"Jah, I'll call them and get a message to William not to expect Jared back today." Gretchen walked out of the house to call from the phone in the barn.

WHEN THEY ARRIVED in town and were parked close to the police station, Gretchen announced, "I'm going to have to call your parents and tell them what's going on."

"No, please don't."

"I'll have to. They'll want to know what's happening."

Stephanie sighed.

"Do they have to know right now?" Megan asked.

"Jah, Megan, I think it's best. I'm sorry, Stephanie, but I'm in charge of you and they'd want to know. There's a pay phone over there." Gretchen pointed across the road. "I'll call and then we'll come in and wait for you."

It was useless trying to talk Gretchen out of anything. "Okay call them, but then just wait in the buggy and if I'm not out soon, just leave. I'll make my own way home. I'll get a taxi."

"Just tell the truth, Stephanie," Megan urged.

"Yeah, I'll have to."

Stephanie walked into the police station with her heart thumping hard against her chest. Even though she hadn't committed the crime, she knew about it and had hidden the money.

She walked up to the man behind the front desk and told him she had a confession to make. He had her take a seat while he got a detective. Soon she was ushered into an interview cubicle.

Stephanie confessed everything, about how the robbery had been set up, and even how she'd hidden the money and tried to get it back to the owners. There was no other way she could get

Jared off except by naming Jeremiah and his friends who were involved.

Stephanie had to make an official statement after her recorded interview was over. Four hours after arriving at the police station, she was free to leave. She knew that Aunt Gretchen would've already left, so she walked up the road intending to call a taxi from the pay phone. She could've called from the police station, but preferred to get out of there as fast as possible.

"Stephanie!"

That was Jared's voice. She turned around, hoping he wasn't mad with her.

"Jared, they let you go?"

"Jah, thanks to you, and what about you?"

"They aren't going to charge me. They released me a little while ago. I'd already told Gretchen and Megan to go home and said I'd wait for you. Let's go home."

"Thank you. My buggy is just up the street a little."

"I'm glad it's all over. They're going to charge Jeremiah and his friends from what I overheard."

Jared scratched the side of his face. She could see that the whole mess she'd created didn't sit well with him.

"At least you're finally in the clear. I do feel bad that they're in trouble because I wasn't successful at returning the money," Jared said.

"Don't feel like that. They shouldn't have taken it." She walked with him to his buggy. Once she'd climbed up next to him, she asked, "How did you get caught?"

He carefully moved his buggy out onto the road. "I'm not cut out to be devious, it seems."

"That's a good thing."

"I was in the store with the money and one of the workers thought I was acting suspiciously and alerted the store security guard."

"Oh no."

"Yeah. They asked what was in the bag and I told him it was stolen money that I was giving back. The owner of the store was grateful and didn't want to call the police. The store security officer talked him into it."

"I feel so bad."

"Don't worry," Jared said. "It's over now and we're both in the clear."

"I should never have dragged you into it."

He shook his head. "It worked out for the best. It's all out in the open now."

"I bet Jeremiah will have a different opinion. The police are probably picking him up right now."

"Now that you're free and clear, no more dealings with men like Jeremiah."

Stephanie giggled. "And what kind of men should I have dealings with? Anyone in mind?"

He glanced over at her and smiled. "I might have some ideas."

"What are they?"

"Do you think you might stay on in the community?"

"I'd definitely think about it if I had something to stay for." She glanced down at his hand resting on his leg and wondered if he was going to reach for her hand. He liked her, and she knew it. Too late! Now they were turning into the Grabers' driveway.

The buggy ride was spent in awkward silence.

When they pulled up, Stephanie offered to help him unhitch the buggy.

"Would you be happy if I stayed on here for some time?" Stephanie asked.

Looking over at her, he said, "I would. I think you're too young for a boyfriend yet, but some things are worth the wait."

This wasn't what she wanted to hear. She was nearly eighteen. "I've had a boyfriend before."

He straightened up and now his face was entirely deadpan. "Tell me it wasn't Jeremiah!"

"Oh, I thought you'd figured that out."

His mouth fell open and she could feel an invisible wall come between them. "I'm sorry, Stephanie, but this is just—all too much." He turned away. "I can do all this by myself. Gretchen will be waiting inside for you. You best go and tell her you weren't charged."

She'd blown it! If only she'd never gotten involved with Jeremiah. He hadn't even been nice to her except when it suited him, and he'd dragged her into criminal activity. "Let me explain, Jared."

He straightened up and looked at her. "Okay."

She had nothing to explain. "Forget it!" She turned and walked to the house, mad with herself for being so close to having a lovely boyfriend and now it was all ruined because of Jeremiah.

Walking up the front path to the door, Stephanie kicked the small pebbles that made up the gravel. As soon as she opened the door, she was met with the worried faces of her mother and father. Behind them were her aunt and uncle, and Tara and Megan. They were all anxiously waiting to hear what had happened when all she wanted to do was be alone and cry into her pillow.

She was ushered to the living room where she told everyone the news.

When she had finished talking, Uncle William stood. "Don't doubt that you did the right thing, Stephanie. It was the only thing you could do. I'm off to the barn, if everyone will excuse me. I've got some paperwork to do."

"I don't have to go home do I?" Stephanie asked looking at her mother and father.

"You can stay," her father said.

"Yes," her mother agreed. "Just stay out of trouble. And we're proud of you for setting things right. Call us when you're ready to come home."

Her mother and father left, and Stephanie was relieved she didn't have to go home with them.

"Now, time for chores," Gretchen said steering her into the kitchen.

There were always chores!

Stephanie was too wound up to sleep that night. She wanted to be honest and do the right thing all the time, but why did she have to tell Jared the truth about her relationship with Jeremiah?

CHAPTER 17

Trust in the Lord with all thine heart;
and lean not unto thine own understanding.
In all thy ways acknowledge him, and he shall direct thy paths.
Proverbs 3:5-6

IT WAS at the next Sunday meeting when Stephanie caught a glimpse of Jeremiah. He was heading into the house where the meeting was being held. She kept her head down, hoping he wouldn't spot her. He'd be furious that she'd squealed on him and his friends. The thing was, she'd had no other choice. It was either keep quiet and let Jared take the fall, or inform on the guilty ones who had pointed to her to save their own skins.

Throughout the service, Stephanie kept her head down. Her life was ruined. Jeremiah had led her down a wrong path and now, because she'd been involved with him, what good man would want her? Certainly not Jared, for one.

When the service was over, Stephanie was with the first lot of people who walked into the yard. Now that the weather was getting a little warmer, the yard had been set up with tables for the food and the drinks. Normally she would've stayed with Tara or Megan, but today she wanted to be alone. She spooned some kind of tomato pasta dish onto a plate and made her way to the far side of the yard and sat on a wooden seat by a tree.

After she'd finished only one mouthful, she looked up to see Jeremiah walking over to her. She looked around for an escape route, but before she could stand, he was right in front of her.

"Why did you do it?"

"What?" It was a lame response, but she just couldn't come up with anything else.

"You turned me and my friends into the police."

"I don't want to talk about it."

"I never should've trusted you."

Jared came up beside him. "Hello, Jeremiah."

"Go away, Jared! I'm talking to Stephanie about something that has nothing to do with you."

"Stephanie doesn't want to talk to you."

Jeremiah folded his arms and turned to fully face Jared. "Since when do you speak for her?"

"I'm just saying she doesn't want to speak to you."

Jeremiah looked back at Stephanie. "Tell him to get lost."

"No. Just go away, Jeremiah." Stephanie pushed past both of them and went to find Gretchen. She figured if she stayed by Gretchen, she'd be safe.

Throughout the meal, she heard whispers about Jeremiah's problems with the law. There was talk of him being out on bail and having to face court soon.

When everyone was leaving, she saw Jared in a conversation and she walked over to him. When she reached him, the man he'd been speaking with left.

"Thanks for what you did back there. Getting rid of Jeremiah."

He chuckled. "I've been waiting for an excuse to stand up to him."

"Can we be friends again?"

"We've always been friends."

She looked back at William and Gretchen to see that they were still talking and weren't leaving any time soon. "If I could take back being involved with Jeremiah in every way that I was, I would. I hope this hasn't ruined things between us."

"You're still young, Stephanie."

"You're not that old yourself."

"Jah, I know, but you're still learning and changing. What if we courted and then you grew out of wanting to be with me just as you grew out of Jeremiah?"

"I wouldn't."

He took his hat off and ran a hand through his hair. "You're not a member of the community."

"Not yet, but I could be."

He chuckled and stared at her for a moment. "If you join us, it'll have to be for the right reasons. The bishop questions people who want to join and you'll have to discuss your thoughts with him. Just give yourself some time. You're still young."

She nodded, figuring that was his way of telling her that he wasn't interested. If she said anything else, she'd only embarrass herself.

CHAPTER 18

I will lift up mine eyes unto the hills, from whence cometh my help.
My help cometh from the Lord, which made heaven and earth.
Psalm 121:1-2

THAT NIGHT she thought everyone had gone to bed and, not being able to sleep, Stephanie headed downstairs.

Gretchen was sitting up, sewing by the overhead gas light. Looking up at her, she said, "Why are you looking so glum?"

Stephanie sat next to her. "Oh, that's how I feel, but I didn't know I looked that way."

"*Jah.* And you're completely free. The police said you weren't going to be charged. What worry could you possibly have?"

"It's nothing."

"Looks like it's something to me," Gretchen said.

"You wouldn't understand."

"Try me."

"You'll say I'm just a silly young girl and blah, blah—and all that."

Gretchen moved closer nudging her shoulder. "I was young once. I wasn't born this age."

Stephanie giggled. She couldn't imagine her Aunt Gretchen as a girl of her age. "It's nothing. It's just about someone I like."

"About a boy?"

"A man," Stephanie corrected her.

"I'm sorry. A man. Well, you can tell me."

"All right." Stephanie took a deep breath. Maybe Gretchen could have some insight. "This man I like is a little older than me. He likes me too, but he thinks I'm too young."

"Did he say that?"

"Yes. He said I changed my mind about Jeremiah, so I could just as easily change my mind about him."

"Hmmm. And is this man Amish?"

"Yes, but I'm not going to tell you who he is."

"I didn't ask. You know he can't date someone who doesn't follow the Amish ways?"

"I know that."

"Has he ever had a girlfriend?"

"I don't know. I haven't heard that he has."

"And he knows you like him?"

Stephanie nodded. "I might join the community. Who knows?"

"My advice is to carry on living and forget about him."

Stephanie narrowed her eyes. That was hardly the advice she'd been looking for.

Gretchen continued, "Don't be like that. You want him to think you've forgotten about him and if he really likes you that'll upset him and he'll come after you to make sure you still like him."

"Aunt Gretchen, you want me to play games?"

"Love's no game, Stephanie."

Stephanie giggled seeing her aunt in an entirely different light.

"Your *Onkel* William thought I was too young for him and I had dreadful trouble trying to change his mind. One day, I left him alone. I didn't look at him and didn't talk to him like I normally did."

"You ignored him?"

"Jah, and it worked. We were married six weeks later." Gretchen chuckled.

"Wow! That's a great story to tell your children. Oh, I'm sorry Aunt Gretchen."

"Don't be sorry. It's a great story to tell my niece, too." Gretchen put her arm around Stephanie. "These men give us problems sometimes, don't they?"

Stephanie relaxed her neck and let her head gently nestle into her aunt's shoulder. "They do, but now I think I've found a good one in Jared."

"Jared! You weren't going to tell me who it was."

Stephanie's mouth opened wide and she turned and looked into her aunt's face.

Gretchen's eyes crinkled at the corners. "I couldn't have picked out someone better for you and I don't think you're too young. Love can find you at any age."

"I'll be eighteen soon."

"There you go."

"I'm glad I told you."

"Me too." Gretchen pushed her needlework onto the couch beside her. "Now, I must get to bed so I can wake up early to make *Onkel* William's breakfast."

"Good night, Aunt Gretchen."

Gretchen leaned over and kissed her forehead. *"Gut nacht."*

STEPHANIE SAT ALONE in the living room wishing she could take back the thing she'd said to Gretchen about children. She and

William had never been able to have their own, and that's why they'd taken in foster children.

After Stephanie had carefully mulled over the advice her aunt gave her, she decided that she'd put her strategy into play. It had worked for Gretchen, so it might work for her.

CHAPTER 19

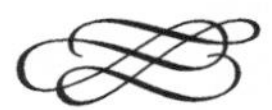

Cast thy burden upon the Lord, and he shall sustain thee:
he shall never suffer the righteous to be moved.
Psalm 55:22

STEPHANIE HAD IGNORED JARED for days. Well, not completely. She answered his questions at the dinner table, but she didn't ask him questions and neither had she gone out of her way to speak to him. The best part was, Stephanie could tell he was bothered by her lack of attention toward him.

As Gretchen and she stood to clear the plates after the evening meal was over, Jared asked, "Stephanie, are you going to the big dinner that Elizabeth's having at her place tomorrow night?"

"I'm not sure yet."

"Oh, you have to go, Stephanie. Elizabeth is having her birth mother and father there, and her sisters and Lyle Junior," Megan said.

"Yes, you have to come, Stephanie," Tara added. "You'll be able to meet my birth father, too, and my little sister and my half brother."

She looked at the three eager faces. "I guess I'll go, then. It'll be nice to meet everyone's families." She continued helping Gretchen and didn't even ask Jared if he was going. That was part of her plan —appearing not to care whether Jared was going or not. Glancing across at him, she saw him staring at her, so she looked away quickly.

THAT NIGHT when everyone had gone to bed, Megan came into her room. "Are you still awake?"

"Yeah, come in."

Megan sat down on her bed and talked about how nervous she was about Brandon going to the dinner at Elizabeth's house.

"You really like him, don't you?" Stephanie asked.

"*Jah.* He's the one for me. Before I met him, I couldn't even talk to a man. I'd literally run away if I had to speak to a man, even in a group of people. With him, everything just flows. And he's a Christian, and he spends his free time helping the church and helping the poor."

"He's your perfect man."

"He is. He truly is."

"Why are you so nervous? It sounds like everything's going fine."

"I want him to like everyone here and I want him to join the community."

"No. I don't think it'll happen."

"You could at least try to give some encouragement or say some positive words."

"I'm sorry. Maybe I should, but I honestly don't think a man who's lived all his life outside the Amish will think it's a good idea to go back in time two hundred years to live how it was back then."

"You'd do it for Jared, wouldn't you?"

Stephanie thought for a moment. "I would, but I've grown up close to it. My father was raised Amish, don't forget, and I've been visiting Aunt Gretchen since I was little and staying here every couple of years. It's different for a man. He's got a job doesn't he?"

"Yes."

"He'd have a lot to give up. I've got nothing to lose. I don't have a job and I've got no particular skills. I'm kind of like a vagrant."

Megan sighed.

Stephanie continued, "What if he wanted you to leave the community? Would it be so bad? Would your life be that bad? He's involved in his church and you could do the charity work together. Someone would look after your bees. Not me, but someone would care for them."

Megan said in a small voice, "I hadn't even thought about my bees."

"Whatever will happen will happen. Don't worry about it. Don't let him go if he asks you to marry him. You must say yes and figure things out later."

Megan slowly nodded. "I don't know if he's even thinking of me in that kind of a way."

"He asked you to go to the homeless shelter with him, didn't he?"

"It wasn't a homeless shelter, but yes, he asked me to go with him in the van to make the deliveries, and I saw how they prepared the food. He showed me around the Mission and he even asked me if I wanted to come and see his house sometime."

"See? He wouldn't have bothered with all that if he didn't like you."

"I hope you're right. I feel in my heart that he likes me, but I've never had a man in my life, so I can't trust in my feelings."

"I'll watch him with you tomorrow night and I'll tell you what I think."

"Would you?"

"Yeah."

THE NEXT NIGHT, Jared went alone in his buggy while Tara, Megan and Stephanie went with Gretchen and William.

While they traveled, Tara explained how Elizabeth's father found her in a coffee shop and thought she looked like one of his daughters, not knowing that she *was* his daughter. The more Stephanie listened to how everything unfolded she learned how unsettling it was for Gretchen's foster girls not to be acquainted with their birth parents. Her mind drifted to her own upbringing. She hadn't been the easiest child to handle growing up and she regretted what she'd put her parents through. *It's no wonder they kept sending me to stay with Aunt Gretchen and Uncle William.*

Uncle William pulled up the buggy outside the house alongside a row of buggies. Closer to the house were three cars.

"It looks like everyone's here already," Gretchen said as she climbed down from the buggy.

As they walked to the house, Jared joined them, having just pulled up in his own buggy.

"Stephanie, can I speak to you a moment?" Jared asked.

Stephanie stopped while the others continued to the house.

"What is it?" she asked sweetly.

"I've noticed you've been acting a little different toward me and I'm wondering if I've done something to offend you."

"No. You've done nothing. You helped me with that money and everything, and I'm really grateful for that."

"Nothing's wrong?"

She shook her head. "Nothing."

He looked down at the ground and then stared into her face. "Would you like to come home in my buggy with me tonight when we finish here?"

Stephanie could barely keep the smile from her face. She wanted to leap high in the sky and give a couple of hollers, but she restrained herself. "I'd like that."

A smile slowly spread across his face. "Good." He looked at the house. "We better get inside."

She walked with him into the house, pleased that Gretchen's advice had actually worked and it hadn't taken too long.

CHAPTER 20

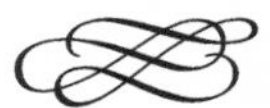

The Lord is my strength and my shield;
my heart trusted in him, and I am helped:
therefore my heart greatly rejoiceth;
and with my song will I praise him.
Psalm 28:7

When Megan was inside Elizabeth's house, she scanned the room everywhere looking for Brandon. He was nowhere to be seen. She said hello to the rest of Tara's family and then to Elizabeth's family members that she'd met at the wedding. Her heart thumped hard when she heard another car pull up outside, hoping it would be Brandon.

A few minutes later, there he was at the doorway. Tara raced over toward him and introduced him to everyone. When the introductions were over, he looked across the room and smiled at Megan and then made his way to her.

"Hello."

"Hi. I thought you mightn't be coming," Megan said.

"I wanted to meet some of your friends and Tara's friends. I've already met Gretchen and William."

Brandon had often collected Tara and taken her to the Tuesday night family dinners. It was on one of those occasions that he'd met William and Gretchen.

"I really liked going with you in the van the other night."

He laughed. "I've been thinking about that. It wasn't a good choice for a place to take you."

"Oh, it was."

"I was thinking that I should take you out somewhere properly, like out to dinner if you'd be interested."

"That sounds good to me."

"Okay. How about tomorrow night?"

"Tomorrow?"

"Too soon?" he asked leaning toward her.

"No. I think tomorrow would be just fine."

At that moment, Megan knew that Brandon liked her just as she liked him. Relief was what she felt. "I should see if Elizabeth wants some help in the kitchen."

She was nervous around him for the first time and she thought she hid it rather well. Brandon hadn't mentioned her seeing his house, but going on an actual date was even more of a step forward.

Walking into the kitchen, she saw that Elizabeth had everything under control. The food was already lined up on platters along the long wooden table. Nerves and excitement would prevent her from eating anything at all that night.

"Have you seen what we've done to the *haus,* Megan?" Elizabeth asked.

"*Nee.* I haven't."

"I'll show you around if you want to see."

"Of course, I do."

"We'll start upstairs."

"Now? Isn't dinner about to start?"

"Not yet. We're waiting on a couple more people. Come on."

When they got upstairs, Elizabeth pulled her into her bedroom and flopped down on the bed. "That was just an excuse to have a rest."

Megan giggled. "Your family seems nice."

"Most of them are. I'm still not close to my father's mother yet. My parents wanted to buy me furniture, but Joseph said we shouldn't accept. I suppose he's right. He wants us to do everything on our own."

"His parents gave him this *haus,* though."

"One thing you'll find is that men don't make much sense. It seems that we can take a helping hand from his family, and not from mine."

"Ah, I see. His are in the community and yours are not?" Megan inquired.

Elizabeth nodded. "Possibly that's it."

"Do you like being married?"

"I do. It's one of the best things to have happened to me. Sit down now, and tell me everything that's been going on with you."

Megan sat down on the bed and was glad to tell her about Brandon. "Well, what do you think? He's not in the community, and Stephanie thinks he'll never join."

"Have you asked him?"

"Nee. He might think I'm rushing things if I ask him that."

"You need to know everything upfront, Megan. You don't want to waste your time with him if he's not going to be a part of our family."

Megan knew Elizabeth was referring to the larger family of the community.

Elizabeth continued, "You'll save yourself a lot of heartache if you get that out of the way before you get too involved with him."

"You think?"

"Jah. I do. In fact, I know it."

Megan sighed. "I guess you're right. He asked me to dinner, so I'll talk with him about it then."

"Perfect. Now let's go downstairs and get this meal started. If the other guests haven't arrived, too bad. Everyone's hungry."

WHEN THE NIGHT WAS OVER, Jared walked up beside Stephanie as she was helping Elizabeth finish up in the kitchen.

"Let me know when you're ready to go, Stephanie."

"You can go now, Stephanie. Thanks for your help. You didn't have to work so hard. You were supposed to be enjoying yourself. There's not much to do now," Elizabeth said trying to keep the smile from her face.

Stephanie had been putting her best foot forward. She knew that Jared would want her to be helpful to others.

Gretchen and William had left minutes earlier, and Brandon had taken Megan home, and Tara had left with Caleb.

"Are you sure?" Stephanie asked.

"Of course. *Denke* for coming." Elizabeth glanced over at Jared. "Both of you."

He smiled. *"Denke* for a lovely dinner, Elizabeth. It was nice to meet your family."

When Stephanie walked outside, she shivered in the cold night air.

"Do you want my coat?" Jared asked.

"I'll be okay. It's not far to the buggy."

As they walked, he said, "I hope I didn't offend you by anything I said the other day about your age."

"You could never do that."

"I mean you're not that young."

"I know that. I was waiting for you to realize it."

When they pulled up at the house, he said, "Go into the kitchen and I'll be there in about fifteen minutes. I've got a surprise for you."

"Really?" Stephanie loved surprises.

"*Jah.* Don't look so shocked."

She laughed. "Okay. I'll be waiting." When she was inside, she was pleased to see no one in the kitchen. She would be able to have some private time with Jared.

CHAPTER 21

I cried unto the Lord with my voice,
and he heard me out of his holy hill. Selah.
Psalm 3:4

Several more minutes, Jared poked his head through the back door.

"Come in," Stephanie said.

"Is it safe?"

"We're alone."

He pushed the door open and he had something in his hands.

"What's that?"

He placed it down in front of her. "This is your double caramel latte."

"You remembered?" She stared at the hot drink in the glass.

"Yes."

"You made it just for me?"

"I did. I've been practicing to get them just right. Taste it."

She picked it up and took a sip. "Mmm. It's excellent! Just the way I like them, and it's in a glass. I can't believe you've done this for me."

"Well, I did. And I've got a few things to tell you." He settled down in front of her.

"What?"

"To start with, I'll have to go back to when I first saw you a couple of years ago. I liked you back then and I never forgot you."

She resisted the urge to tell him she felt the same.

He continued, "I made the mistake of telling Jeremiah I liked you. You obviously don't remember him from your visit to the community two years ago, but I can tell you that he must've known who you were when he met you on his *rumspringa.*"

"Really?"

"That's right. We were friends once, but a year ago things soured between us, just before he left."

"What happened?"

"Just a series of small things. I get along with everyone else in the family except for him."

"Do you think he only got involved with me to get back at you?"

"I'm not saying that. Who wouldn't want you as a girlfriend?"

"You?"

He shook his head and touched the glass of latte. "I made this to show you that there'll be nothing you'll miss if you'll join the community. I can make you as many of these as you want. Six a day isn't too many."

She laughed. "You want me to?"

"I've always wanted you to. I just was worried that you might not be ready, or that you might be too young to make a decision for the rest of your life." He reached out and took hold of her hand. "I had to tell you how I feel. You've been on my mind since the last time you were here. I hoped you'd be back and here you are."

She looked away from him. "I feel like a fool for being involved with Jeremiah and the whole robbery thing."

"Forget it. You wouldn't be human if you didn't make a mistake."

"Doesn't it bother you?"

He chuckled. "It doesn't make me happy, but *you* do. I don't want to put pressure on you, but I couldn't risk you leaving again without me telling you how I feel. When do you turn eighteen?"

"In three months."

He closed his eyes for a moment, and when he opened them, he said, "Would you marry me? You'd have to join the community."

"Yes, I will."

He reached out and took her hand. "If you feel the same when you turn eighteen, we'll marry the day after."

She giggled. "I'll feel the same."

"Are you sure? This is a serious life long decision."

"I do. I'll definitely feel the same. I've always remembered you too, from the last time I was here."

When they heard a car pull up outside, Jared said, "I should go."

"What shall we tell everyone?"

"They'll figure it out soon enough, when you spend every moment with me."

She looked into his deep hazel eyes and he smiled as he squeezed her hand. Before he rose to his feet, he leaned over and kissed her on her forehead.

They heard the front door close.

"That sounds like Megan has come home."

"Good night, Stephanie. I'll see you after work tomorrow and we'll do something together."

"Okay. Good night."

After he had left, Stephanie looked at the latte. She sipped it, but it had gone lukewarm.

Minutes earlier.

WHEN MEGAN GOT in Brandon's car to go home, Elizabeth's words played on her mind. She could feel herself falling in love with Brandon, and she had to know where he stood about things and what he was thinking. She cleared her throat and began the conversation as he pulled his car out of Elizabeth's driveway on the way to take her home. He glanced over at her as though he knew she had something to say.

"Brandon, I'm wondering what you think about the Amish."

He laughed. "I've always been charmed and fascinated by the lifestyle."

"You have?"

"It's a simple way of life with no distractions everyone helping each other and living in a real community. I've often wondered if I could do it."

"Live in the community you mean?"

"Yes, that's what I mean. I've never had any serious thoughts about it before I met you just thoughts in passing."

"So, what you're saying is — "

"What I'm saying to you is that if things progress in the right way between us, I will look into joining your community."

"Really?"

"Sure. Will I still be able to do my charity work?"

"The Mission would be too far to travel to in the buggy, but you could do other charity work closer to home."

He nodded. "I'm glad we had this conversation that tells me that you're a woman who is straightforward and I like that."

She smiled and looked at the dark road ahead grateful that Elizabeth had prodded her into talk to him to gauge his intentions.

"Is your bishop available for an outsider like me to have a conversation with?"

"Yes, of course, he is."

"Well, I think that's something I'd like to do soon."

When he stopped the car outside her house, he turned off the engine. "Don't go just yet."

She removed her hand from the door handle and looked at him.

"I want you to know that I'm serious about you, Megan. I know we've only just met, but I know we're heading in a good direction. I'm not passing the time with you. That's not why I've wanted to spend time with you. I think you and I have a future together."

She smiled at him. That's all she'd wanted to know. Now that he said he'd consider joining the community and was going to speak to the bishop, she couldn't ask for better news.

"Thank you for letting me know how you feel. I've been thinking the same things."

"Good. I'll see you soon." He leaned over and gave her a quick kiss on the cheek.

Her body tingled at the feel of his lips, and she wanted to feel his arms around her and kiss him properly. All that would come in time.

"Bye, Brandon."

"Good night, Megan." She opened the car door and hurried into the house.

"ARE YOU STILL AWAKE?"

Stephanie turned around and saw Megan walking into the kitchen.

"Yeah," Stephanie answered.

"Where did you get that?" Megan looked at the latte as she sat down.

"Jared made it for me." Stephanie couldn't keep the smile from her face. "He wants to marry me."

"What?"

"Jared wants to marry me."

Megan laughed. "I heard. I'm just surprised. Stephanie, that's wonderful news and so sudden. I've got some good news, too."

"What is it?"

"Tonight, Brandon and I had a talk. He said he's not against the idea of joining the community, but he'd have to find out more. He's actually going to talk with the bishop."

Stephanie leaped out of her chair and hugged Megan. "Megan, I'm so happy for you!"

"I'm happy for you too. It's not for certain with Brandon, and I don't know what's going to happen in the future, but I feel confident. I know he's the man for me and *Gott* will make a way for us to be together. Just like he made a way for you and Jared."

Sitting back down, Stephanie remembered her prayer when she first arrived at Aunt Gretchen's house. Also, she thought back to her recent talk with her aunt; Aunt Gretchen had said that love could find her at any age, and it had.

Thou hast turned for me my mourning into dancing:
thou hast put off my sackcloth,
and girded me with gladness;
Psalm 30:11

The End of Book 3

THE NEW GIRL'S AMISH ROMANCE

AMISH FOSTER GIRLS BOOK 4

CHAPTER 1

"HELLO? MISS, HELLO?"

It took an effort for Asha to open her eyes. When she did, she saw a young man standing over her. As she blinked, he leaned closer, peering intently into her eyes. The realization hit her that she was on the ground.

"Miss, you've been in an accident, are you hurt?"

Her head was fuzzy. All she could do was stare at the man, watching his mouth open and close as though in slow motion while his words reverberated around her. She could almost see the words in the air, like butterflies swirling in a large jar. She put her hand to her throbbing head.

"Miss, are you okay?" he asked again.

"Ahh, I think I am." As Asha tried with all her might to sit up, all went gray and everything faded into darkness.

She heard the words, "I'll call the paramedics." That jolted her back to awareness.

"No! Don't. I'm okay." With all her might, Asha opened her eyes. "Don't. I'm okay," she repeated.

"Move your toes," he ordered.

Asha moved her feet and her legs. "See? No harm done."

"I can't say the same for your car. I can call a friend to tow it to a workshop."

"Yes, please. I'm okay. I'll rest here for awhile on the ground." She closed her eyes. "Just leave me here."

"You need to be checked over. You must have a concussion, being knocked out like you were."

Asha lifted her hand and tried to grab his arm, but she had no strength. Just lifting her arm had been hard enough. "No. I can't go to the hospital."

"I can't leave you here." Asha could see him trying to decide what to do. Then he leaned over, carefully picked her up and carried her, and that was when everything faded around her once again.

When Asha opened her eyes it took awhile to remember the accident and to figure out that the young man had taken her to...wherever she was. She was in a cozy bed; the smell of freshly baked bread and freshly ground coffee met her nostrils. Wherever she was, there was a strange sense of calm.

She sat up, blinking, and figured she must be in a farmhouse. Pain gripped her and she looked down inside the white sheet wrapped around her to see a dark bruise following the line where her seatbelt had been. That seatbelt must've saved her life. Looking down at the fabric wrapped around her, she realized it was a nightgown of sorts.

Noticing a small window, she pulled her legs over the side of the bed and that's when she noticed iodine on her legs; then she saw the same on her arms. Someone had been caring for her. On wobbly legs, she managed to make it to the window and she looked out. There was nothing but fields for as far as she could see, not another house or building in sight.

She held her head and sank to the floor when she recalled speeding over the hill and swerving to avoid an Amish buggy. The next thing she remembered was her car tumbling over the side of the hill.

Thankfully, the car had come to a stop upright, she recalled, which allowed her to unbuckle her seatbelt and crawl away from the car. Then the blackness, and then that man. He must've brought her here.

Heading back to the warm bed, she was pleased that she'd gotten away from her life, away from her manager... Who was also her cheating boyfriend, Nate Berenger.

She knew she should've felt grateful to be alive, but she didn't. She didn't care. Maybe if she'd died, Nate would've been sorry for how he'd treated her, and she'd be free of pain—free from the pressure that her life had become.

Everyone on the outside looking in, thought she had the perfect life; she had platinum records and every new song became an instant hit. Her tours were always sold out, and now Nate was negotiating a movie deal where he promised she'd play opposite some big Hollywood names. No one understood the never-ending pressure that came from being on top. Sometimes she felt she was suffocating, with no relief in sight.

Closing her eyes, she remembered the scene—the last straw—that had led her to driving such a long distance that night.

Asha had walked into the busy bar, becoming annoyed that her drink wasn't waiting for her. She scanned the dimly lit nightclub for her manager and boyfriend, Nate. He was nowhere in sight. All eyes were on her from the moment she'd walked in, but that was nothing new. She was used to being the center of attention and would've been worried if she wasn't.

"Asha, can I have your autograph please?" a fan called out, waving a book and a pen.

"Not tonight, sorry. Maybe another time," Jason, Asha's bodyguard, did his best to deter the autograph hunters while bouncers moved between Asha and the anxious fans. "Sorry, Asha, we tried to make the bar for VIPs only tonight. I guess it didn't work."

"Thanks, Jason. Have you seen Nate?" Still looking into the crowd of people to see if she could spot him, Asha grew more annoyed. He'd always booked her for too many shows and didn't give a second thought to how run-down she was.

With Nate missing, Asha grew jealous. Was he with another woman? She wasn't normally a jealous person, but she knew he had a wandering eye. The fact that he was tall and handsome, with sandy blonde hair and blue eyes, and now very rich, thanks to her, didn't help matters. When the flashing lights lit up a corner of the otherwise darkened bar, she saw him...huddled next to another woman.

Anger rippled through every fiber of her being. He'd promised, sincerely she'd hoped, to be faithful and to stop flirting with other women, but that was clearly a lie. It made a fool out of her when people saw him with someone else. Everyone knew she and Nate were dating.

In a rage, she charged toward him and when she got closer, she saw that the woman he was whispering to was her best friend, Julie Rose. Both of them looked shocked and guilty when they turned to see her.

"Real best friend you are, Julie Rose! Both of you, just forget my number. And Nate, you're fired as my manager and... And everything else! I'm leaving the industry."

Nate lunged forward, sending Julie Rose flying, and grabbed Asha's arm. "Hey! Wait!"

Julie Rose stood up and laughed. "He never loved you!"

Nate was talking about contracts and how she wasn't able to

fire him, but Asha wasn't listening. The two people closest to her had betrayed her. She wondered how long it had been going on between them. There was no use asking, she'd heard enough lies for one lifetime.

Asha stepped back, pulled her arm away from Nate's grasp, and walked away. She'd call her lawyer tomorrow and get out of her contract with Nate, and find a new manager. There were two names she'd been given when she last made inquiries. Either one of them had to be better than Nate; next time she wouldn't mix business with personal relationships. She'd learned that lesson the hard way.

"Asha! Wait! Stop, I'm sorry! It won't happen again."

It was too late. Asha ran through the bar to get away and as she did, she felt all eyes on her. She ran to the elevator to get back to the safety of her room and as she waited she felt a hand slip around her waist.

"Let go of me now!" She knew it was Nate.

She screamed as he yanked her closer toward him. Without thinking, she turned toward him, balled her hands into fists and punched. Some punches connected and others flailed about in the air. Her anger was burning deep and her face burned with rage. This was not the life she'd asked for.

Then Jason, all six feet six of him, grabbed Nate. "Go, Asha," he said as the elevator doors opened.

Nate struggled, which made Jason put some kind of hold on him that sent him to the floor.

"Run, Asha, I'll be right behind you," Jason yelled.

As the doors closed, Asha heard Jason tell Nate he knew it wouldn't be long before she dumped him. At least Jason was on her side.

Once out of the elevator, she charged into her room and slumped down on the bed. As the tears rolled down her face, she was consumed with hopelessness.

She was rich and she was famous, so why was she so unhappy? From the time she'd been a young teen having singing lessons and singing into a hairbrush, she'd dreamed of this life. It wasn't supposed to be so unhappy.

All Asha could do was sob into a pillow. This wasn't the first time she had finished a show and gone to meet her boyfriend, only to find him all over someone else. Now two people had betrayed her at once. She always knew Julie Rose wanted him; seeing them kiss was no surprise, not really. They'd probably been hooking up the whole time.

They can have each other now! Asha thought.

There had to be more to life than this. The tears continued as she recalled how hard she had worked to pay for those singing lessons. Time and time again she'd heard she'd never make it. How happy she was when she finally got signed to a record label. *Easy days from here,* she'd thought. How wrong she had been.

Not content to wallow in self-pity, Asha decided to take action. She had to get away from her life and the people who surrounded her. She leaped out of bed and headed to the bathroom. Her red lipstick was smudged, and her mascara-smears gave her a panda-eyed look. She ran cold water over a washcloth and wiped off every trace of makeup. Her long blonde curls were matted and her tight white dress was now stained from tears and makeup. She pulled off the dress and threw on an old pair of jean-shorts and a t-shirt she only wore between public appearances.

Everyone always told her how beautiful she was, but what use was that? It hadn't made her happy. All the money, the makeup, the clothes, the hair, it didn't mean anything to her anymore. Neither had the thousand dollar shoes and the five star hotel rooms. Life hadn't been good before she became famous, but it was better than what she had now and there had been no pressure attached.

A change had to be made. She had to get away. Asha picked up the phone and ordered Nate's car to be brought to the front of the building. They told her it would be there in five minutes. That was just enough time for her to pack some belongings into a small bag. She'd get away by herself and Nate could explain to her fans why she quit her tour. Even though she didn't like letting her fans down, she was in survival mode. If she didn't get away, she knew she'd die. She pushed away suicidal thoughts, she wouldn't let Nate be the cause of that, but could she ever get away from the life she'd created? Everyone would know her wherever she went.

Nate burst into the bedroom and looked down at her bag.

"Where do you think you're going?"

"Away from you."

"Don't be ridiculous. I'll move into another room if that's what you want."

"I'm leaving for good. I'm getting out of the country for a while, and I'm finding peace. Now leave me alone." She'd made certain to pack her passport.

He pulled her arm. "We can work this out."

"Get away!" she hollered.

Jason walked into the room. "I'm sorry, Asha. I tried to keep him away."

"Get back, or I'll fire you," Nate said to the bodyguard.

"I work for Asha," Jason said before he dragged Nate out of the room.

Asha grabbed her bag and headed to the elevator while Nate was restrained.

She jumped into the car at the front of the hotel, and sped away. Asha had no idea where she was going, hoping she'd know when she got there. When Nate finally realized she had his car, she'd be long gone. Anyway, he could go home in the tour bus, she figured.

After a couple of hours, her tears stopped flowing, slowing down to a trickle. Now she was out in the country, surrounded by trees and then fields. Time to speed up, now that she was away from the city. There'd be no police to book her for speeding in these parts. She pressed her foot to the floor.

Driving fast gave her a sense of power, of control, that she didn't have in her day-to-day life. Behind the wheel, *she* was in control and no one could tell her how to drive. When she came to a slight rise, she eased off the gas a bit. As she crested the hill, directly in front of her was a buggy with flashing lights. Asha hit the brakes and swerved to avoid it and lost control of the car. The last thing she remembered was the bite of the seatbelt as she was thrown around inside the tumbling car.

CHAPTER 2

"OH, I see you're awake! How are you feeling?"

It was an older lady in Amish clothing. She'd heard about the Amish and knew they were peace-loving and quiet people.

"Um, my chest hurts." Asha looked down at the bruise running diagonally across her chest.

"The seatbelt saved your life. You had a car accident, and my eldest son brought you back here. My name's Patsy. The doctor will be here to check on you soon."

Patsy was a small lady with a friendly face. She seemed kind. She reached over and put the back of her hand against Asha's head. *"Ach, nee.* You're quite hot. I'll fetch you a cup of hot tea and something to eat. Don't move."

"Thank you," Asha said as the old woman plumped up her pillows. "What's your son's name?"

"John Williamson. He's anxious to know that you're okay. He'll be back from milking the cows soon."

"You dressed me in this?"

The old lady chuckled. "I did. I'll wash your clothes today, but they were torn and badly soiled."

"Oh." She knew she'd had a bag in the car. "The car?"

Patsy shook her head. "John is getting a friend to help him get it towed to a workshop. John will see to it. Don't concern yourself." She turned and pointed at Asha's handbag. "There's your bag."

"Oh good. Thank you, Patsy. You're very kind." Asha put her head back on the pillow, feeling strangely peaceful.

"I'll get you that breakfast."

Patsy hurried out of the room, and Asha closed her eyes. Her thoughts stayed on the car. It wasn't her car and whatever happened to it, it'd serve Nate right. As long as they didn't trace the car back to Nate, she was perfectly safe. And with the car off the road, it would be safe if Nate had reported it as stolen.

She relaxed and listened to the strange sounds of... Of silence. She couldn't hear a thing. There had never been a more pleasing sound than none at all. Finally, she was away, "Far from the Madding Crowd," to quote the film title, away from the hustle and bustle where everything buzzed with the fast pace of life. She'd have to think of a way to prolong her stay. Patsy seemed kind; maybe she wouldn't mind if she stayed longer.

Patsy came back and placed a tray on the bed next to her. "Here you go."

There was a cup of hot tea, and toast with butter and a choice of jams.

"Thank you. This is appreciated. I'm so hungry."

"Go on, eat."

Asha smiled at Patsy who was standing there staring at her. She took a sip of tea and then spread the butter over the toast.

"Do you want me to spread it?" Patsy asked.

"That's okay."

"I didn't know how much butter you'd like. I like a lot, but many people prefer a scraping. The butter and milk are from our cows. That surprises city folk."

Asha nodded. She had just bitten into the toast and couldn't reply.

"What's your name, dear?"

Asha swallowed. It had been a long time since anyone had needed to ask her name. She was professionally known as Asha with no last name, although she was born Ashleigh Kemp. It had been Nate's idea to change her name to just 'Asha.' She tilted her head and put a puzzled look on her face. "I don't remember."

"You don't?"

"I must've bumped my head." She needed to stay somewhere where no one knew who she was. There was no way she could have a rest if anyone found out her real identity. Asha figured there was a strong chance this was her only way to escape reality. "Thank you for this." She took another bite of her toast.

"I was going to ask if you wanted to call anyone. We've got a phone in the barn, you see. Oh dear. Don't worry, the doctor will be here soon. You just finish eating, and then rest."

"You have a doctor? I didn't think Amish people used doctors or had communication with the outside world?"

"Of course we do. We're still human, we still get sick and need medical assistance." Patsy took a little step toward her. "Do you remember the accident?"

Asha took a moment and then shook her head, wincing when that increased the headache pain.

When Patsy left the room, Asha felt bad for worrying her. She took another sip of the hot tea and tried not to worry about anything other than having a rest. After she finished all the food on the tray, she threw aside the quilt and went to look out the window again. She felt a little bit steadier now.

Looking out at the fields that stretched for miles, she saw a blue sky and a small herd of cows grazing on the grass. Asha had never seen anything more beautiful; every shade of green was featured in that field. The sky was a deep blue with not one cloud. Toward the far horizon, the sky faded to a softer, lighter blue.

Beneath her vantage point of the upstairs window, she saw a horse and buggy approach the house. It was a young man driving the buggy. Could this have been the young man, John, who'd taken care of her? She had to thank him. Her eyes were fixed on him as he jumped out of the buggy. Under his hat, she saw his hair was dark and his frame was tall and strong. This was someone she had to get to know.

She couldn't go downstairs in the sheet she was wearing. She looked around the room and saw dresses hanging on a peg. Hopefully, whoever owned the dresses wouldn't mind if she wore one of them. Quickly she slipped out of the 'sheet' and into a pale yellow dress. On the dresser, she found a brush and dragged it through her long blonde hair only to find it full of tangles. Realizing it would take some work, she sat down on the bed. Once the brush moved through her hair freely, she looked around for a mirror to see how she looked. There was none in the room. She always carried lipstick in her bag. With a clean dress, her hair brushed and a smear of lipstick, she hoped she looked presentable and ventured downstairs.

The wooden stairs creaked as she walked down them, and at the bottom, she found herself in a large, sparsely furnished living room. Hearing noises from one end of the house, she headed that way.

Suddenly the front door swung open and she jumped.

"So sorry. I didn't mean to give you a scare."

She let out a sigh, glad to see the handsome man standing in front of her. "It's okay. I wanted to thank you for bringing me here. Your mother has been so kind. You are John, aren't you?"

He smiled. "I am. How are you feeling?"

"Fine. Considering..."

"I'm glad to hear it. My friend towed your car and he's finding out what it takes to fix it. He can give you a quote."

"That would be good."

Asha remembered books she had read about Amish people. "I didn't think Amish drove cars. Do you?"

"My friend, Mick, is on *rumspringa,* a time of living outside the community. A rather extended *rumspringa,* it turns out. He's working as a mechanic."

Time away from Nate and the paparazzi was just what she needed. "You're very kind for helping me and bringing me here, and your mother is extremely kind also."

"It is our pleasure. It's not often that something like this happens. You are welcome to stay here as long as you need. I'm certain my mother would say the same thing."

"What are you doing out of bed?" Patsy had come from the other end of the house.

"I feel better."

"You must go back to bed until the doctor comes." She looked at her son. "The young lady has lost her memory."

John's jaw fell open. "Really?"

Asha nodded. "I'm certain I'll be all right soon. I just need to rest."

"Back upstairs with you then. John, call the doctor and see how much longer he'll be."

"Yes, *Mamm.*"

John walked out of the house and Asha stared after him.

"Upstairs," Patsy ordered.

Asha realized she had been lost in thought, and shook her head before remembering it would hurt. She wasn't used to taking orders from anyone. "Is it morning?"

"It's close to midday. Now, back upstairs with you, and lie down."

Asha smiled. "I'm going right now." Once back upstairs, Asha climbed into bed wondering whose room it was. Neither John or Patsy said anything about her wearing the dress. When she heard the door open and close downstairs, and then John's voice, she walked to the door to listen.

"They said they're too busy to come out. I'll have to take her to the doctor. Dr. Martin said to take her to the hospital, but I think she's terrified of hospitals. I was surprised; you heard last night how scared she was of that."

"Just take her to the doctor. He should know if she's okay."

"Shall I fetch her?"

"*Nee,* I'll do it. You get the buggy ready."

Asha climbed back into bed and waited for Patsy to come back up the stairs.

"We have to take you to the doctor."

"That's fine. Oh, I didn't ask you. Is it okay that I wear this dress? I saw it hanging there."

"Yes. That's Becky's, my daughter. She's on *rumspringa*. Borrow anything of hers you want."

"Thank you." Asha nodded. "Yes, I've heard about that. I think I know what it is."

"John's waiting in the buggy for you."

"Okay." Asha looked around, grabbed her bag and saw her high-heeled shoes. They didn't exactly go with her outfit, but footwear hadn't crossed her mind when she'd run from Nate.

Patsy was watching Asha. "You can see if you fit into Becky's shoes. She won't mind." Patsy leaned down and handed her a pair of stockings and also retrieved a pair of lace-up black shoes.

Asha had never seen anything so ugly since she'd had to wear similar shoes for one of the schools she attended. "They look about the right size."

"Try 'em."

After Patsy placed them on the floor, Asha pushed her feet into them. "Perfect."

"Good. Then put your stockings on and you'll be ready to go."

"Thank you."

As soon as Patsy walked out of the room, Asha pulled the stockings on and then pushed her feet into the black shoes. After she'd laced them, she knew no one would know her in these clothes. Seeing a hair tie on the dresser, she grabbed it and pulled her hair back tightly away from her face. She was even more certain she was not recognizable like that.

Patsy was at the bottom of the stairs ready to escort her out to the buggy. When she climbed up next to John, she thanked Patsy again as the buggy headed away from the house.

CHAPTER 3

"I HEARD something when I was upstairs. Was I conscious last night? I don't remember anything except you after the accident. Did I say not to take me to the hospital?"

"Yes. You must've had a good bump on your head not to remember that, or who you are."

Asha sighed and leaned back in her seat. She'd never ridden in a horse-drawn buggy before and found the cool breeze on her face refreshing. It was a hot day and the scenery was so beautiful. She closed her eyes to smell the fresh air and the scent of the meadows, the trees and the wildflowers. Opening her eyes, she saw more green fields and they passed small plots of farming land.

He glanced over at her. "It's about a thirty minute ride into town. I hope you feel comfortable."

"Look. I don't think it's necessary that I see a doctor, I'm fine. Really I am."

He shook his head and looked Asha straight in the eyes. "You've no memory. I'm sure Dr. Martin is going to send you for tests."

Asha would have to delay those tests somehow. They'd want to see some form of ID and then her cover would be blown. "I suppose you're right."

As THEY WALKED through the doors of the doctor's surgery, she saw a petite young woman with strawberry blonde hair sitting behind the counter. As soon as the young woman spotted John, she jumped up to greet him.

"John! How are you? What are you doing here? Are you sick or hurt?"

Asha looked over to see John's amused face. It was clear Asha wasn't the only one who admired this handsome man.

"I'm fine, Sally. This is my friend."

John trailed off as he looked at Asha and realized he didn't know her name and, apparently, neither did she.

"Call me Jane," Asha quickly replied. John gave Asha a quick smile and turned back to Sally.

"Jane is here to see Dr. Martin."

Sally looked Asha up and down and, with a dissatisfied look and an uncertain stare, advised them to take a seat. She said the doctor would be with them shortly. Her expressions made Asha feel insecure. Did Sally know who she really was? Asha was only in her early twenties as well, and her music reached out to the young people. She tried to shake off the nerves and turned to face John.

"You don't come here much, do you?"Asha smiled at John.

"Not if I can help it."

Asha looked around the room; there were two other ladies. One old lady wore purple glasses and had pale-purple hair, and was half falling asleep, and a young-looking woman on the other side of the waiting room was reading a magazine.

They continued to wait in silence and Asha noticed Sally staring at her, and then quickly looking away so as not to make eye contact. This made Asha nervous and she was glad when the doctor opened the door and called her into his office. As Asha walked past the doctor who was holding the door open, he said hello to John.

The doctor was a small old man with gray hair, glasses and a large stomach. He had a big friendly smile that instantly made Asha feel comfortable. He advised her to step behind a curtain and change into a gown and then a nurse came into the room.

As the doctor checked her over, he asked questions about the accident. She said she didn't recall much at all. And then he mentioned that John had said she didn't remember her name.

Finding nothing physically wrong aside from bumps and bruises, the doctor advised her to get more tests done at the hospital.

"I have a fear of hospitals. Is it absolutely essential?"

"That's my advice. Of course, I can't force you to go. You can put your clothes back on and throw the gown into the hamper."

As Asha did so, she could hear him scribbling on a pad.

When she opened the curtain and sat back down, he ripped off the top sheet and handed it to her. "Take this to the hospital, if you go."

"Thank you." Asha took the piece of paper, feeling guilty for lying.

"Take a few days to rest. You've been quite shaken up. I can see that Patsy has taken good care of your cuts and scrapes."

Asha nodded as she looked at her iodine-stained arms and legs. "Yes. She's been very kind."

"Good luck, Jane. Come back if I can help with anything more."

"Thank you, Dr. Martin." Asha walked out of the room, and John jumped to his feet. Asha paid for her visit in cash, thankful that she'd had some in the purse she came with. She also had a credit card, but if she withdrew money, someone would know where she was. There was only one thing for it, she had to make the cash last as long as possible.

"What did he say?" John asked on the way out of the building.

"He said, "Rest," and that my memory will come back in time. And if it doesn't, come back in a few weeks. If my memory hasn't returned in a few weeks, he wants me to go to the hospital and have some tests run."

John nodded. "I thought he'd have told you to go sooner."

"No. He said it's my decision, and I just need to rest."

As they made their way back to the house, Asha asked, "Was that a good friend of yours back there?"

"That's Sally. She's a friend of my sister."

"The one who's on *rumspringa?"*

"Yes. Becky. My only sister."

"She was acting so concerned, like she was your girlfriend or something." Asha giggled.

"No. There's only one woman in my life."

"Oh?"

"Sasha is her name," John replied

"That's a nice name." Asha's heart sank just a little at the thought of John having a girlfriend. Why couldn't she ever attract a nice man like John? She could tell he was good. All the men who had come her way were men like Nate. Not wanting John to notice her disappointment, she asked, "I suppose she's Amish too?"

"I guess. In a way... She is now."

Asha frowned at him and his stumbling answer to her simple question. "What do you mean?"

He smiled. "Sasha is my horse. She's beautiful, isn't she?" He nodded to the buggy horse.

"She certainly is." Asha giggled as she admired the gray horse with dapples on her rump, and her long white mane and tail. "She's such an unusual color."

"I love horses, and she's the best one I've had."

"It must to nice to be around animals all day, feeding them and looking after them."

"Do you think you've got family looking for you? Should we stop by the police station? They might have reported you missing."

"No! I'm sure that's not the case. I mean, I don't feel I'm being missed by anyone." She looked down at her finger and then held out her hand toward him. "As you can see, I'm not married. There's no ring on my finger. And I'm older than eighteen, so I'm not a child."

He nodded. "I guess you're right."

When they arrived back at the house, John took care of the horse while Asha went back inside the house. She was met at the door by Patsy.

"What did Dr. Martin say?"

"He said to rest, and if I still don't have memory in a few weeks I should go to the hospital and have some tests run."

"I'm glad you're okay. Sit down on the couch and I'll make you a hot cup of tea."

Asha sat down and wondered where she could stay. She then got up and followed Patsy into the kitchen.

"Patsy—"

Patsy swung around and hurried to pull out a chair. "Sit."

"Thank you." As she sat, she said, "I wonder if there might be a bed and breakfast I might be able to stay at for a few days, maybe a couple of weeks?"

"You could've stayed here but with my four boys, it wouldn't be a good idea." She spun around leaving the water running into the kettle. "There's the Grabers. They had three foster children and now they only have two, so I know they've got room."

Patsy turned off the tap.

Asha didn't like the sound of that. She would've preferred somewhere she wouldn't have to interact with people. "I don't want to put anyone out."

"You wouldn't be."

After Patsy put the kettle on the stove, she sat down at the table. "I'll call them today and if they say it's okay, I'll have John take you there tomorrow." Patsy leaned forward. "Don't worry, you'll like them. Everyone likes the Grabers."

Asha smiled and nodded, figuring she might be harder to find deep within the Amish community. At a bed and breakfast, it'd be easy for Nate to find her, as she'd have to show ID and pay with a credit card.

"Thank you. I'd appreciate that."

"They've got a double wedding coming up soon. Their last two girls are marrying."

"At the same time?"

"Yes. And both are marrying lovely young men. And if I'm right, that means their house will be empty."

"As long as I'm not intruding. I don't want to bother anyone."

"Just let me speak with them after we have a cup of tea." Patsy stood up when the kettle whistled.

While Asha sat at one end of the kitchen at a long wooden table, she took a moment to have a look around the room. The floor was gray linoleum with a pattern of small tiles, the kitchen cabinets were also gray and there was one sink and one small stove. Near the stove was a wooden island counter, and against the wall there was a fridge, which she knew had to be powered by natural gas or propane.

Patsy placed tea in front of her and a plate of cookies.

"These look delicious," Asha said reaching for one.

"If the Grabers can take you, I'll make up a suitcase for you of Becky's clothing since you don't have anything of your own here. Becky won't be back for months."

"I didn't even think of that. Thank you."

"I try to be a practical person."

Asha munched into the cookie. In the past she always had to watch what she ate, but now she didn't care. The cookie was as good as it looked. "Did you make these?"

"I had a visitor yesterday who brought those ones. I make cookies about once a week. I have to fill my boys up with something. You should see how much they eat."

"I guess they need a lot when they're growing, and I suppose they work hard."

"They do." Patsy took a sip of tea.

Asha stood up suddenly. "Oh, such a pretty colorful bird was just sitting at the window."

"We get so many pretty birds here. John's got feeders by the barn."

After Patsy talked about birds, they exchanged small talk for some time. Then Asha offered to wash the dishes, but Patsy wouldn't hear of it.

"Sit and have a rest," Patsy insisted.

"I think I just need a bit of fresh air."

"There's a chair out on the porch."

"Okay." When Asha headed outside, she heard singing. She walked down the porch steps following the sound that drew her toward the barn.

Was that John singing? When she got to the barn, she saw that it was John, cleaning out one of the buggies while he sang.

She was taken aback by the power and beauty of his voice, and closed her eyes to enjoy it more. The song continued and then stopped abruptly. Suddenly she opened her eyes to see him looking at her.

CHAPTER 4

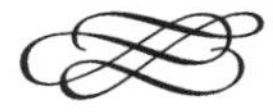

"OH, I didn't mean to interrupt. You have a beautiful voice. What is that song? I've never heard singing like that before."

"It was one of our hymns in German."

"I would love to listen more."

He laughed. "I don't think I can sing with you looking at me. I'd like to ask you a few questions if that's okay?"

"Sure; no worries."

John walked over to the hay and pulled out a bale for Asha to sit on. After she sat down, he pulled one out for himself and sat opposite. A cat sprang onto her lap, causing Asha to yelp in fright and the cat to jump off just as fast as it had come.

"That's only Paws."

"I like cats, but I didn't see him coming. Can I pat him?"

"Sure. He's one of our barn cats. We've got three who stay in the barn and spend most of the day catching mice. If they're not doing that they're sleeping in the sun somewhere."

"'He... so this one is a male?"

"Yes."

"I thought he was. He looks like a boy. Maybe it's because he's so big." Asha walked over to the cat and leaned down to pat him. He purred, curling around her legs.

"Pick him up if you want. He likes to be petted. He'll take all the attention you can give him."

Asha picked him up and sat back down with him in her lap. "He's a heavy boy."

"Yeah, he's a big cat." While the cat sat in her lap, John asked, "How are you feeling after seeing the doctor?"

"I'm feeling okay, just a little headachy and sore from the seat-belt, but I'm sure that'll go with some time and fresh air."

"Surely you have someone who will be looking for you?"

"I... I don't remember who I am."

"I know, but I think if we let the police know, then—"

"I don't remember where I came from, but I feel like I have been alone and that no one will be looking for me. Your mother says she's going to call the Grabers to see if I can stay there."

John drew his head back. "I was hoping you'd be able to stay here."

Asha remained silent. She'd prefer to stay there too. "Your mother mentioned your brothers. Will they be home soon?"

"Later. They're with my uncle today. They'll be home in time for dinner. If you do end up staying with the Grabers, would you mind if I visit you?"

"I'd like that very much. And I'll have to find out where my car is."

"I'll take you there in a few days. Where were you going in such a hurry when you nearly ran me off the road?"

"I don't remember." Asha needed to change the subject. "Is it hard to live without electricity?"

He smiled. "I've never lived *with* it, so I can't say. If you're wondering, we don't have electricity because that would be allowing the outside world into our lives. We prefer things to stay as they are. We don't want TVs or video games because that takes away from the family."

Asha nodded. "I can see the sense in that." If Asha had a family she would've wanted to spend time with them. Jess was the only family she had ever known, and neither of them had experienced what they considered a real home. She felt a pang of anxiety, thinking that her sister had no idea where she was.

"There you are," Patsy said as she walked into the barn. "I'm going to call the Grabers."

John stood and Asha stayed seated, as the cat had gone to sleep on her. "Er, well, I'll go sit on the porch." She held onto the cat, lifting him as she stood up, and then placed him where she'd been sitting.

"Good idea," Patsy said while reaching for the phone on the wall.

Asha walked back to the porch and sat down. The sun warmed her legs as she waited to find out if the Grabers had any room for her.

When Patsy came out of the barn smiling, Asha guessed she'd heard good news.

"They said you're very welcome to stay with them. John can take you there tomorrow."

"Good. Thank you."

"Now you sit out here and rest. Close your eyes and something might come to you."

"Okay." Before too long, Asha found herself restless and made her way back to the barn, where she spent most of the day talking to John as he worked on the buggies and cleaned and oiled the leathers.

When the sun was getting low in the sky, Asha went back to the chair on the porch. She watched as a buggy came into the yard and stopped near the barn. Three young men jumped out and started walking toward the barn.

John stepped outside the house and said to her, "My brothers."

Asha felt nervous to meet these new people, until a sense of calm come over her as she reminded herself how lovely and kind John and his mother had already been to her.

"Are you sure it is no problem that I am staying here tonight? I hope I am not intruding."

"We can't leave you out on the street now, can we? It's no problem at all. I can show you around the farm tomorrow before I take you to the Grabers'."

The boys started toward the house.

"Are you ready? Here they come," John said.

The boys' pace slowed when they saw Asha.

"She won't bite," John said. "This is the lady who was in the accident. Her name is Jane—that's what we're calling her. She lost her memory. The doctor said it should return within a few weeks."

The boys stopped a couple of yards away.

John continued, "She'll be staying with us tonight, and then she'll be staying at the Grabers'."

One young man stepped forward. "Allow me to introduce myself, Jane. My name is Scott. I'm sixteen and if I do say so myself, you're quite stunning." Scott's face beamed, causing Asha to giggle.

"Easy, Scottie," John warned.

Scott was taller and skinnier than John. He had light brown hair and green eyes, and had dirt on his face from where he must've been working in the fields.

"Pleased to meet you, Scott. I can tell you're quite the charmer."

"Quite the fool, if you ask me," one of the other brothers replied as he elbowed Scott, making the other brothers laugh. "My name is Brad, twenty one years old. Very nice to meet you, Jane. I hope you make a quick recovery."

Brad had more of a bulky build than the other boys, and his eyes were golden brown.

Asha smiled at Brad, but before she could reply, the smallest brother, with hazel eyes introduced himself. "And I am Toby, seventeen years old. I hope you find your stay here enjoyable."

"Thank you. It's nice to meet all of you. Everyone's been so kind and your mother has looked after me well."

The boys headed inside and Asha wondered where their father was. "Do you have a father, John?"

"Yes. He's inside. He came through the back door earlier. You were probably still sitting out here. He's a little shy and doesn't talk much. Some people think he's rude, but he's not. *Dat's* just quiet."

"I'll remember that. I'll see if I can help in the kitchen."

"*Mamm* might like some company. She likes to have women around now that Becky's gone."

Asha believed him. With all those boys around, Patsy probably was pleased to have a female in the house. Asha went inside with John, and while he went upstairs, she went into the kitchen. "Can I help you with anything, Patsy?"

"No. You have a rest and just keep me company. Everything's under control. Did you meet the boys when they came home?"

"Yes. They're lovely and polite. And so handsome." Asha sat down at the kitchen table.

"Well, they do have pleasant faces, and I'm happy they are polite."

Scott and Brad walked into the kitchen, and Scott said, "*Dat* will be down soon, *Mamm,* he's just freshening up before dinner."

Patsy looked over at her son pointing to dirt on his forehead. "Maybe you should have thought to do the same, Son?"

Brad laughed, leaving Scott with a dissatisfied look on his face. "You could've told me," he said to Brad, giving him a shove.

"It hid your ugly face, so I thought you wanted the dirt there."

"Brad! Enough!" Patsy said.

As Scott pushed past Brad, Brad hung his head. "Sorry, *Mamm.*"

He yelled after his brother, "Sorry, Scott." There was no reply from Scott. "I was just having a bit of fun, *Mamm.*"

"You don't have fun at other people's expense. What will Jane think of us?"

Brad looked at Asha, and she didn't know what to do or say. "Maybe I should wash up before dinner, too?"

"There's a washroom through that door." Patsy pointed to a door off from the kitchen.

Jane headed to the washroom and washed her hands, disappointed that there was no mirror to check her appearance. She washed her face and then dried her face and hands on a fluffy towel hanging on a hook.

When she went back into the kitchen, all the boys were sitting at the table and Patsy was pulling a large chicken from the oven.

CHAPTER 5

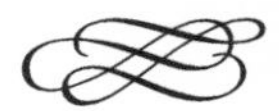

ASHA WENT to pull out her chair, and John quickly jumped up and pulled it out for her. This set off the butterflies in her stomach again. He was so caring and so thoughtful.

"Thank you, John," Asha said with a smile.

"Ohh, 'Thank you, John.' You don't fancy John do you, Jane? I could take care of you too, you know," Scott said with desperation in his voice that once again made his brothers laugh.

"Don't mind him, Jane, he tries too hard with every girl," said Brad.

"That's why he never gets any of them," added Toby.

Asha smiled as she looked over at John; he was trying not to laugh and Asha gathered this was so as to set a good example for his younger brothers.

"What is this fuss?" their father said as he walked into the room.

John said, *"Dat,* this is Jane."

John's father walked around and held out his hand. "Pleased to meet you, Jane. I trust you're feeling better?"

"I am; thank you," Asha said as she shook his hand.

"You can call me Joe."

"Okay, Joe."

"I trust you've been well looked after?"

Asha looked at John and was quick to assure Mr. Williamson of the hospitality she has been shown. "I am so grateful to you and your family. You have all made me feel very welcome. John has been taking care of me all day. He took me to see the doctor. I can't thank you all enough."

"Good to hear." Joe smiled and nodded at John.

The man didn't seem to be so quiet as John had said.

Patsy finished placing all the food in the center of the table. There was a lot of food. There was roast chicken, roast vegetables, fresh bread with butter and all different kinds of jam, and freshly squeezed lemonade. The aroma of the food made her tummy rumble.

John leaned over and explained, "Before we eat, we each say a silent prayer of thanks."

Asha nodded and closed her eyes along with the others. While she was there, she'd follow their customs. When she opened her eyes, she saw they all had theirs open.

"Chicken, Jane?" Patsy asked.

"Yes, please."

John placed some chicken on her plate.

"Look at you boys holding back," Patsy said with a laugh. "Normally, it's a scramble for the food."

"Don't hold back on my account," Asha said. And with that, the boys dove for the food.

"Jane, you better jump in or you'll miss out," Joe said.

"Here, I'll fill your plate," John said, taking her plate from her.

He placed it back in front of her filled with food, and then proceeded to get his own.

"This all looks so good, Patsy."

"I hope you like everything, Jane. If you don't like something, don't feel you have to eat it. There are most likely food here you haven't tried before."

"I'm sure I'll love everything." Asha had eaten food from all over the world, and there was almost nothing she disliked.

She observed the brothers and watched as Patsy kept bringing bowls of food to replenish the table. Their accents and clothes still made her aware of how different they were, but seeing them laugh and make gentle jokes about each other made her think of her sister, Jess.

Asha felt her tummy sink when she realized that her sister would be so worried about her. Jessica and Asha were only one year apart. Jess was twenty four and had always looked out for her. They were adopted out when they were young and had no memory of their real parents. Nor did they know whatever became of them.

Their childhood was spent going from one foster-care home to another. That was why it felt so odd that Patsy had arranged for her to go to the Grabers'—another foster home. Jess and she had been lucky enough to have been kept together when they were little. As they got older, they had refused to go anywhere without the other, which made them spend most of their time in a county-run youth center.

It was having nothing to her name when she was young that had made Asha determined to achieve fame and make something of herself. She worked from age fifteen and it was then that she'd begun paying to take the vocal coaching lessons.

In the last few years, Jess had become Asha's stylist. They saw each other every day and worked well together. Jess had slightly darker hair than Asha, a light brown ashy color, and she had it cut to her shoulders with thick bangs. She never left the house without heels and always wore the tightest jeans and skimpy shirts. Not only had she made it big as Asha's personal stylist, but also with her own clothing line. They had both been determined not to let their past dictate their future.

She pushed Jess out of her mind, only because she had to. Tomorrow at the Grabers' she might be able to use their phone to call Jess and tell her she was okay.

Soon her life would go back to the way it had been, so she pretended that this was her family. This was her life, and John was her husband.

The conversation flowed over dinner, mainly with the boys making jokes. They made Asha giggle and she got to know their personalities more. She started to adore Scott as if he were her own little brother, and Todd as well. She always wondered what having a brother would feel like.

"Tomorrow, before I take you to the Grabers', I can show you around the farm. I hurt my leg in the accident, so I will be off work for a few days." John advised Asha.

"I'm sorry! I didn't know about your leg."

"It's nothing. I'm just taking the opportunity to rest," John said with a smile.

"Meaning he's faking it," Scott called out and the other brothers agreed.

Asha smiled. "I would like to learn more about your culture and lifestyle."

This made Joe sit up straighter in his chair. "You'd like to know more?"

Asha nodded.

"I'm so glad to hear it," he said with a warm smile softening his weathered face.

"Yes, and one day you might come back from the Grabers' to visit me and I'll show you how to make jam. Unless you already know?" asked Patsy.

"I would love to learn how to make jam. I've never done anything like that."

Patsy's face beamed with delight. "Good. I'll have John fetch you one day and bring you back here."

Dinner was delicious. She could tell it was all homemade. Even the butter tasted delicious. So flavorsome. The chicken was moist and the bread was soft. Asha felt her heart opening the more she spoke with the family. She enjoyed how they were relaxed and didn't appear to be worried or concerned over anything.

After dinner, Asha collected the plates to help Patsy with the dishes.

"Oh no you don't; you need to rest some more. Up to bed and we'll see you in the morning."

"Thank you, Patsy. This was a wonderful meal."

Asha looked to John who was wiping his face and hands. "Thank you, John. I have enjoyed meeting you and cannot thank you enough for your help."

John gave Asha a warm smile. After saying goodnight to the family, she was half way up the stairs when she heard a voice yell out.

"Sleep well, Jane!"

That made Asha giggle. "Good night, Scott," she said as she heard the boys cackling.

"Oooh, someone's in love," one of the brothers teased Scott.

As she lay in bed, her mind raced once again and her heart rate escalated.

The anger started inside her as she thought of Julie Rose and Nate. Feelings swirled in her head about how badly Nate had treated her. She pushed him out of her mind and replaced him with images of kind and gentle John. He was tall and friendly and so nice to look at.

And then she did her best to put all the worries out of her head before she slipped between the sheets. Even though it was still early, she welcomed the chance for sleep. It wasn't long after she pulled the quilts up around her shoulders that she fell into a deep sleep.

CHAPTER 6

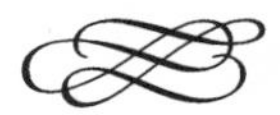

When she woke the next morning it was peaceful, with only the sound of birds singing. She dressed and went downstairs, hoping she could make herself useful before she went to the Grabers'. When she walked into the kitchen, she saw it was just Patsy there.

"Good morning, Patsy. Where is everyone?"

Patsy swung around from the stove. "Good morning. They have all left long ago except for John. He's in the barn or doing something with his horse."

"I was hoping to get up early enough to help you with the breakfast."

Patsy chuckled. "You would've had to get up a lot earlier to do that. Can I make you some pancakes?"

"Oh, yes please."

"Take a seat."

Asha pulled out a chair and sat down at the table. "Have you always lived here? I mean have you always been Amish?"

"Yes, both Joe and I were born into the faith."

Patsy poured the pancake batter into the hot frying pan and Asha took delight in listening to it sizzle.

"Coffee?"

"I'd love a cup. Just black with no sugar."

Patsy made a funny face. "How can you have it black and with no sugar?"

"Well, that answer came out automatically. I think that's how I normally drink it."

"At least you can remember some things. Have you had any other flashes of memory?"

She shook her head. "No."

"Perhaps God wants you to stay in the community for awhile," Patsy said with laughter in her voice.

"Perhaps that's true. I'm looking forward to meeting the Grabers."

"You'll like them, as I told you yesterday." Patsy placed a mug of coffee in front of her. "The beans are freshly ground."

"I can smell it. It's very strong."

"If it's too strong, I'll put a little hot water in it. Or you should try a little milk."

Asha sipped the coffee. "It's perfect. Just right."

"Good." Patsy turned her attention back to the pancakes and flipped three pancakes over.

John walked into the kitchen and sat down. "Good morning, Jane."

"Good morning."

"Good idea. I need some coffee too." He sprang to his feet and poured himself a cup.

When he sat back down, Asha asked, "Are you still going to have time to show me over the farm?"

"We'll have plenty of time. Do you want to go to the Grabers' with me, *Mamm,* when I'm taking Jane?"

As Patsy slid the pancakes onto a plate, she said, *"Jah,* I'd like to visit them."

"Good. Shall we leave at eleven?"

"Okay." Mrs. Graber put a plate of pancakes in front of Asha.

"Thank you." There was already maple syrup and butter in front of her.

"Would you like cream or jam or anything else with the pancakes?" John asked.

"No, thank you. I just like butter on my pancakes, nothing else, and this butter is so nice."

"It's from our cows," John said.

"I know. Your mother was telling me that yesterday."

AFTER BREAKFAST, John walked over part of the farm with Asha.

"How big is it?" she asked.

"It's nearly eighty acres."

Asha giggled. "I've really got no idea how big that is. Is that big, or average?"

"It's fairly average around these parts. Most of us in the community try to grow our own food, as much as we can anyway, and we also trade with each other."

"That sounds like a good idea."

"And what's left over generally ends up at the markets."

John showed her their five cows, the chickens, the goats and the few sheep.

"How many horses do you have?"

"We have four buggy horses. One's getting old so we don't use him much anymore; he's pretty much just put out to pasture. That's him over there."

Asha looked to where he was pointing. "The black one?"

"That's him. Do you want to go over and say hello?"

Asha shook her head. "No. I'm a little scared of horses. They're so big."

"He's as quiet as any horse can be, so he's a good horse to help you get over your fears."

"I think my fear is there for a reason — to keep me alive."

"Trust me. You can stroke his nose; it's very soft."

"Okay, but if he charges at me, I'm pushing you in front of me so he'll get you first."

"That sounds fair."

They set off into the pasture, and the black horse stopped eating grass and watched them approach.

"What's his name?"

"Blackie."

Asha shook her head. "That's original."

John laughed. "My father let me name him. I was only five at the time. What else would a five-year-old name a black horse? Now I can think of some better names, like Shadow or Midnight, but he'll always be Blackie."

As they walked closer, Asha walked slower and John turned around and looked at her, following a few paces behind.

"Don't tense. He'll sense it and think there's danger around, or you're going to hurt him. Just relax."

Asha nodded and did what he suggested and when she drew level with John, they continued walking toward the horse.

The horse took a step to them.

"He's interested, curious enough to come and say hello."

John put his hand out for the horse to sniff.

"Now you do the same," he instructed.

She put her hand out and the horse sniffed her too, placing his nose on her palm. "You're right, his nose is so soft."

"Now do you feel brave enough to touch his nose like this?" John lightly stroked Blackie's nose.

"He likes it."

"Go on. Try it."

Asha did what John said.

"Aren't you glad you did this?"

"I am."

"Well, that might be enough for one day. If we don't leave at precisely eleven *Mamm* will get really upset. She is a stickler for being on time."

As they walked back to the house, Asha said, "Thank you for showing me the farm. It must be lovely here with the animals, and so relaxing. I've got an idea that my life before the crash was anything but relaxing."

"I hope your memory starts coming back soon."

Asha nodded. "Me too. I'm sure it will."

When the house came into view, they saw Patsy waiting in the chair on the porch. She had a black cape around her shoulders and a black over bonnet on her head.

John said, in a low voice, "What did I tell you? I pulled the time of eleven out of my head and the Grabers aren't even expecting us at any particular time, but because I said eleven it must be eleven."

Asha giggled.

When they got closer, Patsy stood up. "Jane, I've packed you a bag."

Remembering Patsy had said she would pack her bag of her daughter's things, Asha said, "Thank you very much, that is very kind of you. I'll bring them back when I'm ready to leave."

"No hurry."

"Are we late, *Mamm?*"

"It is five minutes to go before eleven o'clock and you haven't even hitched the buggy yet."

"I'm doing that right now."

While John headed to the barn, Patsy said, "You can wait next to me on the porch here, Jane."

CHAPTER 7

On the way to Gretchen and William Graber's home, Patsy told her as much as she could about the family.

"For the past few years, Gretchen and William have had three girls living with them. Let me see now. There was Elizabeth, and Tara, and Megan. I would guess they were all with the Grabers for five or six years. Wouldn't you say so, John?"

John shrugged. "I thought it was more like ten or something."

"Anyway, now Elizabeth is married to Joseph and Tara married Caleb not so long ago."

"Didn't you say there was a double wedding coming up?" Asha asked.

"I did, yes. The double wedding is Megan's and Stephanie's. Megan is marrying a man called Brandon. He used to be an *Englisher,* but he's taken the instructions and now he's living with an Amish family until they marry."

"How lovely. He converted for her?"

"That's right," Patsy said.

"And who are Megan and Brandon getting married with?"

"Gretchen's niece, Stephanie. Now she was a little bit of a handful, in and out of trouble. Her father sent her to live with Gretchen, his sister. While Stephanie was there she was reacquainted with Jared who she met while she was staying with Gretchen years ago. And now Stephanie and Jared are getting married. The two girls became quite close and Stephanie decided to continue living with Gretchen and William. Stephanie's family had left the Amish years ago, but now she's back with us."

"And when is the wedding?"

"The wedding is not this coming Thursday but the Thursday after that," John said.

"It's very kind of them to let me stay there."

"You'll fit in nicely with the girls. You're around about the same age. Do you remember how old you are?"

Asha shook her head at the woman who was turning around from her front seat to look at her.

Patsy turned back around. "I'm sure your memory will come back to you soon."

"And if it doesn't, I'll take you to the hospital for those tests, Jane."

"Thank you, John."

"And I'll come back and visit you soon."

"I'd like that."

When they stopped outside the Grabers' house, Asha was surprised how small it looked compared to the Amish farmhouses that they had passed. Patsy took her by the arm and led her inside to meet everyone.

A woman appeared at the door. Asha saw right away that Gretchen Graber had a lovely kind face and immediately made her feel at ease. This wasn't like the foster homes she and her sister had been in and out of. She was certain these people would be different.

"Welcome, Jane."

"Thank you so much for having me. I hope I'm not putting you out with the two weddings coming up."

"We've always got room for one more. You can call me Gretchen or Aunt Gretchen as the other girls call me."

"Okay." Asha glanced around at John who was doing something with his horse.

"It's just me at home. I sent the girls shopping. When they're at home, Megan is out somewhere in the fields. She has beehives that keep her busy, and Stephanie's off somewhere doing something." Gretchen gave a little laugh. "I fixed us up some tea."

Asha and Patsy followed Gretchen into the living room where there was a small table covered with cakes and cookies, and a teapot with several cups around it.

John stuck his head through the door. "Hi, Gretchen. Is Jared around?"

"No, he's off with William. You'll have to join us ladies for tea and cake." He stepped through the door rubbing his hands together. "I won't say no to that."

After everyone was seated with a cup of tea, Gretchen said, "Jane, Patsy tells me that you had a dreadful accident and you've lost your memory."

"That's right. I don't remember who I am or where I come from. The doctor said my memory should return soon, and if it doesn't I have to go to the hospital. I think I just need some peace and quiet and then everything will come back."

"Yes, I hope so."

"I nearly collided with John's buggy," Asha added.

"You wouldn't remember, but you clipped the back of it."

Asha gasped. "I'm sorry. I didn't know."

"I saw you coming when I heard the car in the still night, and I thought you were going to run into me so I leaped out of the buggy."

Patsy said, "John! You shouldn't have done that. You could've been badly hurt! She could have run over you."

"God was watching over me."

"I'm sorry about that—your leg and your buggy. Let me know how much it costs to fix."

"Don't worry about that. It was just some scratches and I can fix it. Anyway, you've got your car to worry about."

"It sounds like God was watching over the both of you," Patsy said.

Asha nodded.

"Do you have any belongings, Jane?" Gretchen asked.

"I packed her a bag of Becky's clothing."

John said, "I left that in the buggy. I'll get it before we leave."

"Help yourself to the cake and cookies, don't be shy, Jane."

"They do look delicious." Asha leaned forward and took a chocolate chip cookie, took a bite and then balanced the rest of the cookie on the saucer that held the teacup.

After they drank their tea, it was time for Patsy and John to leave. Asha was nervous to see them go.

John hurried and brought the small suitcase, putting it next to them on the porch. "I'll see you soon, Jane, and hopefully I'll have news about your car."

"That will be good. Thanks, John."

As the buggy drew away from the house, she stood alongside of Gretchen watching them.

Asha hated talking about money; Nate had always done the negotiations on her behalf, but she knew she had to raise the issue. "Gretchen, I just want to let you know that I don't expect to stay here for free. As soon as I know who I am I will have access to my bank account, no doubt, and then I can pay you for staying here."

"No need to worry about that. Whenever you're ready you can contribute for the food, but only if you want to." The woman smiled kindly at her.

Asha made a mental note to pay the woman handsomely when she got back to reality.

"Is there anything I can do to help with the wedding or anything?"

"Not right now, but there will be in the coming days. It's always good to have an extra pair of hands about the place. You could help me now by clearing the dishes if you feel up to it."

Together they carried the dishes to the sink. Gretchen placed the uneaten food away while Asha did the washing up.

"You've been a foster parent for a while?" Asha asked.

"For quite some years. William and I could never have children of our own and we knew that was because God had a plan. There are so many children out there who need love and attention. If we'd had our own, then those who came to us might have gone where they were neglected or uncared for. God has had His hand on every child who came to us."

"And the last two girls you have here are getting married? And then you and William will be on your own?"

"Megan was a foster child of ours, but Stephanie is my niece."

"Oh, that's right. I remember Patsy telling me that on the way here."

Asha could see how genuine Gretchen was about looking after foster children and she wasn't doing it for the money the government gave her to do so, as she suspected with some of the foster parents she'd been placed with. Most of her experiences had been bad.

"And I suppose you don't remember how old you are?"

"No, I don't."

Gretchen studied her face. "It's hard to say. You've got beautiful skin, and you're a very pretty girl. I would say you're in your early twenties somewhere."

"Possibly," Asha said. "So your niece was an *Englischer?*"

"That's right."

Asha was now worried that Stephanie, Gretchen's niece, might recognize her.

"Her father is my brother and he left us many years ago. He turned to me when he couldn't control Stephanie. She's lively, but Jared has calmed her. They're truly good together and well suited."

When they heard a buggy, Gretchen rushed to the window and looked out. "Here the girls are now. Stephanie and Megan. Come out and I'll introduce you to them."

CHAPTER 8

ASHA KNEW full well that this could all be over soon if one of the girls recognized her, but would anyone know her in these clothes and without makeup? She followed the small Amish woman out to the porch.

"Where are they?" Asha asked.

"They're in the barn now. They won't be long."

Asha couldn't see them, but now she could hear them talking and giggling. She hoped she would get along with them. Several minutes later, two girls wearing Amish clothing walked toward the house.

"Girls, this is Jane. The girl I told you about who'll be staying with us for a while. Jane, this is Stephanie and this is Megan."

The girls said hello to one another.

Stephanie stepped forward. "You look a lot like Asha. Except her face is slightly different."

"Who's Asha?" Megan asked.

"Don't worry about it," Stephanie said shaking her head.

Phew, that was a close call! "I hear you're both getting married soon, and at the same time?" The girls looked as though they were still teenagers.

Stephanie said, "I'm marrying Jared, and Megan is marrying Brandon."

Megan nodded. It was clear she was the quieter of the two.

"Where are my groceries?" Gretchen asked.

The two girls looked at each other and then burst out laughing.

Stephanie said, "We left them in the buggy."

"Well, go and get them."

"Do you need help?" Asha asked, trying to make friends with them.

"Yeah, okay. We've got quite a few bags," Stephanie said.

Asha walked with the girls around the corner of the barn. It opened up to a large area where two buggies were kept.

"Is that too heavy?" Stephanie asked after she handed Asha two bags.

"No, I can carry more."

Stephanie gave Megan some bags and then Asha another one. Then with their hands full, the three girls walked to the house.

"How long are you staying with us, Jane?" Megan asked.

"Maybe a couple of weeks. I'm trying to get my memory back."

"You don't remember anything?" Stephanie asked.

"No, I don't. I remember a little before the accident and that's it. The doctor said I should get the memory back over a short time."

"You don't remember your family or anything?" Megan asked.

"Nothing." Asha thought it might be a good idea to block out the past. What if she had really lost her memory and didn't know who she was, and she wasn't Asha, the famous singer. If she had really lost her memory, she could have a chance to start her life over again. Who would she become? One thing she knew for certain was that she didn't want to be famous.

The girls made their way into the kitchen and placed the bags on the wooden table.

"Stephanie, you can help me in here and Megan, you can take Jane to the spare room and help her settle in."

"Jah, Mamm," Megan said, while Stephanie didn't look too happy to be the only one helping in the kitchen.

As Megan was walking down the hallway carrying the small bag, Asha said to her, "You called Gretchen, '*Mamm?*'"

"Yes, that's how we Amish say Mom."

"You feel that close to her that you call her that when she's your foster mother?"

"Yes, I've called them *Mamm* and *Dat* for a long time. I've never known any mother or father. They're the only ones I'll ever have and they're the closest people to me. I went from foster home to foster home before I came here." She nodded to a room, then walked toward it and pushed the door open. "This is your room."

Megan's story was similar to her own. "What was it like in the foster homes?"

Megan placed the bag down and sat on the bed and Asha sat next to her.

"No one wanted me. I can't even count how many foster homes I was in. And then for a long time I just remained unclaimed, uncared for in the orphanage. No one wanted to adopt me because I was sick all the time when I was young. And I don't know why that was. I must have had something that I grew out of."

"Unless you were allergic to something."

"If I was allergic to something, I've never found out what it was."

Asha said, "It was a good thing you came here to live with Gretchen, then."

"God had his hand on me."

"Were you Amish before you came here?"

"No, none of us were. Stephanie is Gretchen's niece and her father is Tom. He was raised Amish and then he left the community so Stephanie was raised an *Englischer* for most of her life."

"That's interesting," Asha said even though she'd heard that three times now.

"I can't even ask you any questions because you can't remember anything."

"That's right. It's quite a strange feeling not to have any past. So I don't know who I am." She was lying about not remembering, but she wasn't lying about not knowing who she was.

"I used to think that if my mother ever came to find me that I would know who I was, but then I realized that you are who you are and it's got nothing to do with your parents. We are all individuals. Brandon was looking into finding my mother for me for a while, because I thought I wanted to know, and then I had to tell him to stop."

"Why?" Asha asked.

"If I found out she was dead, I thought it would be too much pain to deal with, and if she is alive, why hasn't she ever come to find me?"

"So you feel more comfortable not knowing?"

"I guess so." Megan nodded. "Now you know all about me."

Asha wished she could share her story, too. As Megan said, it shouldn't matter who your parents were or where you came from. Asha too had decided not to find out more about her parents. Maybe one day she'd want to know, but for the past few years she'd been too busy pushing herself to get to the top of the music industry to worry about her parents and why they'd given her and her sister away.

After having a nice talk with Megan as they unpacked her bag, Megan went to help with the meal while Asha stayed in the bedroom.

Asha sat on the bed looking around the bare room. On the walls there was nothing but a small sampler with cross-stitching that read, "God is Love." The bed seemed comfortable enough and there were two pillows on it, which made her happy.

Her thoughts soon turned to Jess. The Grabers surely had a phone in their barn, the same as at Joe and Patsy's house, but how was she going to get to it? She knew she was going to have to wait until tomorrow. She couldn't risk sneaking out at night in case someone saw her. In the day, it would be much easier to say she was going for a walk and then she could slip into the barn and make that telephone call.

Hearing the lively chatter from the kitchen, she headed back to join them. Soon she was sitting down with the girls as they peeled vegetables for the dinner. The conversation was fun and lively and these girls didn't have a care in the world. Asha knew she had to make her life like theirs. She'd gone against the odds to become a famous singer; she could do it again and have a different life.

Soon William Graber and Jared arrived home for dinner. Jared was clearly taken with Stephanie and could hardly keep his eyes from her. It was sweet to see young people in love, Asha thought.

After dinner the girls pulled their wedding dresses out to show Asha. They had matching blue dresses that ended below the knee, white organza capes, prayer caps and aprons. The clothes they were wearing to their wedding were pretty much the same as they wore every day, just a little bit fancier and brand new.

That evening they hand sewed the dresses of their attendants, who were also wearing matching blue dresses but in a lighter shade.

The girls explained to Asha that they had sewn most of the dresses on a friend's gas-powered sewing machine, and they were only sewing the hems by hand.

When William and Gretchen went to bed, Asha stayed up with Stephanie and Megan.

"Do either of you work?" Asha asked.

"I work part-time at a coffee shop, and Megan sells her honey and works for someone at the farmers markets."

"Oh yes, I've heard about your bees, Megan."

"Really?"

"Yes. I think Patsy told me that you keep bees."

"I can show them to you tomorrow."

"There's not much to see. They are just boxes with bees buzzing around," Stephanie said.

"I'd love to have a look at them," Asha said.

"I have to leave for work really early in the morning but I can show you when I get home."

"Good. I'm not going anywhere as far as I know." Asha had already told them over dinner about the accident and her car rolling down the hill after clipping the back of John's buggy. "John said he would come and get me and then we'll both go and see about my car."

"That's one thing I miss — cars," Stephanie said. "Buggies are so slow."

Megan said, "Now that you're in the community, Stephanie, you don't have to hurry anymore."

"Everything's a lot slower," Stephanie said.

"What else do you miss?" Asha asked Stephanie.

"Nothing else. I would miss Jared if he wasn't here, but now since he's in the community and I'm in the community, I have everything I want."

"That must be a very nice feeling," Asha said.

CHAPTER 9

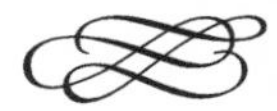

THE NEXT DAY, after an early breakfast, everyone except Gretchen left for work and Asha excused herself after helping clean the kitchen, saying that she needed to get some fresh air and would go for a short walk.

As soon as she slipped through the door of the barn, she spotted the phone. Taking a deep breath, she picked up the receiver. She wasn't exactly sure what she was going to tell her sister. She knew Jess would be an absolute mess and looking for her everywhere. It only took a few rings before she answered.

"Hello?" a nervous voice answered the phone

"Jess, it's me."

"Where are you?" Jess replied in a panicked voice.

"I've had to get away for a while."

"Are you okay?"

"Yes."

"Why are you whispering? Whose number is this?"

Oh no! She hadn't blocked the caller ID. "Jess, you must not call back on this phone. I'm staying with some people and they've got no idea who I am. Promise me?"

"Okay. Just tell me where you are."

"I can't. I'm okay. Don't tell anyone I called you."

"Nate's been frantically worried. He's about to put out a press release."

Asha sighed. "Okay. Tell him I called you and I'm okay. I'm taking a vacation."

"Just tell me where you are."

"I can't. You've got to trust me. I'll call you back in a day or two. Just don't tell Nate where I am."

"You haven't even told me."

"I wrecked Nate's car and—"

Jess gasped.

"I was just banged up, nothing broken or anything. A nice man found me, an Amish man. I'm staying with his family. They are lovely and they're letting me stay here until I feel better."

"What? Have you gone mad? Do you know how sick and worried I've been, thinking my little sister has been abducted, if not killed, and this whole time you've been more than okay?"

Asha understood Jess's point, but for the first time ever, she didn't let the guilt overtake her. For once she was putting herself first. For once, she was doing what she wanted to do and not living her life to please others while sabotaging herself.

"I understand and I am sorry, Jess. I'm not exactly 'more than okay,' though. I'm still recovering from the car wreck, and what came before it. Just tell Nate I'm taking time off. I saw Nate making out with Julie Rose, and that was the last straw. I had to run. I can't go back to him, or to that lifestyle. I need time to sort myself out."

"Asha, you've got commitments. You've always known what Nate was like. And I told you not to trust Julie Rose."

"I love you. I'll call again soon. Remember what I said, just give me some time."

"No, Asha, you don't understand. Nate has gone mad; he's gone crazy. He's drugged himself and been in the hospital because he was so stressed and worried about you. He only woke up yesterday and he has to be heavily medicated because when he remembers, he goes crazy again. It's weird, it's like you were a drug to him. He needs you."

"Not badly enough to be faithful to me. And I don't need him. This time I need to look after myself." Asha couldn't believe what she was hearing. Sure, it would've been stressful for him to cancel the tour and she guessed he would've had to make an announcement that she was ill. That would've created stress for him.

"Ash, you there?"

"If he cared about me, he wouldn't treat me like that. I've got to go, Jess, love you." Asha replaced the receiver. She could've done without knowing anything about Nate, and it most likely wasn't true anyway. Nate would've made her sister say all that just to worry her.

Asha walked out of the barn and headed toward the fields. Maybe a walk in the fresh clean air would help to clear her head and her emotions. When she heard a buggy she stopped still, and then turned around to see John's buggy heading toward the house. She walked over to meet him.

"Hello," she said, trying to hide her smile. She was pleased to see him.

He stopped the buggy. "Hello, Jane. How are you on this fine morning?" A smile twitched at the corners of his lips.

"I'm doing well. I was just about to take a walk in the fields."

"My mother sent me over here to see you."

Asha had hoped that John was there because he wanted to see her.

"She's got it into her head that you're going to help her make jam."

Asha giggled. "She did mention something about that."

"Well, what do you think? Do you think Gretchen will mind if you spend the day at my house? I think my mother misses my sister. She said it was nice to have some female company around."

"I'll see. I'll just ask Gretchen if she'll mind. I'm sure she won't."

Asha hurried into the house and once she talked to Gretchen, she grabbed her bag and shawl and headed out to John's waiting buggy.

"She doesn't mind at all."

"Well, let's go," he said, letting his smile light up his face.

Asha climbed up next to him. "Gretchen dropped a hint about bringing some jam back to her."

John chuckled. "I'm sure that can be arranged." He turned the horse around and started back down the driveway. "So, what do you think of the Grabers?"

"The girls are really nice. And so are Gretchen and William, of course. I've gotten to spend some time with Stephanie and Megan." Asha wondered why John hadn't gotten together with either one of those girls. Perhaps she might find out one day soon. She didn't know him well enough to ask him.

"Before I came here, I stopped by to talk to my friend—the mechanic. He has to order some parts for your car and then the car will need the dents pounded out before they touch up the paint. That can all be done at the same place he works."

"That sounds expensive."

"He'll do a quote."

"That's fine."

"It's Saturday today so he's not working, but did you want to stop there and talk to him about your car or anything one day early next week?" He glanced over at her.

"That would be good, if you don't mind."

"I'd be happy to take you there."

"Good."

"So, how are you feeling?"

Asha rubbed her shoulder. "The bruise from the seatbelt is

going down a bit and my scrapes are healing well, but I haven't remembered anything yet and there's still a bit of headache."

"My brothers are all home today."

"That's right, it's Saturday."

"They work most Saturdays, but they're not working today because we're preparing the house for our meeting there tomorrow."

"At your house?"

"Yes. We have our meetings every second Sunday, and we take it in turns to host them at our houses."

"I see. And tomorrow is your turn."

"That's right."

When they got back to the Williamsons' house, Asha felt more comfortable being there, almost as though it was home. He stopped the buggy behind the barn.

"You go on ahead. I'll unhitch the buggy."

"Okay." Asha walked toward the house, and then stopped to pat the large cat she'd met. "Paws," she remembered "Ah yes, that's your name, isn't it?"

He purred loudly in response.

When she walked further, she spotted John's brothers carrying wooden chairs and tables from a big wagon into one of the barns closest to the house.

CHAPTER 10

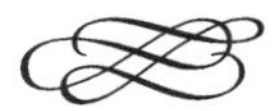

Asha wandered over to John's brothers to watch what they were doing. Scott spotted her as she approached, and a large smile creased his face.

"Jane! My dearest Jane. How are you this fine morning?"

Scott made Asha laugh at his eagerness to please. "Hi Scott. I'm fine, thank you. How are you?"

"Fine."

"What are you guys moving all this furniture for?"

"The meeting is here tomorrow."

"And you have it in the barn?"

"Yes. The house can't hold that many people."

Asha peered through the large barn doors to see what must've been over fifty long benches. To the other side were chairs and tables. "How many people will be coming?"

"About one hundred and fifty to two hundred."

"Wow! Keep working. I'm off to help your mother make jam."

"She's excited about you helping her with the jam," Scott told her.

Asha headed to the house. As she walked through the doors, the scent of freshly baked cake wafted to her. It was her favorite smell and, she thought, just how a home should smell. "Hello," she called out.

"I'm in the kitchen, Jane."

Patsy was mixing something on the counter and turned around to face Asha.

"Hi Jane, and good morning. I'm making food for tomorrow before we start on the jam. Would you like to help mix some more cake batter?"

"I'd love to help." Asha walked over to the table. "And good morning to you, too."

"Thank you. I've already finished two. We have four more to make, including the one I'm mixing, and then we'll go on to the main meal," Patsy replied as she put the cake recipe in front of Asha. "Everything you'll need is here." She pointed to a counter covered in eggs, flour, sugar and milk. "If you could finish these, that would be a big help for me."

"Sure. Patsy, Scott told me there are over one hundred and fifty people coming tomorrow. So every time you hold church at your house, you cook for one hundred and fifty people? Alone?"

Asha saw Patsy give a small smile as she looked in her direction. "Becky always helped me before, and I'm thankful you're here today. Everyone in the community helps. Most people bring food to contribute to the meal after. But the family holding the meeting will provide most of the food. It's a blessing to have it at our house."

Patsy's dedication to her family and the Amish community was something that inspired Asha and made her start dreaming of her own family that she could care for in the same loving way. While she was here, she would learn all she could from them.

"I am looking forward to church tomorrow. I guess the Grabers would be going?"

"Yes, of course."

"Good." Asha read the cake recipe.

"I am so pleased to hear you want to come, Jane. You seem to be settling in very well."

"Patsy, I feel that I really don't want to leave here. I fear that the life I was living before was horrible. I'm not so sure I want my memory to return."

Before the accident, she was not living like a good person, especially compared to them. She drank every night, and spent all her money as fast as she made it. She didn't care about life, she was looking for an escape in any way that she could find it, and this led her to bad lifestyle habits. A tear fell down her face and Patsy noticed, dropping everything in her hands. She walked over to Asha, wrapping her in her arms.

"Oh, dear, it's okay. The Lord teaches us not to live in fear. I'm certain everything is going to work out okay for you, my dear Jane."

Asha felt so comfortable in Patsy's arms.

"Do you want us to pray together now?" Patsy asked as she stepped back.

Asha sniffed and nodded. "I'd like that."

Patsy closed her eyes. "Thank you for bringing sweet Jane into our lives. We come before you today to pray for strength. Strength and hope for Jane and her life. We pray that she finds all that she is looking for, we pray for her health and ask you to bless our lives and restore Jane's health. Thank you, Heavenly Father, Amen."

Asha fought back more tears. She was so moved, so touched. No one had ever prayed for her. She had goosebumps all over her body.

When Asha opened her eyes, she said, "I will pray for a family like yours one day. You are all so kind, so loving and warm. I want a house like this, I want children like yours and I want a beautiful man in my life, like your husband."

Patsy smiled at Asha. "Then say a prayer to God and He will give you what you ask for. All you have to do is believe."

There was a loud bang at the door and Patsy and Asha looked over to see that John had just closed the door with his foot.

"I'm sorry, was I interrupting something?" John asked. As he looked into Asha's face, it was clear she had been crying. "Jane, are you okay? Did you remember something?" John dropped the bag he was carrying and quickly walked toward Asha.

"I'm alright, John. No need to worry." Seeing John care so much about her made her feel happy inside.

Patsy said, "It would've been nice if you could've stayed here, Jane, but you can visit whenever you'd like. You'll be here tomorrow, too, and I have something for you."

"For me?" Asha asked.

"*Jah,* for you." She walked out of the room and came back holding a black book.

"A Bible?" Asha asked.

"It is." She handed it to Asha.

"Thank you. No one has ever given me anything like this."

"I thought you might like it."

John said, "Do you have a Bible, Jane?"

"No, I don't think I ever had one, but I do now," Asha said, staring at it in wonderment. What if the key to having a good life was somewhere in that book? If it was, she was determined to find it.

"You can leave it on the shelf there so it won't get jam or cake mix all over it."

"Yes, okay." Asha walked over and placed the Bible on the shelf Patsy had pointed to.

Patsy stared at John, who was still looking at Asha. "Do you plan on helping us in the kitchen today, John?"

John whipped his head around to face his mother. "I'll get out of your way."

Asha and John exchanged smiles before he left. She knew John liked her and she was pleased about it. He was a genuine man and would never treat her like Nate had. If she married a man like John, her life would be complete. In the short time she'd been with the Amish, she had come to know their world was real. Not fake, like her world that was built on falsity and vanity. No one in that world took time to care for anyone—everyone was out for themselves.

After half a day in the warm kitchen getting to know Patsy better over cooking and jam making, John drove her back to the Grabers.'

As the buggy clip-clopped down the winding narrow roads, she looked down at the Bible in her hands. "It was so nice of your mother to give me this. I shall read it tonight."

"What, the whole thing?" He laughed.

"Well, not all of it. I'll work my way through it and read a little every night. Your whole family is lovely."

"Thank you."

"They *are*."

"I guess they are. They're the only family I know."

Asha giggled. "You've done well to land where you have."

"You could have a family out there somewhere."

Asha sighed and looked out across the green fields as the descending afternoon sun shone its warm glow upon them. "I don't feel as though I have. Deep down, I don't feel it."

"You'll soon find out. I'm sure."

She looked over at his kind eyes as he faced her. "I hope so."

"And if not, you'll have to stay on in the community."

Asha laughed.

"It wouldn't be so bad, would it?" he asked smiling a little uncertainly at her.

"I think it would be lovely."

"Really?" His face brightened.

Asha nodded. "It's so peaceful and there's no falsity among anyone. Everyone is just as you find them, and so kind and good."

"We're God's people. It's God's love that you're seeing."

"I'd like to know more about God. I've never given Him much thought. I always thought if God was real there wouldn't be so many people suffering."

"There are things that are hard to figure out, that is for sure and for certain. But we know He is real, and that He loves each of us."

CHAPTER 11

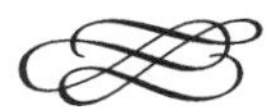

THAT NIGHT, Asha couldn't sleep. As she tossed and turned, negative thoughts crept into her mind. John had told her about *rumspringa.* What if some of the young people coming to the meeting had been on *rumspringa* and knew who she was? How long would it be before she was found out?

Nate would've had to go public by now, and make a statement about why she wasn't going ahead with the tour. Thousands of dollars worth of tickets would need to be refunded. She knew Nate would be furious with her. Wherever he was, she could almost feel his rage reaching out toward her.

She sat up, leaned over, switched on her lantern and reached for her Bible. She opened it and started reading. The words she read said she shouldn't be afraid and to thank God for all He has done. When she turned to another page, her eyes fell to a scripture that told her God would fight her battles. That sounded good to her. After she opened a few more pages and read the verses where the pages had fallen open, her eyelids grew heavy.

She closed the Bible, turned off the lantern, and lowered her head into the pillow.

A change had to be made in her life. Maybe all of the things that had happened to her had been deliberately set in place by God to bring her to know Him? Could she really find peace in her life? Closing her eyes once more, she prayed, promising that she would give her life over to Him if He would give her peace. Not knowing about God or how to pray, she asked God's forgiveness if she was praying in the wrong way.

THE NEXT MORNING, Asha awakened to find the Bible resting on top of her. Had she fallen asleep before setting it on the table after reading it the night before? She recalled all that she had read, and she felt a sense of deep inner peace and understanding. She immediately thought of John. She was excited to see him today, and wondered if he felt the same about her.

Asha couldn't hear any noises and wondered if she was the first to wake. She got ready quickly, putting on the borrowed clothes from Patsy; a plain green dress which, at first, she had felt unattractive in. Now she was used to it because the other women all wore the same sort of dresses.

Once she had dressed she headed to the kitchen. To her surprise everyone was there except for William.

When the three women had greeted her, Gretchen said, "We have cereal on Sundays and we don't do much other cooking."

"Sunday is our day of rest," Stephanie explained.

Jared walked through the back door, and handed a mug to Stephanie with a little head nod.

"Morning, Jane," Jared said.

"Good morning."

Megan explained, "Jared fixes Stephanie her favorite coffee-shop-style hot drink every morning."

"Jah, and he better do it after we're married too," Stephanie said.

"Of course I will," Jared said. "As long as you do everything else in the kitchen."

Stephanie smiled. "That's a good exchange."

"Do you live close, Jared?"

"I live in the quarters by the barn. When Stephanie and I marry, we'll be moving to a small house. Are you coming to the meeting, Jane?"

"Yes."

"Will this be your first Amish meeting?" he asked.

"First of many, I hope," William said as he walked into the kitchen.

Everyone said good morning to him and he sat down at the table with them.

"Coffee, *Dat?"* Megan asked.

"Jah, please." William shook cereal into a bowl and then took up the jug in front of him and poured milk on top.

Stephanie said, "This is our last meeting before we get married, Megan."

"Jah, it is."

"You're all leaving me," Gretchen said.

"We'll visit most days," Megan said while placing a cup of coffee in front of William.

"I hope so," Gretchen said. "I'll certainly miss you girls."

Soon they were traveling in two buggies to the Williamsons' house. Jared and Stephanie were in one buggy, while Megan and Asha rode with Gretchen and William.

When the buggy stopped, Megan went to find Brandon and Asha wandered over to the house. It seemed they were early, as there were only five other buggies parked.

She looked inside the barn to find the boys still arranging furniture.

"Morning, Jane!" Todd exclaimed as he was lining up chairs.

"Morning, Todd."

"Excited for the meeting?"

"I am, actually. I've never been to a church before, ever. These are all new experiences for me."

"Hi, Jane."

Asha turned around to see John. "Hello."

He pointed to one side. "The men sit on that side and the women on this one."

"Oh, I didn't know."

He laughed. "I figured you wouldn't."

As the people started coming in, she noticed how similar they all looked and not because they were all wearing the same clothes, but because they all had that same certain energy within them.

"Ah, you must be Jane."

Asha turned around as she heard a friendly voice. "Yes. Nice to meet you." The man had brown hair and blue eyes, and he had a similar build to John's.

"I'm Gabe, John's cousin. I've heard a lot about you. John and I work together when he's not pretending to have a sore leg."

John and Asha laughed.

"I'll remember that. Just you wait," John said.

A young boy ran up to Gabe and held his hand, glancing shyly at Asha.

"Oh, is this your son?"

"No. This here is my little brother, Luke. And somewhere around here is his slightly older sister, Miriam. If you see a little girl running everywhere and creating havoc, that'll be young Miriam."

"I'll keep that in mind."

The families kept coming in and greeting Asha, and she found herself yearning for what they had—a family. They all looked so happy and at peace. Makeup, clothes, and other material objects didn't matter to them. There was no one better than the other and they all greeted each other with such joy and laughter. It wasn't too long before they all took their seats.

CHAPTER 12

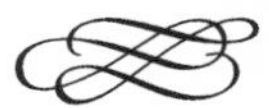

Asha looked around to find somewhere to sit, and Stephanie stood and beckoned her to sit with herself and Megan in the back row. She hurried over, relieved to be able to relax, sit back, and watch the proceedings.

She looked up to see Scott peering back at her from the front row. He gave her a big smile before he turned around.

"Looks like you've captured a heart," Megan whispered to her.

The room went quiet and then she saw John standing at the front. He looked in her direction, gave a small smile and started singing. It was such a beautiful song. She felt goosebumps come all over her body and she closed her eyes to enjoy the song more fully. She opened them to find John once again staring straight into her eyes.

The moment she couldn't stop thinking about was happening again. She looked back into his eyes from across the room. He looked so handsome, and she loved that he also loved to sing. She felt her heart starting to open wider the more she listened. The song finished and John didn't move, he didn't blink, he kept staring straight at Asha. He only moved when the bishop stood.

Feeling her face grow hot, she looked down to her hands.

"Looks like you've captured more than one heart," Megan whispered.

Asha gave her a small smile. John's actions confirmed that he liked her too.

When the bishop spoke, Asha tried to take it all in. She found it hard to understand, but she knew in time it might make sense.

When the bishop finished talking, another man stood and made announcements, and then a third man closed the meeting in prayer. Then everyone stood and moved to the other side of the barn. The boys moved some of the benches away and replaced them with tables, leaving the remaining benches to sit on.

Asha joined Patsy in the kitchen to offer her help. All the women ate on the run while they took plates of food out to the barn and then returned shortly after with empty plates. For the next couple of hours, Asha was in the kitchen helping the women, and she found she enjoyed it.

"You've done enough work for one day, Asha. I've made you a hot cup of tea. Take a seat on the porch or somewhere."

"Thank you, Patsy." She took her cup of tea outside and was surprised to see John on the porch with a spare chair next to him. "I brought you a cup of tea," she said, offering it to him.

John broke his gaze and shook his head as if he'd been off in a distant memory and was coming back to reality. *"Denke,* Jane. That was kind."

She handed him the tea. "Mind if I sit?"

"I'd be happy if you did." When she sat, he asked, "How are you enjoying the farm life?"

"To be honest with you, I love it. I feel at home here, a certain peace that I don't think I've ever felt before in my life, like I was saying yesterday."

"Can you remember anything yet?"

"No. I'm not sure I want to. For some reason, I feel that wherever I came from, I didn't really want to be there. If that makes sense."

He took a sip of tea. "I think so."

"Can I ask you a question, John? And if I am being too forward, please feel free to let me know."

"Sure."

"I noticed the way the woman looked at you in the doctor's office the other day. I am sure you could have been married with a family by now if you wanted. May I ask why you still live at home with your parents? Don't you want your own family?"

Asha saw John swallow hard.

"I-I'm sorry, it's none of my business. I'm too nosey for my own good," Asha said.

John breathed deeply. "It's okay, Jane. I just haven't found the right woman I want to raise my children with, and spend every day with. My family is important to me. I'd rather be here helping them, setting a good example for my brothers. When I find the right someone, sure, I will be happy to marry, but that hasn't happened yet."

Jane gave John a smile and they both stared off into the distance together. Asha couldn't help but feel there was more to the story but she respected John's privacy and didn't let her curiosity get the better of her.

"My leg is better now, so I will be back in the fields with Gabe tomorrow. I've enjoyed these past few days getting to know you, Jane."

"I've enjoyed it too, John."

"I will see you about the car, though. And take you to see my friend to find out what he can do about the car. That might be tomorrow or the next day."

"Yes, that's good." When Asha looked up, she saw the Grabers heading to the buggy. "It looks like we're going." Asha stood. "I'll say goodbye to your mother."

When Asha came back out to the porch from saying goodbye to Patsy, John was no longer there. She hurried to the buggy so she wouldn't leave them waiting.

"Jane."

She turned to see John walking toward her. "I just wanted to let you know I'm glad you came here."

"Me too. Where did you get to? I came out to say goodbye and you'd gone."

"One of my annoying brothers called me over." He shook his head. "I shouldn't speak about them like that, but they are annoying when they interrupt my time with you."

Jane couldn't keep the smile from her face. She glanced over at the Grabers' buggy to see William give her a wave to hurry up. "I should go," she said as she turned back to John.

"I'll see you soon. Maybe Tuesday, I'd say."

"I'll look forward to it."

As she hurried to the buggy she heard John call after her, "Me too."

It was a refreshing change to meet an open honest man like John. There were no games, no guarding himself against hurt like so many of the men she'd dated, no having to guard herself. There was frankness and honesty in everything he said.

CHAPTER 13

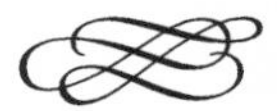

It was Tuesday when Asha saw John again.

Asha climbed into John's buggy and sat next to him.

"He's still waiting for quotes on your car. I'm sorry it's taking so long."

Asha was pleased about any delay that would cause her to stay longer. "That's okay."

"I can take you to see it."

"That's okay. I don't need to see the car, do I?"

"No, I guess not. In that case, would you care to spend the day with me? I've got a whole free day."

"I'd like that very much."

"Good. I've got something to show you."

"A surprise?"

"Yes."

"I like surprises."

Thirty minutes later, he stopped the buggy in a clearing and Asha didn't see anything particularly special-looking around them.

"Where are we?"

"Near a creek." He jumped down from the buggy, and pulled some things out of the back.

When Asha got out, he met her and handed her binoculars while he held a pen and a book in his other hand. "You can use these."

"What are we looking at?"

"Birds. I often come out here by myself and watch them."

Asha frowned. "Really?"

"Don't look like that. I thought it would be boring at first, but then I got interested. My aunt and uncle got me started and it was through their excitement that I got curious."

"Okay. I'm willing to give it a try. What's the book for?"

"I note down anything I see, and if I see something rare, I let the bird society know."

"Ah, and then all the birdwatchers flock here to try to catch a glimpse of it?"

"Something along those lines, but mainly so we can track what birds are where. It can help with maintaining their species, protecting their breeding spots and things like that. So it's not just for the purposes of seeing an unusual bird."

"Okay." Asha slipped on the muddy trail and John quickly put both hands out to steady her, dropping his book.

When both feet were firmly planted on the ground, she looked into his eyes. There was a brief moment between them before he quickly withdrew his hands.

"Thank you," Asha said.

He leaned down and picked up his book, which now had mud on it.

"Oh no! Your book."

Brushing off the dirt, he said, "It's fine. I was more interested in saving my binoculars."

She looked down at the binoculars she was still holding. "Yes, I knew that. I didn't think you were worried about me."

They exchanged grins.

"Let's go." He strode off. "I know a good place to watch from."

When she caught up with him, she asked, "Will this involve a lot of walking?"

He chuckled. "A little. Do you have something against exercise?"

"Not really. I haven't done a lot lately." She had to stop herself from telling him how Nate had made her work out every second day.

"What do you know about birds?" he asked.

"Not much. They eat and fly around, and the ones in the city seem to look for clean cars to mess up."

He laughed. "You might learn something today. I'm looking for a Western Grebe. They aren't supposed to be in this area, not this far east, but one of my cousins saw one here last week."

"I've never heard of a Western Grebe. What do they look like?"

"They're a water bird. They look like a swan but with a long beak. Another name for them is a Swan-necked Grebe."

As he talked more about these birds, Asha was pleased that he was interested in nature. Nate had only been interested in money and how to make more of it. The other boyfriends she'd dated had been impressed that she was a famous singer and none of them had any particular interests other than going to nightclubs and drinking. John was different because he took pleasure from animals and nature, and he liked her for herself.

"Well, I hope we see one of the Swan-necked Grebes," she said.

"It's not likely, but you never know what else we might see."

"What are your favorite birds?"

"I like the ruby-throated hummingbird."

"I hope we see one. I think I saw one at your house the first day I was there. You had a special bird feeder there for birds who like nectar. Your mother was telling me about them."

"Did you like it?"

"Yes. The one I saw was so pretty, a beautiful shade of green. It had a red neck and it was very small, and its wings were flapping at a hundred miles per hour."

Asha hardly remembered any birds in the cities where she'd gone on tour except for pigeons, who were treated as pests as they swooped on tourists and nested in inconvenient places such as rooftops and eaves.

The trail opened onto a river and Asha could see that it continued along the riverbanks for some distance. "At least it's drier underfoot here." Movement from the water caught Asha's eye. "What's that?" She saw what she thought was a duck of some kind.

"That's a Green-winged Teal"

"Is it a duck?"

"Yes, a small one. It's proper scientific name is Annas Crecca. Sadly, the population of the American Black Ducks, a larger species, is in decline."

"Now you're showing off your knowledge."

He laughed. "There are a lot of the teals around here. Look, there's another one."

She looked to see another Green-winged Teal waddling on the other side of the bank before it slipped into the water.

He looked up to the sky. "There are usually more birds around here."

"I might have scared them away."

A little further on a bird flew overhead. "What's that? A hawk?"

"Yes. It's a Northern Farrier. A medium-sized hawk. That might be why there are fewer birds around."

"Are you going to write that down?"

"No. I only write down birds I don't normally see."

"I hope we see something rare."

He laughed.

"What's funny?"

"You might be catching the bug."

"The bird-watching bug?"

He nodded.

"I like to watch them. You're right, I might be catching it."

They walked on for another hour while John kept pointing out the different birds and telling Asha what they were.

"Look there. It's an Eastern Bluebird."

"Oh, I love it! Such a beautiful color."

"And they have a glorious voice. A few years ago I didn't see any, and now I'm seeing them more often. It might be that the weather has been warmer these past years. And some of the farmers are building houses especially for them. They are picky about where they nest, and they eat lots of insects so we like them around our farms."

The trail moved away from the water and continued up a hill.

"Have you had enough, or do you want to keep going? I'm not carrying you up that hill."

"Maybe we should head back because of your sore leg."

He laughed. "My leg is better."

"We can't be too careful. If we go up that hill, you might strain it."

"Okay, we'll head back."

When they turned and started back, Asha said, "Thank you for bringing me out here. It's nice to learn more about you and what you like to do."

"It's me who should be thanking you. I usually come here by myself. It's much more enjoyable to be here with you."

She glanced over at him to see him smiling at her.

"Are you hungry?"

"Starving."

"I brought us some food. Just in case you wanted to spend the day with me."

"You did?"

"Yes. Well, my mother packed it for me."

"She's so nice."

"She's a pretty good mother."

When they got back to the buggy, John brought out a picnic basket and handed Asha a blanket. "You find a good place for us to sit."

"Shall we keep the binoculars out?"

"Yes. You never know what we might see."

Asha found a grassy place and spread out the blanket. When they were both sitting down, John opened the basket.

"Now let's see what *Mamm* has packed for us."

"She knew this was for me too?"

"Jah." He pulled out a bottle. "This is ginger beer." Then he handed her two glasses. "You can pour while I set out the food."

When the food was arranged, Asha saw there were sandwiches, cold chicken, salads and cold potatoes. "I love cold potatoes."

"Really? To me, potatoes should always be hot and mashed."

They stayed there for the next two hours, eating and drinking, and they were so busy talking that no more birdwatching was done.

When neither of them could eat any more, Asha started packing the basket.

"I suppose I should take you back to the Grabers'."

"I suppose. I've had the best day I've had since… Since… I'm not really sure. Maybe the best day ever."

He chuckled. "I hope you get your memory back soon. Well, I do and I don't. I don't if that means you'll leave, but I hope for your sake you do. Then you can reconnect with your family and friends."

"Something tells me I might not have many of those." Asha closed the lid of the picnic basket and tapped it. "There. All done."

Together they drove back to the Grabers'.

When Asha got down from the buggy, John said, "I'll see you at the wedding. I guess that's the next time I'll see you."

"Yes. I'll see you then. Bye, John, and thanks again."

"Bye, Jane. I had a lovely day."

Asha walked to the house knowing that the longer she stayed there the deeper she was going to fall in love with John.

CHAPTER 14

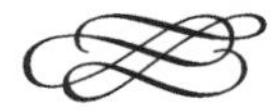

IT WAS the Tuesday night before the wedding, and Asha was having dinner with the Grabers and Stephanie and Megan.

"This is the last time we'll be having dinner like this," Megan said looking sad.

"We can come back here when we're married and have dinner," Stephanie said.

"Yes, you're welcome back here whenever you want."

"We're in for a busy day tomorrow," William said.

As she knew, the next day was the day before the wedding. "Why, what happens tomorrow?"

Gretchen explained, "Our house is too small, so we need a huge covering going from here almost to the barn for the guests in case it rains. And I've only got this little stove, so we need more stoves for the cooking and the heating up of the food. We've got extra hotplates coming."

"And that all happens tomorrow?"

"*Jah,* it'll all need to happen tomorrow. I've got about thirty workers coming to help out," William said.

Asha hoped that John might be coming, but then she recalled he said the next time he'd see her would be at the wedding on Thursday.

Asha asked, "Wouldn't tonight, I mean tomorrow night be the last dinner you have?"

Megan shook her head. "All the workers and their families will have dinner here tomorrow night. It will be fun, but it won't be the same as how it is now."

Asha nodded. It seemed a lot of work to have all those people for dinner the day before the wedding, but she kept her opinion to herself.

"I'm going to have an early night," Gretchen announced. "It might be the last I have for a while."

"We'll do the dishes for you, *Mamm.* You just relax before you go to bed."

"Thank you, Megan."

When the dinner was over, Gretchen and William left the kitchen, and the girls cleaned up and washed the dishes.

"It must be so exciting for both of you to be getting married. And did it take a long time for Brandon to convert to Amish?" Asha directed her question to Megan.

"A few months. He had to live with an Amish family for a few months first to make sure he was making the right decision, and then he had to take some lessons. And then it was a few more months after that before the bishop allowed us to marry."

Asha nodded. "I suppose that's best. Did he believe in God before that, or before you met him?"

"Yes, I suppose that's what attracted me to him. He did a lot of charity work with the church he belonged to and helped to feed the homeless. Not just feed the homeless and the people who don't have much money, but he became a friend and listened to their problems. That's when I fell in love with him. And he was pleased that he could continue his charity work, because Amish do a lot of that and fundraising too."

Asha nodded. Her impression of the Amish had been totally different before she lived with them.

"Are you thinking of joining us, Jane?" Stephanie asked as she picked up a plate to dry.

"It's crossed my mind. I'm sure I'd be happier here than where I was before. Although I can't remember anything yet, I've got the feeling that I wasn't very happy with the life I was living. And I was probably even trying to escape from it."

"I guess you'll only find that out when you get your memory back."

"I guess so. So, did you finish sewing your dresses?"

Stephanie and Megan smiled at one another.

"Yes, we have," Megan answered.

"We've got all the dresses ready, so we just have to help Gretchen with the food tomorrow."

"And the cleaning," Stephanie added.

"Would I be able to help too?"

"Of course. An extra pair of hands is always welcome."

"Before we do anything else, Gretchen has ordered us to clean the house as soon as we wake up in the morning. That will take a couple hours."

"I'll help with that," Asha said, pleased to be included. She hadn't cleaned in the last few years, but when she was living with her foster families, she'd always had chores to do.

WEDNESDAY PASSED SLOWLY. With every new buggy that arrived at the house, Asha hoped that she would see John, and every time she had been disappointed. She tried to push him out of her mind, but every time she heard a bird chirp, she thought of him and the lovely day that they had spent together. Then she'd recall his smile and the way his strong arms had caught her before she fell.

THAT NIGHT ASHA stayed up with the girls and heard details about their relationships with the men they were about to marry. She listened to many stories about how they had met them and what they had thought of them. She'd learned how Megan's father had died, and her mother was ill and had no money and had to give her up. She'd heard the story before, and was sad all over again for Megan, that she'd never met her mother or her father. Megan's mother could've been out there somewhere still alive, although Megan said she had a feeling she'd died.

The story Stephanie had was slightly different. Stephanie told of all the trouble she got into and everything she had put her parents through. Now that it was all in the past, her stories were funny, but Asha was certain that Stephanie's parents hadn't found them funny at the time. Now all that was in Stephanie's past and she was about to begin a new chapter of her life with Jared.

ASHA WAS the first of the girls to wake the next morning. They'd all fallen asleep in the same room. She opened her eyes and then felt something across her face. It was an arm. When she pushed it off, Stephanie woke.

"What time is it?" Stephanie asked as she sat bolt upright.

"I don't know. Where is Megan?"

Megan wasn't on the bed and then the girls both saw Megan asleep on the floor. They giggled at the sight, which woke Megan.

"Are we late?" Megan asked sitting up.

"I doubt it. If we were late Gretchen would be in here yelling at us."

"Should I go down and put the kettle on?" Asha asked.

"Yes please, Jane. I won't be far behind you," Stephanie said.

Asha headed into her room and pulled on a bathrobe before she headed downstairs. When she walked into the kitchen, she saw Gretchen leaning over the sink and crying into a handkerchief.

"Gretchen, what's wrong?"

Gretchen turned around and shook her head. "I feel like I'm losing a daughter. That's what Megan has been to me."

Tears stung at the back of Asha's eyes. She would have no one to cry for her when she got married. It touched her to see the bond between Megan and Gretchen.

Asha put her arm around Gretchen's shoulders. "She won't be going far. And then she'll have lots of babies and bring them back here for you to help look after."

That made Gretchen giggle. "I keep telling Elizabeth and Tara to hurry with the babies. Maybe they'll be beaten by Stephanie or Megan."

"That's right."

"We're having cereal this morning because we've got so much work to do. People will be coming soon."

"Cereal's fine with me. I've just come down here to put the tea kettle on the stove."

"It's already boiled."

A very tired Megan and Stephanie walked into the kitchen. Asha was used to surviving on very little sleep, often having to perform concerts while feeling the effects of jet lag.

TWO HOURS LATER, hundreds of people were there for the wedding.

"Where have all these people come from?" Asha asked Gretchen. There were far more people there than at the Amish meetings.

"Near and far, far and wide."

Asha walked into Megan's bedroom and saw both girls in their blue dresses. It was odd to see people getting married in such clothing.

"You two look beautiful," Asha said.

"Thank you," both girls chorused.

"Is there anything I can do?"

"No, but thank you so much for helping over the last few days. We have really appreciated it," Megan said.

"Yes, thank you," Stephanie said.

"It was lovely getting to know you, Jane. And I'm glad we had that chance."

Stephanie nodded in agreement at what Megan said.

"And you really do look a lot like Asha," Stephanie added.

"Yes, people say that all the time. I better get outside and take a seat."

Asha headed back outside and took a seat on one of the back benches. All the while she was looking for John, but couldn't see him anywhere. She saw Gabe, his cousin, first and then she saw John behind him. John appeared to be looking around and she wondered if John was looking for her. Then their eyes locked and he waved. *Question answered.* She smiled and waved back.

Now she felt like her insides were glowing. Seeing him filled her with peace and happiness.

When all the guests were seated, both girls came out of the house and waited, greeted by their future husbands. Both couples walked to stand in front of the bishop.

John stood and sang a song in German. Asha closed her eyes and listened to his voice. They could sing wonderful songs together. She'd been told that the women didn't sing out in front at the meetings, that only men did that.

When John's song finished, a man who had been standing near the bishop opened in prayer. Then the bishop gave a long talk that went on and on. Asha was so far away she could barely hear what was said. She tried very hard to stop her mind from wandering but her eyes wanted to stay fixed on John.

When the couples were pronounced married, people jumped up to congratulate them. Some of the men started changing the furniture arrangement, bringing long tables to replace some of the benches.

Asha went to help the women in the kitchen, but she was shooed away by Patsy who told her she needed to rest after the work of the past couple days. She headed back to the crowd to find someone to talk with. She didn't want to appear too obvious by going straight to John—the only person she wanted to talk to.

She was helping herself to a glass of soda when she felt someone standing beside her and looked up to see John.

"Hello, John. I really enjoyed your singing."

"Thank you."

"You've got a lovely voice."

"You're going to have to stop complimenting me over my voice or I will get a big head." He chuckled.

"I'll keep that in mind."

"I guess this is the first Amish wedding you've been to?"

"I'd say so. It's doubtful that I'm Amish, or that I've been to a wedding like this."

"If you were Amish we would've heard that there was an Amish woman missing. And you weren't wearing Amish clothing."

"Well, there you go then."

He laughed. "It would make things a lot easier for me if you were Amish."

"Why's that?"

He scratched the back of his neck. "Then I'd only be competing with other Amish men. Not Amish and *Englisch* men."

She laughed. "Do you think men would be competing for me?"

"For sure."

Asha shook her head. "I'm positive there was no man in my life. I wasn't in a relationship before I came here."

"How can you be so sure?"

She put her hand over her stomach. "It's something that I just feel."

He smiled. "I hope so."

Asha spent most of the day in John's company.

CHAPTER 15

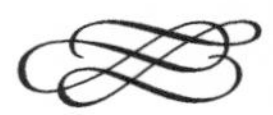

THAT NIGHT, Gretchen was alone in the kitchen and Asha approached her.

"Gretchen, I really enjoyed the wedding. How would someone become Amish? Does your community take people who want to convert? I have heard that you do, that Brandon converted."

Gretchen dropped the plates in her hand back into the sink and turned to face Asha.

"My dear, that is wonderful news! We would love to have you here, but are you sure? When you remember where you came from, don't you think you might want to go back there?"

"No Gretchen, there is a knowing inside me, something telling me that this is where I am supposed to be. This is the life I am supposed to lead. Even if I have done wrong in the past, I want to make amends for that and I believe everything I have read in the Bible. It's like I always felt something missing, but now I have found it."

Gretchen walked over to Asha, grabbing her shoulders. "I am so happy to hear you say that, Jane. You will have to attend classes to be inducted into the Amish life, if you are serious. You have to study for a few weeks and then be baptized. You need to learn everything about us, and then make a decision after your studies."

"This is great. I want to learn more!" Asha replied.

"Would that have anything to do with a certain young man? A man named John?"

"How did you—"

"I saw the way you both looked at one another today. Sit down and I'll tell you some things about John you don't know." When they sat down, Gretchen continued, "When he was eighteen, he courted Lindsay May. She went on *rumspringa* and never returned. She just forgot about him, didn't even bother to send a letter. Broke his heart, it did."

It all made sense and Asha now realized why he had been so worried that she too, might return to her old life once she regained her memory.

OVER THE NEXT two weeks Asha and John saw each other every second day. John was delighted when she shared news that she was thinking of joining the community. When she was informed the car was ready, she knew that something had to be done. Should she confess her lies? Or should she stay in her happy bubble for as long as she possibly could, knowing that it would burst? When it burst, she knew it would not end well. How could it, when she'd lied to people who'd only shown her love and kindness?

That morning, she waited for John to take her to her car. Nate's car...

"That's him now," Asha said looking out the window.

"Take a coat. There's mine by the door. It'll be cold out."

Asha stood. "Thanks, Gretchen."

"You can bring the car back here and leave it in the barn if it's ready."

"Thank you. It'll feel strange to drive a car after being in the buggies."

Asha grabbed the coat and headed out to meet John.

"Good morning, Jane."

"Hello," she said as she climbed in next to him.

"Do you mind if we take a detour before I take you to your car?"

"That's fine. You're the driver."

"I will be dropping off some vegetables for my uncle's stall at the farmers market.

"You seem cheery today."

"It's been a good day so far and it can only get better. It's about a forty-minute ride to the markets. I hope that you will enjoy it. You'll be meeting my Uncle Steve.

Asha smiled at John, and then looked at the view. They were passing a frost-covered field that was sparkling in the morning sun.

"John, look how pretty it is."

He looked over. "It is. Mornings are my favorite time of day. Especially the sunrise."

Asha nodded and tried to recall how long it had been since she'd been awake to see the sun rise. "I'll have to try that. I haven't been up that early in a while."

He chuckled at that.

"I'm going to talk to the bishop soon about joining the community."

He took his eyes off the road to stare at her. "That's great. But, you haven't got your memory back yet. Have you?"

"No. I just know this is what I want."

"Good. I'm happy to hear it."

When they arrived at the farmers market, she noticed small stalls selling fresh produce and various other items. There were many Amish people, and they all smiled and said hello as they walked by.

Asha realized how judgmental and unkind she had been about the Amish. She'd seen them as outcasts and extremists. Now, living amongst them, it all made perfect sense. As they continued walking, she heard a woman's voice from behind, yelling out to John.

They turned around to see Sally from the doctor's office

"John! Hi, how are you?" Sally said, over-enthusiastically.

"I'm good thank you, Sally, How are you?"

"I'm great!" Sally continued, completely ignoring Asha, "I've been speaking with your Amish bishop about joining your community."

Asha narrowed her eyes at her and had unkind thoughts before she could stop herself. Sally was only thinking of joining the Amish because of John. Then a thought occurred to Asha. Was she doing the same?

"That is good news," John said.

"He said I'm to stay with a family first. Any ideas?"

"Well, Jane here didn't stay with my family, she's staying with the Grabers. I'm sure the bishop will find you a family to stay with."

Sally looked at Asha. "You do look awfully familiar. I can't put my finger on it, but I know I've seen you somewhere before."

Asha felt her heart sink and the anxiety instantly came over her. Surely, she wouldn't be able to tell who she was in a plain Amish dress and no makeup. Asha would never have been seen out in public before without designer clothing and her professional makeup.

Laughing, Asha said, "I get that a lot from people. I think I have one of those faces. You'll be pleased to know that we might be taking those classes together, Sally," Asha advised, trying to change the subject.

Sally's face went blank. "You mean you're turning Amish? Why is that, may I ask?" she enquired looking toward John.

"Jane will be speaking with the bishop soon, Sally. It'll be good for you both to have each other. We have to get a move on now, " John said as he touched Asha's arm to guide her in the other direction.

At his touch, Asha's heart beat faster.

"Bye, John," Sally yelled out from behind.

"Bye," John said, half-turning back.

"John, how are you?" A large man smiled as they approached his fruit stall.

"I'm good, Uncle Steve. This is Jane, she's new to our community and will soon be taking the instructions," John informed him as he smiled in Asha's direction.

"Ahh yes, Jane, I remember seeing you on Sunday. I have heard a lot about you. I apologize for not introducing myself sooner."

"Nice to meet you."

Uncle Steve gave a small smile, and then he and John continued to talk about produce and the setup of the stall. As they unloaded vegetables from the crate John had brought, Asha took a seat behind the stall and her mind started to wonder again. *What should I do?* If she told John the truth, he would surely see her as untrustworthy, a liar, and all of this would be over in a second. But then she remembered what she read in the Bible.

Do to others as you would have them do to yourself. God forgives all of those who repent.

She knew when she repented and was baptized, all her sins would be forgiven. *It will all work out,* she thought to herself.

The exchanges of smiles continued between John and Asha and she found herself sitting on the stool, getting lost in him once again. He was so tall, so sun kissed, his brown hair and green eyes made him so unusually beautiful and his singing was just as beautiful. She imagined what their babies would be like. She hoped they took after him and had bright green eyes and brown hair opposed to her blonde hair and blue eyes.

As they headed to the garage to see about the car, Asha asked, "Why do you think Sally is joining the Amish?" Pangs of jealousy pricked her heart and she couldn't stop them. She only hoped John didn't know how she truly felt about the woman who was trying to win him over.

CHAPTER 16

"I HAVE no idea why Sally would or would not do something. I'd rather not think about it, but I am glad if she is doing it for the right reasons," John replied.

"Noted, and what would the right reasons be?" Asha asked, ashamed of herself for the jealousy she felt.

John took a moment to reply. "There could be many right reasons to do it, but the heart has to be in it. A burning desire from within, a knowing that it is the life you want to lead. I respect people who join us. Turning to God and the simple life is not a choice everyone wants to make."

"I should make a time to see your bishop and put things into place."

When the buggy stopped at the car workshop, Asha got out and waited for John to secure his horse. "I can't see any cars," she said when John walked up to her.

"They're all out in the back."

John walked in and asked to speak to Mick, his friend.

A few minutes later a young man in grease-covered overalls headed toward them.

"Mick, this is Jane."

"Hi." He nodded. "Won't shake your hand."

Asha smiled when he lifted up his dirty hands.

"How's Jane's car?"

He sighed. "We're gonna need an expensive part. Sorry about this, Jane. It's not your run-of-the-mill car. I thought we'd be finished. The dent-pounding work and spray painting are all done."

"Good. I'm not in a huge hurry for it."

"Can you pay a deposit today? You'll need to check at the office to see how much it's going to be. You could take it to a Mercedes workshop, you know."

Asha knew the dealership might be able to look up who owned the car. "No. It's fine. You come recommended by John. Do you take a card?"

"Yeah. Jenny at the office will fix you up."

Asha left Mick and John talking while she headed to the office. When she walked in, she heard one of her songs playing.

The woman looked up and gasped. "Are you Asha?"

Asha gave a laugh. "I get that a bit. I'm here to pay a deposit. You're fixing my car."

The woman tapped some keys on the computer in front of her. "Name?"

Asha was pleased the name on her credit card was not Asha. She handed her card over.

"Is it the black Mercedes?"

"Yes."

"Can you leave four hundred?"

"That'll be fine."

The woman ran the card though the machine.

When Asha joined John back at the buggy, John said, "Jane, you have a credit card?"

She'd blown it. Swallowing hard and thinking fast, she said, "I do."

"Then you would know your name." His speech was slow and deliberate.

She looked directly into his eyes. "I don't think I want to be whoever I was before. I feel that deep in my soul. God put me here to find the community. And to find you." Asha reached out and grabbed his hand.

His eyes fell to her hand on his and he smiled. "What is your name?"

"No. I don't want to be her anymore. Please understand. Just trust me that this is something I need to do."

He covered her hand with his other hand. "I'll trust you, but you must tell me this truthfully. Do you remember who you are? Where you're from?"

"No." She shook her head.

He nodded. "Do you want me to keep calling you Jane?"

"Yes."

"You know it would be easy to find your friends and family now that you know your name from the card?"

"I know that, but I feel I've been put here for a reason."

He smiled. "Me too. I knew as soon as I saw you there was something about you."

"You felt that too?"

"Yes. I think you're the woman for me, Jane. Is it too soon to say that?"

"No it's not too soon at all," Asha confessed, "I felt that way about you the next day after the crash, when I saw you at your house."

He drove her back to the Grabers' house and she was pleased they'd expressed their feelings, and that she'd gotten out of a sticky situation with fast thinking.

As they pulled up to the house, the smell of freshly baked bread and hot roast pork reached their nostrils.

"Mmm, smell that?"

"Jah. Can you stay for dinner? If it's okay with Gretchen and William?"

"I'd love to.

Gretchen had made a delicious meal of pork, roasted vegetables and salad. Sitting down for a meal with the man she liked and William and Gretchen, Asha felt she had a real family. She knew this wouldn't last and things could very soon get ugly. Asha had lost count how many times she'd lied to John and he was a man with such integrity, she feared he'd never forgive her.

CHAPTER 17

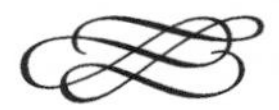

IT WAS A WEEK LATER, and John was taking Asha back to get the car.

"What will you do with it if you join us, Jane?"

She had to get the car back to Nate somehow. Maybe Jess could catch a bus to see her and then drive his car back. "I'll have to sell it, I guess."

With John alongside her, Asha stepped into the office to pay for the work.

The office lady took her glasses off and said, "The owner of the car has already paid." She nodded to the other side of the office, and sitting there was Nate.

Nate leaped to his feet.

Asha gasped and ran out of the office, followed closely by Nate.

Asha swung around. "Go away."

He stayed back and John ran to Asha. "Jane, who is he?"

She held her head. "No one."

"No one?"

Nate strolled over. "I'm her manager. What the heck are you doing in those clothes?" He laughed at her.

"I'm not going back."

"Jane, what's this all about?" John asked.

"Jane?" Nate looked at John and then turned to Asha. "Yes, *Jane,* what is this all about? And what did you do to my car?"

"Your car?" John looked from Nate to Asha and she looked away.

"It didn't take you long to forget about me, Asha," Nate said.

Asha shook her head. "It's not like that."

"Jane, will you tell me what's going on?" John urged.

Asha looked into his face. He still trusted her after she lied to him. She didn't have the heart to tell him the truth.

"I'll tell you what's going on, farmer boy. This woman's mine, got it? Now go back home and grow your corn or whatever it is that you do."

John frowned and ignored Nate's rudeness and simply pointed out, "Jane's lost her memory."

Nate threw his head back and laughed. "She's a liar. She remembers me all right." Nate nodded to a black car with dark windows. "Get in the car, Asha. Your little vacation has come to an end. Fun's over."

"I'm not going."

"Is this your husband, Jane?" John asked, now looking doubtful of her.

"Her name's Asha, and she's a singer."

"No, he's my manager. *Was* my manager. I'm sorry I lied to you. I just wanted to stay a little longer around you and your family—also the Grabers. I've never felt so wanted or appreciated."

"What a load of rubbish! You don't feel appreciated? What about your millions of fans who buy your music? They've spent millions on you. Talk about spoilt. Thousands of singers want to be where you are. You don't know when you've got it good. Now get in the car!"

Asha looked at John's face.

"Is it all true?" John asked.

Asha hung her head. "Yes."

"You never lost your memory? You were lying to me this whole time?"

Asha nodded. "But I want to stay. I don't want to go back."

John took a step back.

"Get in the car, Asha."

"I can't believe you lied to me. You made it all up."

Nate grabbed her arm and pulled her to the car and she went with him. She couldn't stay, now that she'd hurt John so badly. His eyes told her how much she'd hurt him.

As they zoomed away in Nate's hired car, she asked, "How did you find me?"

"Your credit card was used there. Oh, and thanks for wrecking my car. I'll send someone for it when it's finished." He glanced over at her. "Your sister's worried out of her brain and so was everyone else."

"And especially Julie Rose?"

He growled, "She was never a serious thing."

Asha shook her head. Her peace was shattered and it was back to reality. At least she'd had a small piece of happiness in her life.

"Do you know how many people depend on you? And how many people haven't been paid since you skipped town? There's your sister for one, and your security team, and the list goes on. We all depend on you to put food on the table. Do you know how much money we've had to pay back because you ditched the tour?"

"No, but I'm sure I'm going to hear about every dollar of it."

"And what are you wearing?"

Asha trembled. "Just don't talk. You're hurting my head."

"You're so selfish. After all I've done for you. I made you, and this is the thanks I get."

"God made me and gave me my voice. Not you."

"Ptf!" he spat out. "I had a press conference and told them you were in rehab."

Asha's jaw dropped. "What?"

"Someone caught your outburst on their camera, loaded it onto YouTube and it went viral."

"What outburst?"

"The night when you left, when you attacked me in the nightclub."

"I was trying to get away from you if I remember correctly."

"TomAtoes, TomAHtoes—whatever. Anyway, it's cost us a fortune, you running away like that. You'll have to make it up to your fans or they'll never trust you." He patted Asha on her leg. "You can do that when you get out of rehab."

"I'm not in rehab!"

He shrugged. "You can have a few days off and then we can catch the last few days of the tour, so we'll need to be on a plane to Amsterdam."

"I've quit. I'm not going anywhere."

"We'll talk after you have a rest and after you talk to your sister."

Nate had always been able to make her do whatever he said, but not this time.

Nate delivered her back to the hotel, and before he let the valet park the car, he said, "Get out of those clothes as soon as possible. No one can see you in those." He twisted around and handed her a black coat from the back seat. "Cover yourself with that. Don't talk to anyone and head to our room."

"My room!"

"Our room."

"No. There is no more 'our' going on. I need my own room. We're through!"

"Okay, calm down. I'll get another room; you stay in that one.

Here." he handed her the key. "We should go separately and looking like that, hopefully, no one will know it's you. Go now!"

Once she stepped out of the car, she swung the coat over her shoulders, kept her head down and walked to the elevator. Thankfully there was someone just stepping out of the elevator, so she slipped right in. When the doors opened, she hurried to the room next to hers, which was Jess's.

CHAPTER 18

After she knocked on the door, her sister opened it.

Jess grabbed Asha and hugged her. "Where have you been?" She stepped back and looked her up and down. "You look dreadful."

"Thanks."

"Where were you?"

"Trying to escape."

"Did you stay at the Amish place you were calling me from?"

"Yes, and they were lovely. I want to go back and live there."

Jess grabbed both of her shoulders. "You're not being yourself. You're having a breakdown."

Asha wiggled out of her hold. "I'm not. For the first time in my life I know what I want."

"You've always known what you wanted. To be a famous singer, and you are!"

Asha walked over to the bed and sat down. "I've found God, or He's found me, and this life I've got is a fake life."

"You've what?" Jess sat next to her. "What did you say?"

"Found God."

Jess sighed. "They've brainwashed you."

"No, Jess. My brain's been washed."

"Same deal, if you ask me. Where's Nate?"

"Getting his own room."

Jess sighed. "At least that's a step in a positive direction."

"I met a man."

"Ah, now it makes sense."

"It's not like that."

"Isn't it? You've always been manipulated by men. Look how Nate treated you and you put up with it. Now you're onto someone..."

"You have to trust me."

Jess shook her head. "Do you know what you've put us all through?"

"I called you."

"Only once. I've been worried sick and I've hardly slept."

"I'm sorry, but I felt I would die if I stayed here any longer."

"It's not all about you all the time, Asha. Do you know what I've been through, all my life, to try to keep you safe and look after you? Then you run off without a care."

"I'm sorry. Just listen to me, and please try to understand."

Jess sighed again. "Tell me everything from the start."

Asha told Jess everything, starting from seeing Julie Rose with Nate, and running away in Nate's car, about the accident, about pretending to lose her memory so she could stay among the Amish, and about moving to the Grabers.

When Asha had told Jess everything, Jess said, "So, what were you doing? Were you lying to people, pretending to be someone else? What's going on with you? You never lie."

"It's not like that, Jess. The life I have here is not me. I'm not that girl. Everyone back there treats me different and they all called me Jane. I want to be Jane. I want to be Jane and marry John. Well, that's what I wanted. He won't want me now that I betrayed his trust. I didn't expect to fall in love, it just kind of happened."

Asha felt a tear fall down her cheek and Jess pulled her in to hug her

"It's okay. We will work everything out." Jess tried to comfort Asha

"Yes, but Jess, you don't understand. Sally is only turning Amish so she can be with John. I know it and she'll probably end up marrying him."

"You've got to forget it all."

"I can't. I can't."

"Well, why don't we go back there? And you can go back as yourself and talk to John and tell him the truth."

"He already found out the truth from Nate. You should've seen the hurt look on his face."

"If John loves you like you love him, then I'm sure he'll forgive you."

"I don't know how John feels anymore. We never talked about it after he heard Nate's story. He never said anything more after that. Before, he'd said maybe I was the woman for him. Anyway, I've ruined everything." Asha took a deep breath. "I can't go back. I lied right to John's face. He asked me if I remembered anything and I said no."

"Aren't Christians supposed to forgive?"

"Yes, but they might not forget. How will he ever trust me again?"

"Forget about John."

"I can't."

"You didn't let me finish. In your head, take John out of the picture. Would you still want to join the Amish if John wasn't there?"

"Oh. It wouldn't be the same without him."

"He could marry someone else even if you go back," Jess pointed out.

"Oh, thanks. Are you trying to make me feel worse?"

Jess shook her head. "I want you to see things for how they are. You can't change your life for a man. This change must be for you. What do you want?"

Asha bit her lip. Jess was right to ask her that. She had always thought she knew what she wanted—fame and fortune. But it hadn't given her freedom. Fame and money had restricted her and made her life miserable. "I just want a normal life. I don't want to be famous. And what does money matter?"

"Everyone needs money, Ash."

"I'll need to give everything a lot of thought."

Jess nodded. "Good. You can't rush into anything. Get a good night's sleep."

"I walked out on everyone. I didn't even take Patsy's daughter's clothes back to her."

"Just go to bed. Things always look better in the morning."

CHAPTER 19

ASHA RACED into Jess's room the next morning. "I'm going back there. I feel that's where I belong."

"Oh, Asha. Give it more thought than that. You haven't even been home a day."

"My mind is made up and you know that I never change it."

"I know."

"Come with me and meet everyone. Oh, I hope they'll all forgive me."

"Just tell them the truth and say that you're sorry. People only get upset if there's more deception after your apology."

Asha nodded. "You're such a wise older sister."

"I know."

"Will you come with me?"

"Can you really leave everything behind? Give up everything you've worked for?"

"Yes."

"I'll come with you. I want to see what all the fuss is about. We can take my car."

. . .

ON THE DRIVE to Lancaster County, Asha told her sister about the community and the people in it.

"We'll stop at Patsy's house first. That's John's mother."

When they drove up to the house, Jess looked at the farm. "It's beautiful. I can see the attraction to this place."

"Patsy will be the only one home. The others will still be out working. I guess I will speak with her first."

"Okay, Ash, do you want me to wait here?"

"No, I don't think I can do it alone. I need you there."

Together they walked to the front door.

Patsy opened it and when she saw the girls, she smiled brightly. "Jane, what are you doing home? And you've brought a friend."

"Yes, Patsy" Asha said in a small voice, "This is my sister, Jess. And there's actually… there's something I need to tell you."

Asha noticed Patsy's smile fade from her face as she gestured for them both to come inside and take a seat.

Asha took a deep breath before continuing. "I am so sorry. I don't know how to tell you this after you have been so kind to me and so loving. But I never lost my memory. I remembered who I was this whole time. I just didn't want to go back to my life. I am so sorry." Asha broke down in tears and Patsy rushed to her side

"Please don't cry, child, it is okay. I had a suspicion you never lost your memory."

Asha looked up at Patsy through her tears. "What do you mean?"

"It was just a hunch I had. You didn't seem worried about losing your memory and you wouldn't go to the hospital, or to the police to see if anyone had reported you missing. Do you still want to join our community?"

"I do, but I feel I've ruined my chances in that regard."

"As long as you are sorry for your sins, we forgive and forget. I will just say that it is easier for some to forgive. Others find it not so easy. The boys will be home in a few hours. You will have to tell them and they might not be very impressed with what you say."

The thought of John's reaction weighed heavy on her heart. "John knows."

"*Jah,* he told me."

"I didn't get a chance to explain everything."

"You'll soon have your chance." Patsy said.

While they waited for the others to arrive home from work, Patsy made the girls tea and biscuits. Jess and Asha spoke to Patsy about their lives and the reason why Asha wanted to stay with them so badly.

Before they knew it, the men were walking through the door. Asha's heart sank when she heard the door open. Patsy advised the boys to be seated in the living room, and there Asha found herself surrounded by the whole family. As there were not enough chairs to accommodate all, John was standing across the room, directly in front of Asha.

"So, what's this big news you have to break to us, Jane?" one of the boys asked.

Asha looked at John; he was staring her straight in the eyes with a serious look on his face.

"I don't know how to say this to you all so I just want to start by saying that I've lied to all of you." She took a moment to stare straight at John before she continued.

"This here is my sister, Jess."

"Go on. Tell them," Patsy gently urged.

"I never lost my memory. I remembered the whole time. My name is Asha, and I am a famous singer in the outside world. I pretended to lose my memory because I don't like my life back home. I don't like being famous. All the pressure, all the stress, all the negativity and all that comes with it. I felt lost, that's why I was speeding so fast that night. I was..." Asha stopped to wipe a tear.

Patsy patted her shoulder, and Asha found the strength to

continue. "I was speeding so fast to get away from it all. Then I found you all, and then I found God. I always felt like something was missing in my life. My sister and I grew up in foster homes, but mostly in an orphanage. I have never felt love like you have shown me. All I have ever wanted is a family like yours. When I found it, the only way I knew to hang onto it was to make up lies. I am so sorry."

There was a silence in the room, Asha looked down at her feet and couldn't bring herself to look anyone in the eyes.

Before long, Mr Williamson broke the silence. "Well, are you sorry for what you've done?"

"Of course I am. I say sorry to God every day."

"Well that's good enough for me. You've made your confession and we give our forgiveness. There's not one among us who has not sinned."

"Yeah, Asha, I like your name better than Jane! You can still stay with us, no worries!" Scott added enthusiastically.

Scott always had a way of making her laugh and feel at ease. She smiled in Scott's direction and then looked up at John's face. He was staring at a spot in front of her feet. He looked as though he did not know what to say.

"John?" Asha said in a croaky voice. "May I speak with you in private?"

He nodded and they walked outside together.

John spoke first. "I'm pleased you came back. It shows great courage and so does admitting what you did."

"I'm so pleased you're not angry."

"I believe you did what you did for the right reasons, not the wrong reasons. I know you're a good person. I'm pleased to know that you want to stay. You do want to stay, don't you?" John's body stiffened.

"Of course I want to stay. I came back to ask forgiveness and also to talk to the bishop about joining."

He took hold of her hand. "I was leaving tomorrow to find you. I hadn't told anyone. I'd bought my bus ticket."

"You were coming to find me?"

He nodded.

She knew he loved her as much as she loved him. "Oh, I'm so pleased I came when I did. I might have missed you."

"*Gott* is in control, not us."

"I'm beginning to see that," Asha said.

"He caused everything to happen so we would meet."

"Do you think so?"

He squeezed her hand. "I've never been surer. I've prayed for a long time for a bird-watching partner. It's not much fun by myself."

Asha laughed. "I'll happily be that for you."

"That's what I was hoping you'd say." He shook his head. "I'm so glad you're here."

"I'm so glad you forgive me."

CHAPTER 20

Over the next few months, Asha stayed with the Grabers while she took the instructions. In that time she grew even closer to John.

When a suitable time had passed, the bishop gave his permission to John that he and Asha could marry.

As the wedding drew closer, Jess decided to stay close by, at a place in town to help Asha with the wedding plans. Asha was certain this wasn't the only reason. She suspected Gabe, John's cousin, might have been another reason Jess wanted to be close by.

Every time she mentioned Gabe, Jess seemed a little too interested to hear the sentences that would follow.

Two days before Asha's wedding, Jess and she decided to go for a walk and have a picnic at the river. Once Asha was married, she knew she couldn't be too close to an outsider, even a birth-family member. The community was her family now.

The sun was shining bright, the birds were singing and the water was babbling and so clear.

"Beautiful, isn't it?" Asha said

"Surreal," Jess added

Asha looked at Jess as she gazed into the distance, and admired how truly beautiful her sister was. Her sandy blonde hair was tied back into a ponytail and she hadn't worn makeup since she'd been staying here.

"You know, I understand why you decided to stay here, Asha." Jess broke her gaze and caught Asha's eyes "It's wonderful here. We never had a family like this, and now you've got one. I'm so happy for you."

"Thank you, Jess."

"But won't you miss the outside world? When they find out you've turned Amish, everyone will be trying to come here to find you, the press will go mad. You'll be all over the tabloids."

"Well, then, let's make sure they never find out." Asha smiled. She knew Jess had a good point, but she simply didn't care. She had learned already that worrying did her no good. She wasn't going to live in fear of other people any longer.

"I'm happy now, Jess, and that's all that matters. Well, I guess being right with God is the only thing that matters. Now I feel I have it all."

"Then I'm happy for you too, Asha. I just worry sometimes... especially about Nate. I know he won't stop trying to make you come back."

"He'll give up eventually." She was surprised at herself, how much she had changed. How much her faith in God had changed not only her beliefs, but the person she was. She had often thought of Nate, and all she felt for him now was compassion. He was stuck, he was sick. She had found a way out, but he was still stuck there. "And what about you Jess?" Asha elbowed Jess, teasing her.

"What about me?" Jess said, pushing her back playfully.

"I see the way you look at Gabe," Asha replied with a wink

They both burst into laughter and Jess made her confession. "Okay, he is pretty cute. I like a strong man in overalls."

They both laughed again

"You know, you'd have to join the community to date him or marry him. We could both stay here together." Asha smiled to herself, hoping that maybe someday her sister might consider it.

"Don't hold your breath, Ash," Jess replied.

When they returned to the place Jess was staying, they saw Nate's black car parked outside.

"Asha, it's Nate."

"What do I do?" she asked Jess, feeling a little panicky.

"Breathe. I will go see what he wants. You wait here."

Asha watched as Jess ran toward the house. What was he doing here? He was going to try to get her back, that's for sure. Would he tell the outside world where she was? There would be a field day here, and the paparazzi would ruin everything. The Amish wouldn't want photographers everywhere.

She had to think smart. How could she keep him on her good side? She heard Jess yell out to Nate in the distance and she watched as Nate turned from the stairs and started to walk toward Jess. She slid down in the seat and watched as they spoke, and then she ducked down lower, out of sight, as he looked in her direction.

Before long, he was back in his car driving away and Jess was running back toward Asha.

Breathing heavily, she said, "It's okay, he's gone. I told him you weren't here."

"What did he say? What did he want? Was he angry?"

"No. He's fine; I think he's just relieved you're alive. He looked sad, like he was about to start crying. I had to tell him that I would take you to see him later on. He's staying at a bed and breakfast up the road. It's your call when you want to go, but if you don't go, he won't leave."

Asha swallowed hard. She felt her anxiety coming back again. Anger started to well within and she pushed it away. "No. We're going right over there now. He's not welcome here or in any part of my life ever again."

"Asha, calm down. I've never seen you so angry. You were so cool, calm, and collected about it all before."

Asha didn't look at Jess. She felt too much anger and pain inside her as she fought back the tears, as the memories of his abusive control over her life bubbled to the surface. "He won't control me any longer," she said as she thought about John and her life here with him.

Jess drove Asha to the bed and breakfast. "There's his car. This is it, Asha. Do you want me to come in?"

Asha thought for a moment before replying. "No. I need to do this on my own. I'll be okay." She tried to reassure Jess, who looked worried.

"Are you sure?"

"Yeah. I won't be long."

She only had to knock on the door once before it opened and she was smack bang in front of Nate.

"Asha! I was so worried" he said as he pulled her tight into his arms. Asha froze. All the hurt, all the pain, all the anger she'd held for him went. He pulled her out at arm's length and looked her up and down. "You're staying here, like Jess said?"

"Yes, I am. I'm sorry, Nate, but I'm never coming back."

"Asha, did you hit your head in the accident? I'm not mad about the mess you made of my car, by the way."

"There's nothing wrong with me. The life I was living was futile and now I've found a purpose for everything."

"That's all very well and good, but people are depending on you."

"I can't live my life for other people. I need to live it for God and for my new family."

"You've gone mad."

"No, Nate, I haven't. I've gone sane." Never in her life had she stood up for herself like this, and especially never with him. She was proud of herself but in the back of her mind, there was a struggle between right and wrong going on.

"What about us?"

This made Asha feel sick and she laughed in his face, sarcastically. "You never loved me. You loved the money. You cheated on me, you hit me, abused me. I have no love to give you anymore." Asha saw the hurt in his eyes and thought she should just get it over with. She took a deep breath before continuing. "I've met someone, Nate. I'm getting married in two days. Bye, Nate."

"So that's it? After all I've done, you're just walking away?"

Nate pulled on her arm. "Who have you met? Some poor guy that came to your rescue and now you're using him to get back at me?"

"It's not all about you, Nate."

"Okay, Asha, I'll leave you alone. Let's just see how long you last without me. It won't be long until you come crawling, begging me to take you back."

Asha hurried to Jess's car and as soon as she got in, she burst into tears. Jess pulled her into her arms and they sat there hugging each other until Asha felt she could cry no more.

"Ready to go home, little sis?"

Asha nodded. "Gretchen said for you to have dinner with us. Did I mention that?"

"No, that's nice of her."

"You will, won't you?"

"Yes. We can spend more time together that way."

CHAPTER 21

"GIRLS, we were starting to worry about you. Everything okay?" William asked, giving Asha a curious look when they walked through the door.

"We're fine, and sorry to worry you."

"Asha got caught up with her manager. He still wants her to come back."

"That's why you look so troubled?" William asked.

Asha nodded.

Gretchen called out from the kitchen that dinner was ready. Asha hurried into the kitchen and apologized to Gretchen for not being there to help.

"I'll have no one to help me soon," Gretchen said with a forgiving smile as they all took their seats at the table. "I guess this was a practice session."

They closed their eyes and said a silent prayer of thanks. Asha's eyes swept across the table, over the salads, bologna, and the mounds of mashed potato. "This is a feast."

"It looks lovely," Jess agreed.

"You'll be married in two days. Stephanie and Megan are married, and I will have an empty house."

"What about me?" William asked with a mock sad face.

Jess and Asha laughed.

"*Jah,* there's always you," Gretchen replied, barely looking in her husband's direction which made the girls laugh harder.

"We might be getting too old to have more foster children," William said.

"We'll see," Gretchen mumbled. "If *Gott* wills it, we'll have more coming our way. Stephanie came our way and so did Asha."

Asha said, "Maybe Jess might end up staying here and marrying Gabe."

"Asha!" Jess said.

William and Gretchen chuckled.

"It's good to see you smiling, Asha," William said.

"I like having my sister around. And now I've told my manager face-to-face that I'm not coming back. I feel a whole lot better."

"Good."

"Jess, tomorrow can you take me to John's house?"

"I can drive you anywhere you want."

"Thanks." The wedding was taking place at John's parents' house. John had rented a small house from his uncle for them to live in and it was just a nice walking distance from there to his parents' house.

THE NEXT DAY AT THE WILLIAMSONS' house everyone was eating breakfast when they walked in. John pulled up some chairs for Asha and Jess, while Patsy poured them mugs of coffee.

"The big day is only one sleep away, Asha. You sure you don't want to change your mind? You could marry me instead." Scott teased Asha and she couldn't help but smile.

"It is a tempting offer, thank you, Scott, but I am more than satisfied with my soon-to-be husband," Asha said, expecting John to look up and react, but he didn't.

Everyone else seemed to notice too, and the room fell quiet with an awkward silence that seemed to make the ants crawling outside sound like elephants stomping.

"Delicious coffee," Jess said breaking the awkward silence.

Asha felt Jess's hand rub her back. She looked at Jess, smiling back at her with a warm smile that said everything will be okay.

Has he changed his mind? Did I do something wrong? After everyone went about preparing the house for the wedding, Asha sought a quiet moment with John.

"Did I do something wrong?"

"Not now, Asha. I don't want to talk about it."

"We're getting married tomorrow. We need to talk about things. If something's bothering you, I need to know."

John looked down into Asha's eyes as he leaned against the barn door. "Maybe it was too good to be true."

"What do you mean by too good to be true? I'm sorry I lied. I just didn't see any other way. I have said I'm sorry for my sins. I've joined the community for you."

"For me? You said you were joining for yourself." He shook his head. "I don't know if I can trust you. What if you run away from me?"

"I won't. We're in love with each other. And I did join for me, but I'd never have found God without you."

"I'm in love with you, Asha. But even your name isn't real, is it?"

"No. I thought of going back to my birth name, but I've been Asha for so long. It's just a name. Tell me if you need me to change back. I'm in this for life. I've made a full and proper commitment, and tomorrow I'll make another sincere commitment to you, in front of everyone."

He slowly nodded.

"What has brought these doubts, John?"

"Something Sally said bothered me."

"Sally?"

"She said you used me and my family, so you could stay here."

"I guess that's what I did in the beginning. John, I am in love with you and I know you love me too. Don't let us go. If I had never lied, if I had never used you and your family, we would never have fallen in love. I wouldn't be here and we wouldn't be getting married tomorrow. Sally has gotten into your head because she wants to marry you, and you know this. Please, John, please?" Asha begged John not to leave her. She dropped to the ground and sobbed. She felt like she was on the ground forever before John's strong hands pulled her to her feet and then into his arms.

"Shhh, shhh, it's okay, Asha. I can't see you like this. I love you. I am sorry, I am so sorry."

Asha was relieved to hear John apologizing. She looked into his eyes and he wiped her tears away. "I guess I let fear get the better of me, and Sally was saying things to me at the wrong time. I shouldn't have listened to her."

"John, we need to communicate; it needs to be you and me, and no one else. No one else should have that kind of power or influence on our relationship—ever. It has to be me and you from now on."

John smiled at Asha. "Okay, Fiancée. That sounds good to me. No more crying for you, and no more fearful thoughts for me. You will believe that I have forgiven you, and I will believe that your words are true."

Asha remembered that his old girlfriend had gone on *rumspringa* and had never returned. "Okay." Asha smiled and buried her head into his shoulder. He was just having a normal 'cold feet' fearful reaction.

CHAPTER 22

ASHA LOOKED at her reflection in the windowpane of her bedroom at the Grabers'. Her hair was tied back and she had a white cap on her head. It was the day of her wedding. Her skin was free of makeup and her dress was plain sky-blue.

She never expected she would get married in a dress showing no skin at all. It was simple, it was plain, and she loved it. She took some time to herself, to review her life. She had gone from having nothing and no money to gaining the world, all the money she could ask for, and then going on to leave it all behind, finding God and a loving husband, finding connection with people instead of connection with her fans.

Caring about others instead of caring about herself. She was pleased with what God had brought to her life. Without Him she would've had nothing. He'd shown her and taught her how to rely on Him. It hadn't been hard to leave everything behind.

There was a loud knock at the door and before she could reply, Jess was bursting through the door

"Oh Ash, you look beautiful! Are you nervous?"

"Hi, Jess." Asha smiled. "No. I'm excited, and you look beautiful too!" Asha looked Jess up and down. She wore a purple dress. It was baggy and covered all of her arms and went right up to the bottom of her neck.

There had been a strong change in Jess too. Before, she would never have been caught dead in a dress like she was wearing, or with no makeup. She knew Jess enjoyed spending time in the community and her best hope was that Jess would join her and call the community her home and her family.

"I love you, Jess." Asha smiled.

"I love you too. Now let's go, or we will be late for your big day."

William was waiting outside in the buggy to take them to John's house.

ASHA WALKED INTO THE WILLIAMSONS' house with William, and her sister followed close behind her. Everyone was seated, ready to watch the wedding take place. It was not the wedding she'd imagined she might have, but she was marrying the best man in the world. A happy-tear spilled from her eye.

Asha looked at John and felt the butterflies going crazy in her stomach. *Breathe Asha,* she thought to herself. Asha looked around; the house was decked out so beautifully with white and yellow flowers. Picked from their very own garden.

She looked back at John; he couldn't keep the smile off his face, and he looked as nervous as she felt. Asha noticed a tear run down his cheek, also.

Everyone stood and a man walked out to the front and sang a song. When it ended, the people sat down. The bishop took over and gave a talk about marriage and how the love in a marriage represents the love God has for His church.

When the bishop finished, he turned his attention to Asha and John. They exchanged vows and were then pronounced married.

The meal after the wedding was set out in the front yard between the barn and the house. It was now midday and the sun was shining brightly. Most marriages, Asha was told were traditionally held at the end of the year after harvest, but that tradition was fading with many of the Amish people no longer living on farms.

Asha and John sat at the wedding table along with Jess and John's cousin, Gabe. Patsy and Joe were at the table closest them and they all chatted cheerfully.

As Asha looked around, she felt her heart open at the love and joy surrounding her. She looked at John's brothers at the next table, now her brothers-in-law, joking around with other Amish teenagers. Smiling, she breathed in the fresh air, taking in the beauty of her surroundings.

When she turned to admire the flowers surrounding Joe and Patsy's house, she noticed Jess and Gabe were deep in conversation.

Mr. Williamson stood and got everyone's attention. "I'd like to thank everyone for coming out today to celebrate my son and daughter-in-law's wedding. We are happy to have Asha in our family. My son, John, we are so over the moon that *Gott* has brought you someone as bright, loving and caring as Asha, and your *mudder* and I pray for His blessing on your marriage and your lives. Thank you for marrying my son, Asha. If you hadn't come along he might've been living at home forever." There was laughter and 'amens' from the crowd and then he sat down.

Asha was struck by the realization that she now had a mother and a father. She couldn't contain her feelings and a tear escaped her eye. John noticed and wiped her tears with his napkin.

"Second thoughts already? It's a little late," John whispered to her.

Asha smiled. "I'm just so happy.

John put his hand over hers and gave it a squeeze. "I'm more happy than I thought I could ever be." He leaned closer and whispered, 'Have you noticed your sister and Gabe?"

"I've been watching them," Asha whispered back.

"Do you think your sister might join us too?"

"I don't know. I hope so."

"This is the happiest moment of my life," John said.

"Are you happier than if you'd seen a Purple Gallinule?"

John threw his head back and laughed. "You've been studying?"

"Yes. If I'm going to be a good bird-watching partner, I have to know what I'm talking about."

"Good. I'd love to see one."

"Me too. It's a miracle we found each other, John. We're perfect for one another. We were from two different worlds and He caused us to find each other."

"I thank *Gott* for you every day, and will continue to thank Him each day of my life."

Asha looked into his eyes and knew that he meant it.

Then visions of the accident flashed through her head. It seemed like it was years ago that she'd run away from her old life and collided with her new one. It was a miracle she had run into John's buggy. She silently thanked God for bringing her home into the fold.

ABOUT SAMANTHA PRICE

USA Today Bestselling author, Samantha Price, wrote stories from a young age, but it wasn't until later in life that she took up writing full time. Formally an artist, she exchanged her paintbrush for the computer and, many best-selling book series later, has never looked back.

Samantha is happiest on her computer lost in the world of her characters. She is best known for the Ettie Smith Amish Mysteries series and the Expectant Amish Widows series.

www.SamanthaPriceAuthor.com

Samantha loves to hear from her readers. Connect with her at:

samantha@samanthapriceauthor.com

www.facebook.com/SamanthaPriceAuthor

Follow Samantha Price on BookBub

Twitter @ AmishRomance

Instagram - SamanthaPriceAuthor